Mob Star

The O'Rourke Brotherhood

Sabine Barclay

OLIVERHEBERBOOKS

 Created with Vellum

"Love is blind despite the world's attempt to give it eyes."
~Matshona Dhliwayo

Find me writing Historical Romance as Celeste Barclay.

Happy reading,
Sabine

Subscribe to Sabine's Newsletter

Subscribe to Sabine's bimonthly newsletter to receive exclusive insider perks.

Have you read *The Syndicate Wars*? This FREE origin story novella is available to all new subscribers to Sabine's monthly newsletter. Subscribe on her website.
www.sabinebarclay.com

Chapter One

Finn

I fecking hate office parties. Well, not mine because my colleagues are my brothers and cousin. When we gather for work, it's never for fun. Since I work with my family, I suppose it's all relative. But these feckers...

My head shoots up from the cocktail I'm mixing. I look to my left to see who made the racist comment about a woman. My hands curl into fists. I will not tolerate bigots in McGinty's.

"Jenny, take these to table five."

I don't even look at the waitress who's waiting for the six drinks I just made. I walk to the douche who spoke. That joke isn't the only one he has, but I don't let him get past the first two words.

"You're done." I interrupt. I'm not having it.

"What?"

Fuck face looks up as though he just realizes he's in public and not jacking off to some shite homemade porn.

"You're cut off, and you're leaving."

"Why?"

"Because I heard what you said. It's my bar, my rules. Out before I throw you out. I'll even give you your drinks on the house."

"What the fuck, bro? Why're you even listening in on my private conversation?"

I have ears like a dog, so most people wouldn't have heard him. But my keen sense of hearing is why I haven't looked like a piece of Swiss cheese many times in my life.

"It's not private when you have it where anyone— *I* —can hear it."

"What's so bad about what I said?"

I look at him as though he's lost his mind. But my attention shifts when one of the most stunning women I've ever seen walks over. She's average build, but that's the only thing average about her. She has pale— almost translucent —green eyes, thick dark hair, and skin that's smoother than— feck, I don't even know what. She carries herself with confidence, and her gaze tells me she's nobody's fool. That's why what she does next surprises me.

She's wrapping her arm around this fucker's waist.

"What's wrong?" Definitely not a New York accent, but it's super subtle. Somewhere on the East Coast.

"This asshole's trying to throw me out."

"I'm not trying. I am throwing you out." I signal to Cormac and Seamus, tilting my head toward the door.

Neither of my cousins says a word before they crowd the fucker and the arsehole's coworker, the femme fatale— she's shooting daggers at me with her sea green orbs —that's the best I can describe them.

"Miss, please move. He's done for tonight. I won't tolerate his comments in my bar."

I don't think his second racist comment about some woman

would have been as bad, but the first one is what got my hackles up. He sneers at me as he stands. He has something more to say, and it's going to piss me the fuck off. I can feel it. He keeps his voice low, but he doesn't even get the second word out.

I reach across the bar and grab a fistful of his shirt, yanking him forward.

"You've pissed off the wrong person. I not only own a fuck ton of bars spread throughout the five boroughs, but I own ones in Jersey and Connecticut. Look at the security camera behind me and smile. You can even say cheese. Not only are you banned from any establishment I own, I'll make sure you're banned from every bar, nightclub, and strip joint worth visiting."

Because either my cousins own them, or members of the other syndicate families do. We don't get along, and we almost never agree. But none of us allow people who mistreat women in our places of business. I don't give a shite that the woman now standing with her arm around this fucker clearly has shite taste in men, since she's obviously way too well-acquainted with him. If he'd made any equally disgusting comment about a man, I'd still toss him on his arse. My bar, my rules.

"I'm not going anywhere until you tell me what he said that was so bad." My mystery goddess isn't going to budge, and my cousins won't force her.

"He can tell you outside."

"It was nothing bad, babe. I swear. I just called you a—"

Those comments were about her? Motherfucker better run.

"Nope. Take it outside."

This time Cormac and Seamus ease in, so Cormac doesn't touch the woman. They each grab the guy by an arm, though either of them could take this arsehole outside without a problem. Together... They won't hurt him, but they will scare the shite out of him.

3

The woman stares at me before she realizes the entire bar is now watching the scene. Her cheeks darken, and she's even more pissed at me than she was before. She didn't rush after the guy, and she didn't put up much of a defense. But there's still more than just colleague familiarity between them.

Her gaze sweeps the bar, and so does mine. There are some regulars relegated to corners since there's about twenty people in here who came together for whatever the hell this office shindig is. It's an enormous bar, so there's more than enough room, but this new crowd has spread out and taken over. They're buying plenty of drinks, so I don't care. Most of them have ordered meals because we're known for generous pours—until midnight, then they get stingier and watered down. Patrons are usually already drunk and willing to pay for what they don't notice is less booze, which makes them buy more — along with our food.

The goddess looks back at me, then glances at the window, looking out to the street, then back at me.

"Was it really that bad?"

"I thought it was enough to kick him out."

"And you won't repeat it?"

"No."

"And it was about me?"

"Yes."

She looks back at the window and nods. We can see the guy arguing with Cormac, who weighs at least eighty pounds more than the DB. That's eighty pounds of muscle because Cormac is the cleanest eater I've ever met. My uncle's been making vegan birthday cakes for him since he was twelve and read some article that made him refuse to eat most processed sugars or most things that aren't plant-based. Fortunately for the rest of us, plenty of vegan foods are delicious, and my uncle's a great baker.

"Shit!"

Green Eyes hurries to the door as we watch the shitbag lunge toward Cormac and try to shove him. I promise you; it was like hitting a brick wall. I have a completely unobstructed view, and I watch Cormac tense just before numb nuts' hands touch my cousin's chest. He's not preparing for impact. He's making his body as hard as he can. The guy's kinetic energy is enough that he rebounds from Cormac and stumbles backwards. Seamus steps up, so the guy lands against him, now boxed in. Neither of my cousins touch him except for where he's collided with them.

I observe as the woman— who's likely a doctor or nurse since everyone else in the party is —walks up to them. She doesn't insert herself into the conversation or try to intervene. She shakes her head at something Seamus says then turns toward the street, raising her arm. She hails a cab and grabs the guy's arm. Now she's talking to him, and the douche follows her to the waiting car. I watch it drive away before my cousins come back inside.

Cormac's lip curls as they come over to the bar. They're not even a year apart since Cormac was two months premature. You'd never guess at the sight of him now. The man's an ox, and so is Seamus. They could be twins like my brothers Sean and Shane. Yes, we are that Irish.

"Can I get some hand sanitizer? I feel dirty just being near a fecker that skeezy."

I pass him one of five bottles I keep under the bar, never mind the two I have attached to the wall behind the bar where all the bottles sit. All the patrons have lost interest in the exchange that just happened. Even the others in the party are more interested in their libations and sustenance. That's what Nana called it to justify her grandsons doing more than having a nip of whiskey on a frosty night. Never mind that she got me the liquor license three months before I turned twenty-one.

"What'd the woman have to say?"

I try to keep my tone neutral and not give away my interest, but they turn matching smirks at me. It's fecking annoying because it's practically like looking in the mirror. They're near replicas of each other, and all of us in the O'Rourke family share the same shade of emerald-green eyes and varying shades of red hair. That's the easiest way for people to tell us apart, besides the fact that Sean has a freckle on his throat that distinguishes him from Shane. This is what happens when three sisters marry three brothers.

Cormac's smirk turns into a scowl. "She apologized and said she'd get him home. By the time we got outside, the drinks were catching up to him. How many did he have?"

"Like three light beers. Not much for a dude his size."

"Lightweight." Cormac rolls his eyes.

"Didn't you smell the scotch on his breath?" Seamus's brow furrows as he looks at his brother, who shakes his head as he frowns.

"I didn't serve him any hard liquor. He must have pre-gamed, which is alarming since half of them are still in scrubs and came straight from the hospital. He's one of them."

When he sat down with his friend, I got the impression they're nurses from something the other guy said. But I don't know about the woman. A doctor or nurse doesn't matter to me if she makes house calls. But if she left with the douche, then they're probably a couple. His comments about what he'd like to do with her weren't just your average misogynistic shite that even I'm guilty of, too. They were more than that. Gross enough to make me certain they aren't related, but I didn't see a ring on either of their left hands. I even checked her right hand.

"They're gone now, so as long as he doesn't come back, who gives a feck?" Seamus, the perpetually pragmatic one.

I nod and go back to serving drinks, but it nags at me. I don't know why the woman created such a lasting impression. When you have the wealth my family has, attractive people have a way of glomming onto you. She's stunning, and I'm definitely attracted, but I'm not used to beautiful women making me think about them for hours after they walk away. Maybe it was a combination of my attraction to her and revulsion toward him. But it just doesn't sit right.

It should be out of sight, out of mind. At least, that's what I'm telling myself as I lock up. But it feels unresolved, and I don't like that.

✕

"Dillan?"

"Yeah. We're in the kitchen."

We used to have an open-door policy at each other's homes for all the cousins. Now that Dillan's with Mair, it's different for them. I texted just as I came through their property's gate. They recently moved into a gated community in Queens. Dillan didn't feel the security was adequate outside his Brooklyn brownstone, and he wouldn't consider Mair's place in Harlem. Now we all have to knock or text ahead of time. The last thing any of us wants is to walk in on his kinky arse with his wife. All our proclivities run in the same direction.

"Hey, Finn."

Mair— Márgrég —grins at me as I join them. She hands me a glass of wine and points to the table. They're just about to have dinner. I didn't realize that. She's more Irish than we are. She was born in Ballycastle, Northern Ireland, but moved to the States as a kid. She goes by Mair— like the horse —when she's with us. Her real name isn't hard for a Gaelic speaker, but it would confuse the feck out of most Americans. It's easy—Mare-greeg. Only Dillan calls her Greta.

I'm letting my mind wander as they whisper something to each other, and Dillan's hand wanders south to her arse. I'd blame it on them being newlyweds, but considering how our parents behave, I think this is inherited.

"I didn't mean to interrupt. I could have come at another time."

Dillan shakes his head as he pulls corned beef out of the oven. It's not St. Patrick's Day. It's not even Sunday. We're that Irish.

"I'm glad you're here." Mair curls her nose. "This way there won't be leftover cabbage."

Dillan waggles his eyebrows. "I'll get you to enjoy cabbage. I have sixty years to do it."

We like to think we're going to have a long life, but there isn't one of us in this family who doesn't know it could end before the sun comes up. It's the life we were born into. No one in my generation or our parents'— or even our grandparents' — asked to be part of the mob. It was decided four generations back when our family was still in Ireland. We can't leave. We *won't* leave. We do our best to have a normal life when we're at home.

So, I'm carving the corned beef right now as Dillan brings over the vegetables, and Mair grabs the apple cake for dessert. It's really a side dish in this family.

We laugh and joke throughout the meal. Mair shares her newest assignment for the newspaper where she works. She's on the National Desk, and it's been interesting since she married Dillan. Even when they were dating. Fuck. Their relationship is complicated. But they make it work. Her editor is still walking on eggshells around her. I had a little chat with the

Editor-in-Chief, Chuck, to make sure he and Gary understand Mair gets treated with the utmost respect just like before she got involved with Dillan.

"I have work to do, so I'll get out of your way."

Mair grabs her bag and heads to her office, which is downstairs but at the opposite end of the mansion. What else do you call a home that can sleep them, five cousins, and three sets of parents? Dillan and I move to his office where we each take an armchair. I naturally settle into the one to his right, and his is closest to his desk. I'm his right hand. Part of it is because I'm the second oldest of the six cousins. Part of it is because we're best friends. But most of it is because we balance each other. It's probably because my younger brothers are a matched pair as twins, and Cormac and Seamus may as well be. I've been Dillan's conscience and DD as many times as he's been mine.

He has a mind for strategy, and I can make Uncle Scrooge look extravagant. I see numbers, and they tally themselves in my head. I'm the family accountant, so I ultimately decide how we allocate our money. Dillan comes up with the plans, and I tell him how much we can spend.

"How're things coming along with Marco?" Dillan crosses his left leg over his right thigh. I look down at my legs. We match. Fecking nature versus nurture.

"Things are falling into place. The FBI and ATF are asking how high when I tell them to jump. Trying to get them to go after Lorenzo was a bust, but Marco is a solid target."

It was more than an inconvenient failure. It's been a long time since I've lost a fight. Enzo came to my boxing gym and fucking lost his shite in the ring. I ended up with a broken nose and ribs that have just recovered from the severe bruising. He thought I was into his now-wife. I thought I kinda was when Enzo started sniffing around. Getting the shite knocked out of me made me realize I literally wasn't going to fight that hard to have her. I might have lost, but he could barely limp out on his own.

"The Mancinellis still haven't guessed our role in the whole Kansas City-Chicago deal. Fucking numb nuts. I can't believe at least Carmine hasn't figured it out."

That fecker. Maniacal genius.

"Yeah, well, Carmine's still living in his newlywed bubble just like Enzo."

Dillan grins at me as he glances toward the door. Gross. "What do we need to do to move things along?"

"Nothing right now. The ball isn't in our court, but I'll take it back if the FBI and ATF feck this up. As long as they keep looking away from us, we're good. Any other direction is better than us."

"True. Where do we stand with the shipment coming from Prague?" Dillan's ready to move on from the Mancinellis, and so am I.

"It's due to arrive any minute now. My brothers are at the docks to meet the ship. They know the customs officers, and they'll make sure they cooperate. Hopefully, all it takes is one look at them. But they have five grand for each."

"That much?" Dillan's sarcasm makes me mentally roll my eyes.

"I told Sean and Shane they better come home with change." I'm frugal, not a miser. I understand just fine that you gotta spend money to make money.

"What's your schedule like tomorrow?"

"I'm going to the clubs for payroll, then I need to pop round to McGinty's. There's another private party, and Shannon's been a little trigger-happy with the pours. I want to make sure she has a jigger glued to her hand. I got a new one just for her. It's not double-sided, so there's no accidentally pouring double what she should after ten."

We have plenty of bottles that line the wall behind the bar, but the ones we serve from are under it. That way, at ten, we switch out and start using the watered-down shite. Their fault for getting too intoxicated to figure it out.

"What about after that?"

"I don't know. I'm hoping to get out of there early. We'll see."

Chapter Two

Thea

It has been a long fucking day. Twenty-four-hour shift. Six newborns delivered in distress. That was just the first thirteen hours. I had to give heartbreaking news to parents that left me crying in the breakroom. It's been a long-ass time since that's happened. Then back to rounds to check on infants who'd recently come out of surgery and were remaining in the NICU along with the other babies receiving ongoing care. All those surgeries were successes, but none of them come without serious chances for post-operative complications.

I really want to go home. I really want to shower. I really want to go to bed and sleep for a week. I really *don't* want to go to Tony's birthday party. I've told him I don't want to go, but he's been insisting since it's his thirtieth. What can I say? I'm a cougar, but what I'm pissed about is he insisted on having it at McGinty's. His brother's dating a bartender. I guess the red-headed guy from the other day won't be there tonight. Even if he isn't, nothing good can come from going back there. But I feel responsible for Tony. Which I fucking hate. I'm not his fucking mother, but I can see how I could turn into her.

We've been going out for two months, but I've known him since I started working at the hospital as a resident. He was one of the first nurses I worked with. He seemed like a nice guy, but I was seeing someone else at the time. I've had four boyfriends — including Tony —since I started at the hospital nine years ago. I broke up with my last boyfriend eight months ago.

I finally said yes when Tony asked me out after he hinted at it for weeks. This was like the third time we've both been single at the same time. Third times the charm. At least for him.

He is completely different as a boyfriend rather than a friend. He's so fucking needy. I can't with him. If tonight weren't his birthday party, I would dump him. His birthday was last week, so I thought I was in the clear to do it, until he announced this party at lunch three days ago. We were sitting with a bunch of coworkers in the cafeteria, and he made a big thing about having me on his arm.

A couple of my friends looked at me, and I just smiled. They know I'm nobody's arm candy. I didn't work as long and as hard as I have to be reduced to a pretty doll a guy takes out to dinner then takes home to play with. Tony is a himbo— ya know, the male version of a bimbo. I didn't think he was before we started dating. He's a fucking nurse anesthetist. But away from work, he's— too much.

Lord, let me survive tonight, then I'll be done with him.

I'm practically dead on my feet now that I've changed into jeans and a cute top. I have ankle boots on, and I feel good about how I look. Too bad it's wasted on a night that I'd rather spend curled up with my pillow. I'm off tomorrow, so at least that's a plus.

I walk over to McGinty's with Tony and a handful of his friends that went to high school with him. They met us outside the hospital. I haven't met too many of his friends, but now that I've met these... It makes so much more sense. They're straight up gumbas. Like complete idiots. They should have left their sense of humor back in middle school. I have nothing in common with them. It wouldn't surprise me if at least one of them is a flat Earther.

As we walk into the bar, I scan the crowd that's already gathered. A woman waves to us. It's Tony's brother's girlfriend, Shannon. She works here, so she's generous when she serves us. If I drink, I'll have fucking heavy head and be asleep in five minutes. Besides, Tony's already talking about getting wasted because he has the next four days off. Drunk Tony as a friend is different from drunk Tony as a boyfriend. He clearly isn't still trying to make a good impression on me.

In all fairness, it hasn't been horrible dating him since day one. It's just gone downhill over the past two weeks. It started just before our last time here. I don't know what he said that pissed the owner off so much.

The owner. The man is the hottest guy I have ever seen. Like if he told me to strip, I'd run around like fucking Lady Godiva. If he told me to bend over a table, I'd clear it with one of those TV arm sweeps. If he wanted to tie me up and do dirty, dirty things to me, I'd hand him the rope.

He was calm and confident as he threw my boyfriend out of the bar. He could have been an asshole in response to whatever Tony said. My soon-to-be-ex-boyfriend refuses to repeat it. I haven't seen the guy he was sitting with that night and don't know him, so he wasn't an option to ask. McGinty's owner seemed like a man while Tony was a boy.

I've bitched about my boyfriend in my head for the last fifteen minutes. I'm ending it in the morning. Let me just get through tonight.

We slide into a booth with five other people, so it's

cramped. We wait for a waitress, but no one comes. It's obvious they didn't expect a crowd like this tonight. The last time we were here, it was an office party. It was booked in advance. Tony might have been planning this for a while, but they must have assumed he wouldn't come. He clearly didn't let them know. He couldn't since he's banned.

"Whatcha want?" Tony's staring at me as though he's annoyed I'm keeping him waiting. I know he hasn't asked more than this one time.

"Gin and ginger, please."

He curls his nose, but I don't care. I watch him cross the bar, and I breathe easier. My friend, Dana, leans across the table to whisper.

"I thought you were going to dump him."

"I am. But I felt obligated to come to this with him since I didn't break up with him before I found out about it."

"I can't believe what an a-hole he's turned out to be."

"Me neither. It's a total Dr. Jekyll-Mr. Hyde. It's weird." I twist to see him at the bar, and my heart sinks. "Fuck me."

"Huh?"

"The red-headed guy over there is the owner. Tony had a run in with him. He banned Tony from here."

"And you let him come back?"

"I didn't let him do anything, Dana. He's a grown ass man. He heard through his brother that the guy wasn't supposed to be here."

"I don't think he's seen Tony yet. Can you get him back over here before he does? It's crowded enough he might not notice Tony. That's assuming Tony stays hidden."

"How fucking ridiculous is it that he has to hide at his own party because he insisted upon coming somewhere he knows he's been blacklisted? Dana, I'm done tonight. I won't make a scene here, but I can't wake up in the morning knowing we're still dating. I have to have some self-respect."

She just looks at me as if to say, "about time."

"Look, you're nice, Ally. You wanted to believe you could go from friends to lovers. It's not your fault that he's actually a frog under his princely disguise."

I laugh. "You hit all the romance tropes, didn't you?"

"Not all. But, yeah, you get my drift."

"I do."

"Shit." Dana points toward the bar.

I don't think Tony's seen the owner— yet —but the owner sees him. I slide out of the booth and squeeze through the crowd, people saying hi as I go. I get to the bar just as Tony says something that makes me freeze.

"She's an Oreo, and I like licking her cream."

My mouth has to be hanging open. He did not just call me that. He doesn't stop with just that.

"Being between her thighs makes me think of caramel swirls—"

It's like slow motion in my head as I watch the bar owner lunge at Tony. He grabs him by the back of the shirt and with only one hand, yanks him off the stool. He'd struck up a conversation instead of getting my drink. Jackass. But I already know that.

"Get the feck out of my bar."

"Feck? What are you? The leprechaun from Lucky Charms?"

I cringe.

"What I am is an O'Rourke."

I'm not sure what that means, but Tony goes stiff as a corpse. He seems to know. I watch as this man spins Tony to face him. He's at least four inches taller than my soon-to-be ex-boyfriend. He's gotta outweigh him by at least fifty pounds of solid muscle. This O'Rourke isn't even as big as the two guys who tossed Tony out the last time. But his tight button down shirt is the equivalent to women's lingerie. The only thing sexier on him— short of nothing at all —would be gray sweatpants. I bet his ass would look divine in those.

I glance down at his shoes, then at his hands. I wonder if everything is proportionate. I shouldn't be thinking about what it would be like for him to lift me onto the bar and go down on me. I shouldn't be thinking about what it would be like to go in the back and suck him off. But it's taking my mind off what Tony said. It hurt along with pissing me off. The comments themselves stung, but for them to come from him? I refuse to allow anyone to see they bother me.

"I banned you from this bar and all the others my family owns. From your expression, you know who I am now. Who should I call first? The Diazes? The Mancinellis? The Kutsenkos? Actually, let's put them on a conference call. That would be a fuck ton faster."

"Be pissy. I'm still the one drinking the milk from that coconut."

What the ever-loving fuck? He's being disgusting on purpose now. He's egging Mr. Gorgeous on, but that he would say any of this for any reason shows me a side of Tony I never want to see again. A side that makes me ashamed to admit I was his friend, let alone dated him.

My hottie hero still has a hold of Tony, but now it's the front of his button down. He pulls his phone out and shakes in front of Tony's face. I creep closer and watch— fuck, I don't have a clue what his first name is —O'Rourke unlock it. He taps something, and we can hear it ring.

"Finn—"

"Enrique, hold on. I'm calling Maks and Salvatore, too."

"Why?"

"Just hold on. You're on speaker at McGinty's by the way."

"Wonderful."

I guess he called the Diazes first. But I don't know why. Finn— that's fucking hot —taps his phone again.

"Sal, you're on speaker at the bar. Enrique's on the line too. I'm calling Maks."

I hear the phone ring twice before a man's Russian-flavored accent fills the bar that is now so silent a pin could drop.

"Mother—"

"Maks, you're on with Sal and Enrique. I'm turning this into a video call. I'm at McGinty's. There's someone all of you need to meet. He's already banned from O'Rourke establishments. I want him banned from yours, too."

The man named Enrique doesn't agree. "You don't tell me who can and can't come to my businesses."

"You'll swallow those words when you hear what he just said to a woman in my bar. A woman he's dating."

"Was dating." I blurt that as I get close. "'Scuse me."

I push my way through two cardiologists who are blocking my way. As they both look over their shoulders at me, I realize they're purposely blocking me. I don't know if they're trying to protect Tony from me. Trying to keep me safe from winding up near a fight if it breaks out. Or just not willing to give up their front row spots. I still make it through.

"I was dating him. Never again. Tony, you can go fuck yourself. And believe you me, there isn't a woman at the hospital who'll want you after they find out what you said about me and hear about your micro dick."

It's not quite micro, but I can promise you, it isn't anything like the outline of what's pressing against the front of Finn's pants.

Finn looks at me and smirks. "Not surprising."

"I'm waiting."

That's Salvatore Mancinelli. The accent is straight up New York Italian. I don't know who he is either, but he sounds like a man used to being in charge.

"Fecker, repeat what you said." Finn looks at me as he speaks.

I want to crawl into a corner. I don't want to hear it again.

"Wait. Hold on." Finn drags Tony with him as he heads toward the back. "I don't want the lady to hear it again."

"That bad?" It's the guy named Maks. He must be one of the Kutsenkos.

Tony and Finn disappear, and I'm left not knowing where to look or what to do. The anticlimactic moment tempts me to grab my purse and make a break for it. But I want to see what happens to Tony. I hope he comes out with his face fucked-up. Finn seems smart enough not to do more than fist Tony's shirt in public. What's happening right now, wherever they went, is anyone's guess. What I want most is to thank Finn for defending me twice. The way he looked at me just now... It made my toes curl. He's pissed on my behalf. But the expression was—reassuring. Like he was silently promising to take care of everything, so in turn, take care of me. It made me feel safe.

Dana walks up to me and hands me my purse. "Wanna split an Uber?"

"I want to know what happens." I need to know what happens.

"It looks like the closest car is like ten minutes away. We've got time. But I'm getting out of here. I'm not associating with Tony anymore. Are you all right? I should have asked that first."

"Yeah. It's not the worst thing I've been called. But it blindsided me."

It makes me feel utterly shitty about myself to know he made some other racial comment the last time we were here, and I gave him a pass. I figured Finn overreacted when Tony downplayed it. But watching Finn tonight— he doesn't strike me as a man prone to overreacting. He strikes me as a man who's methodical in everything. A man who isn't easily rattled or dissuaded from anything.

"I can't believe he's a racist." Dana offers me a sympathetic smile. I refuse to consider it might be pity.

"Neither can I. I never would have—"

"Ally, you don't need to explain. I know you wouldn't. I feel shitty for you. I'm sorry."

"It's not your fault."

"Yeah, but—"

She doesn't get to finish because Finn returns with Tony, except it's not just the two of them. The two guys from last time are back along with identical twins. The five men bear striking resemblances to one another. Finn must be the twins' older brother. Maybe the other two are cousins or something.

Finn hands Tony off to one of his brothers— I'm assuming that's who they are —and turns toward the waitress who said it was okay to be here.

"Shannon, get your stuff. You're done."

She blinks for a moment. "For tonight?"

"For good. You knew I wouldn't allow him back. Not only did you tell him he could return, you served him. Leave. Let your da know I'll be dropping by in the morning."

Why would he go see her father? She has to be in her mid-twenties. She goes white as a sheet, and I take a step toward her. She looks like she's going to faint. She's trembling. Why's she acting like this?

Before I can get to her, Tony calls out to me. "Come on, babe. Let's go home. They're just trying to flex. This isn't about me. He just wants to look like he's got the biggest dick in the room in front of his mobster friends."

I walk in front of Tony and keep my voice low. "He probably does have the biggest dick. Or one of his relatives does. Shut up. Go home. Fucking delete my number from your phone. Come near me again, and I will file a grievance with the hospital." I step even closer and whisper. "Come near me again, and I will make sure no one finds you."

I might make a lot of money now, but I didn't come from money. Where I grew up wasn't rough, but I knew rough people. I have plenty of favors to call in.

I watch as he tries to pull his arm loose from one twin. Needless to say, he isn't successful. Unlike the office party that carried on without us, no one seems interested in continuing a birthday party for someone who isn't there.

"The Uber's pulling up."

I turn toward Dana, then look over at Finn. He's watching me.

"Go ahead. I want to say thank you."

Dana glances at Finn. "Be careful. He looks like he wants to gobble you up."

Chapter Three

Finn

I heard what my green-eyed beauty said. I don't know who she knows, but she sounded pretty damn convinced she could make the arsehole disappear. I watched her as I named the other three families. There wasn't a spark of recognition. There wasn't any when I said the leaders' names or when she heard their voices. She's not affiliated with the Cartel, the bratva, or the *Cosa Nostra*. But she is affiliated with something. If she's a doctor or a nurse and promised to do no harm, I'm guessing she'll do no harm. Doesn't mean someone else won't on her behalf.

She doesn't watch her ex-boyfriend as my brother tosses him out. Shane gives him a strong shove, and he stumbles, then falls. He lands hard. His knees are the least of the pain he'll wake to. The bruises we gave him won't show because we hit him where his clothes will hide them. We also made sure we nailed him in places that didn't hurt as badly as they will tomorrow. No one needs proof we roughed him up. Though, I bet half the people here assumed we would.

"Are you okay?" I almost put my hand on my mystery woman's lower back. Yes, *my*.

"I am. I didn't thank you last time for defending me. Now I owe you double. Thank you."

"I can tolerate a lot, but not shite like that. I won't have a racist thinking he's cool to drink here, and I won't serve someone who speaks about women like that and thinks they'd still be welcome here."

"I—" She looks like she doesn't know what to say next. I get the sense she feels foolish standing with me. She should have broken up with Tony after the fucker's last confrontation with me. I told her it was bad enough I wouldn't repeat it. After hearing what she did, I think she gets why.

"Would you like a drink?"

"A gin and ginger, please."

I look at her for a moment, my head slightly tilted before walking behind the bar. She looks shy now.

"I know it's not everyone's idea of a good combo, but I like it."

"That's not what I was thinking. That's my go-to. I don't know anyone else who drinks it."

She slides onto a stool as she watches me mix the drink. I don't put in as much gin as I could. What I say surprises her.

"You look exhausted. You did when you came in. I'm guessing anything stronger than this will put you to sleep. I'm Finn, by the way. I didn't hear anyone say your name."

"I'm Althea."

I reach across the bar. She accepts my hand. Mine is warm and calloused, while hers is smooth and cool. Mine dwarfs hers, so I'm gentle. It's a firm handshake, but only because I can wrap my hand all the way around hers. I could crush hers. I hope it's obvious I'm being careful not to. I don't want to let go, and neither does she. I have to release hers first, otherwise, she'll have to pull it free. I don't want to, but I let go.

"Are you hungry? The kitchen's open. You didn't get to eat here last time. The food's delicious. All my nana's recipes."

That makes her smile. "What do you recommend?"

"How hungry are you?"

"Actually, pretty hungry. I can't remember back to lunch."

"Have you ever had steak and kidney pie? It's better than it sounds. I promise." Another one of those stick to your ribs meals as my nana called them.

"I'll trust you."

Of all the people she knows, I'm probably the last person she should trust. But I want her to. And that means more to me than I can explain.

"Kate, can you put in an order for steak pie, please?"

My phone vibrates in my pocket, so I ease it out far enough to see it's a text. Shite.

"Sorry. I have to answer this."

"Don't worry. You don't have to babysit me. I'll just sip my drink until my food comes."

Our gazes lock before I lean over the bar. "Nothing about you makes me think you're a child. Just the opposite."

Her cheeks darken, and I want to see what other reactions I can get out of her. But first, this text.

HEIDI

What's the deal? Are you coming?

I've known Heidi since we were kids. We've been fuck buddies for years. She's in an open throuple, so when we want to hook up we do. The woman she's with joins us sometimes,

25

and we were all supposed to get together tonight. I don't have to look at Thea to know that's the last thing I want right now.

ME

Sorry something happened at the bar that I had to deal with. I'm not going to make it.

HEIDI

Tomorrow?

I look at that text, and I realize something that practically knocks me over.

ME

No. You and Louisa shouldn't count on me anymore.

HEIDI

What? You've never said that. Not even the few times you've gone out with someone. You always knew it would end. You always come back.

ME

I'm not trying to hurt your feelings.

HEIDI

You didn't. I'm just shocked. It's cool, Finn. Really.

I believe her. She loves her partners, and I know she doesn't love me. We've just always been sexually compatible. It's never been romantic.

ME

Thanks nite

HEIDI

Nite

I slip my phone back into my pocket as Katie comes out with Thea's food.

Thea. Where did that come from? I heard her friend call her Ally. That's way too generic for a woman like the one sitting across the bar from me. She's just as stunning now as she was the first time I saw her. Her hair's in braids, pulled back in a thick ponytail. Her eyes are translucent, even lighter than before. It makes me wonder if it's because she's tired. Or could it maybe, possibly, just a tiny bit be because she's aroused? I sure as fuck am more than a bit. It's a good thing the bar is hiding my hard on.

"Can I ask you something?"

She hesitates before she nods.

"How long were you with him?"

"Two months."

That's not very long. Maybe that's why she didn't know he was a douche. Or is that her type?

"I never would have gone out with him once, let alone dated him if I knew that's what he was thinking. He and I have been friends for nearly a decade. I didn't want to believe someone I've known that long would say something so hideous about me. I brushed it off last time as you being overly sensitive or blowing whatever he said out of proportion. Now I realize you restrained yourself to only toss him out."

I didn't restrain myself this time. I keep a dozen socks with bars of soap in them for a reason.

"Do you work directly with him? Will it be awkward?"

"No. He's a nurse anesthetist, working primarily in oncology. I'm a neonatologist."

"You save babies' lives?"

"I try to."

I rest my forearms on the bar as I lean forward. "Today wasn't a good day even before you got here."

She stares at me for a moment then nods. "How'd you know?"

"You tried to sound optimistic. But you glanced down for a moment. It's a tell."

"It was a twenty-four-hour day, and I had to break some horrible news to a couple. It was the hardest day I've had in a long time. Probably since residency. Since the first time I had to tell parents whatever birth defect their child had was inoperable and terminal."

I've had to tell plenty of parents that their son isn't coming home. It's horrible being the bearer of that bad news. But it's always news about an adult. I can't imagine what it must be like for Thea or for those parents when it's a baby. I don't catch myself before my hand covers hers on the bar. My thumb slips between her thumb and forefinger. She turns hers over beneath mine. I give it a soft squeeze. Just like last time, she doesn't pull away. We're trying to figure each other out. Our gazes remain locked as she takes a bite of her food. She takes four more, and neither of us has moved our hand.

I have the strongest urge to ask her out. But a) I don't date. Ever. It's way too fucking complicated, and b) she just broke up with a guy thirty minutes ago. I'm not looking to be her rebound, and I sure as fuck don't want to come across as a creeper. But, God, it's tempting. It's only when Katie looks in our direction that we both seem to come back to Earth. We don't snatch our hands away like guilty teenagers, but we're close to it. Katie's been trying to catch my eye since she started working here a year ago. I've never considered her. She's pretty, and smart, and funny, and nice. But she does nothing for me.

Thea, on the other hand, does all the things. Like make

my dick ache right now. I'll be jerking off to the thought of her again. Yeah. I've already done that twice. I'll be doing it a lot more now that I've touched her, even if it was only her hand.

"Finn?"

I turn toward the kitchen and watch Mair step out. She must have come in through the back. I won't say anything to Dillan, but I am going to say something to her. I smile at Thea before excusing myself to speak to Mair. We hug and exchange a kiss on the cheek.

"Did you drive, or did Joey drop you off?"

"I drove."

I just look at her. She huffs and rolls her eyes.

"Your brother was coming in at the same time. You can check in the kitchen. Shane's eating you out of house and home. Rather here than my place."

I thought the guys left after they escorted arselick out. I should have known Shane would come back since there's fresh bread and butter in there. We get the butter from a dairy in Jersey. The soda bread is the same recipe my dad's family has used for like ten generations. However many back to the potato famine. My dad taught us, and I taught our cook who's my cousin Angie from my mom's side. It didn't thrill Da to know I'd let the secret out, but she's family.

"What're you doing here?"

"Sean called and said you sacked a waitress today. Something to do with the guy you banned the other day. I offered to come in. You know I'm capable."

She's definitely capable. She went undercover as a waitress at one of our strip clubs to write an exposé. That's how she and Dillan met. Needless to say, there were some tense moments when we realized she'd set out to ensure we lost money. But her family history is nearly as complicated as ours, and they intersect. Once we understood her rationale, we actually came to admire her even more.

"The aprons are in the back. All the tips are yours." I wink as I turn away.

It's at that moment I realize Thea's been watching us the entire time. Feck me. She has no way of knowing Mair is my cousin's wife. I hugged and kissed her right after holding another woman's hand.

"Finn?"

I turn toward Shane, who's walking toward me with basically a loaf of bread. There have to be only crumbs left in the kitchen. And that has to be half a stick of butter slathered on it. How he doesn't have high cholesterol and high blood pressure is beyond me. How none of us have high blood pressure is inexplicable considering we live under constant stress.

"What?" From his expression, I'm certain I won't like what I hear.

"The douche called the cops. We slipped them some cash, but that was out of my pocket. I need to pay my gardener today."

We're all the picture of domestic tranquility when we aren't engaged in our illegal business ventures. I'm the only one who lives in Manhattan, and my place is a converted warehouse made into luxury condos. It has exposed walls and overhead piping. It's my reprieve from real life and my favorite place. But it definitely isn't everyone's taste. I have overstuffed furniture and a library of books to rival most small-towns', but the walls and ceiling are rough. I like the contrast. The rest of the guys are spread out among Brooklyn, Queens, and Harlem. No one wants to live in the Bronx or Staten Island. Can you blame us?

"Come back to the office. I'll get some cash from the safe. How much?"

"A grand each."

"So, two?"

"Yeah."

"You're lucky I haven't hit the bank yet. I wouldn't have the cash if I hadn't gotten delayed with fuck nuts."

"And the beauty with the eyes."

Shane pretends to peek around me. My left eye narrows. It's my sign I don't find my brother's joke funny. It only makes him laugh harder.

"Leave off, Shane."

"There goes another one."

"The feck does that mean?"

"You know damn well what I mean. When are you asking her out?"

"I'm not. I don't date. I fuck. Rough. She just broke up with her boyfriend thirty minutes ago. And if that guy is any sign of what she values, we aren't compatible."

"Bullshit. Look. She's talking to Mair, and they're both looking over here."

Do I dare turn around?

"You know the code. Get what you need." I jerk my chin toward the hallway leading to my office.

"Why can't you do it all of a sudden?"

"Because I have other shite to deal with."

"What's her name, anyway?"

"Althea." *Thea.* It comes to mind every time I think of her.

"Kinda old fashioned."

"You're one to talk. All our names are old-fashioned, even if they've only become popular again in America in the last thirty years."

"Sure. But my name doesn't make someone assume I'm eighty."

"No. But your name is the equivalent of an Irish Chad."

31

"If I'm a fecking Chad, then you're a damn Irish Brad."

We look at each other. We are hardly either of those. We might be white and started out middle class, but that's about as far as we resemble mediocre frat boys still trying to live out college glory days from a decade ago. No dad bods among us. No dads among us. Though, with the way Dillan and Mair are, it wouldn't surprise me if we aren't throwing a baby shower in a few months. It's a good thing she's Protestant, and we're loose Catholics. Birth control is a must.

"Hello?" Shane snaps his fingers at me.

"I have more important things to think about than your gossiping. I need to sort out how much to pay our agents to make a move on Marco sooner. I want this done within the month."

"It will be. Chill."

"Get your money, little brother."

"Sure, *capitaine*."

The mob doesn't have the same structure as the other syndicates. At some point way back when, someone thought nautical terms would be a good way to distinguish rank. Dillan fucking loathes being called Skipper. He says it reminds him of *Gilligan's Island*.

I look over at Thea. If we're on *Gilligan's Island*, then she's definitely Ginger. I watch her talking to Mair, and I remember Dillan saying his wife reminds him of Mary Ann. I try to appear casual, like I have a reason to be behind the bar again. I pull some bottles out and get the Sharpie from the till. We have the modern touchless payment processors, but the cash register is a holdover from Nana's days. It's more memorabilia than functional.

I stand a few feet from where the women are chatting, and I busy myself marking the liquid lines on the bottles. I like to see just how much liquor goes every night. Shannon should be doing this. It was these markers that told me the liquor was going down too fast from her heavy-handed pours.

That reminds me. I have to pay her dad a visit. He's still actively working for us. He drives a garbage truck and hauls large items people put out at the curb. If it's worth anything, he sells it and tithes to us. If it's not, we take it as a charitable contribution. If he'd like to have a job tomorrow morning, he'll make sure his daughter understands how it goes when you work for the O'Rourkes. We aren't tyrants... As long as you obey.

I catch part of what Thea says to Mair.

"They seem really close. You said you're just filling in for today. Are they always together?"

Mair laughs. "More often than not. My husband and Finn are best friends. You've seen Sean and Shane, the twins. And I heard you met Cormac and Seamus, who are Irish twins. Dillan, my husband, and Finn are the ones without a matched pair. They became each other's pair when they were kids."

"Your husband?"

I can see from the reflection of a mirror across the bar that she turns her head slightly to see me. I pretend to be absorbed with my task. Thea'll clam up if she knows I'm listening. I'm certain Mair knows I have the same keen hearing her husband does.

"Yeah. Finn and Dillan are cousins. Dillan and I got married about two months ago."

"So, you and Finn never..."

"Good God, no. He's hot like the rest of them, but he's like a brother. Besides, my husband would throttle Finn if he came near me like that. They might share most things, but not women."

At least, not these days. Mair knows about a girl from the block who we're all intimately acquainted with. It was back in high school, but she worked at one of our strip clubs until she picked a fight with Mair, and Mair kicked her arse. Maybe that's an exaggeration. But Mair had Maureen pinned to the floor until Dillan and I and the others rushed in. Considering how Mair handled things the next time she had to defend herself, Mo was damned lucky she left with all her teeth.

"That's sweet. The part about you being close to your husband's family and how he sounds just the right amount of possessive."

"He is. He's the hottest of the six of them, though none of them agrees with me. He's wonderful."

"You really are newlyweds."

Mair laughs. "Have you been married before?"

"No. But I have married friends. I remember going through the bridesmaid circuit about five years ago. All my friends sounded like you."

"Do they still sound like me?"

Thea's cheeks darken in that adorable way I've noticed a few times. It's not a full blush. It's just at the apple of her cheek. I still want to know what she'd look like flushed right after she comes on my tongue or my cock.

"Some. From what I've seen of this family, I have a feeling you'll always sound like this. The men are— charismatic."

Mair giggles. "That's putting it mildly. If my in-laws are a clue, then we will be." She beams.

Three sisters married three brothers. Soulmates are real. Neither set of grandparents were, but they loved each other. My parents, aunts, and uncles are just different. Mair and Dillan are the same. I'm confident they'll be just like my parents and Dillan's. Just like Seamus and Cormac's parents. Mair might be blissful right now as she talks about her husband, but she's not blind to who and what Dillan is. She pushes back when she wants, and he listens.

"I need to get going. The food is amazing here. I wish I could have it again."

"You wish you could? Why can't you?"

"After tonight, I doubt I'll be welcome back."

Mair glances at me. She leans forward to whisper to Thea. I can read her lips.

"I guarantee you're not only welcome back, but you'll probably get an invitation."

Chapter Four

Thea

I stare at the woman who introduced herself to me as Margaret. She has the slightest hint of an Irish accent, and it's only with certain words. I felt like I'd been gut punched when I watched Finn wrap his arms around her and kiss her cheek. Now that I think back on it, it was a loose embrace. Not a lovers' embrace. But when you're not expecting it after practically coming from a guy just holding your hand, it hits you hard.

Now that I can think about it objectively, it's nice to see the closeness Finn shares with his brothers and cousins extends to his in-laws, too. I haven't really seen Finn with the other guys since most of the two times I've been here has been spent with Tony getting himself in the shitter. But I can tell. It's a vibe. It's how comfortable they are with each other. It's like they have telepathy.

It's more than just superhuman genetics that have them looking like carbon copies of each other. I don't know any other guys who are that close. At least, not so open about it. It makes me wonder if it's how their parents raised them or if something happened that made them so tight. I love my brothers, and they love me. They were best friends when we were kids, even though I'm in the middle. But I can tell it's not the same.

I don't know what to say to Margaret's suggestion that Finn might invite me back. That's exactly what I'd like, but if I hold my breath, I'll turn blue before that happens. I say nothing and take another bite of the steak and kidney pie cooled while Margaret and I were talking. It's delicious.

"Mair?"

We both look at Finn as he moves down the bar toward us.

"After what happened here, make sure one of us walks you to your car. Thea, the same for you."

"Thea?"

Oh, my god. He's blushing. He's so fair there's no way to hide it. I dart my gaze to Margaret, who looks like she's going to pee her pants from how hard she's trying not to laugh. She croaks a cough and excuses herself. His cheeks practically match his hair, which only makes his green eyes even more piercing. They're holding me captive. I don't know where else to look.

"Althea. Thea. Your friend called you Ally, but that..."

I wait for him to finish. Instead, he shrugs.

"No. You can't stop there. What's wrong with the name Ally?"

"Nothing. I just don't think it suits you."

"Oh?" Should I be insulted?

I wait for a better explanation, but nothing is forthcoming. I can wait. He seems intent on the same thing. I'm stubborn enough that I will last longer than him. But I can also stare him down. I have an unnatural ability to last nearly a minute without blinking. It used to creep my brothers out, so I practiced and got better at it.

"You can stare me down, Thea, but you won't break me."

I don't respond. I just keep watching him. Now I've laid down the gauntlet, I can't back down, even if curiosity is driving me crazy. I want him to admit the reason he called me that, not make me beg to know. When I can't go any longer without shutting my eyes for a second, I shrug as though I don't care. I turn my attention to my food.

"You asked what was wrong with the name Ally. I said nothing, which is true. Ask me why."

There's something in his tone that makes me want to obey. A richness to the timber that makes me shiver and my pussy ache. Now it's his turn to lock eyes with me with an intensity that makes me want to squirm. I can't help it when I glance down. He leans across the bar, his height making it easy for him.

"That's right, *cailín*. I call you Thea because it's as unique as you are. And I'm the only one who calls you that."

He straightens, and I look up. I don't know what that word means. It must be Irish. It sounds like a term of endearment. That he's already come up with a name for me that only he uses— that he can claim any part of me— even my name —as his... It makes me want to jump his bones.

"Why?"

"Because I can."

If it came from anyone else, he'd sound like an asshole. But as we watch each other, something is happening that I can't explain. He's letting me know my attraction isn't one-sided. We're letting each other know we want to do something about it. His self-assuredness is what most people would call cocky. But it's not bravado. Everything about him tells me he has the ability and the certainty that he can back up whatever he says.

"You don't even know my last name."

"You know I'm an O'Rourke. I suppose I am at a disadvantage."

"Gallagher."

He walks around the bar and comes to stand behind me. His hands rest on my waist, and we watch each other in the mirror. We make a striking couple since our coloring couldn't be more opposite. Despite how fair he is with red hair and freckles, there's a perma-tan that tells me he's spent a lot of time outdoors over the years. But it's still a different skin tone than mine. I like to think I'm the best mix of both my parents. People rarely believe my light eyes come from my mom's side of the family because she's Black, and my dad's mixed. But they do.

I wait to see if he'll do more, but he's still. The warmth of his hands seeps through my sweater top. Their weight is heavy, but not in a way that makes me feel trapped. It's reassuring. It's protective. His shoulders are so broad they stick out well past mine in the reflection. Even seated on a bar stool, my head only comes to just below his collarbones. I try to make my shift subtle as I lean back. It must be the only cue he needs because his right arm slides around my waist as he draws me against him.

He leans to whisper in my ear even though no one is close enough to hear. We're not alone, but everyone else at least appears occupied with their own conversations. Despite the noise and people moving around, it's almost possible to imagine we're alone. The way we've talked and are now together feels too intimate be part of a crowd.

"I know you broke up with him today, but I don't want this to be the last time I see you, Thea. When you're ready, I'll be waiting."

His warm breath on my neck tickles. I shy away by instinct, but it just presses me against him more. His arm tightens, and his other hand squeezes my waist.

"I hope I can make you shiver like that again. But not while we're in public."

Our gazes remain locked in the mirror as he continues to whisper to me. Fucking hell. This is the sexiest thing I can remember since starting to mess around with guys when I was fifteen.

"Finn, I've known Tony since I started working at the hospital almost ten years ago. We were friends. Two months ago, we were both single. He finally convinced me to go on a date with him. It was fun. The first five weeks together were great. But thinking back on it, it was probably because we had little time to spend together. Our rotations were pretty much opposite, so we made the most out of the time we had. The last three weeks got worse. Even before today and the last time we were here, things were going sour. I was going to dump him last week, but then he announced this party and how he'd already told his friends I would be there. Hindsight being twenty-twenty, I think he knew I was ready to break up, so he manipulated the shit out of me by guilting me into staying with him. But I'd already decided I was going to end it tomorrow. Then I was going to end it tonight. And you saw how it actually ended."

"Did he ever give you a hint of what he thought about you?"

"Never. That's why I thought you blew things out of proportion when you refused to repeat what he said before. What did he say?"

"Thea, I get why you want to know. But it'll only hurt your feelings, and I don't want to be part of that."

"It's not your fault, and I won't shoot the messenger."

His left eyebrow twitches. It was an infinitesimal movement, and if I didn't know what to look for with neurological responses, I would have missed it. It happened when I said the last three words. Tony called him a mobster... Hell.

"Finn, what does your family really do?"

I expect him to freeze. I expect him to be evasive.

"You heard what Tony called us. Do you know who those men were on the phone?"

"No."

"If you google my family, you'll find plenty. Thanks to some not-too-distant relatives, we've wound up in the news a lot more than we like. It's no secret. The other families are less conspicuous these days."

"I don't understand. Was what Tony said about you and yours friends being mobsters true?" My heart is racing, and right now, it's not because I'm turned on. Just the opposite.

"This is my bar, and most of the people in here are regulars. They come here for a reason. But I'd rather explain that reason in my office than out here for anyone to overhear."

"You want me to go into an office alone with you to discuss whether you're in the mafia?"

He looks duly insulted that I insinuated I'm not safe with him. But how the fuck should I know?

I should know because he's done nothing but defend me since before he even saw me. Just the knowledge that I existed was enough for him to be protective. Now that we've met— the way he's holding me is protective, as well as erotic. But I suddenly feel too confined, and I pull away from him. He releases me immediately, and that feels worse. I swivel on my stool. When I'm facing him, I nod, and he helps me down.

"Mair, I'll be in the office."

"No worries."

"Is Mair a nickname you gave Margaret?"

Does he give all the women in his life nicknames?

"No. Her parents call her that, so we started to as well. Her husband calls her Greta. Margaret is the English version of her Gaelic name. They mean the same thing. The modern version of her Gaelic name is Mairghráid. Mare like the horse and grade like in school."

"Then why'd she introduce herself as Margaret?"

"Because that's what she goes by professionally and with most people outside the family."

Sounds complicated. I'm interested, but not as much as I want to know what the deal is with his family. Finn punches in a code so quickly I can't catch what it is. I suspect he did that on purpose. The door unlocks, and he pushes down on the handle. I don't know what I expected in here, but definitely not something as inviting. There's an overstuffed couch I bet Finn's napped on— passed out on —more than once. There's a fireplace that looks like he uses. His desk chair is ergonomic but comfortable. He has family photos lining the walls. Maybe this is why he brought me in here. I'm super curious now.

Finn gestures to the sofa, so I sit. I want him to sit beside me. I want him close, and I can't justify why when he's about to tell me something that's likely to scare the shit out of me. But it would make it an awkward angle to talk. That's what I'm telling myself as he leans against his desk. I'm growing more nervous by the second, so it feels like a chasm is opening between us. I'm worried about falling in.

"Thea, when Tony mentioned me being a mobster, he wasn't wrong. But I'm not Al Capone. I'm not Bugsy Segal. I don't sit around smoking cigars and plotting bank robberies or putting out hits. I could deny what he said, but like I told you, my family's been in the news enough lately that you'll find stuff on your own. I'd rather explain it. When he said I was in the mob, it made me suspect he knows of the other families. Those men you heard on the other line are the leaders of the other major syndicates. It was a calculated risk to make that call in front of your friends and coworkers. I've never admitted to anyone what I'm telling you right now, but neither can I hide who I am or who my family is thanks to the internet. But I said nothing in public that can be held against me or my family. The other people here know exactly who we are. They're here because they either work for us or their family has been connected to mine for generations. I wish I had a different explanation, but I don't."

That creates an avalanche of questions that sweep me away. I just sit here. Mute.

"Thea?"

"Hmm." I'm still digesting what he said.

"Do you have questions?"

"Plenty."

I'm looking at his chest as though I can see through it to the wall. I'm staring into space as I try to wrap my mind around this. This man I've met twice, who I'm inexplicably drawn to, just admitted he's a criminal. A well-dressed criminal in his slacks and button down shirt with the sleeves rolled up and just enough of his chest showing to make me want to run my hands over his muscular pecs. His pants are just tight enough in the back for me to know I could bounce a dime off that ass.

Just what sorts of things has he done? Do I truly want to know? Is he dangerous to me? I told him I would trust him earlier. Yeah, that was about picking food. But can I trust him with anything else?

You have trusted him. You've trusted him more than once. You're alone in here with him.

I can ask myself those questions, but I already know the answers. I can trust him, and no, he's not dangerous to me. But I don't want to know what being a mobster means. I don't want that world near me. I've been adjacent to it before, and I don't want to go back to it.

But the longer I sit here, my mind whirling and Finn letting me think in peace, the more I realize my answers to those questions are the ones I think I'm supposed to give. The ones I feel obligated to give, especially as a doctor. How can I even consider a man attractive who probably does some horrible shit when I've pledged to do no harm?

Because the pledge was about me. It wasn't a pledge to stop other people. I know no specifics, yet I'm trying to decide. I wouldn't use speculation to diagnose or cure a patient. I would gather facts and observe. Those decisions might happen in a split second sometimes, but I can do that through using fact and observation.

"Finn, why did you tell me that if you've never admitted it to anyone else? Is it because other people already know, so you don't have to?"

"Sometimes. But I could have kept quiet. I could have lied. I could have done a lot of things besides confess that to you. I told you because I don't want to lie to you."

"Why does that matter to you?"

He stares at me. He can confess he's part of the organized crime world, but he won't tell me why he admitted what he did. He's looking at me as though I should already know the answer.

Margaret said he would probably invite me back. He said he wouldn't do anything because I'd just broken up with someone. He said when I was ready, he'd be waiting. He wrapped his arm around me, and when I watched us in the mirror, I pictured us as a couple. Feck, I've even thought our kids would have amazing eyes.

Feck. I noticed he'll say fuck when he directed it at Tony. But he won't swear in front of me.

"Were you serious when you said you'd be ready whenever I am?"

He scoots closer to me, but he continues to lean back

against the desk. "Thea, I've been attracted to you since the moment I saw you. You're beyond beautiful. But it's something about the look in your eyes. I don't need to know you're a doctor to know you're intelligent. You're poised even when you're threatening to kill someone. You take things in stride, but you'll also disagree with me without exploding. Knowing you're not only a doctor but one who takes care of babies in distress tells me more about you than I think you realize."

"Such as?" I want to know probably more than I should.

"You're responsible for people's lives and those of the people who love them most. You're calm in stressful situations. You're calm when talking to people in crisis. You're calm and make immediate decisions based on knowledge and observation. You have an inquisitive mind that likes to solve puzzles, even if they're not crosswords or jigsaws. You can find solutions to things most people would think are unsolvable. You care about others and will sacrifice for other people's wellbeing. You're used to being part of a team and will take advice from others as knowledgeable or more than you." He smiles at me. "I can go on."

"You can tell all that from meeting me twice?"

"I can deduce it from knowing what you do. Everything about your bearing tells me you're confident in public because you have to be. As a doctor, even when you have doubts, you must project that air of confidence in your decisions. I don't know what you're thinking right now or what you thought the last time you were here, but you're listening to me. That tells me you're curious, but fair."

Wow. I am those things. Like, if I had to get specific describing myself, then those are the things I'd say. But I haven't given much thought to it before. He said all of it so practically. As though how he described me is a given. He's not blowing smoke up my ass.

I've already told myself the answer to what I'm about to ask. But I need to hear it from him.

"Finn, am I safe with you?"

He watches me for a long moment, and I don't know why he isn't answering. He's looking at me as though he's evaluating what to say. I don't like it.

I'm unprepared for him to scoop me off the sofa and settle me on his lap. His left hand takes both of mine, and they rest on my lap. I should try to get up. I should push him away. Instead, I want to lean against him and shut my eyes. I want to melt against him. I feel safe with him like this. Like— I don't know— like he'll take care of me —protect me. His right hand glides up and down my right arm. It's so soothing that I give up trying to keep my body away from his. I lean against his chest and exhale as I let my eyes drift closed.

"Thea, you are safe from me. I will never intentionally hurt you. You know that. That's why you haven't jumped off my lap, screamed, or hit me. I told you. I don't want to lie to you. I can't promise you'd always be safe with me. I'll do everything I can to protect you no matter what. But I am a dangerous man."

Chapter Five

Finn

I have lost my goddamn mind.

It's not like what my family does is some well-guarded national secret. We've run the mob for generations, and the mob is the oldest syndicate in the U.S. Ironically, Mair is the one who made sure most parts of the world know who my family is. It wasn't her fault her articles leaked before she could delete them from her cloud. It also means denying my connection is futile. But I have never in my life admitted to someone I'm in the mob. People have insinuated. People have guessed.

What I just confessed could not only wind me up in prison, but it could take my entire family with me, including my mom and aunts. It's not like I've never been on a date. Heidi pointed out in her text that I do sometimes. But I don't have relationships. Her family and the woman's she's involved with have been in the mob for at least five generations. I don't have to hide that from them. I can— could— past tense —cancel on short notice, and they would think nothing of it.

Telling Thea is an entirely different story. She's a virtual stranger to me and knows nothing about this life. Yet, here I am, bringing her into it. There's only one reason I would: I want her. I want her for more than a few dates and a few good fucks. That makes her sound like a toy. A possession. Something for me to play with until I don't want to anymore. That couldn't be further from the truth.

The way I described her is exactly how I see her. Those qualities are ones she'll need if we have a future. And a future is exactly what I want because she's all those things. She's the first woman I've met who I can imagine coming home to, imagine having the strength to endure what life with a man like me means.

I won't suggest we elope tonight. I'm not in love. Yet. But I could easily fall in love with her. I don't know that because I've been in love before. Just the opposite. I know because I've never felt this way about any woman. I noticed all the qualities I described the first time I met her. I've thought about her more than I should have, and I secretly wanted dipshit to return. Not because I wanted another confrontation. I only wanted it because I prayed she'd come with him. I prayed she'd come alone. My mind has been working overtime since numb nuts left, and she stayed.

She's not the only one who makes split-second decisions. I make them way more often than I can count. I wouldn't even want to try. Too depressing if I did. But I have to. It's my life. It's my brothers' lives. My cousins' lives. My men's. If I can't assess and decide in an instant, then we all wind up dead. It's been like that since I was sixteen and went on my first mission. I wasn't supposed to be there.

I was in the wrong place at the right time. My dad and uncles were headed out with their men for a rendezvous with Enrique, but we weren't invited guests to his negotiations with a Brazilian cartel. I was impetuous and naïve. I jumped into one of the SUVs at the last minute. I didn't realize it was the one my dad was in. Holeee shit. He exploded. He was switching between English and Irish so fast there were entire sentences I didn't catch. Curses came out in a jumble. I thought he might have an aneurism. But it was too late. I was there, and I had to do my part. I did.

And my mom wouldn't speak to either of us for a week. She couldn't. My dad and I infuriated her too much. And she couldn't get past her fear for me. Every time she saw me, she burst into tears. She knew what life held ahead for me. But she also knew what everyone else— including me —knew. I wasn't ready. I hadn't had enough training for that kind of situation. I'd been doing small time hustles. I'd been extorting people twice my age. But I'd never been in a gunfight. If my dad and uncles hadn't been there to watch out for me— to pull me back into shelter —I would have died.

I learned a shite ton that day. Taking more than two seconds to decide means death. One second means getting shot at or stabbed. Having hours to consider Thea is a luxury. Even the minutes we've had talking today is a lifetime in my world. Even these thoughts are buzzing through my head at warp speed.

Thea's looking at me with a mix of curiosity and fear. I told her the truth. I am a dangerous man. I live surrounded by it, and I'm violent when I have to be. Very violent. Ruthless. Conniving. Intolerant. These aren't my natural inclinations. They're what this world made me. I can wish I were someone else, but I don't regret who I am. I have no remorse for the things I do to our enemies. But I'm sorry I'll bring any of it around Thea. But I guess I'm also a selfish arse to want her with me, anyway.

When she opens her mouth to say something, I can't begin to imagine what it will be. I don't think it'll be a refusal.

"Finn, I've sensed you're dangerous from the moment I spotted you. You're not arrogant or cocky. Those— those imply an attitude that can't be backed up. Bravado. An over-inflated sense of importance. Misplaced ideas of grandeur. Those aren't you. You radiate well-earned confidence in yourself. Strength, and not just physical. You command a situation with ease, and I'm positive that comes from experience. This is your bar, and I'm certain the police leave you alone most of the time. You could have pulverized Tony out back either time. You don't strike me as someone who lives this life for shits and giggles. You strike me as a man who can be ruthless and cunning, but that's because you have to. You strike me as a man who is usually even-tempered, thoughtful, insightful, and kind. And I'm not saying this about how you are with me. I saw the way you were with Mair. You could have lost your shit with your waitress, but you didn't. You saw things in Tony I should have but didn't. You could have repeated what he said, but you didn't because you knew it would do more harm than good. You are an enigma. You are two men in one body."

"You're the insightful one. I am two men. I'm the one I have to be, and I don't want him anywhere near you. I'm the one I choose to be. That's the one I hope you want to be with. But you have to accept both, Thea. There's no way around it."

"Why? I mean, not the part about there being no way around it. I mean the accepting it part."

I tighten my hold on her, and she relaxes even more. I'm looking down at her, but I can't see most of her face. I can tell her eyes are closed. She's responding the exact opposite of how she should. How most women would. It's not chasing the thrill of being with a man like me. It's like the more I tell her the truth, the safer she feels with me. The more she's letting down her guard. She knows I'll protect her, even if I haven't said it.

"You know why, *cailín*. It's why you haven't run from here and straight to the police."

She leans back so her head rests against my shoulder rather than my chest. Her mesmerizing eyes lock with mine. It's slow, but she nods. She cups my cheek, and her thumb runs over my cheekbone. I might be a ginger, but I can grow a full beard. She brushes my five o'clock shadow.

"What does that mean?"

"Little girl."

She doesn't shy away from that. I've heard Dillan call Mair that. It seemed sweet, but I didn't give it much thought. I know his proclivities since they're the same as mine and the other guys. None of us are into DDLG, but we like our kinks.

But it's not that. That word isn't about domination and submission. It's not because Dillan thinks Mair is a child, and I definitely don't think Thea is. She's all woman. It means I want to take care of her and protect her from this world— not just my life. She's physically smaller than me, too. I'm taller. My shoulders are broader. I'm stronger.

"Like how Shemar Moore calls the IT genius woman 'baby girl' on the TV show?"

"Yes. I don't see you as anyone younger than who you are. I'm not looking for that. I know some couples with that relationship, but I'm not a Daddy Dom."

"But you are a Dom, aren't you?"

"Why do you ask?"

"You brought up a BDSM dynamic most people wouldn't know about. You radiate that kind of control."

"You looked down earlier. You didn't object to me putting you on my lap, and you haven't tried to get up. Are you a sub?"

"Answer my question first, Finn. Don't deflect. Don't decide how you want to answer based upon mine."

My eyes widen. "I wasn't. I got curious and forgot you'd asked. I am not a Dom with any kind of arrangement. I've never been in a committed BDSM relationship of any kind. Thea, I haven't been in a committed relationship since I was a junior in college. My life isn't conducive to that romantically, and I'm not interested in that purely sexually. But I have a dominant personality, and I know you can understand why. I don't expect you to be a sub."

"But you'd like me to be."

"No."

"You can't easily put two dominant people together. One of them has to submit."

"You can submit without being a submissive. I don't want you to obey me, and I'm not into domestic discipline. You can argue with me, and you can do the things you want. I want an equal."

"But you want me to submit to you intimately."

This conversation just went from zero to sixty in one-point-five seconds. We may as well discuss it because if we can't agree on this now, then we won't agree on it later. I'd rather we're on the same page before we even go on our first date than have a great time going out on a few dates, then discover we don't want the same things.

"I think we both want that."

She watches me for what has to be at least a minute.

"You said you don't want domestic discipline. But you would like to spank me. You would like to command me if we have sex."

"Thea, if we date, there is only one instance where I will ever spank you as discipline. If you endanger your life or others. I won't tolerate it. There are precautions we will have to take because you don't know this life yet, and there are dangerous people in this world. If you stay with me, you will learn how to navigate this. Whether you knowingly or accidentally endanger yourself, I will spank you. Hard. If you do things that risk the lives of men assigned as bodyguards, I will spank you. Hard. But if you don't want to do something, I won't punish you for saying no. I admit I've had some kinky fucking thoughts about you."

"I've had some kinky fucking thoughts about you, too. I've never been in a submissive relationship. Not romantically or purely sexually. But I have been— am —into BDSM. Not with every partner." She gives me a pointed look that means Tony. "I have submitted physically and to an extent mentally. But I see my submission as not a true power exchange. I always have the right to say no. It's my choice what I submit to. I still have control of myself, and I suppose I have control of the situation."

"You do. I may take the lead and control what we do, how we do it, and even when we do it. But you can always express what you do or don't want. And you ultimately have the last word. I will never ignore or refuse your limits. If this isn't what you want now, or it becomes something you don't want later, then you tell me. Thea, I don't have to have this part of a relationship to want a relationship with you."

"A relationship?"

"We are not negotiating sex, and you know that."

"True. You said you haven't been in a relationship since you were— what —twenty-one— twenty-two. Did you have this conversation with that person back then?"

"No. We sensed we were into similar things, but I knew she wasn't someone I would be with for long. She wasn't someone I thought I could share my life with. My real life. She saw what I wanted her to see."

"You want me to see the good, the bad, and the ugly."

"Never the ugly. You may have a clue what that is. But I will never tell you. I was honest when I said I don't want to lie to you. That doesn't mean there aren't times when I will. I will lie about where I am, who I'm with, and what I'm doing. I will lie to keep you safe, to keep my family safe, and to keep the people who depend upon me safe."

"You didn't say you would lie to keep yourself safe. You didn't forget to say that. You put other people ahead of you. You aren't selfish. You're a leader."

"I am selfish. I'm the definition of selfish to even consider wanting you. I'm selfish to ask you to be part of this."

"You said you'd lie about who you're with."

"I will never be unfaithful to you. I will not sleep with someone to get what I want. Not you. Not anyone else. But I do business in some pretty shady places, and they often involve half or completely naked women. They are not who I'm there to see. They are not who I'll be looking at. I don't go to strip clubs for the shows. Besides, there would be a line eleven deep of family members to castrate me if I did something so disgraceful as to cheat."

She shifts to straddle me, so we can look at each other more easily.

"Can I break up with you and walk away whenever I want?"

"Always. No matter what type of relationship it is. How casual or serious it is. No cement shoes. No sleeping with the fishies. No hits put on you. None of that. I told you. I'm not Al Capone or Bugsy Segal. I'm not Hollywood mob."

"You definitely are not that. Can I tell you what I think?"

"Always. I want to know."

"I think you are a man who makes me feel special. You say I'm beautiful, and I appreciate it. I don't see myself that way, so it feels good for a man as hot as you to think that about me. I—"

"Wait. I get you might not see yourself the way I see you. But does it surprise you that I think you're good enough for me?"

"Maybe not you, but the rest of the world will think our attractiveness is unbalanced."

"Thea, you have to be kidding. I don't see myself the way you do me. But no one in their right mind would think I'm more attractive than you. You're stunning." I pull her hips toward mine. "You have to have felt that since the moment you sat down. I want you, Thea. I want to fuck you, and I have since the moment I saw you. I want to be inside you. I want to taste you. I want all the things we can think of. I'm attracted to you physically, but I want you to know it's more than that."

"You have. You've been clear about what attracts you to me. I appreciate that. It's more than superficial. But it still feels good to know you also want me because you think I'm pretty."

"Stunning. A kid's doll can be pretty. You take my breath away."

Her smile is soft, almost self-conscious. It's sweet. It's enticing. But I won't rush her. I know I said I would control things, but she has to come to me. I never want her to feel forced or trapped.

"Finn, may I kiss you?"

"You never have to ask, little one."

She leans forward and tilts her head. Our lips brush, and the surge of lust that shoots to my dick makes it throb. She feels it and presses her hips forward. I swallow my groan. My hand cups her neck while the other grips her hip. Together, we move her hips to rub against me. The moment she parts her lips, I plunge my tongue into her mouth. Sweet Baby J. She's sucking lightly on my tongue, and she knows exactly what it's doing to me. Fecking hell. I'm going to come in my pants if this keeps going. But I don't want to stop her.

The kiss keeps going, and it's getting more heated by the second. My cock's telling me to lay her on the sofa, strip off her pants and panties, and feast on her pussy then thrust until I explode inside her. My mind is telling me to slow down. Neither is communicating with the other. I settle for both hands on her arse, pressing her against my cock but not letting her rock.

"Finn." She sighs my name as we come up for air.

"I've never had a kiss like that before." I didn't mean to blurt that out.

"Like what?"

"Like nothing else in the world exists but us. Like I'm floating out of my body, looking down on us and wondering how the feck I got so lucky. Like I want to keep doing that until we're too tired to keep going. Then I want to do it some more."

Well, fuck. Why not confess every fecking thing? I may as well tell her it wasn't Sean who broke my parents' wedding flute when I decided to see if I could drain a glass of beer without holding it. Yeah, I let my baby brother take the fall for that, and he never ratted me out. My parents still think it was him.

"I've never had a kiss like that, either."

"Yeah?"

"That didn't feel like a first kiss. Like— it was so natural. Like we've been doing this for longer than a few seconds. But it was definitely more momentous than any other first— any — kiss at all."

I lean in for another one, this time taking control from the beginning. Her hand tunnels through my hair as the other grips a handful of my shirt. I roll us, so she's beneath me.

"I won't take this any further. My brothers and cousins have the code to this office. There are other people here. And

I'm not having our first truly intimate encounter be in a bar. But I want to. I want all of you."

She flexes her hips and grins.

"I know."

I sorta break my promise. I skim by hand down her pants and beneath her panties. When she doesn't stop me, I slide my fingers between her pussy lips before I pull them out. I suck the tips of them.

"You want me too."

"What're you going to do about it?"

Chapter Six

Thea

I can't believe I just issued that challenge. I meant it. I just can't believe I said it. The wolfish expression in his eyes tells me he'll take me up on it. I can't wait. I want this way more than my common sense says I should. But Finn draws me inexplicably. It's like this is where I've always meant to be. Talking to him. Sitting on his lap. Kissing him. Being beneath him. The feeling of all that— physically and emotionally —is like I'm breathing easier than I ever have before.

I widen my legs, and he settles his cock completely against my pussy. Fucking hell. I could tell he was endowed, but dear God, he could be a porn star. I don't have tons of experience, but I have more than enough to know he's bigger than average. Fuck.

I'm a damn doctor and have seen all sorts. You don't go straight from med school to your specialty. I had rotations in other departments. I did all the standard ones. Neurology, internal medicine, general surgery, and family medicine were where I got some field experience on men's dicks. OBGYN and pediatrics were when I knew I wanted to be a neonatologist.

"Finn." I moan his name a second time and move restlessly beneath him. I'm horny as a fucking toad. We both have clothes on, and all we've done is kiss and press our bodies together, but I ache. I want to feel him inside me more than I have ever wanted another guy.

"I know, *cailín*. I want it too."

Little girl. The way he says that endearment. I don't feel like a child. But I feel precious. The more he told me, the less scared I felt. More worried about him and what could happen, but less scared about the unknown. By the time he finished, I wanted to curl up like a content little kitten. I didn't want to curl into a defensive ball. I felt completely relaxed. I know that no matter what happens— we date— we date and break up— we don't date —he will protect me. I thought I wanted no part of it, and I didn't before he explained.

As our lips fuse once more, I give myself entirely over to the kiss. The rest of the world vanishes. It's Finn and me. That's it. He's holding my thigh, pinning it against his hip as he rocks against me. The hint is almost excruciating in how it teases me. But it's like we both come back to reality at the same time. He pulls back, and I sit up. My lips feel plumper, and I wonder if the skin around my mouth is red from his stubble.

He lifts me like I'm a feather, which I am not. I'm thick, and from the way his hands are running along the outside of my thighs, his fingers tight, he likes it. I sink against his chest, my head once again against it. It feels so natural to be with him like this. I can hear his heartbeat. It's definitely rapid, as though he needs to catch his breath. But it's steady and strong. It's incredibly soothing after the intensity of passion.

"Thea, will you go out with me?"

"Yes." No brainer.

"When? What would you like to do?"

Besides you?

"I don't know when you're free. I'm off for the next three days. Then I have a thirty-hour shift. I'm not really off after that. I'll still be on overnight call a couple times. One night on and three off, so that's ten hours off between shifts. I sleep at the hospital a lot of times."

"Do you sleep most of the day after your shift? You said you just came off a twenty-four-hour one, and it was a harder day than usual because you had to give some bad news."

He paid attention. Not just that it was a rough day, but why it was. He's thoughtful.

"I usually pass out for a solid ten hours, then I'm back to normal."

"Is tomorrow night too soon?"

He sounds like he's trying not to sound too eager. I grin and shake my head.

"Tomorrow night is perfect."

"What would you like to do? Dinner?"

Jump your bones.

"That sounds nice."

"I own a comedy club, and there's a great woman on tomorrow night. But the show doesn't start until nine-thirty. Is that too late? Are you into that sort of thing?"

"That sounds perfect. I could do with a few good laughs."

"Dinner at seven-thirty?"

I nod. He hesitates for a moment, unsure if he should say what he's thinking.

"I don't know what's easiest for you. We could meet there. I could pick you up. I could send a driver."

"I'll be in Jersey tomorrow afternoon with my parents. I can meet you."

"Have you been to La Petite Fleur?"

That's not super fancy, but it's definitely a higher end restaurant.

"A couple of times. I like it."

"Then seven-thirty at La Petite Fleur."

We stare at each other. Neither of us moves. We look at each other's mouths, the temptation thrumming between us. We laugh as we both sigh. I get up, and he follows me. I glance at my watch. It's already eight-thirty. I've been here two-and-a-half hours. It doesn't feel that long. We must have been making out for a while.

He rests his hand on my lower back as he opens the door and lets me pass through it first. I have a moment of embarrassment as we step back into the main bar area. We've been in his office a long time. There are people still here who know we went back there together. But no one pays us any attention. That makes me wonder if they're used to Finn taking women there.

"*Cailín*, the people here know not to be nosey. They don't ask questions, and they don't make assumptions. It's not that I fuck women back there so often they don't notice."

I look up at him in surprise.

"I know how it looks if you don't know who frequents this bar. But the people here know I don't hook up with random women. They know I don't take any women back there to fuck. All of them are regulars."

"You read my mind."

"Sort of. I scanned the crowd to see who was here and who was looking in our direction. I know almost everyone here and have for years. The few people I don't know wouldn't know to think there's anything odd about me coming out here with you."

I breathe a little easier until I spot Mair. She knows we went back there. She knows how long ago that was.

She's serving drinks at a table, but now I'm doubly embarrassed.

"Mair won't think anything of it. She knows me."

That doesn't sound good. Won't think anything of him taking a woman back there?

"Thea, she knows I don't screw around. She won't think less of you for being back there. She won't assume it was some quickie that wasn't so quick. If I hadn't gone back there to talk to you, she would be the one telling me I'm a dumbarse for missing my opportunity with an amazing woman."

I'm looking up at him while he speaks, but now I'm looking back at his cousin-in-law. She shoots me a friendly smile, and it eases my worry.

"Did you drive?"

"Yeah. I'm parked around the corner."

"This is a good neighborhood, but I'd feel better walking you out. Especially after earlier."

"I appreciate it."

We head out and walk the half block, and he tells me he inherited the bar from his grandmother. The kiss is over too fast, but there are plenty of people on the sidewalk. Then I'm home, passed out, dreaming about the hot red-head.

"Mom?"

"Hey. I'm upstairs."

I hang up my jacket and purse and head up to find my mom. She's folding laundry in her room, and I notice a couple of shirts that belong to my older brother. He moved out before I did. Why's Mom doing his laundry?

"Hi, Ally." My mom gives the best hugs. Maternal hugs. Finn's hugs feel entirely different, but fuck, they are the best

I've felt from a man. He gave me one just before I got in the car last night.

"Hi."

"Why do you have some of Jamie's shirts?"

"He and Asher had the kids over, and Skyler had an explosive diaper. Twice. You know they both always have an extra shirt for themselves in the diaper bag. Jamie went through both and wound up going home in one of Papa's."

My brother and brother-in-law have four kids, and the youngest is six months old.

"How's Skyler doing?"

My mom hesitates. It's only for a second, but I know it.

"What happened at the last appointment?"

"The cardiologist wants to do some more tests."

"Dr. Rodesman is the best pediatric cardiologist I know. If he wants more tests run, it's because he wants to be absolutely certain of his diagnosis. It doesn't automatically mean something bad."

My nephew has a congenital heart defect— CHD. In the grand scheme of things, it's mild. But it's going to take ongoing care, not just because of the heart itself but because of the related medical and developmental challenges it will present. I was at the hospital the day he was born. I didn't know Skyler was the baby in distress when I got the page. Thankfully, there were two other neonatologists on call at the same time. I didn't have to be my nephew's doctor. Instead, I was able to explain to my family what was happening.

That was the worst day of my life. *That* was the worst day of my career. I made it through the first twenty-six hours of Skyler's life, having to come in and out of the postpartum room where my family and the biological mother were because of my own patients. I finally got five minutes to myself. I have never cried so hard in my life. Then I had to pull myself together and do my rounds.

"Asher says the doctor has been amazing with Skyler. But it's hard, you know?"

"I do. Jamie and Asher know I'm happy to talk to them after any appointment."

"They do. Thank you, sweet pea." My mom's been calling me that for as long as I can remember.

"How's everything else going?"

My mom's even slower to answer that. I raise my eyebrows and wait.

"We weren't going to say anything until you all came over next Saturday."

"Weren't going to say what?"

Next Saturday will be my first day off again after the three I have now. It's Wednesday, so that's a week and a half. My mom puts down the socks she just rolled. If she can't fold laundry at the same time as talk to me, there's something wrong. She could fold laundry while grounding me for two weeks from TV when I did something wrong as a kid.

"Your dad lost his job last week."

"Last week?!" And they were going to wait another week and a half to tell us?

"Yes. The company says he's underperforming."

"How? He still puts in the same long hours plus overtime that he has since he started working on the fabrication floor. He never takes sick days. The people under him respect *and* like him. Is it agism?"

"Yes. You know your dad's arthritis is getting worse, so they're saying he can't do all the parts of his job description."

"That's ridiculous. His job doesn't involve him being a welder anymore. He supervises. What does the union have to say?"

"They're doing what they can, but it's slow going. And Papa isn't sure he'd even want to be reinstated there."

"Can he go on disability?"

"He qualifies, but at his age, if he goes on, who would hire him if he goes off it? He's not ready to be home all day, and you know we need his income."

I sit on the edge of their bed. The same one I climbed into and scooted down under the covers between them when I had a bad dream or didn't feel well. The same one my mountain of a father used to play tickle wars with me on.

"He's not that old."

"He's fifty-seven."

"So, what now?"

My mom resumes folding, which is a good sign. "We're going to tap into our retirement, take the penalty, and hope he gets a new job or his old one back."

"No."

My mom looks at me askance. "What do you mean 'no?'"

"No. I'm a lot further away from retirement than either of you are. I have way more time to save aggressively if I take a break now. You are not tapping into a fixed income when you both might live another thirty-odd years."

"And in thirty years, you'll be ready to retire too."

"Mom, no. If Papa can't get disability or a new job, then I am helping you with whatever unemployment doesn't cover. You live a modest life. It's not like I'd be floating your jet-setting lifestyle. You know I have the means to do that."

"You're still paying off med school."

"I am. And I'm actively saving for my retirement beyond what the hospital matches. I can reallocate those funds for now."

"We're not—"

"So, you're going to consider the alternative. That's what you're not telling me."

My mother's eyes narrow at me, and I feel like I'm six again and just put stickers all over my little wooden rocking chair.

"You know that isn't what we're going to do."

"And when he finds out and comes knocking? Then what? You won't be able to say no."

"He won't find out."

I scoff at that. "Uncle Corey will absolutely find out. And he will absolutely come knocking. Or worse, he'll send a half dozen guys to smash your windows and key your cars. He doesn't give a hoot that Papa is his own nephew."

This is what I feared being with Finn would bring back into my life. That being around the mob would be like the motorcycle club my dad's uncle leads. My grandfather was a member too. My dad had no choice but to run with them when he was in his twenties. But he beat the shit out of his cousin for something he said about my mom when my parents were dating. It was along the lines of what Tony said about me— the caramel swirl part. Papa put his cousin in the hospital for three weeks with so much internal bleeding everyone was certain he would have died. When my dad said he wanted out, they showed him the door.

But that hasn't kept Uncle Corey from making an appearance from time-to-time. I also know he's been extorting my parents since they got married. They might have let my dad out, but he pays for the privilege of staying out. It's that monthly payment that worries me more than if they can keep the electricity on. My mom makes enough to support them. So did my dad. But the moment Uncle Corey knows they're having a hard time, he'll up the payments. He'll make sure they have other hardships, like needing cars or the house repaired.

Then he'll loan shark them. I've seen him do it to other people in our family.

"Ally?"

I twist to look at my dad in the doorway. "Hi, Papa."

I go over to him and hug him, too. He's as tall as Finn, at a few inches over six feet, but he's a mountain. His forearms are the same width as the bottom half of my calves, which are not thin. He was a welder for nearly twenty years before he became a supervisor. There isn't a ton of hand fabrication that still goes on, but there's enough custom that his arms show the years of using a hammer and anvil. He's as in shape now as he was when he beat the shit out of his cousin. I've seen photos from when my parents dated.

"I told Ally." My mom sounds so defeated.

"I know. I could hear you as I came up the stairs. Ally, you are not taking care of us. We're not feeble quite yet."

"No one's saying you are. There are plenty of cultures where this is totally a normal part of intergenerational families. Why does it have to be different here? I have the means."

"Because you have a future to consider, and as kind as your offer is, it's short-sighted."

I take a deep breath. I won't convince them otherwise. This is why my mom gave in and told me alone. She knew I would insist, and it's actually better that I'm here alone than with my brothers. They'll make the same offer, but they both have families. I'm the only single one with no one to support but myself. I'm also the highest paid of all three siblings.

Jamie and Asher are both associate professors who went through funded PhD programs, but they have kids, one of whom has severe medical issues. My other brother, Rod, is married with one kid. He's an entrepreneur with a fleet of new trucks to pay for as an outsourced delivery service provider. He has thirty people working for him who need to get paid every two weeks. He's also paying off his MBA. His wife is a nurse at the same hospital as me and is going through a doctoral program for Nurse Practitioners. This isn't the time for either of my brothers to help, though I know they will insist. I'm the one who can do this, and I will. This isn't the hill I'll die on today, but it is the war I will win.

"Just keep it in the back of your mind, okay?"

My parents nod, and I know that means fat chance. But both of my parents combined still don't equal how stubborn I can be. They know that, so I don't meet either of their gazes, or they'll know I have no intention of relenting. Truth be told, they already know that. I just don't want them to see how deep I'm digging my heels in.

"Are you ready, Mom?"

She just finished folding the laundry, and my dad will put it away. We're going to find a graduation gift for my sister-in-law. We could order something online and probably will, but it's a good excuse to spend time with my mom. They don't live far outside the city in Long Branch, but I don't come out here that often because of work. Sometimes they come into the city, but neither of them likes it much. I give my dad another hug as I walk past, then my mom and I head out. This wasn't what I expected to hear today.

"How was your day?"

Finn holds the restaurant door open for me, and I barely keep from grimacing. I let the subject rest with my parents, but when my mom and I were looking at gifts, it was a silent albatross around both our necks.

"It was nice."

He glances down at me and draws me aside before we can

get to the host's stand. He's watching me, and I feel like he sees into my very marrow.

"What happened, *cailín*?"

"Nothing."

"Tell me you'd rather not say. Don't tell me nothing because I know it's something."

That's not disconcerting as fuck.

"How can you tell?"

"Nothing about how you said nice sounded genuine. It's how someone deflects when they don't think the other person wants to hear how shitty something was. When I asked what happened, you glanced down. You did that at the bar yesterday, and I told you it was a tell. You only shifted your gaze to my shoulder for a second, but I saw it."

"Are you always that observant?"

"Yes."

I wait for more, but he's not forthcoming. Now who's turn is it to be evasive? But as I look at him, it dawns on me. He's probably got eyes like a hawk because of whatever situations he winds up in. The ones he'll lie about.

He wraps his arm around my waist and draws me close enough that we can speak without anyone else hearing. His hand on my waist feels good.

"Thea, this is our first date. We still don't know each other, but I told you there are things I'm going to lie about. It's hypocritical of me to demand you tell me everything. I won't. Your thoughts are your own and always will be. But I won't lie to you if I don't have to. Please don't lie to me. Just tell me you don't want to talk about it, and I'll respect that."

"Thank you. I just got some news today that was upsetting. It's nothing catastrophic, but it's going to take some sorting out."

"Is there anything I can do to help?"

Whack my dad's uncle? Not quite the request you make on a first date.

"No. But thank you for offering. It means a lot." And it does.

He puts his forefinger underneath my chin and nudges upward. He presses a soft kiss to right beside my mouth.

"Neither of us would be here if we wanted to be fuck buddies. I've told you I don't date or do random hook ups. You know what I am. You wouldn't be anywhere near me if you thought this would be a couple dates or a few amazing fucks. If there's anything I can do, tell me. You don't have to ask, little one. Just tell me."

As my green eyes meet his green eyes, I know he's telling me the truth. Our different shades of green are a fitting metaphor. We're very much alike, but at the same time, we are so completely different. He pulls back, and I go on my toes to steal a quick kiss before we walk to the host's stand. The man standing behind a stack of menus looks at me as though my tits and ass are hanging out like an invitation. I'm in a knee-length dress that fully covers my cleavage. Then he looks at Finn and freezes. I glance up at Finn, and his expression is enough to make the devil run away. His arm goes back around my waist, and the vein in the maître d's left temple jumps out. He looks like he's going to shit himself.

"Mr. O'Rourke—"

"Do not."

Do not what? Speak? Apologize? Finn didn't bark an order, but it was clearly a command. The man just dips his chin and gathers two menus. I walk between the guy and Finn. The maître d' reaches for my chair, but Finn gets to it first. I can feel the anger pulsating off him as he moves aside to let me get to my seat. He's gentle as he pushes it in. The man hands me a menu first then Finn, but Finn puts it on the table without a glance.

"Have you been here before?" I shift my gaze from Finn to the maître d when he makes a strangled sound at my question. His face is so red, I'm actually alarmed. I'm ready to stand and offer the man my seat.

"I own this place."

Oh! Now I nearly laugh in the maître d's face. No wonder he looks ready to shit himself. He looked at his boss's date like I'm Julia Roberts out of *Pretty Woman*— a hooker. Since I'm appropriately dressed, I suppose I can take his lasciviousness as a compliment. It was poorly shown appreciation.

Nope. From the way Finn's still looking at the man, then the way the guy beats a hasty retreat, I would say that isn't remotely how Finn sees it. I suppose I shouldn't either.

"I'm sorry, Thea."

"That wasn't your fault. I suppose I could even look at it like a compliment."

His jaw clenches.

"You are a beautiful woman, and I'm going to have to get used to men looking at you in a way I admit makes me want to bash their teeth in. But there wasn't a damn thing respectable about what he just did. It's as much about you being my date as it is me being unwilling to tolerate him behaving that way in front of other guests. Not on a moral principle or a business principle."

Who would have thought a man in the mob could have such scruples? I could tell from the moment I saw him he has no patience for bullshit. I never guessed he'd have such a strict sense of morality.

"Thea, I wouldn't want him to look at my mom or aunts like that. I wouldn't want him to look at Mair like that. If I'd find it objectionable that he did it to them, then I have to find it objectionable that he looks at any woman like that. The fact that you're my date, and he only fixed his attitude because he saw me, tells me things about him I didn't know before. I'll give him one more chance. If I find out he acts like this on the regular or does it again, I won't have it. I won't have any employee feel uncomfortable around their manager, and I won't have any patron refuse to come back because of it. He will not cost me good wait staff or customers. Plus, he's a dick."

I chuckle at the last part. "I don't disagree. What do you recommend?"

"The entire left side of the menu tonight, and the entire right side the next time you're here. Besides McGinty's, this has the best food out of all the restaurants and bars I own."

"Do you have many? I didn't realize you're a restauranteur."

"I'm not. I'm an accountant and a day trader. But I like good food that I don't always have to cook. Since my mom refuses to cook for my brothers or me because we eat too much, I have to go elsewhere. She only cooks for us when it's my parents' turn to host our Sunday family dinners."

His eyes crinkle at the corners as he speaks, so I know he's joking. I can hear it in his tone. It's sweet how he talks about his family. It matches the little I've seen of him with his brothers and cousins. He was loyal and defensive a moment ago when he said he wouldn't tolerate disrespect toward the women in his family, but now he sounds lighthearted talking about his mom.

"Do you have Sunday family dinners every week?"

"Usually. Not everyone can always attend, but we rotate. My parents and uncles and aunts made sure we could all cook before we left home. They survived the teenage years with six boys raiding their fridges. They said we were on our own once we moved into our dorms. We could eat at the university cafeterias or cook for ourselves, but they were all off the clock except for once every nine weeks when their turn comes up."

I like that idea. My family has meals together a couple times most months. But it's nothing set in stone. They'll go to Jamie and Asher's to see the grandkids or Rod's to see my niece, but my schedule makes it hard to be included often. Until hearing Finn talk about it, I didn't realize I feel excluded. No one means to, and it's never bothered me to just see pictures or hear stories. But it gives me a little sad twinge.

"Do you have siblings?"

"Yeah. An older and younger brother."

This is a good time to test the waters. Things could be dead in them right now depending on how he reacts.

"My older brother and brother-in-law have four kids. The youngest is six months old."

"That must make Christmas fun. And loud."

He doesn't drop a beat. He's been open minded about everything so far, but I don't know if and where there's a limit.

"Thea, I was raised Irish Catholic. But no one in my family is the stereotype of anything."

My cheeks are ablaze. I inwardly cringe. He reaches across the table and covers my hand just like he did on the bar yesterday.

"We're getting to know each other. It's okay to want to make sure I'll accept your family. Feck knows I'm asking a lot of you."

He's definitely not any of the stereotypes of mobsters I've heard or seen in the news or the movies. All I can do is smile and nod as our waitress approaches. I skim the menu and pick something.

"Do you know what you'd like, Thea?"

"Yes." I close my menu and look up at the waitress. "The poulet à la provençale, please. Is your Riesling sweet or dry?"

It's one of my favorite dishes. Chicken with herbs de Provence. Rosemary, fennel, thyme, and oregano.

"Sweet."

"A glass of that, please."

The woman looks at Finn, and I get what he meant about wanting to bash someone's teeth in. She looks like she'd like to have him for dinner. Finn's hand is still covering mine, and she's still looking at him with unmasked interest. Do they have a past?

"The steak au poivre with a glass of Malbec, please."

He doesn't even look at her as he orders his steak with cognac cream sauce. I almost ordered that instead of the chicken. But I had the steak and kidney pie last night, so I wanted something a little different.

We hand her the menus, and she turns away. I force myself not to watch her. It hurts when he pulls his hand away, but then he's moving his chair to be next to mine instead of across. He laces his fingers with mine.

"How many hours are your shifts? Are they usually twenty-hours or longer?"

I almost answer "huh." I wasn't ready for that. It's not that he's trying to avoid me thinking about the waitress. I think he truly didn't care enough about her for him to give her a second thought. I wish I could be that blasé.

"It was a short shift because I filled in for someone. Mine are usually at least thirty-six hours."

"Do you have any mandatory breaks? I mean, I assume it's not a fifteen-minute break for every four hours you work. But do they have to let you rest or sleep or anything?"

"Haha. No. Definitely no mandatory breaks of any kind. I eat and sleep when I can. I usually start the morning with rounds. I'll check in with the nurses who were there overnight and the doctors coming off rotations. I'll examine some babies and observe the others for a bit. I'll make any medication or treatment changes needed. I try to spend a couple minutes talking to all the parents there. They watch their babies like hawks, so they see things we might miss because their care teams can't be beside the babies all the time like their parents are. I can be called away for a delivery at any time, but usually we manage our duties, so those on rounds can finish them before being on call for high-risk deliveries or newborns in distress."

"That must be exhausting physically and emotionally, but it must be amazing to save a baby and know they're going home with their family."

"It truly is. Sometimes it's weeks or months before they go home, but that feeling makes up for the days that don't go so well."

"Like yesterday?"

He keeps his voice soft when he says it. It's like he doesn't want to reopen a wound, yet he wants to acknowledge that he remembers what I told him.

"Yes." I actually feel like sharing with him. I rarely want to talk about work outside of work if something went wrong. "I had to tell a couple their baby won't be coming home with them. It's a matter of when, not if, she'll pass away. They need to decide whether they wish to cease care now or prolong life. Either way..."

That's as much as I can say, so I shrug. I was at that delivery. Mom and Baby nearly died. The mom will never have more children, and it was their first one. The baby was only three weeks early, so considered full-term. But there were a lot of issues that were undetectable through the regular ultrasounds that aren't even done that often unless there's a reason to. Everything seemed so normal until it wasn't.

"I'm sorry you went through that. It never gets easier to let someone know their child isn't coming home. I can't imagine having to tell a baby's parents that."

I meet his gaze, and he's giving me a strong fucking hint without saying what he means. Men— his men —die around him. Because of him? Directly or indirectly, and he has to be the bearer of the bad news.

"So, you catch naps and meals when you can? Do they have break rooms like they show on TV?"

"Sort of. Hospitals vary, but there's usually an on-call room. Some places call it a doctors' mess, like the navy type of term. There's at least one couch or a set of bunk beds. The one I use has a locker room attached with showers."

"Are they at least comfortable?"

"Maybe. I'm usually not awake long enough to think about it. My head hits the pillow, and I'm out until I get paged, or someone wakes me."

"Can you sleep anywhere?"

"Once I got to med school, I learned to."

"That sounds like Cormac. The man could sleep standing up and wake up fresh as a daisy. Is the cafeteria any good?"

"It's okay. Better than it was when I started there as a resident. I pack food most of the time because the cafeteria is often closed when I have time to eat. You said you're an accountant and day trader. What made you get into that?"

"I have a thing for numbers. I can look at them and arrange them however I need them to calculate or find patterns with little effort. Things just stand out, and I can do mental math without giving it much thought. I've been that way since I was a kid. I'm also the most budget oriented of all of us. I wouldn't say I'm obsessive about making accounts balance, but I don't like it when I can't account for more than five cents."

He makes it sound like he's the family accountant. I guess— I suppose the mob is a family business.

"Thea, we all own multiple businesses. I'm the accountant for *everything*. My cousins also trust me to invest their money because I'm good with patterns. I can project how stocks are going to behave because I remember past performance and that helps me predict what's going to happen. It's a good thing we own the casinos I have to go to. Otherwise, I'd get banned for counting cards and picking slots with the highest payouts. Since I don't gamble often, and I wouldn't gamble at a place we own, everyone is better off."

"Don't do it often?" That makes me wonder if he means there are other types of gambling. Like gambling with his life.

"I can hear your thoughts from here. I told you about the other families. All four families own casinos in Atlantic City, Vegas, and Reno. Sometimes I've gone to ones that belong to another family and won a shite ton of money to piss them off. But it's tit-for-tat. Each one of them has a savvy accountant who can practically do what I can. No one else has the numbers thing I do. But each accountant comes close. And yes, there are other things I have to take a gamble with. I'm not impulsive, *cailín*. There's a lot of risk, but they're measured."

I don't have a chance to say anything because the waitress arrives with our food. I don't know that there is anything to say.

The woman can barely tolerate me, and I'm surprised she isn't baring her teeth at me. I'm lucky my meal doesn't land in my lap. Finn finally pays attention to her, and I watch how she drops her gaze when he does. Fucking hell. I've just lost my appetite. I sit back in my chair and pull my hand away from Finn's once she turns her back. I look toward the door.

"Thea?"

"You brought me somewhere I'd meet one of your subs."

"No. I did not. I have never had sex with Rosalee. I've never done anything sexual with Rosalee. But I know she is a sub, and I know her Dom."

"If she has a Dom, then why did she look like she wanted you as her main course?"

"Because she's approached me more than once at the club I belong to, and I've turned her down. We aren't into the same things, so I've never been interested."

"And she works here."

"Yes. It's never been an issue before, and I didn't know it would be. But I've also never come here on a date. I don't know what her deal is, but she knows I'm going to bring it up to her Dom."

"Is that— would you normally —Mmm?"

Fuck me.

"The man she's involved with is a friend of mine. They have a 24/7 dynamic. He'd want to know that she acted in a way we all know she shouldn't have. Plus, I don't like that she'd eye me or any other man when she's involved with my friend. That's not cool."

"You belong to a club?"

"Yes. Thea, you said you're into BDSM. Do you belong to one?"

I shake my head.

"Have you been to one?"

I shake my head again.

"Do you want to go to one? Do you want me to take you there?"

I want to say yes, but I don't know what to expect. Will it be like Cheers— or McGinty's —where everyone knows his name? Will I run into women he regularly scenes with? I don't even know what he's into. What did he mean when he said he and Rosalee aren't into the same things? Like which one of them likes it more extreme? Or was it the whole 24/7 thing?

"You don't have to decide right this minute. I'll take you

there tonight, in a week, or never. It's up to you. But I'm not going back unless I'm with you."

Well, that just unleashes another slew of questions. Why doesn't he want to go back? Does he assume I'll be into all the kinky things he is? Does that mean he wants something monogamous? Do I want that? What if I'm not into what he is? What if—

He leans over to whisper in my ear, and I love that we have what feels like secrets that are just between us. Like how he's the only person who calls me Thea.

"We will take this as fast or as slow as you want. If you want to see or be with other people, I'll—" He pauses. "—figure out a way to be okay with that. But I don't want anyone else."

I turn my head, and our noses brush before I press a kiss to his lips. "I don't know what speed I want to go yet, but I only want it to be with you." And it's true.

Chapter Seven

Finn

I have lost my goddamn mind.

That's the second time in as many days that I've thought that. But I have. I just invited her to a sex club on our first date. The devil has possessed me. Shocking, considering all the other things I've done in life, now's when he decides to take up residence. What else can explain what the fuck is wrong with me to offer a woman who's never gone to a BDSM club an invitation to debauchery before we've taken our first bite?

She's not shocked or running away. That's a plus. She even seems curious, which I'll count as a blessing. But she would have found out about my membership sooner rather than later, so I'd rather she knows I'm not going there to meet anyone else. At some point, I'm going to have to tell her about my arrangement with Heidi and that it's over. That's another item on the to do list. Making sure Heidi truly gets I'm not going back to her. She'll accept it, but I want to be clear. I don't want her popping up unexpectedly.

"I know you said you have another long shift, and next Saturday is your first day off. Do you already have plans that day?"

She hesitates before she nods. Sadness creeps into her eyes, but she blinks it away.

"I have a family dinner that night. But I'm free earlier if you could do lunch or something."

"I'll make sure I can."

The conversation moves on to more about our more recent past. She tells me about undergrad and med school. I tell her about majoring in finance and getting an MBA with a focus in finance. All the things adults in their early thirties discuss. Nothing especially fascinating, but so completely normal. It's a reprieve from so many conversations I have. It's nice to forget my role for a little while. But it comes slamming back into me as we leave the restaurant.

"Carmine, Serafina."

Carmine Mancinelli and his wife are the last people I want to see while I'm on a date. But we own neighboring restaurants. Irony is a bitch in this life. We've known each other practically our entire lives. We used to play little league and peewee sports together. I actually liked Carmine more than any of his cousins until we were about eight or nine. Then things changed, and he became the douche he is now.

But for the sake of the women with us, we grin and bear it. Serafina knows more than most wives since she's *Cosa Nostra* on her mother's side and *Bela de Menta* on her father's— Venetian Mafia. They both look at Thea and smile. It's genuine from Serafina, though I have seen her shoot looks at men twice her size that have practically frozen my blood. Carmine's is the same douchey one it usually is. He'll be running to tattle to his uncle the moment they're in the car.

"Hey, Maria."

I look down at Thea before looking at the couple that just stepped out of the restaurant next to mine.

"Ally? Hey." Maria Mancinelli is the only one in their family I can tolerate. She's the only biological one who actually has a humane bone in her body and isn't trying to dick everyone over. I watch as she and Thea embrace.

"Hi, Matteo."

What the ever-loving fuck? How does she know Maria's husband? I watch her embrace Maria and Matteo. She looks back at me, and a flash of worry crosses her face as I step forward.

"Maria, it's nice to see you. Matteo."

That motherfucker. He nearly killed me during a shootout not too long ago. Fucking aiming for Niko Kutsenko and nearly nailed me. His dumbarse needs more time at the range. I wasn't anywhere near Niko. I was at least two feet away.

It's Maria who asks what all the Mancinellis want to know and what I wish we could avoid.

"Are you here with Finn?"

"Yeah." She's hesitant to answer as she tries to sense what her response will mean.

I slide my arm around her waist, and I feel her relax. She's scared I'm angry that she knows them. I give her waist a squeeze, and she leans against me.

"Finn, Maria and I went to med school together. We were in residency at the same time, but at different hospitals. We work together now. I had lunch with her yesterday."

Isn't that a lovely complication?

"That must be nice to work with an old friend." What else am I supposed to say?

The six of us are standing on the sidewalk, all knowing normal people would have more to say, but none of us do. The men are judging whether we're going to get out of this without an argument. We'd never have a physical altercation with women around. Our families would execute us— slowly and painfully. Our mothers still terrify us. Serafina and Maria are probably wondering how long the standoff is going to take and just want to leave before they get bored. And Thea is trying to figure out what the fuck is happening.

I can tell the moment it dawns on her. She must remember what I said in the bar yesterday when I mentioned the family names. She must not have connected Maria to these Mancinellis. She's one two times over. Her husband is the son of her father and uncle's adopted second cousin. There isn't an easy family tree among us. A fecking forest.

Blessedly, Maria saves the day. That's one thing I can count on. She fucking majorly saved my arse when she was in med school, and I was in grad school. We wound up at the same party, which had only happened once before. That was an even bigger disaster. Cormac and Seamus sold the hosts some fentanyl right before it started. The girl I was with took some while I went to get us drinks. Maria did everything she could to save her, but she didn't have NARCAN with her. I know she carries it everywhere now.

"Ally, are you going to that medical conference in Chicago next month?"

That perks up my attention. We've been doing some business there that's specifically fucking over the Mancinellis. Thea looks up at me before she nods. I don't know what she's thinking.

"I am. I'm presenting a paper I co-wrote with Dr. Vasserwine and Jordan. As you know, it'll only be Wendy and me going."

Maria flinches, and I know why. Carmine and Matteo immediately go on the defensive. I tighten my arm around her, ready to step in front of her if either of them even looks sideways at her. So much for saving the day.

"Maria?" Thea senses the shift because it's practically knocking us all over.

"I had some trouble with Jordan just before he passed away. He's not a topic my family likes to discuss."

Neither is the bastard's sister. They were both pieces of shite that got what they deserved. I rarely say that about women, but it's true. They targeted Maria because of yet another twisted branch of their family tree. Neither lived to tell the tale.

Thea nods, but then she stiffens again. Maria's gaze is locked with Thea's, and she nods at my date. Maria can tell Thea knows who she's on a date with. She's acknowledging who her family is, and that they were involved with dealing with Jordan. No one will say that aloud, but I suppose it's a level of acceptance into our world that Maria's admitting it, albeit silently.

"It's nice seeing you. I'm off for the next few days. I think we're on similar rotations. My nephew's got some tests coming up, and I'm pretty sure Rodesman is going to order imaging."

"I'll keep an eye out for them. How's Skyler doing?"

I don't know what they're talking about.

"Better than a month ago, but he still has a lot of appointments coming up."

Maria steps forward and gives Thea hug, and I watch as Thea leans into it.

"Let's have lunch together next week. If I happen to have questions about a six-month-old with CHD, I'll be sure you're the doc I go to."

"Thank you." It comes out choked as Thea steps back. I still don't understand, but Thea's upset. She's trying not to show it, but she is. I draw her back, so I can press her against me, but she turns and wraps her arms around me. She's standing side-ways, but her head rests on my chest. It surprises everyone, but none of us let it show. I hold her as we say our goodbyes.

"I'm sorry."

We're alone as she apologizes. I cup her jaw as my thumb brushes her cheekbone.

"What for?"

"That got heavy fast. I'm usually more composed. I should have expected Maria's kindness, but considering what I just figured out, it was extra special."

"I strongly dislike Carmine and Matteo. The feeling is mutual, but Maria is the kindest person I know. She's known no life but being a Mafia daughter, but she's never let that jade her. She doesn't let the rest of her family define her. Never underestimate her. She's deadly if she has to be. But she will put everyone ahead of her every day of the week and twice on Sundays. If she's a friend, she's a good one to have."

None of that is an exaggeration. There was only one other person like Maria. It was Dillan's sister, Colleen, before she was killed. She was a veterinarian and was so much like Maria that they were friends until the day my cousin was murdered. No one in either family dared object.

"Do you still want to go to the show? Or would you let me take you home? I have a driver around the corner."

"A driver?"

Thea glances toward the street where the Mancinellis are getting into an SUV. There's clearly a man in the driver's seat and another standing beside an open backdoor where the women are climbing in. Carmine is on the far side, and Matteo is next to the bodyguard.

"Finn, is that necessary?"

"Necessary? No. Wise? Yes. For all Carmine's and Matteo's faults, no one matters more to either of them than their wife. There's no limit to what they'll do to protect them, so if an extra bodyguard makes them breathe a little easier, then it's worth it."

"Do you have a bodyguard?"

"Sometimes. I mentioned a security detail in passing yesterday. It's something we'll need to talk about more. Are you all right?"

She nestles against me, and I can't describe the happiness it brings me to know I can offer her comfort. That she wants comfort from me. She's letting her guard down around a man she barely knows because I make her feel safe. Protected.

"I will be. I'd appreciate a ride home. But later. I wasn't in the mood for the subway."

Now it's my turn to tense.

"Thea, it'll be at least midnight before the show ends. I really don't like the idea of you taking the subway that late at night and alone. I'm sure you do, but it bothers me a lot."

It makes me want to crawl out of my skin. I know the Mancinellis won't do anything to her since she's friends with Maria. But we're out in public together. If we ran into them, then we could run into someone else. Or someone else could see us. My mind runs to the worst scenario, so I can make contingencies.

"I can take a rideshare if you prefer."

That's marginally better. Since my family owns the three biggest cab companies in the five boroughs, there's a good chance she would catch one of ours. Even if she were to get into a cab from another company, it would take one call from me to deal with whoever it was if Thea arrived at her place with a hair out of place.

"A rideshare still bothers you, doesn't it?"

It surprises me she can tell. I haven't moved or said anything.

"Finn, your heart is racing. It sped up when I mentioned the subway. Now it's racing."

"I understand you might not want me to come back to your place, but I'd prefer it if you'd let one of my drivers take you home. I know you can catch a cab, or take the subway or a rideshare just fine on your own. But I can also admit it makes me anxious now that I know you."

"Because I know you?"

"Because you're gorgeous."

"Thanks?"

"Traveling alone in the city at night isn't something to avoid just because it's New York. But your appearance is eye-catching. You must draw attention. The idea that something could happen to you that's avoidable when I have chauffeurs available makes me anxious."

"You seriously overestimate my attractiveness. It's flattering, but no one else is paying that much attention to me."

"*Cailín*, just because you don't notice doesn't mean other people don't. I've seen the way people look at you when we walk past."

"That's because they can't figure me out."

I know there's an element of truth to that. Her complexion, her eye color, and her hair probably lead people to want to know more than is any of their business. They make her alluring, and in just the time we've been at the restaurant and outside, I've seen how men and women look at her. It's not all rude curiosity. A lot of it is appreciation. I mean, fecking hell. Louis nearly lost his job and half his teeth.

"Or they're attracted to you just like I am. Except I'll always accept no from you. I'm not trying to be controlling, but I get that's how I sound. I'll back off. But you can always have a car take you wherever you want. Let me know, and it'll be there any time. Day or night."

We've started walking to the comedy club that's two blocks away. We're holding hands now, and it feels so completely natural. I'm not sure if I took hold of hers or the other way around. Our fingers just wound up entwined.

"I don't think you're being controlling. I think it's sweet that you worry. You haven't issued me ultimatums or threatened to punish me or coerce me. You aren't guilting me into anything. You're expressing your concern, and I know there's a ton I don't know about the world I'm entering. I'll defer to you."

We're at the club's door, and there's a line. I don't bother looking at the end. I walk straight to the door. Just as the bouncer's about to greet me, the arsehole at the front of the line has something to say about it.

"Hey, dude. Back of the line."

I ignore him.

"I said the back of the line, dude. You and the bitch can go and wait like the rest of us."

"Mikey, send him home."

I grin at the bouncer who's shooting the guy a warning expression. But fuckface isn't paying attention. The teddy bear at the door— he's the size of a grizzly and looks as fierce but is a complete gentle giant when he's not on the clock —opens it for us. The guy grabs the sleeve of my suit coat and yanks. I'm wearing my gun holstered at the small of my back. It's been a bit awkward, but I've kept Thea from wrapping her arms low enough to feel it. If my gun were holstered under my arm, like it often is, everyone would see it. This is why it isn't.

"Let go." I stare at him, but my usual intensity does nothing to the guy who's now enraged.

Before I can stop her, Thea's hand goes around the guy's wrist. She gets a pressure point, and he releases me.

"You're an idiot to attack the club owner." She turns away from the guy. "Hi, Mikey."

She acts as though she's been here every day of her life as she takes my hand and draws me in after her. It completely diffuses the situation. Or at least long enough for us to get inside. Mikey'll take care of whatever we left in our wake. The guy won't be enjoying a show here ever again, and that means the pack of twats with him. They all look like the stockbroker type.

"Thea, he could have hurt you."

"He won't get feeling back in his hand for at least ten minutes. And no, I don't know martial arts. I know human anatomy."

"Promise me you won't do that again. Please."

"No."

"Thee—"

"I refuse to promise not to intervene if someone's threatening you. I know you weren't in any danger, but I ended what was about to be a standoff or the idiot getting his face bashed in by your bouncer."

"He could have swung at you."

"He could have, but I don't think he was quite that stupid."

"You can't be sure."

"But I can be sure your reactions are way faster than his. He wouldn't have gotten close enough to touch me."

I sigh. "You have a lot of faith in me."

"I do."

I pray it isn't the most misplaced thing in the world. But it means everything to me. My family has a ton of faith in me. My men and their families have faith in me, but I'm obligated to protect them. I can't imagine not protecting my family. But Thea's is entirely voluntary. I have her trust until I lose it. The idea I might gives me chest pains.

I guide her to the seat I reserved for us. I told the manager we'd be here. I also sent the comic a text warning her not to target Thea. She can have a go at me, but she'll never work in New York again if she says a syllable at Thea's expense. It's the risk anyone takes sitting in the front row, but I'll be damned if I sit anywhere else in a place that costs me more a month to run that most people earn in a year.

"What would you like to drink, miss? Mr. O'Rourke?"

The waiter offers Thea a courteous smile, but he winks at me.

"Gin and ginger, please."

"Same, Taylor."

"You're breaking my heart, O'Rourke."

He saunters— yes, motherfucking saunters —off. That's after he winks at me again.

"Finn?"

Thea has no idea what to make of that. She isn't sure if Taylor is teasing me about snagging Thea or not.

"I've known Taylor a long time, and he knows he isn't my type. But it doesn't stop him from teasing me once in a while. He never takes it too far, and he's hilarious with what he comes up with. I've never brought a date here, so he's got something new to needle me about."

"Oh."

She watches Taylor at the bar. I am, too. Heidi's working tonight. She must be picking up some shifts for her sister. Heidi's usually at 4Play, one of our strip clubs. She's a waitress there. She's danced in the past, but she prefers not to.

This is not my night.

Karma is dancing a fecking jig. Heidi's staring straight at Thea, who has noticed. When Heidi's gaze shifts to mine, she offers me a tight smile. I'm still convinced she has no romantic feelings for me, but she's not happy to see who she assumes has already replaced her. Sex has always been great with Heidi. We've been fuck buddies for ages. But she loves her partners, not me. That said, I'm certain she assumed the arrangement would last until she no longer wanted it. Not the other way around.

"Finn?"

"Yes, *cailín*." Here it comes.

"Is she one of your subs?" Her voice is barely above a whisper.

"No. I haven't had any. I told you that. I've done scenes, but I've never had a formal or even an informal arrangement. That's Heidi. I've known her since we were kids. We had a mutually agreeable arrangement until yesterday. Now it's over."

"Yesterday?"

"Yes." In for a penny, in for a pound. "That text I got yesterday was to confirm our plans for last night. I told her I wouldn't make it, and she shouldn't plan for me to join her in the future."

I pull out my phone and unlock it. She puts her hand over it.

"I really, really don't want to see it. If you're willing to show me, then it's what you said. You were friends with benefits."

"Yeah." That's a politer term for it.

"And you have been for a while."

"A few years."

"Did you date?"

"Never."

"Then how'd—" She shakes her head.

"We were attracted to each other physically. We have next to nothing in common beyond that. She's in an open relationship with a man and woman. Before you ask, yes."

She nods. She was wondering if I'd had threesomes. That was my past before I met Thea, but I don't feel great admitting it.

94

"Should I confess any parts of my past?"

She didn't say it maliciously. But it makes my stomach churn.

"If you feel you should."

"Before Tony and I started dating, I had a mutually beneficial arrangement too. When Tony and I first started dating, before we decided we'd see each other exclusively, he joined us a few times."

I think I'm going to vomit.

It's bad enough knowing the last man she was with. Knowing what she's done with other guys feels shitty. But it's her past, just like I have one.

"I didn't say it to make you feel badly, Finn. I said it because it felt like the right time to tell you. I'm sure it would have come out at some point. If I didn't say it now, you'd wonder why I kept it from you."

"True. Maybe we can let our past stay there for a while."

She leans over and kisses my neck before whispering to me. I love that we already have private things, like a normal couple.

"Finn, neither of us can ignore that we both have past partners. But I'm not interested in anyone but you. I've never met a hotter or more considerate man in my life. I'll accept your past as long as it stays there."

"It will. Thea, I want an us. I'm not going anywhere until you tell me to. Either to come with you or to leave you alone."

"I'm keeping you to that. And only the first part matters. The part about wanting an us. I wonder what your favorite breakfast food is."

Chapter Eight

Thea

The things that come out of my mouth. What's his favorite breakfast food? Who am I?

This is moving way too fast. I'm letting myself get caught in the tidal wave that is Finn O'Rourke. He surged into my life, and I'm about to be pulled under, spun around like the rinse cycle, and probably spit out like a beached whale.

The problem is everything about being with him feels right. It was weird, then tense, when we ran into Maria and her family. Finn isn't wrong. She is a kindhearted person, and now, realizing who her family is makes me appreciate her even more. You would never guess she comes from one of the wealthiest families in NYC. They must be. Her husband didn't hover any more than Finn did, but it was obvious he wouldn't take his eyes off Finn for even a second. I'm not sure if any of the men blinked during that entire brief conversation.

The other woman, Serafina— I think that's what I heard Finn call her —remained quiet, but she was just as observant as the men. I don't know what her story is, but she didn't strike me as ignorant of who Finn is or the family she married into. Just the opposite. I sense she and Maria are very much alike. I know Maria's close to her cousin Carmine, but I didn't know he was married.

Taylor brings our drinks just as the show is about to start. I glance over my shoulder and am relieved to notice Heidi isn't looking in our direction anymore. She's busy making drinks, but as soon as I turn around, it's as though eyes are boring into my back. I want to squirm, but I won't give her that satisfaction if she is looking. It's probably my imagination.

Finn and I are quiet as the opening act takes the stage. The guy is hilarious, but it's the headliner that has me nearly snorting my drink a couple times. I watch her look in our direction a few times, then quickly look away. She finds some way to tease everyone else in the front row, but she studiously ignores us. Did someone tell her the owner was in the audience?

It's just as well. After what's happened so far tonight, I appreciate flying under the radar for a bit. It's amazing how fast the next three hours zoom by. Finn and I hold hands for part of the show, and he has his arm draped over the back of my chair for some of it. But a lot of it has his hand resting on my thigh. He does nothing more than leave it there, but it's enough to make me shift a few times. Each time I do, his fingers press against my inner thigh. Then he eases the pressure. He knows what he's doing to me.

"That was great. Thanks for this, Finn. I haven't laughed that hard in ages."

It's true. What's there to laugh about? My nephew's condition? No. The babies at work? Rarely. The shit with Tony? No. The shit with my parents? No. This felt good for my soul. I needed it.

"I'm glad you enjoyed it. I heard this comic was good, but it can be a bit hit or miss, you know?"

"I do. But, Finn, are you why she said nothing about us?"

"She knows I'm the owner."

He's being cagey. I think he must have, but it doesn't feel worth pushing him on. He wanted to be sure I enjoyed it and wasn't insulted. Again, considerate. He helps me on with my jacket. But just as we get to the door he gets a call. He apologizes but has to step away. It leaves me looking around.

"He's into you."

I turn around to find Heidi right behind me. What do I say to that? I know?

"I'm into him." It's true.

"Finn's a good guy. If he's with you, then he wants to be *with* you."

I don't understand, and it must show.

"The O'Rourke men don't date casually. I can tell he told you about our arrangement. He ended it yesterday, and I get why now. He'll look at me like a little sister, and that's cool. There were more years that he was like an older brother. But let me give you a word of advice." She pauses. I nod. "I can tell you know what he is. If you can't accept giving all of yourself to him but never getting all of him back, leave now. It's unfair, but you'll break his heart. He doesn't deserve that."

"Heidi?"

Finn walks up behind me, and I don't know if he heard any of what she said. I turn toward him and smile. He looks nervous. Then I look back at Heidi.

"It was nice to meet you. I think you're right."

She nods and walks away. I know Finn wants to know what I meant, but he won't ask. He's told me he'll respect me not wanting to share my thoughts. But this isn't something I want to keep from him. I don't see any reason to.

"She was being nice, Finn. She said you'll look at her like a little sister, and she'll go back to looking at you like a brother. That you guys were like that for longer than you weren't."

"She's right."

"She also gave me a piece of advice that I think I'll heed."

He still doesn't ask me to share. But he appears curious. When I offer nothing, he turns us toward the door. We step outside, and we're more alone than a moment ago. I step around him and turn.

"I don't completely understand Heidi's advice, but I think she's right. She told me I have to accept giving all of me to you but not receiving all of you back in return. If I can't live with that, then I should walk away."

He glances back at the door, and now he really doesn't seem thrilled that she spoke to me. I put my hand on his forearm.

"She's right, isn't she?"

"Yes. I'd just hoped to get through the first date without having to explain more about my life that I wish didn't exist. I hoped to end the evening on an uneventful note."

End the evening?

"Thea, I can't escort you home. I have to meet with my cousins. Something came up with Shane's import/export business. A shipment of rugs from India got lost in transit. I need to run some numbers to see what the losses will be and what we want to claim with the insurance company."

That sounds shockingly legit.

"*Cailín*, this is aboveboard. But it's going to take several hours. With the time difference, it's already the workday there. Joey's my driver tonight. I'd like him to take you home, please."

He's basically asking. This sounds like a shitshow he's going to have to deal with. I don't want to make his night worse. It was good during the times we were alone, but it wasn't great

when we weren't. If knowing I made it home safely is important to him, then I'll accept graciously.

"I'd appreciate it."

We walk to the town car that's parked at the curb. A man
gets out of the driver's side, but Finn shakes his head. We stop
next to the back door as the man gets back into the vehicle.

"The privacy glass will be up when you get in. You can
lower it and tell Joey your address. He'll escort you to your door
and wait until he's certain you're inside safely. Do you live in
an apartment building?"

"Yeah. Condos, but I'm all the way on Staten Island."

"That's not a problem. Joey will take you."

Traffic between Manhattan, where the hospital is, and
Staten Island, where I live, is the reason it's usually not worth
trying to go home for my ten-hour break.

"Finn. I know you trust Joey or else you wouldn't send me
with him. But I'll text you when I get into my place."

I get my phone out and unlock it. I pull up a contact and
put his name in before handing it to him. He punches his in,
and I send him a text, so he has mine. Neither of us is in a hurry
to end the night, but it's just as well. The tide is ebbing, and I
have a chance to think rationally before I do something I can't
take back. I don't usually sleep with guys on the first date. I
have, but I don't usually. I want things with Finn to work.

We need to slow down a little and build a foundation that
isn't purely sexual frustration. I see that now, but the moment
his lips meet mine, all restraint disappears. If he were taking me
home, I bet we'd be fucking in the backseat.

He opens the door for me, then closes it softly once I'm
inside. I roll down the privacy glass and tell Joey my address.
He raises the glass, and I lower my window.

"Thanks for a great night, Finn."

"Same to you."

"I'll text when I'm home. I promise."

"Thank you, little one."

I thank Joey when he holds the door open to my building. I can tell he's scanning the lobby before I cross the threshold. I could tell he surveyed the area when he helped me from the car. I look back as I get into the elevator. He dips his chin, then the doors close.

ME

Thanks again for a wonderful night. I had a fantastic time.

It's a couple minutes, but then my phone vibrates.

FINN

I did too. I'd like to see you again the next time you're free.

I could tell him I'm free the next two nights, but I'm not sure if I should see him so soon if I want to pump the breaks a bit.

KIMMY

Hey! How'd the date go? Are you going to be answering me in the morning?

I don't expect my friend's text to come in before I can respond. Before I'm done reading, another text pops up from her.

KIMMY

A bunch of us are going to Tropicals tomorrow night. Do you want to come?

A casino in Atlantic City. I'm not much of a gambler, but I like roulette and blackjack. It's been ages since I've been there, and the buffet is amazing. That's the real reason to go. I think about Finn, then my family dinner next Saturday. I'd really like to see him before that. Maybe the night after tomorrow.

I tap over to Finn's text.

ME

I'd like that too. I have plans tomorrow night. But are you free the next night?

FINN

Yeah. Let me know what you'd like to do. I picked this time.

ME

Let me think about it. I hope everything works out tonight.

FINN

Me too. Thanks. Sleep well, cailín.

That makes my toes curl into my carpet. I really love it when he calls me that. I want a name for him, but I can't think of anything special. I have time.

ME

I will. You too.

Fuck. I know what I almost typed. No. I cannot call him that.

I tap Kimmy's text and go back to that.

ME

Sounds good. What time?

KIMMY

I wasn't sure you were going to answer.
Buffet opens at six. You know the line. Do you
want to make a day of it? We can get a suite
and go out to the beach. Then get cleaned up
and head down for dinner then the casino.
It'd be you, me, Dory, Samantha, Nicole, and
Terry.

They're a mix of doctors and nurses. They're all from OBGYN, so I work with them all the time. Kimmy's the person I'm closest to at work. She's a doctor, but you'd never guess the reserved woman who looks up vajayjays all day is the wild woman who'll dance on tabletops without a drop to drink first. Then again, she's said the same thing about me minus the vadges. I see plenty, I'm just not looking up them.

The water'll still be frigid, but it's been unseasonably warm this spring. It'll be nice to get some Vitamin D now that winter's over.

ME

Sounds good

KIMMY

Want me to pick you up?

ME

That'd be great. Who else is riding with you?

KIMMY

Sam and Nikki.

Thank God. I like Dory a lot, but not in an enclosed space like Kimmy's midsize Lexus. That would be a *loooong* two and a half hours.

> What time should I be ready?

KIMMY

> Let's say 9:30. I'll make a reservation right now.

ME

> Cool

I have something to look forward to rather than worrying about my parents. I can tell myself that, but at least it'll occupy my mind. And it'll distract me from thinking about what Finn's doing and how many hours it'll be before I see him again.

I toss clothes in a bag along with some toiletries and shoes. It's already just past one, so I'm asleep as soon as my head hits the pillow.

"*Hola, chica.*"

I move over to let the guy next to me have more room at the roulette table. It was a great afternoon on the beach with the girls. I definitely ate way too much at the buffet, and I'm up a hundred dollars at this table.

"Whatcha drinking?"

I slide my plastic cup over. "Just a soda."

I am. I slept super well, but the last few days have caught up with me. If I drink any more than the wine I had at dinner and the couple of cocktails from earlier, I'll fall asleep where I sit. I already have a strong case of heavy head. I feel like putting my head down and closing my eyes. But I also want to see if I can make back my part of the suite and the drinks I bought today. That'll make it a good night.

"That's boring. Let me get you something better."

"No thanks. I don't drink."

"That's not true. I saw you out at the pool today. Looked like a couple Blue Hawaiians went down easy."

The way he looks at me tells me he means something entirely different. Gross.

He's not bad looking or even that much older than me, but he's skeezy the way he's coming onto me. I look at Terry, who's sitting across from me. She's trying not to laugh. I feel like sending him over to her. I feel like sticking my tongue out at her.

"I'm done for tonight. Thanks though. Excuse me."

I reach to place my bet, and his hand brushes my arm. I ignore it. But when his leg nudges mine, I pull away.

"Come on, *chica*."

Why is he calling me that?

"*Permítame pagarle una copa.*" Let me buy you a drink.

My Spanish isn't great, but I understand him. I ignore him. I play a few more spins, and I'm still up. I signal to Terry that I want to leave, so we gather our chips.

"*¿Se van tan pronto? Vamos mami. Trae ese culito puertorriqueño apretado aquí.*" Leaving so soon? Come on, *mami*. Bring that tight little Puerto Rican ass over here.

This isn't the first time someone's confused me for Puerto Rican, though it's just as often Dominican. When he stands and tries to brush his hand against my ass, a security guard appears.

"Leave the lady alone." The security guard's voice is so low it could be Barry White but gravely, like Bruce Springsteen.

"Mind your own business."

"She's getting up to leave, and she's already been ignoring you. Leave the lady alone."

"She's with me. Aren't you, babe?"

"I'm—"

"I'm pretty sure my girlfriend is with me."

I spin around to see Finn walking over. He appears relaxed, but there's that energy vibrating off him that first attracted me to him when he threw Tony out the first time. I'd only followed Tony because I felt obligated to when it looked like Cormac and Seamus were going to play pinball with him.

"Bullshit, she's your woman. Why was she leaning over me like that if she didn't want me looking at her tits?"

"Because you were in the way, and she was polite enough not to shove you off your stool. You're cut off. Todd, escort Mr. Juarez back to his room. Make sure he's tucked in for the night."

"Who the fuck are you? I'm not done playing."

"I own this casino. You're about to be thrown out altogether. Go to your room on your own or have my guys toss you out on your arse. You'll find every place in Atlantic City that isn't some roach motel is suddenly booked up."

"You can't do shit."

"I own three other casinos, and I'm well acquainted with the owners of the other six worth staying at."

Is there anything he doesn't own?

Terry's come around the table to stand beside me, but she's remaining quiet as she tries to figure out who Finn is and why he just called himself my boyfriend. Did he just say it for this douche's sake?

The big guy, Todd, steps forward and puts out his hand as though he's going to take the DB's arm. The DB pulls away so hard he nearly falls over. No one moves to help him. He stumbles, and how drunk he is becomes obvious.

"Lenny?" A woman with so much collagen that she has her own life preservers walks over. "Lenny, baby. What's going on?"

"Is he yours?" Disgust drips from Finn's tone. Things just went from bad to worse.

"Yeah. Why?"

I look at Finn and shake my head, shooting him a pointed look not to tell the woman what really happened.

"Take him up to your room. He's too drunk and causing a disturbance."

"What kind of disturbance?" The woman doesn't relent.

"The kind that's making other guests uncomfortable."

Great. Now she turns her sights on me. She looks me up and down, and it's clear I don't pass muster. I'm in a cute dress with ankle boots and a cropped jacket. I think I look nice. But it's also obvious I'm not spending my days at a plastic surgeon's office. She turns her nose up and looks at Lenny.

"Lenny, what did you do?"

"Nothing. The bitch wanted it."

The woman shrieks, and Finn's ready to lunge at Lenny. He doesn't after all. But he gets in Lenny's face, having to look down since he's half a head taller than the jackass. I can barely hear him over all the noise of the slot machines, but I'm close enough.

"You do not want to call my girlfriend another thing. You want to walk out of here on your own two feet before I break them both. You want to take *your* woman up to your room and stay there. If you don't, I will make sure you're escorted off the property. It's awfully dark tonight, and the lighting isn't so good once you're off the casino grounds. I'd hate for you to fall."

Finn pushes his shoulders back, and for the first time I realize just how big he is. He doesn't have poor posture, but neither does he impose his size. With his chest and back fully expanded, he's nearly as big as Cormac and Seamus. He steps back and reaches for me. When I go to wrap my arm around his waist like I have before, he moves in a way that traps my arm at my side. Weird. He just defended me, but he doesn't want anyone to see me with my arm around his waist.

Todd follows the couple toward the elevators. When we see them get on, Finn steps around, so we can look at each other.

"What did he say to you?"

"He was just being a jerk. He wanted to buy me a drink and didn't want to take no for an answer. I ignored him. He tried to brush up against me a couple times, but I ignored that too. I was winning, so I stayed. Finn, this is my friend Terry."

I turn toward Terry, who's been watching all of this play out. She smiles at Finn, and I can tell she's about to do her diagnostician thing with about a thousand questions and hypotheses the moment we're alone. She's an OBGYN and specializes in high-risk pregnancies.

"Hello." Finn smiles at her and offers her his hand.

"Terry, this is Finn." I don't know if I should say he's my boyfriend. I don't know if I should say his last name.

"Nice to meet you."

Before Terry or I can say more, Finn smiles down at me.

"Ladies, let any of the staff know if you need anything. I'll let you continue your night. I'm glad I recognized you when Todd said there was a drunk guy on the floor bothering a woman."

What the fuck?

Did I just get the blow off? Why'd he defend me if he's just going to pretend like we barely know each other? Now I get why he didn't want me to wrap my arm around him. He was just pretending. That stings.

"Do you want to find the others, Ally?"

"Sure. Thanks, Finn. It was good seeing you."

We're standing with our backs to a wall, and I don't think Finn maneuvered us like that on accident. When Terry turns around, his hand goes to my ass.

"You look gorgeous, *cailín*. The things you make me think about. I don't know if you've told your friends anything about dating someone new. I don't even know if you told them you ended things with Tony. But I'll be counting the hours until our date tomorrow. Did you pick something to do?"

I shake my head. I step away from him, so Terry doesn't get that far ahead of me. But I twist to see Finn.

"Thank you. Terry's going to have a shit ton of questions. Can I tell her your full name?"

"Of course."

"Are we dating?"

"If that's what you want."

"Okay."

I hurry to catch up with Terry, who shockingly doesn't ask me a million questions. She looks back at Finn, then at me.

"He's hot."

"Yeah, he is."

"He's not your boyfriend, is he?"

She does have some.

"No. But we've gone out, and I'm seeing him tomorrow night. He knew saying he's my boyfriend would make the guy back off."

"He likes you. A lot."

"Why do you think that?"

"Because he would have come over as just the casino owner if he didn't. He's a hundred percent better than Tony. You deserve someone good after him. I heard what he said at the bar. Fuck him."

"I'd rather not. I broke up with him, so I don't have to." I laugh, and Terry grins.

We find our friends, and the rest of the night is fun. We all come out ahead when we head up to the suite. We got two, so we all have our own room."

FINN

What time would you and your friends like breakfast?

I just finished brushing my teeth and was about to climb into bed.

ME

I don't know. Check out's at eleven, so probably like 9:30-10. Why?

FINN

Your suites are comped. I'll send up whatever you want whenever you want. Mimosas?

ME

You don't have to do this. He was a drunk idiot.

FINN

It has nothing to do with him and everything to do with spoiling you

ME

It's not necessary.

FINN

I know. That's what makes it spoiling.

I don't feel like he's trying to impress me or even buy my—affection —or whatever. I think he genuinely wants me to have a good time here. I wonder if gift giving is his love language. Or maybe this falls under acts of service.

ME

You're very sweet did you know that?

FINN

Only my mom says that. And she has to.
She's my mom.

ME

Well she's right

He sends me the emoji with the heart eyes, and I giggle. I look toward the bedroom door, and I'm tempted to invite him up. The other bedrooms are across a sitting area. Kimmy and Terry would never know.

FINN

I hope I didn't overstep tonight I didn't make it weird with your friend did I?

ME

No. I appreciate what you did. She understood. She even pointed it out.

It's too soon to really call us a couple or say that we're dating. He's not my boyfriend, yet we've said we don't want to be with anyone else. I guess that makes him that. I don't know. I don't know what to make of most of this, but I'll go along. When you're in a rip tide, you don't fight it. You swim parallel.

FINN

I have to go. There's a problem on the floor that I need to deal with. Sleep well little one

ME

You too.

Again, I have to keep myself from typing the word that comes to mind. But it's on the tip of my tongue every time I think about him. What would he say if I called him what I'm thinking?

Chapter Nine

Finn

Last night was as unexpected as everything has been since meeting Thea. I was in the security room, watching the screens because one of my dealers reported someone was possibly slipping cards in at one of the poker tables. I recognized Thea as soon as I saw her. It was the same time the guy sat down next to her. I watched him, not wanting to cause a scene if I didn't have to. But I radioed Todd to get closer. When he told me the guy was trying to brush up against her, I decided I would deal with it personally. So, I did.

I got to Dillan's this morning after I scheduled breakfast to go up to her suite. She's probably just waking up since it's not even nine yet. I made sure she knows check out at eleven doesn't apply to her. They can stay as long as they like, and everything is comped.

"Finn?"

"Yeah. I'm here. Where are you?"

I can hear Dillan, but his new house is fucking huge.

They've furnished most of it, but it's still empty enough that sound echoes in some parts.

"We're in the sunroom. Grab something to eat and join us."

I head into the kitchen and make a bowl of cereal. Dillan and I have been eating the same brand of granola since we were in high school. I look in the fridge.

What the feck is this shite?

Oat milk? Gross.

I pick up the carton and shake it. There's not much left. I look farther into the fridge and find the gallon of whole milk. That's better. Once I have a spoon, I head out to the sunroom that's attached to the kitchen at the opposite end of the dining room.

Mair tries to get off Dillan's lap, but he pins her in place. I want to roll my eyes. I know exactly why he doesn't want his pretty bride to stand up right now. It's not entirely sweet. It makes me think of Thea, and that just makes me hurry to sit down before I'm in the same boat as my cousin.

"How'd things go last night?" Dillan's question is genuine. It means he hasn't gotten the morning report yet.

"There were two incidents at Tropicals last night, but everything was quiet."

"I wouldn't let Ally hear you call her an incident."

Well, feck me. I guess he did get the report. I'll have to thank Sean for crowing at dawn like a fucking rooster. He's in charge of all our security systems at every business we own. He's got our places bugged better than every foreign embassy in America. He's also our intelligence collector. I can hack and program, but he's the super sleuth. He might not work for the government, but he puts his degree in national security to use. In many ways, our family governs a small empire. So, running it isn't entirely different from running an oligarchy.

It is an oligarchy.

We need to be on top to stay on top. That means knowing more about everyone else than they know about us. We might not know the last time the Pope shat, but we know just about everything else. We let the other syndicates think we're barely above dirt farmers and kneecap busting dock workers. They know there's just as many of us with Ivy League educations as in the other families, but they forget that when they see the personas we want them to see. They think we paid our way in while the rest of them earned their places in those hallowed halls. Let them. It's convenient.

"She isn't an incident. The douche who bothered her is. I dealt with that and the guy trying to trade out cards. He was sly and good, but he didn't realize we have cameras at each table. It was easy to see."

We have them to keep the dealers honest and to keep an eye on the patrons. I'm glad Sean insisted upon them. I didn't want to approve the expense. I thought it was exorbitant, but he's proved me wrong many times over. Every once in a while, my baby brother gets it right.

I change the topic because I don't want it going back to Thea. I'm not ready to talk about her, and Mair is way too perceptive. She's a journalist and can sniff a lie from a mile away.

"Is everything squared away with the rugs?"

I can mention it in front of Mair because they're items we're bringing into the country legally. What she doesn't know is what we have stitched into them. They'll be unwoven to get to the nanochips disguised in the patterns.

"Shane said he tracked them to Indonesia. They got on the wrong freighter."

I cock an eyebrow.

"It was a legit fuck-up."

It would have cost us millions and put a strain on our relationship with one of the Triads in Hong Kong. We hadn't yet taken possession of the cargo. It was on one of their ships when it went missing. We sure as fuck aren't paying until we have the goods. Our refusal is justified, but they won't like it. But I'm not paying a penny until the goods are ours, and I have the customs declarations to prove it.

"I need to get to work, Dill." Mair stands up, and Dillan swings his legs under the table.

She bends to give him a kiss, and I think his eyes might roll back in his head as he peeks down his wife's blouse. Fucking worse than a sixteen-year-old. But it's cute. Losing his sister really fucked with him. They were as close as my twin brothers in many ways. She was a year and a half younger, but they were totally in sync. I pulled his head out of his arse more times than we've admitted to anyone while he was grieving. He and I have always been closest to each other, but it wasn't until we lost Colleen that Dillan and I became practically inseparable.

Mair gives him a lot of the balance he lost when Colleen was murdered. I have a feeling he tells his wife more than he probably should, but he did the same thing with Colleen. He trusted his sister's advice, and he trusts his wife's. He's not wrong, even if that trust was highly questionable at first.

"I love you. Have a good day."

I can't hear Dillan call Mair *cailín*, but I can read his lips. They exchange a quick kiss, then we're alone. I keep eating my cereal, waiting for what I know is coming.

"You won't like what Sean found."

"There wouldn't be anything to dislike if you hadn't insisted on the background check."

"Yeah, well after what happened with Mair, call me justifiably paranoid."

Shane's background check was thorough, but not as deep as it could have been when Mair applied to be a waitress at 4Play.

We didn't know her real background until shite hit the fan. By then, she and Dillan were halfway in love. Fortunately, finding out what we did made it easier for us to accept her. If we'd learned her full history first, they might not be together. Blessings in disguise, I suppose.

"Is it something dire?"

"No."

"Is it something that'll likely come out through the course of dating her?"

"Probably."

"Then don't tell me until it becomes necessary. I'd rather get to know Thea on my own like a normal guy."

"Fine. Do you want a detail assigned to her?"

"Yes."

I stare at Dillan. It's a natural question, and he knows I was going to request it today. But something gives me the feeling that him asking so quickly is a hint that she might need the bodyguards. My hand curls tightly around my spoon, but I don't press my suspicions. He'll tell me if whatever he knows becomes a genuine threat.

"Consider it done."

"I have news about Hollands and Spiegel."

Director Hollands of the FBI and Agent Spiegel of the ATF are more than just brothers-in-law. So very much more, and Hollands' sister— Spiegel's wife —hasn't a clue that while the cat— her —is away, the mice —them —play with each other.

We're keeping their secret in exchange for them helping us with a little project. We had our sights set on causing trouble for Lorenzo, Maria's next oldest brother, in Chicago. It worked, but it didn't last nearly long enough. He resolved it without too much fuss. Annoying.

Now we're setting in motion our plan for Marco, Maria's second oldest brother. The FBI and ATF would love nothing more than to get their rocks off by busting our families. They know they don't have nearly enough evidence to go after the leaders, so Dillan, Salvatore, Maksim, and Enrique are safe.

They know going after the heirs or seconds-in-command isn't wise either. That leaves me out. Luca— Maria's oldest brother and Salvatore's oldest nephew —therefore his heir —is also out. Aleksei, the second oldest Kutsenko brother, is Maksim's second and heir until he decides what to do when his toddler son gets old enough to join. Pablo is Enrique's oldest nephew and heir. He's safe too.

Marco is the perfect mark. He's the third highest ranking member of the family, if you exclude his father. His dad's the family's *consigliere.* He's also Salvatore's younger brother. He's the chief advisor and not in the line of succession. He'd be a good person to snag but getting him won't weaken the Mancinellis as much as it will taking out a young man who could wind up running the *Cosa Nostra* one day. Luca only has an infant daughter.

We're putting a lot of resources behind this, but Marco's fucking shite up by dating Lorenzo's new sister-in-law. Two sisters with two brothers. Sounds pretty familiar. They're fucking inseparable. We don't want the bust to go down when she's anywhere near him. The goal isn't to scoop her up too. But now that the ATF and FBI have the scent, they're baying at the moon. We still have a leash on them, but they're tugging.

NYC isn't as big a city as people think. Not when it comes to who you know. We have a new stockbroker who handles most of our trading, but not all of it. The shite I want really kept secret— the billions of dollars of rainy-day money — doesn't get touched by anyone but me. It's routed through so many offshore shell accounts I'd forget where it was if I didn't have an eidetic memory. This new stockbroker is none other than Lorenzo's new brother-in-law. Yup. The two sisters have a brother who works for us. He also does some odd jobs for the Kutsenkos he thinks no one knows about. Of course, we do.

He's still on probation, so I've given him enough money to earn us some good returns and to think he can hurt us if he runs with it. He thinks he knows more about our portfolios than he does. He has just enough rope to hang himself.

My cousins hated playing Monopoly with me. When I was almost ten, and Maria was almost seven, we were both side-lined from soccer. I had a broken wrist, and she had a sprained ankle. We had to go to games with our siblings and cousins, but it was boring. She brought Monopoly one Saturday afternoon. Our parents watched each other like hawks, but they didn't stop us from playing together. I explained the rules to her, and she got it right away.

Within half an hour, we completely forgot there was anyone around or that we were at a soccer match. We were so engrossed in being real estate moguls. It ended in a draw when it was time to go. We both thought we were so smart when we pulled out our cash. We were definitely fucking smart. But we were the same kind of smart.

We each had cash we let each other see. We had cash we hid behind our backs that we could draw from, thinking the other hadn't kept count. Then there was money we were sitting on that we never touched. When we added it all up, we had exactly the same amount of cash and our properties with houses and hotels were worth the same.

We were both back in the game two weeks later, and I was home with a cold in between. We never played anything together again, but we used to laugh about it in school because I'm three years ahead of her. We were both our class treasurer throughout middle and high school.

Steven, the stockbroker, only gets the money we want him to see. He thinks he knows what's in the stash I'll pull from. He has no idea about the money I'm sitting on. We'll see if he passes the test.

"Earth to Finn."

"Huh?"

"Hello. You're not even fecking listening, are you? Thinking about a particular green-eyed angel?"

"Actually, no. I was thinking about how Steven could become a problem if his sister gets caught up in the shite with Marco. I want Sean to warn him off. Tell him his family needs to get away from the Mancinellis. They get one friendly heads up, and that's it. But give them the chance to keep her out of the FBI's and the ATF's crosshairs."

"I talked to Sean this morning. He thinks *Tres J's* wants to target Marco, too. I don't know if they got a whiff of us or if lightning struck twice, and they had an original thought among them. We can let them take the fall for this and let them face Marco. But if they get in the way, they'll feck up months of planning."

"Shouldn't they still be at their aunt's hospital bed? I heard it's dire." Dillan and the rest of us can be sympathetic to a point, especially when it's about one of the moms.

"From what I heard, it is. I don't know if the cancer's terminal, but that's the feeling I got."

"Did our moms send anything round to them?"

"Yeah. They took over some meals a few weeks ago. I'll remind mine, and she'll set something up with yours and Aunt Saoirse to send some more stuff soon."

Women and children were supposed to be off limits. It was an unwritten law for generations. The shite was supposed to be between the men. But Uncle Donovan and Declan fucked that up and opened a door no one's been able to shut. The Kutsenkos think it started with them, but it didn't. It started with Colleen. Declan's the reason she's dead. His own death couldn't have happened to a more deserving piece of shite.

Mrs. Diaz used to bring tres leches cake to games for any kid's birthday, regardless of their family. She used to slip me extra frosting when my mom wasn't looking. It was fine because my mom used to give Mrs. Diaz's younger son pieces of brownie. That shite bag is dead too thanks to the Kutsenkos. He deserves a seat next to Declan in hell.

That's the sort of fucked-up world I grew up in. We played kids' sports together. Our moms and dads were the snack parents. We celebrated birthdays together until each boy turned twelve. Then we got knives to stab each other with. Saturdays and Sundays were truce days because other families were around. The men got along for the sake of the women and children.

My family fucked it up and ruined that. We're doing what we can to restore the old way, but it's like trying to build a snowman during an avalanche.

However, our moms will still do the right thing. They will have safe passage to the Diazes' house in Jersey to drop off enough food to feed all of them for a month. They know it's not much, but if it makes it one less thing for Mrs. Diaz to worry about, then it's worth it. If we hadn't thought Maksim would throw anything they brought over straight in the trash, they would have taken food to Laura when she had the twins.

People think we're completely devoid of all ethics. That we're morally gray on our best days but morally black most of them. But they don't understand the world we live in. There are exacting standards for behavior, and codes of conduct that should never be violated. Once they are— well, our family is proving it's damn near impossible to regain respect once it's lost.

"Finn? For feck's sake. Could you pay attention?"

"I was thinking about Margherita. If that happened to one of our moms, do you think the other families would send anything to us?"

"Yes."

That was an immediate answer. I sigh and nod.

"I'll text Sean and tell him to make the call. Once I know he's spoken to Steven, I'll get things going for the bust."

"Fine. I want to go over the rental properties in Maine."

Dillan and I spend the next hour discussing the property taxes and real estate investments we have with some vacation rentals along the coast in northern Maine. That money's part of the pot no one outside the family knows about because I never touch it. I have it going to a Swiss account to silently accumulate compound interest.

Once Seamus and Cormac arrive, we spend another two hours discussing various legal issues. We have some men awaiting indictment who Seamus's representing. The DA's dragging their feet now that they know Seamus's involved personally. There's some issue over exculpatory evidence. Cormac's handling three big acquisitions we have going on in Poland. The Polish here in NYC are cooperating because they know we'll go after their families in their mother country and just take what we want if they try to dick us over here.

I head home to run some monthly P&L statements. I find an account that isn't reconciling within my five-cent standard deviation limit. I use my own program I designed. There isn't a chance I'm using some commercial accounting software that's easy to hack. My shite's encrypted to the moon thanks to Sean. I find the entry error I made two weeks ago. I don't know what I was doing to distract me, but I inverted two numbers. I make mistakes, but it's rare. By the time I'm done, it's midafternoon, and I still don't know what Thea wants to do.

ME

Did you have an enjoyable morning?

I don't expect an immediate response, but five minutes turns into ten turns into twenty turns into an hour-and-a-half. Am I getting the blow off?

THEA

I'm so sorry. I just saw this. I'm at the gym. I missed it vibrate, so I didn't check to see if anything came through. I had a glorious morning. That was the best breakfast I've had since I was in the UK a couple years ago. How's your day going?

I like that she asks. I know it's a common question, but I appreciate that she cares enough to ask.

ME

Busy with work. Lots of numbers floating in front of my eyes. Are we still on for tonight?

THEA

Yeah. I had an idea but

I wait to see if there's more, but nothing comes.

ME

???

Instead of a text, my phone rings.

"Thea?"

"I don't know how this works. Are there things I shouldn't — can I —um —are our calls and texts private?"

She wants to know if someone's tapping my phone. Not an unreasonable question.

"I'm home, so we're fine to talk about whatever you want."

We have technology to jam anyone trying to listen in when we're in our homes and vehicles.

"I had an idea, but I don't know if you'd be into it. I don't know if it's—"

"I'll tell you if it's something I don't want to do."

"I just don't know if I'd offend you to suggest it."

Now I'm really curious.

"I'm worried it might be too much like some of your— work. I —I don't want to make assumptions. But I also don't want—"

"Thea, just tell me. I won't be upset by whatever it is. I don't like you being scared to tell me something. Especially something you want."

"I want to go ax throwing, but is it too much like your work?"

The entire sentence came out as basically one long word. I try not to laugh because she won't understand why I am. I get why she's worried. I've never taken an ax to anyone. I have used bone saws, though.

"That sounds like fun. Is there a place around here?"

"There's one in Queens. I looked it up. Finn, is this really okay? I don't want to make you do anything—"

"Thea." I infuse command into my tone.

"Yes, D—"

I can practically hear her teeth clack as she cuts herself off. What was she going to say?

"What time do you want me to pick you up?"

"I can be ready at six."

I glance at my watch. An hour and a half. That's going to feel like an eternity.

"Sounds good."

It's long enough to jack off a couple times, so I don't maul her the moment I see her. What didn't she let herself say?

Chapter Ten

Thea

My entire drive home, I chastise myself for suggesting something that probably is like work to him. A weapon. Throwing it. Hacking at something.

Then I tell myself I'm stupid for thinking ax throwing is anything like what he does when he's being what he called the ugly side of him that he hopes I never see. I'm going around in my head about what an idiot I sounded like stammering on the phone. I know he was trying not to laugh at me. Once I'm in the shower, I have plenty of other thoughts. I close my eyes and let the hot water run over my back and tits, thinking about what it would be like to be in here with Finn. To go down on him or have him go down on me. To brace my hands on the wall and stick my ass out for him to fuck my pussy or my ass. I get myself off three times before I hurry to get clean.

I took longer in the shower than I realize, so I've barely finished getting dressed when the doorbell rings. I glance at my watch. He's early. I'm about to open the door without looking through the peephole. Something tells me I should. That is not Finn.

"Ally, I know you're home. Open up."

I remain silent. I fervently pray Uncle Corey is gone before Finn gets here. One of them will end up dead.

He bangs on my door a few more times. I barely take a breath, certain somehow he'll hear me.

"Ally, I heard you running to the door. Who are you expecting?"

Go away, go away, go away.

He hammers on the door three more times.

"Fine. Jamie's the next person on my list. He and the kids should be home by now."

My hands are shaking as I pull out my phone.

ME

Are you home? Answer me now. Urgent.

JAMIE

Almost. What's wrong?

ME

Where's Asher? Where're the kids?

JAMIE

Asher's teaching a night class. The kids are at Mom and Papa's. What's going on?

ME

Uncle Corey is outside my door. He said he's going to you next.

JAMIE

What the fuck? Why is he in town?

It's too long to tell you over text. You need to get to Mom and Papa and all of you need to leave. Now.

"All-eee! All-eee!" He's sing-songing my name.

I glance at my watch again. I don't think Finn is the type to be late. He'll be here any minute. I try not to scream when something hits my window, and I hear it smash. I don't go near it, dropping to the ground instead. I see the brick. I'm on the third floor. Who hurled that all the way up here?

"I'll check on you tomorrow, Ally."

I lie on my floor for a couple minutes before crawling over to my window. It didn't shatter the whole thing, but there's a hole in it. There's a note wrapped around the brick.

I'll be seeing you in all the old familiar places.

That's Uncle Corey's calling card phrase. I raise my head just high enough to peek out the window when I hear three motorcycle engines rev. I watch my great-uncle— my dad's uncle on his dad's side —and two of his henchmen ride away. I watch as they disappear around the corner. Before I can get anything to clean up the glass, a black town car pulls up.

Fuck.

I grab the brick and run to my bedroom. I shove it under my bed and run back out to get the broom and dustpan. I've just finished and calmed my breathing when I hear another knock. I tiptoe to my door and peek through the peephole again. I nearly burst into tears when I see Finn and not Uncle Corey. I take a few more deep breaths before I exhale a slow one. I open the door and smile. He's about to smile back when his gaze pierces me.

"What happened to your window, Althea?"

He doesn't push past me, but I couldn't stop him if I wanted to. He storms across the room and looks at the hole in the glass. He spins around and stalks back to where I'm still standing by the door. I'm unprepared for him to slam the door shut then back me against it. His kiss is almost too much. I reach for him, but he grasps my wrists and lifts them over my head, pinning them to the door just like he has my body.

If it were any other man, I'd freak out. It would terrify me. With Finn, I want more. I open to him, letting him into my mouth, letting him press his thigh between mine.

"I'm going to get you off, Thea. Do you know why?"

I shake my head.

"Because you are mine. Mine to pleasure and mine to take care of. I'm going to hear you moan my name as you come."

His free hand grips my hip hard enough that his fingers bite into my flesh and hurt. I don't want him to stop. He guides me to ride his thigh. When I'm moving at the pace he wants, he reaches behind me and yanks down the zipper to my dress. He pulls it down one shoulder before he kisses the top of my breast. He pulls the bra cup down, then he's lifting my breast to his mouth. His tongue toys with my nipple until it's a tight dart. Then he's sucking on it. His mouth is open as wide as it can, and he's practically inhaling me. He can tell what that does to me. How much it turns me on.

I'm moving faster on his thigh as he drives me to the brink. I'm rubbing my pussy against his thigh as hard as I can. I want to come so badly. I want his fingers in me. I want his cock in me. I want something in me. But he replaces his mouth with his fingers. He pinches my nipple, twisting and pulling.

"We're not ready for me to fuck you for real. But I will, Thea. You are mine."

"I know, Finn."

He's kissing my neck, and it pushes me past my limit to control my body. I feel my orgasm coming, then it slams into me.

"Finn!"

He picks me up and carries me to the sofa. I straddle his lap and lean forward, panting. His hands are running over the outside of my thighs beneath my dress. His hands rest on my ass and push me closer, so I can feel his hard on.

"I want to touch you, too."

"I didn't get you off, so you'll return the favor. I did it because I wanted to feel you in my arms. To know that whatever just happened to that window didn't hurt you. To show you I'll take care of you. You didn't answer me before, and to be honest, that freaked me out more than the window."

"You surprised me. I didn't expect you to notice so fast."

"I noticed from outside, but I couldn't tell for sure. Joey would have called the other night to tell me if you had a broken window. He knows I'd be pissed if he left with it like that."

"I didn't expect you to call me Althea. I don't like it."

I think that's the real reason I didn't answer his question. It wasn't even that I don't want to tell him the truth. It shocked me to hear my full name, and I didn't like his tone. We barely know each other, but he's never called me that. He refuses to call me Ally. Anything other than Thea, *cailín*, or little one feels wrong.

"That's your name."

"But it's not what you call me. I'm not a child. I don't need to be reprimanded."

He cups my face. His hands are warm, and his touch is soft, even though I can feel the slight callouses.

"I didn't mean for it to come across that way. I didn't even realize I had. I guess I wanted you to know how serious I take this. What happened?"

"A bird flew into it."

I've been going over that lie since the moment I saw the brick. Clearly, I didn't practice enough. Before I know what's happening, he's lifting me off his lap, then I'm over it. My dress is over my back, and his hand lands hard on my ass.

"OW!"

"You lied. I've already told you more than once that you don't have to tell me your thoughts. You can tell me you don't want to say. But I also told you I will punish you— hard —if you do anything to endanger yourself. There isn't a fecking bird on the ground. I didn't see one when I walked up, and there wasn't one when I looked down. Hitting a window hard enough to break it like that would have killed it. And that isn't even how glass breaks from a bird dive-bombing it. That was a fecking brick."

He keeps raining down spanks, and I'm kicking my feet.

"Tell me the truth, Thea. Staying silent is no longer an option. You will answer me."

"The truth is I don't want to tell you. Stop, Finn. It hurts."

"Of course it does. It's a punishment. I didn't think the first time I spanked you it'd be because you're risking your safety by lying to me. I thought I'd spank you before fucking you. Did this happen because of me?"

The fight goes out of me. He's scared for me, but he's also scared this is his fault. He feels guilty. The spanking isn't about allaying his fear. It is about me risking my safety. But he's frightened.

"Finn, stop for a moment. Please. You can finish, but I need to sit up and see you while I talk."

He stops immediately. He helps me up until I kneel beside him.

"This has nothing to do with you. But I'm not ready to talk about it. I understand you want to keep me safe. I need you to trust me about this, please. I need to sort some family stuff out. I trust you, but I'm still getting used to that. My instinct isn't usually to lie."

"Thea, I won't pry if this has something to do with your family. It's not my business unless you want it to be. But I won't relent on your safety. Either you accept my expectations and the safeguards I want to put in place, or we can't go forward. But either way, you are going to have a safety detail until *I'm* convinced you're safe. Someone, at the least, wants to scare you. More likely, they want to hurt you, and they're letting you know it's coming."

I close my eyes as I nod. He's not being unreasonable. I stand and lie across his lap again. I reach back and lift my dress. His hand rubs my ass cheeks, taking away some of the burn. He massages, squeezing and rubbing. I expect more to come, but he helps me to sit up. He settles me on his lap with my ass between his open thighs, not putting any weight on it. He kisses my forehead as he holds me. I'm relaxed, but he isn't. He's all hard bone and muscle, even when he's at ease. But he's coiled so tight, he feels like a spring about to pop. He's respecting my boundaries, but it might kill him to do it. He really doesn't like not having control of this situation, and it's stressing him out. But I don't want him involved with Uncle Corey. Nothing good can come of them meeting.

We hear my phone buzz where I put it on the counter. "I have to get that in case it's work."

He helps me up, and I pull my dress back into place as I cross the short distance.

JAMIE

We're going to Gamma's. Asher knows to join us.

Our grandmother lives in New Jersey. She's our mom's mom. I don't agree that they should go there. I glance at Finn who's watching me. I shoot him a smile, and his face appears less taut.

ME

Keep me posted. I don't think Gamma's is a
good idea. He'll think of it as fast as you did.

JAMIE

She lives three doors down from a police
station.

ME

So?

I don't get a response. I don't want to fight with him. I want
my family safe. For now, that may be the best choice.

"Everything okay at work?"

"It was my brother." I won't lie. "It's fine."

That was sorta the truth. It is until Uncle Corey finds
them.

"Your nephew?"

He stands, but he doesn't walk over. He never hesitates to
come near me if that's what he wants. I think that as though we
have some long history together. We don't. But he doesn't move
closer. He's giving me space, so he can't see my phone. He
thinks I'm going to lie again.

"No. Skyler's okay as far as I know. We were talking about
something earlier, but Jamie was in the car."

He looks over at the window, then at my phone in my hand.
He nods.

"Will you let me have one of my guys board up the hole
until I can have the glass replaced in the morning? Your neigh-
bors won't appreciate the noise if a guy does it now."

"You don't have to do that."

"Shane owns a construction company. He's in real estate
development. It'll take one of his guys like fifteen minutes."

I know it'll take longer than that, but I won't turn him
down. He's really trying. I slip my phone into my pocket. I walk

back to him and go to slide my arms around him. His longer arms wrap around me below mine. It's awkward, but I step into his embrace.

"Finn, can we still go out?"

"Of course. If you feel up to it, then of course we can. Are you angry at me for spanking you?"

I lean back. "If I wasn't okay with that, you would know. I agreed to your rule when you told me about it. I didn't object to you doing it, and I knew I could. I knew if I said stop and really wanted it over, you would accept that. I'm sorry I've lied. I hope you can understand why I have."

"I do. If anyone can, I do. I already told you I know I'll be a hypocrite. I'll lie to you, yet I demand you be honest with me. It's not fair. Whatever is going on, you don't want to talk about it for your family's sake. I, of all people, get that. But I'm here if and when you need or want me. I'll let this go, but only for now, Thea. If anything else happens that scares me again, I will push you until you tell me the truth. I'm giving you fair warning."

I pull one arm free and put my hand over his heart. "I don't mean to scare you, Finn."

"I know, little one. Let's go throw some axes. We'll probably both feel better." He grins as we walk toward the door. I grab my purse, and he opens the door for me. I lock up and pray a broken window is all I come home to.

I smile at Joey, but his expression is grim. He's looking up at my window. Maybe he saw Finn in it, and that's how he knows which unit is mine. He walks around the car and speaks to Finn as he opens it.

"I already texted Shane. He can have someone over in the morning. I can get a couple of boards, nails, and a hammer while you're together. If there's time, I can swing over and do it."

I look at Finn who's looking down at me. He's waiting for

my answer. I look back at Joey, and I wonder what he thinks happened. He knows Finn well enough that he didn't bother to wait for Finn to call Shane or tell Joey to text him.

"Grab what we need. I'll do it when we get back." Finn's still watching me, so I nod.

I won't turn down the help, but I think he knows it would make me uncomfortable to have strangers in my place. I slide into the car as Joey gets out his phone. He closes the door behind Finn as whoever it is— presumably Shane —answers. I reach for my seatbelt. When I twist to fasten it, Finn cups my jaw. He says nothing. He just sweeps his gaze over me as though he's not convinced I'm all right after all. When I click the buckle, he lets go and puts on his own belt.

I don't want to keep things a secret from him, but this is private family business. I'm not ready to tell him what's going on. It would piss my parents off. I'm not exactly embarrassed, all things considered. But it's not a part of my family tree I'm excited to share. If I want things to work with Finn, I must figure out how to navigate not lying to him— which feels crappy every time I do it —and not divulging crap my parents would lose their shit over. This also makes me realize I'm not a compulsive liar, but there are very few people I trust enough to tell them really important stuff. I'm used to deflecting or bending the truth a little to avoid answering.

I don't want Finn to walk away because he thinks I'm dishonest. I see the irony, considering what he's already told me will happen. But just because he has to protect me and others, which means lying, doesn't mean it gives me a pass.

I'm lost in my thoughts, so I don't notice how I cover his hand with mine where they rest between us. It's not until he turns mine over to lace our fingers together that I realize what I did. It's comforting.

"You were very generous to my friends and me. Thank you.

We were already having a terrific time, but we felt like royalty when breakfast arrived."

His thumb sweeps across the back of my hand. "I told you I wanted to spoil you."

"You did." I don't want him to think I'm a gold digger and will expect more of this lavishness. I stretch to kiss his cheek.

As I sit back, I hear a motorcycle behind us. I hold my breath as it passes us on my side. It's some crotch rocket, not a chopper like my uncle's motorcycle club prefers. He has a few of the bikes made for speed, but he prefers the ones with the higher handlebars when he's cruising and making sure the people in his neighborhood get a good, long look at him. As though any of them could forget the person extorting them for protection money every month.

I dart my gaze to Finn, and I wonder how I'm able to accept Finn being part of an organized crime family with such ease, but what Uncle Corey does makes me think he's little more than pig shit. Am I a snob? Do I have more respect for a man who commits international crimes than someone who's limited to the Mid-Atlantic area?

Finn's family runs a small empire from what I can tell. They have thousands of people who must work for them. They might commit crimes— probably some really fucking heinous ones —but nothing about him makes me think he does it for the jollies. My dad's uncle absolutely does it to feel superior to regular people who just want to live their lives in peace. He picks on people to see their fear. Finn probably terrifies most people he knows, but I think it's likely with reason.

What the hell do I know? I barely know Finn, but nothing about him makes him even remotely on the same plane as Uncle Corey. He strikes me more like a ruthless corporate mogul than some two-bit criminal.

"How'd you find this place?"

Finn's question breaks me out of my trance. How long have I been staring off into space? I'm being a crappy date.

"Terry— my friend who was at the roulette table with me — suggested it a while back. We had a particularly rough week, and she said it would be a great stress reliever. We never made it, but I remembered."

"Are you into things like panic room escapes?"

If I say no, then I'm lying again. If I say yes, will he think I want to go to one with him? Is that like work for him?

"*Cailín*, it's not a trick question. I think they're cool. I enjoy solving puzzles like that."

Survival training?

"Thea, I can practically hear the gears grinding in your head. No, I don't use them as practice. No, it isn't like work. No, it won't bother me if you say you like them, too."

Our gazes meet, and I wonder how he can read my thoughts so clearly when so few can. Most people say I have a resting poker face. They don't know what I'm thinking until I'm ready to share it. I need it to break bad news to people. I have to appear calm and unfazed when I walk into a room with terrified parents.

"I haven't been to a panic room escape before, but I'm intrigued. I think they look cool, and those are the kind of logic problems I like to figure out." Better than diagnosing some rare condition.

"That's why I asked. You spend your days figuring out solutions to problems, so I know you excel at it. I thought this might be something you're good at but isn't work." He lifts our hands and kisses the back of mine. "I live a normal life most of the time. I don't want you to walk on eggshells, worrying that things remind me of a part of my life I've never admitted to anyone. Most people have no clue. I go about my business and do regular things. I use the rumors to my advantage, but most people assume the truth is exaggeration. I only admitted things to you because I didn't want you to walk away once I'm— we've been dating for a while."

What was he going to say? Attached? In love? Hopelessly devoted? I hear that song from *Grease* in my head. But that's what I wonder.

"I'm glad you told me up front. You've been giving me choices you could have easily kept from me. I want to be with you, and I'm going into this with my eyes as wide open as I can."

We pull up to the industrial park with the warehouse that someone converted into this ax throwing place. It's not very industrial anymore, considering there's a wine bar, a vape place, and three food trucks parked in the lot. I spy a group of motorcycles parked at the far end, and it makes my heart race. I can't see license plates or even that much detail to tell if I should be scared.

When we walk in, there's a group of men in black leather vests. I want to bolt.

"Hey, Finn!"

The biggest guy waves at Finn as he gets off his stool. He's gotta be three-fifty easily. The doctor in me wonders what his blood pressure must be, and if he should eat oatmeal for high cholesterol rather than drink an IPA.

"Hey, Hank." Finn holds out his hand to a guy who totally looks like a Hank. "This is—"

"Dr. Gallagher."

I go still. How the hell does he know my name? I feel a clammy sweat break out along my back.

"Hello."

I do the polite thing and offer my hand, and we shake.

"I'm certain you see hundreds of faces every day. My daughter and son-in-law had a baby three years ago who was born with the cord wrapped around her neck. You were her doctor because she was blue and not breathing well when she came out. You saved my little half pint's life."

I chide myself for my paranoia as I smile. "I'm glad I could help."

"You did more than help, Doc. My daughter and son-in-law had been trying for eight years. She'd lost four pregnancies already. She was high risk because of her own health. We didn't think they'd ever have a child. She was a miracle, and you kept her alive. Thank you doesn't seem enough."

I reach out and put my hand on his tatted forearm just like I've done with countless family members who need just an ounce of reassurance to make it through another day.

"Hearing stories about the kiddos growing up is the thanks." I give his arm a quick squeeze, then let go.

"All the same, Dr. Gallagher, you helped make my family whole." Are those tears in his eyes?

He turns back to his buddies and plonks down on the stool next to one of the high-top tables. There are four lanes, so there are places to sit when it's not your turn. Finn and I walk over to the desk and sign all the necessary waivers. We wait for a target to come available, so we snag a loveseat near the back wall. There are a few of them pushed against the walls, along with the stools. I glance up at Finn and notice his eyes are scanning the crowd. He's taking in everything and everyone. He's not on edge. Just the opposite. I think he's pretty relaxed. It takes me a minute to realize it's because he can see everything from the front door to the back emergency exit. There aren't any windows except next to the main door. Our backs are to a wall, and anyone not throwing is easy to watch.

What is it like to be on guard constantly? Isn't it exhausting to always have to be situationally aware to the nth degree? I sense his need to control everything around him, but I never get the sense that he's controlling. It sounds like a contradiction. But it's not. He doesn't make anything feel oppressive or restrictive. Instead, it puts me at ease. I can let my guard down because I know Finn will watch out for me. It's not like I'm paranoid or too anxious to go out. It's not like I assume something horrible's going to happen, so I only feel safe with him.

It's because I'm a single woman living and working in NYC. I'd be foolish not to pay attention to my surroundings. With Finn, I feel totally in the moment. I choose to trust him. I choose to follow his lead. I choose to be with him. So, since it's my choice, I have no problems letting him have control. Plus, I want him to have a good time. If being on guard actually lets him relax like he is now, then why question it?

His hand rests on my thigh over my dress. His thumb rubs the outside of it absentmindedly. He leans to whisper in my ear.

"It's sexy as feck seeing someone come over and thank the beautiful woman on my arm for saving a baby's life."

I turn my head to whisper back to him. "That's what you think is sexy? So, I don't need to worry about my lingerie?"

The look he shoots me makes my legs tense. His grip tightens.

"I think it's sexy that you're brilliant, and kind, and sacrificing. I think it's sexy that you're gracious, patient, and humble. And as for the lingerie, you don't need to worry about it because you don't need to wear any."

His hand slides up my leg like a centimeter. Just enough for me to feel without it being inappropriate. The weight of his hand settles heavier on my thigh as he continues to whisper to me.

"I haven't enjoyed your pretty pussy nearly enough. That means when I want it, I will have it. No more panties."

I hold my breath for a second. That's the hottest fucking

shit. But only because it's Finn. It would sound arrogant and disgusting coming from someone else. His matter-of-fact tone doesn't make it sound dismissive or overbearing. It makes me feel physically desirable after he made my heart melt with his compliments. Like he wants all of me. Like I want to let him have all of me.

"Finn?"

An employee calls out his name. He helps me off the sofa and holds my hand as we weave among the tables to where the woman has four axes in her hands. She leads us to our lane and explains the rules. Finn steps back, and I suddenly get nervous. What if I make an utter fool of myself and don't even hit the target?

I watched a couple videos before I suggested it, so I at least know the technique. I stagger my stance with my dominant hand holding the handle. My less dominant foot out in front. I wrap my other hand over the one holding the ax. I raise it until I point the blade at the bullseye. I inhale, transferring the weight to my back foot. Then I pray I don't make an ass of myself, shift my weight forward, and exhale as I bring it over my head and release. I'm tempted to squeeze my eyes shut, but I watch as it thuds against the board. It embeds above the bullseye but in line with it.

Okay. That wasn't as hard as I feared.

Finn's hand comes to rest on my lower back. "That's awesome."

I turn my head to look at him, and our lips practically brush. He kisses my cheek instead. I step aside. I make sure I'm out of his way so he can bring the ax back over his head. Except he doesn't. He holds it in his left hand; his stance clearly showing he's been an athlete. He brings the ax up and throws without having to practice lining up his sights. It digs into the target just left of the bullseye. My eyes narrow. I knew he was left-handed, but...

"You missed on purpose." I'm not asking. I'm telling.

He looks over at me, his brow furrowed. The picture of innocence and confusion. Fuck. He's going to be a good liar. Far better than me. Neither of us says anything as I pick up my second ax and take my position. I focus again before hurling the ax with more force than I planned. I'm annoyed.

It hits dead center; the blade embedding deep into the wood. It'll take some prying to get it out. I step out of the way again, but this time, I'm practically glaring at Finn. I don't want pity shots to make me feel better. It makes me feel belittled instead. He watches me as he raises his hand. He doesn't take his eyes off me as he sends the weapon sailing through the air and into the target at the very most center part of the bullseye.

"Thea, I own an Irish bar. I used to go there after school when I was in elementary school. I did my homework there while Nana babysat my brothers and me. I've been throwing darts since I was nine. I wanted you to have a good time."

Fuck. I'm a bitch.

He wraps his arm around my waist and pulls me against his body. He presses the softest kiss to my lips. It's so gentle after watching him do something— violent if we weren't here— manly —impressive —that makes me want to jump his bones. That is Finn. A contradiction.

"Thank you. I should have been gracious like you said I was."

"No. I made you feel like I did a pity throw. And I did. Not because I don't think you're good at this. You impressed me the first time. A little scared of you now after the second time. I did it because I didn't want you to think I was showing off and being a dick."

I cup his face. I'm falling into infatuation. He's too good to be true. My kiss is not a mere brushing of our lips. It's hard and fast. I want to be somewhere private. I want to take off my panties and let him do what he wants with my pretty little pussy.

Instead, I sweep my thumb over his light stubble. "Thank you for always putting me first. I'm sorry I assumed the worst."

"You didn't know why I was good at it, but I shouldn't have tried to hide what you obviously already knew."

"I want to try it single-handed, but I'm not sure I'm strong enough. I don't want to embarrass myself by having it land on the floor halfway to the target. Will you show me, please?"

"You're strong enough to make it across that space. It's not that far. I think you're worried you won't throw hard enough to get it to stick. Considering how you just threw the last one, you definitely are. I think what's really your concern, though, is the timing, so the blade is facing the right direction when it hits the wood."

I nod. My fear of embarrassment is all of that. That I won't be strong enough with one hand to make it sink in, but I also don't feel confident that I can throw it so that it hits the wood at the right rotation.

"*Cailín*, I think your nerves are telling you that you have to do everything perfectly. Instead, they're making you feel less coordinated. It doesn't have to be a bullseye every time. It doesn't matter if you don't even hit the target. Everyone is busy doing their own thing. People aren't watching us. And even if they are, there are plenty of other people who aren't doing so great at this. You wouldn't be alone at not being an expert."

All of that. It's why I take forever to bowl a decent game or play pool well. It's not until I practically give up trying to be any good and just play that I hit pins and shoot balls into pockets.

I keep my voice low for only Finn. "It's not exactly that I

resist doing things I can't be sure I excel at. I mean, there are some cases of that. But I was game to try this, knowing I have no experience with it. It's not that I think you would look down on me for missing every shot. I'm used to being good at most things I do. When I get to something I don't think I do well, I overcompensate. Then I'm way worse. I have to get to a point where I don't care that I might not be good enough. And that 'enough' is some ridiculous self-imposed standard."

I just admitted something that makes me feel kinda vulnerable. All I see in his gaze is— I'd say love if we were that far along in our relationship. I guess it's respect and acceptance and —I just don't know. It's something I can't articulate. But it makes me feel warm and gooey inside. I'd stepped back a little to talk to him, so he pulls me close again.

He whispers in my ear. "Fate gave me a gift the day you walked into McGinty's."

He lets go of me and fetches the axes. We take turns for the next hour until our time is up. I'm at ease during each of my turns, and I get progressively better with the one-handed throw. Moving my way from the right side of the outer-most ring to the bullseye. I don't hit it dead on, but I get much better each time.

I excuse myself and slip into the restroom. There's a stall open, so I go straight in. I want to surprise Finn later, so I'm pulling off my panties as I hear two women talking.

"Did you see the guy with the red hair and green eyes? What I wouldn't give to be his girlfriend."

"How could I not? The man is fucking hot as hell. He looked so sweet and in love with her. She's so lucky."

"I know, right? He's gorgeous and is obviously the perfect boyfriend. I wish he was whispering whatever he was saying in my ear. His girlfriend is stunning. They could be like in a movie or something."

"Why do gorgeous people always fall in love with other

143

gorgeous people? I'm not surprised she's with such a hot guy. She's straight and out of my league."

I hear them flush each toilet. I remain hidden. It's not that I'm eavesdropping— okay. I totally am — I don't want to embarrass either of them. It would be awkward, wouldn't it?

The second woman speaks again as I hear water running. "I just can't get over how loving he was. Like, she's his entire universe. The place could have burned down around us, and he wouldn't have taken his eyes off her. And it was obvious she feels the same way. I didn't see any rings on their fingers. I definitely looked at her hand. I wonder how long they've been together. It's gotta be years."

"Yeah. Not that new relationship everything's roses and passionate sex. It was like a lifetime together, but they're still only in their 30s." The first woman sounds like she's directly outside my stall.

"Maybe college sweethearts or something."

I can barely hear the first woman as they walk out. "Maybe."

I realize I need to hurry because I've been in here too long. I stuff my panties in my purse and rush to wash my hands. Good thing I didn't actually need to go. Finn's outside the door, flashing a quick smile to the women as they walk past. But he's looking at me as I step out. He doesn't expect me to slide my arms around his waist for a hug, so he doesn't get his arms under mine fast enough.

I freeze.

Chapter Eleven

Finn

And there went an amazing date.

Thea's staring at me as we embrace. I don't know if it's she's simply too shocked to move or too scared. Probably both.

"Will you let me explain in the car?"

"Let you?"

"Yeah. Please don't bolt."

She blinks three times before her brow furrows. She lowers her arms and nods. I guide her out of the converted warehouse and out to the town car. I open the door, but she doesn't get in.

"This isn't something I want anyone to overhear. We won't leave. We'll just sit and talk. If you want to end the date, then I'll make sure you get home however you want."

"We haven't decided where to have dinner."

Now it's my turn to blink and furrow my brow. *Huh?*

"Finn, I thought we were going to have dinner, too. We just never talked about it."

"You still want to have dinner with me?"

"You asked me not to bolt. I haven't. You asked me to let you explain. I will. But wouldn't it be more efficient for you to explain in the car on the way to the restaurant? I admit I'm a bit hungry."

She turns and slips into the car, and I'm left catching flies with my mouth open. I slide in after her and pull the door shut. Before she can fasten her seatbelt, I lift her onto my lap. I lower the privacy glass just enough to tell Joey the name of a restaurant. I don't own it, but Cormac does. It's the best Japanese restaurant in Queens. He has the best chefs and everything.

"You're not scared of me now? Scared of what it means that I carry a gun on a date?"

"I've never been scared of you. I don't believe for a second you will ever physically hurt me. I don't think you'd intentionally do that to any woman."

Physically hurt me. She's worried I'll hurt her emotionally. I probably will. But I pray it's not enough for her to end things. I pray if it happens, it's something we can work out.

"I only want to keep you out of harm's way."

"I know. But I suspect that, now I know you're carrying a gun, you always have one."

"Not always. I didn't at McGinty's either time you were there, but that's a controlled space for me."

"But you did at the casino, right? And on our last date, right?"

"Yes."

"Are you always in that much danger? Am I now in that much danger? Will I be a target?"

I want to sigh and run my hand through my hair. Instead, I tighten my arms around her hips.

"I live with constant threats, so yes, I'm always in danger. But I still go about my life like I don't. I just take precautions. There was a creed among the families that women and children

146

were off limits. My family broke it. No one living did it by choice. The men responsible for that are dead. But it's changed the rules. The best I can answer your last questions is possibly. If I believed with certainty that you'd be a target, I would never have come near you. I'm selfish in bringing you anywhere near me. I'm selfish to know I'll lie to you and want you to accept that. I also know I don't want either of us to walk away."

"Maria. Her family is one of those families, right?"

"Yes."

She sits contemplatively, and I have no idea what's on her mind. I give her time to work through whatever she's thinking.

"I know she has bodyguards with her, even at work, but I assumed it was because her family is uber wealthy."

"They are."

She looks toward the privacy screen with my driver/bodyguard on the other side. "You are too."

"We are."

I still don't want to push her. But I'm desperate to know what's going through her head. She hasn't hopped off my lap or demanded we stop. She got into the car with me.

"She goes to work and clearly goes out on double dates with her cousin. If I didn't now know who her family is, I would have assumed they were just two well-off Manhattanite couples. Totally normal."

"In many ways, they are."

Except Carmine and Matteo have both tried to kill me, and I've gotten even closer to killing them. Four times.

"We're doing something totally normal, too. I mean, ax throwing isn't one-hundred percent normal, but we're having a normal date. We did last time, too."

"I want us to." There's nothing I want more right now.

She leans against me, her head against my chest. I rest one hand on her arse while the other runs up and down her back.

"What do I do if something goes wrong? Like if you have to shoot someone, or they're shooting at us?"

"You get away as fast as you can. I don't care if you think I've lost a speck of blood or gallons of it. You do not try to save me. You get somewhere crowded where you can blend in, or you go to McGinty's. As you get to know other members of my family, you'll know where to go if you're near enough. If you have to hide, my family will come and get you. Either way, they will protect you. Always."

And they will. The guys haven't given me as much shite as we gave Dillan when he was into Mair, but not yet dating. They know I have a far lower threshold for teasing. It's not that I'm thin-skinned. I just won't tolerate it. I'll walk away or hang up. They know I won't put up with a single thing that might be a jab at me that comes at Thea's expense.

"Could I get arrested for dating you?"

I don't want to tell her what happened to Mair. "It's possible. But it's very unlikely. The cops and feds know we don't involve women in the business. It's patriarchal. It's archaic. It's misogynistic. And we won't have it any other way. All of us were born into this. No one in my generation or my parents' asked to enter a syndicate. The legacy that's passed down should only be the men's burden since we created it."

"But they could go after me to get to you."

"Yes."

She nods against my chest. "Am I going to find a lot of scars?"

"I have more than I'd like. I know you'll recognize I've been shot before. You'll see some that you can likely guess came from a knife. We have a family doctor. Short of a ruptured organ or paralysis, we do not go to hospitals. Our doctor stitches us up."

"Because GSWs and stabbings require the hospital staff to call the police."

"Which leads to questions none of us will answer. Can you accept this?"

When she pulls the hand away from her arse, my heart tightens. I don't expect her to guide it beneath her dress, up her thigh, and to her pussy. She's so fucking wet.

"Have you been like this for me all night, *cailín*? I notice your panties disappeared."

"Yes, and they did."

"Do you want me to make you come?"

"Yes."

"Why?"

"Because it's your pussy to play with."

I slide two fingers into her, and she clamps her legs closed. She sits up enough to pull her dress down and lift her tits from her bra.

"Finn, what you told me is fucking scary. It should make me run away and never look back. I'm not wet for you because I have some bad boy, danger seeking fantasy. I'm wet because everything about you turns me on. Your acceptance of duty. Your loyalty to family. Your willingness to protect what matters. Who you are is just as hot as how you look."

She lets her legs fall open again. I slide a third finger into her cunt and work her as she pinches her nipples and pushes her tits together. Her skin is so smooth it invites me to lick and nip at her neck. She shifts to straddle me so I can finger fuck her and suck on her tits at the same time. She's riding my hand just like I want her to ride my dick. But I don't want our first time together to be in a car. That's way too cliché.

"Finn, more. Please."

I increase the pressure as I rub her clit. She's rocking against my hand and my hard on. Fuck, she'll make me come before I get her off if she keeps doing this. I lift her and roll her onto her back as I follow her. I steal a kiss before I shift to kneel half on and half off the seat. I push her dress up and gaze upon the promised land. Her skin is silky smooth everywhere. I lave my tongue along her pussy lips before flicking her clit in a rhythm that soon has her writhing on the backseat. I slide three fingers back into her. She grabs my wrist and tries to push me deeper. I pull out instead.

"Finn!" She lifts her head to look at me with surprise.

"I decide how I'm going to get you off. I also decide when I'm going to get you off. Now I'm going to take even more time."

She whimpers but lays her head back down. Saying nothing, she lifts her hands over her head and grabs the end of the leather. She knows she needs to do this to keep from grabbing me again.

"Would you like me to cuff you to my bed and fuck you until we can't keep our eyes open?"

"Is that what we're going to do tonight?"

"It can be. Is that what you want, little one?"

"Yes."

"What else do you want?" I put my mouth back to her clit and suck.

"I want you to fuck every part of me."

I slide my free hand beneath her arse and let my fingers dip between her arse cheeks. "Here?"

"*Every* part, Finn. I want to jack you off, suck you off, feel your cum dripping out of me. You decide where you finish."

I bring her to the edge and let her jump. Her body tenses as she comes. God. The temptation to fuck her right now is pushing me past the point of reason.

"Finn, I have an IUD, and I tested right before I started seeing Tony. He always wore a condom. I insisted."

"I'm clean too. I tested a month ago." Because it's a requirement for my BDSM club. "And I haven't gone bareback since college. Is that what you want me to do?"

"I want to feel my pussy full of your cum as we walk into the restaurant. I want to know that's our little secret."

Fuck. That makes my balls ache.

I glance out the window. We still have at least thirty minutes before we get to the restaurant with the way traffic is right now. I move her legs and sit on the seat again. As I unfasten my pants and push down my boxer briefs, she yanks her dress off and unfastens her bra.

"Holy feck, Thea. You are gorgeous. Every part of you."

I run my hands up her ribs and over her tits until I cup her neck. I tug her toward me as she straddles my hips. I'm so damn hard that I'm sticking straight up like a fucking telephone pole. She slides down me, and we both groan. I pinch her right nipple while my other hand keeps her head in front of mine. I tighten my grip slightly. She lifts her chin, lengthening her neck for me. I squeeze, but not quite hard enough to be breath play.

"I am going to fuck you until you're screaming my name. Your cunt belongs to me just like my cock belongs to you. I'm going to fill you with my cum because I can. I have a dominant personality, but I am not a Dom. My cum is yours whenever you want it because you can. Just because I want control doesn't mean you have none. Hell, if you want to fuck, I'm hard the second I'm around you, so just pull my dick out and take me."

"I'm always willing to submit to you because I know I have the control to say no. If you give me free rein of your cock, you better be sure you know what you're saying. If I want a good fuck, and you said I can have it whenever I want, I will accept the offer."

"Good."

Our kiss is beyond passionate. I wonder when— not if,

but when —she'll accept that offer to sit on my dick whenever she wants. She rides me, and I have to take some deep breaths when we pull apart. I'm going to embarrass myself with how fast I come. I was hard while I spanked her. I was semi hard while we threw the axes. I've had a raging boner since the second she sat on my lap. Since she sat where she belongs.

We push each other, fucking as hard as a backseat with allow. I pin her hips in place as I thrust over and over, making her tits bounce. Just like I did a few minutes ago, I turn us, so she's lying down. I keep her hips up and pound her like a motherfucking jackhammer. I can't stop. I rub her clit.

"Finn, I'm so close... Yes... I'm going to come... I'm coming, D— Finn."

D— Who the fuck's name was she about to say? That ought to kill my libido. It doesn't. Just the opposite. I'll fuck whoever she's thinking about out of her mind.

"Say my name, Thea. Say it."

"Finn."

"Say it."

"Finn."

"Who's fucking your cunt? Whose cum are you going to wear down your thighs until *I* say you can wash it off?"

"Yours, Daddy!"

We both freeze. That's what she was about to say. That's what she stopped herself from saying the last couple of times she nearly let it slip. I lean forward and rest my elbow next to her ear. I go back to fucking her.

"That's goddamn right, *cailín*. You're going to wear Daddy's cum until *I* wash it away. Tomorrow morning. At my place. In my shower. After I spend all night filling you with more."

I punctuate the short sentences with thrusts. She's gripping my arms during the last five hard thrusts when I tell her this is going to last all night.

"Daddy!"

She keens the word as her entire body tightens so much she trembles. Perspiration beads along her forehead. She lifts her head so I can brush her braids out from beneath her shoulders and back. I watch her suck in lungfuls of air for a moment before she comes back to me.

"I want to make you come, Finn."

I don't care what she calls me right now. Either Finn or Daddy work for me. I keep going, and I feel her doing Kegels around my cock. I can't hold back. With a grunt, I hold her hips in place as I explode inside her. My cock pulses over and over, and I know this is the hardest I've ever come. I scoop her up and move with ease as I take my seat for the third time.

"I'm not a Little, Finn."

"You definitely are not. Calling me Daddy isn't about age play for us."

"No, it's not. But I've never called a man that. I don't know where it came from."

"Have you thought it was hot in the past and just never said it?"

"Kinda."

"I call you *cailín* which means little girl. Seems a logical response."

"You've made sure I understand the risks I face. You've also made sure I understand you want to watch out for me and take care of me. You spoiled me at the casino. I've heard it in porn, and I guess it all fit together, then came out of my mouth. I think it's super-hot that I'm naked and you're still in jeans and your sweater."

"I don't want to be your Dom. And I don't want you to be my sub. But I loved hearing you call me that."

"You thought I was going to say another man's name."

"Can you blame me?"

"No. Keep fucking me like this, and there'll be no space in my memory for anyone else."

I'm still balls deep inside her, but I can feel myself softening. Neither of us moves. Her head is back where it belongs: against my chest. Her hand is resting over my heart, and she's pressing soft, quick kisses to my neck. I know we're almost to the restaurant, but I don't want this moment to end. So much for not wanting to be a cliché. It's just the two of us, and it's so fucking peaceful. There's nothing happening besides basking in the post-coital glow.

Damn. We're here. Thea realizes it too because she tries to scramble off my lap, desperately reaching for her clothes.

"Thea, no driver will open the door until the passenger raps on the window. For all they know, the passenger could be on a call not meant for their ears. It's okay. Joey won't see you naked. That's only for me."

But she bites her lip, then nods.

"Thea?"

"Yeah?"

"You look like you want to disagree with that. We haven't stated it plainly, but I want to be a couple. An exclusive couple. If that isn't what you want, we need to talk."

"I definitely don't want to date anyone else."

"But you aren't on board that I'm the only man who sees you naked. Or is there a woman you're also involved with?"

"No woman. I just have a fantasy that's all. And since it's obvious you're into BDSM, I thought you might know somewhere we could roleplay it."

Second date, and we're discussing going to a BDSM club.

"Do you want people to watch us?"

Her cheeks darken, and now she's hesitant to answer. Did I sound judgmental? I didn't mean to.

"Thea? You can tell me anything you do or don't want. Sexual or not."

"It's way too soon. I shouldn't have brought it up."

"Is it a fantasy you've always had?"

"No. It just came to me."

"If it's something we can make happen, then we will. What do you want?"

"You're going to think I'm—"

"What I'm going to think is whatever you're about to tell me is going to make me fuck you a second time in ten minutes, never mind what the fantasy actually is. Tell me, Thea."

"I want you to fuck me while other people jack off."

She's mortified. I shouldn't have pushed. She ducks her head.

"Sweetheart, look at me."

She does, but she's reluctant.

"I know where we can make that happen. If we do anything voyeuristic, it has to be like this. I have to remain clothed. My tatts are too distinct."

I lift my sweater up, so she can see the shamrock with the O in the center on my left pec. It's a rite of passage that I earned. I'll never tell her how many people I killed on that mission to join the ranks. I have other ones that would stand out to people, but that's the recognizable one.

"I can live with that. Would it be at a dungeon?"

"Yes. A BDSM club. I'm a member, Thea. If you decide you don't want this, then I will cancel my membership. If you want to try the club but not the voyeurism, we can do that too. Whatever we decide, I am not going there without you."

"I think I want to experience that. Can we wear masks or something?"

"Yes. Always. I won't go in without one. Neither will you."

"How would it work?"

"The place has a private viewing room in the center of the sectioned off space. Around the viewing room are smaller ones where individuals or couples can go to watch. It's double-sided glass. The voyeurs can see what's happening, but people on stage can't see who's there."

She flexes her hips and rocks. My dick is swelling again, so it's only a moment more before she's riding me.

"Finn."

It's a whisper as she shatters again. I'm there with her a couple thrusts later. Then I'm helping her get dressed before she climbs off. I fasten my pants and give her a quick glance. She doesn't look like she's been well fucked, even if I'm certain Joey knows that's exactly what's happening back here.

Hell, it wouldn't surprise me if my parents didn't conceive me in the back seat of one of our family cars. Half my cousins and even my brothers probably were too. Our parents can't keep their hands off each other. And more than once, I've arrived at an event in a separate car from my mom and dad only to see my dad straightening his tie or my mom fiddling with her hair as they get out.

I knock on the window, and Joey opens the door. I get out, pulling my sweater down in the back just to be sure. Then I reach in to offer Thea my hand.

"Do you want me to get the supplies?"

"Yes, please."

Joey wouldn't have left us alone at the ax throwing place, even if I'd suggested it. Which I wouldn't with Thea with me. But I know we're well guarded at Cormac's restaurant.

Thea and I head inside and stop at the host stand.

"Hey, Finn."

"Hi, Tom. Table for two, please."

"Do you own this place as well?" Thea whispers as she looks around.

"No. Cormac does." I grin.

I nod to a few people I know as we make our way to a table in the corner. I pull out Thea's chair. I don't love her back being to the windows, but at least I can see everywhere with my back to the wall. I don't need to look at the menu here, but that's not because I've been here so many times. It's because I know what rolls I like. I stick my hand out, palm up. Thea smiles as she puts her hand in mine while she looks at the choices. It only takes her a moment before she closes it. After the sex we just had, how do we come up with something normal to talk about?

Feck me.

"Look who we have here."

Chapter Twelve

Thea

Whoever these men are, Finn isn't happy to see them. Who starts a conversation with a cliché greeting like that? Finn doesn't let go of my hand, instead, giving it a little squeeze.

"Hollands. Spiegel."

I wait to see if he'll say more, but he remains quiet. He didn't even use these guys' first names. The taller of the two men takes a step closer to the table. Bad choice, dude. Finn straightens and pushes his shoulders back. He never hunches, but neither does he make his actual size obvious. I remember seeing him do that for the first time at the casino. He could be a pro athlete or pro bodybuilder for his size. I haven't seen him naked— yet —but I know he's all lean, chiseled muscle. He's making sure these guys know. He doesn't like them encroaching.

"It's not office hours, gentlemen. I'll speak to you on Monday."

That's one way of dismissing them. Do they work for him?

Nothing about them makes me think they're underlings, but Finn certainly just treated them that way.

"O'Rourke, aren't you going to introduce us?"

It's the one who took the step forward. He's pushing his luck. I sense these two men know exactly who Finn is, and that's why they came over. I'm watching Finn, not them. I know the guy got closer from my peripheral vision and the darkening of Finn's expression.

"Spiegel, my cousin owns this restaurant. You know that means cameras. Do you really want to do this right now? Because if you do, say cheese."

I shift my gaze because the air just changed. There's a smugness to Finn that only just now came out. Both men appear on the defensive rather than the offensive. Through it all, I'm not tempted to say a word. I'm content to be the pretty arm candy for this. They look like FBI agents or something. I didn't notice that at first. It makes the hair on the back of my neck stick up when I realize Finn issued a threat that's tanta-mount to extortion. These men either don't want to be seen here, or they don't want to be seen together. Actually, it's likely both.

I glance at the men's left hands. Wedding rings on both ring fingers. The silent guy angled himself slightly in front of the guy who started all this. A defensive position since he was farther away from us a moment ago. They're lovers, not husbands. At least, not to each other.

"When we talk on Monday, I'm certain you'll be the bearers of good news. It would be nice to start the week right." Finn's piercing green eyes bore into them.

The silent one nudges the other guy, and they leave without another word. I want to turn and watch them walk away, but I don't dare. Instead, I lean forward.

"They're having an affair, aren't they?"

Finn's eyes widen, and his jaw tenses. Then I'm the recipient of his stare.

"What makes you say that?"

"They're wearing wedding rings, but they don't match. Not even similar. The similarity part is just incidental. The quiet one moved to a defensive position to stand in front of the loudmouth. Two men that size rarely need to protect each other during a conversation. A more dominant lover will. Just because he wasn't the pushy one doesn't mean he isn't a top."

"You got all of that just from how they stood?"

"Of course. You already know that, and that's what you have on them. They wouldn't want any proof they were out together."

"They're brothers-in-law, so them hanging out isn't implausible. But you're right about the rest. And no, they would rather I not use proof to go along with what I could share."

"They thought to embarrass you in front of me, and they wanted to use me as a shield to issue thinly veiled threats to you. They assume I know nothing."

"Which you don't. I won't tell you their first names, Thea. You figured out something that impresses me, but it's something dangerous. This isn't how I wanted to prove there are risks to being with me. As much as they don't want anyone to know they were out together, they know I don't want your name or face splashed around. They were using you as a shield. That pisses me off."

I can't help but wonder what it means when someone pisses Finn off. Like is that an understatement, and they're going to have concrete shoes? Or is he mildly annoyed? I attempt to keep my expression impassive, but he smiles.

"I'm not putting a hit on them, Thea."

Yet? "Okay."

I return his smile as the waiter comes to our table. The rest of the meal is shockingly normal. We chat about what a typical workday looks like for both of us and how our jobs have evolved over time. Maria came up naturally in conversation. It wasn't like he asked. He's known her pretty much her entire life. At least since they were old enough to play rec sports. Will I ever get used to how fucked-up their world is? That their parents used to stand around on Saturdays and watch their kids play together. Then Monday rolled around, and they were trying to kill each other— figuratively or literally.

We're about to step out of the restaurant when Cormac comes in. "I was looking for you."

How'd he know we were here? Cormac wouldn't randomly drive around.

"I stopped by your place, then remembered you were out. I was going to go to my office to call you." The look they exchange says more than they'll say aloud.

"Should I head to the car?"

Finn's gaze sweeps the restaurant before he looks out the door. He doesn't like either option. I think he knows how awkward it would be for me to just stand here.

"I'll walk you out. Cormac, I'll be right back."

Joey opens the door for us. I saw him having dinner at the sushi bar.

"I'll try not to take too long."

"Take as long as you need." I kiss his cheek and give his forearm a squeeze.

He looks torn, but he nods and heads back inside. I think this is a look into the life I'm accepting. He wants to put me first, but family and the mob will always take precedence. I can't blame him, but I think it's going to hurt. A lot. Often. At least in the beginning. It's something I have to be okay with. I'll get there. Part of why it sucks is I know it means whatever's happening is something at the very least illegal, but far more likely dangerous.

I've already rationalized why I can accept what Finn does, but I can't accept what Uncle Corey does. I'm in the car with the door shut, looking out the window at the restaurant. I pull out my phone and do the thing I told myself not to. I search the internet for anything about his family.

Immediately, shit shows up. A lot of shit. I open another tab and search the Mancinellis. Just as much. I try Diaz and mafia. That's too common a name not to search something specific. Tons come up for them, too. I comb my memory for the fourth family's name. It takes a moment, but I search Kutsenko. They're the only ones who seem to turn up only articles about legal shit. They're corporate moguls. I noticed that the dates for the Kutsenko articles were only within the last ten or so years. The dates for the other families go back further.

I toggle to the tab with results for the O'Rourkes. With trepidation, I click the first link.

Mob Boss Dies in Plane Crash

Which of Finn's family members was this? Looking at the dates, my guess is an uncle or grandfather. I scroll and read. It names the victim as Liam O'Rourke. It said he died at sixty-three, so my guess is Finn's grandfather. The article hints it was one of the other syndicates. That whoever organized it made to look like a mechanical failure that caused something in the fuel line to ignite, then explode. My heart breaks for Finn as I think about how traumatic that must have been.

Then I keep reading. The article names several court cases filed against Liam. They accused him of some pretty fucking heinous shit! Like holy fuck! If he did what the article claims, then he was a fucking sociopath.

I look up from my phone and stare out the window again and toward the restaurant. Juries acquitted Liam because something always came out that benefited the defense in each case, and double jeopardy prevented the government from prosecuting again. I'm certain they made sure no one filed civil suits. Is this what Finn does?

I can handle the extortion, the racketeering, the money laundering, the coercion. Why I can is something I truly need to dig deeper into, but I can. But if he does the things they accused Liam of... It's not just shooting someone in the head or heart. It's torture. But there were never any bodies to identify or gather physical evidence from. The lack of those things is largely why he was exonerated, but there were also allegations of witness tampering and intimidation.

I go back to the search results and click another article. This one is about an explosion at the docks about three years ago. It happened in an area where the article alleges several shipping companies with affiliation to the mob operate. It names Shane as an owner of one of the largest ones. Whoever it was targeted his company. It says law enforcement suspects it was a rival syndicate. It doesn't specifically state the Russian bratva, but it hints heavily that it was them. Once again, there was no evidence at the scene to make any definitive claims. Shane declined to comment each time reporters approached him.

The reporter noted it was around that time that an obituary posted for Declan O'Rourke. I click over to that. Whoever wrote this was blowing smoke up everyone's asses. It sings his praises like he was fucking Mother Teresa. It definitely doesn't match how they describe Declan in the article. It pretty much made it sound like he was a chip off the old block from his uncle, Liam. I try to piece together how everyone is related. Since they're all O'Rourkes, I assume it's through Finn's dad's side of the family. They list the cause of death as a heart attack while he was working out. He was fifty-seven. Possible but improbable.

I return to the search results yet again. The next article is one about Finn and his cousins. They're at some gala, all wearing tuxes. I find genetics fascinating. While we don't do genetic testing on every newborn who has a difficult condition to diagnose, the tests we perform can provide crucial information. I also think it's super cool how some inherited traits are absolutely predictable, and others are like roulette. Looking at this black and white photo of Finn, his brothers, Cormac, Seamus, and Dillan, they could all pass for one another. From a distance, I know they could pass for one another.

The American Academy of Ophthalmology says— and let me tell you, those reports are just scintillating reading —green eyes are the rarest. Yet, all six men have them. Red hair is also the rarest color. All of them have both. Genetic lottery of hot recessive genes.

I return my attention to the article after letting my mind wander. Fuck that's a lot of money. It says the family donated fifteen million dollars to support the ASPCA and the AVMA— American Veterinary Medical Association —during a fundraising project to raise money toward rescue services for abused animals. Not exactly the big-name type of philanthropy, but it's sweet. Apparently, they not only donated the massive sum, but they also sponsored the entire event. They worked in conjunction with the organization to raise an additional fifteen million dollars. They did a donation match. I can't fathom having that much money. It says the donation came from their personal assets and not any businesses.

The contradiction is mind-boggling. One moment, I'm reading articles about their relatives being worse than fucking Pol Pot or Vlad the Impaler. The next, I'm reading that they shut down puppy mills. Then again, it's proof of what I've already seen. I know what they do, but I also know how the guys I've met have been around me. You wouldn't guess if you didn't know.

I move to the next article, and there's a nearly full-page image of Finn dancing with one of the most gorgeous women I have ever seen. The way they're holding each other shows more than simple familiarity. They're smiling at each other and completely at ease. I glance at the caption. Finn and Colleen O'Rourke. The photog took it at Salvatore and Sylvia Mancinelli's wedding reception thirteen years ago. He would have still been in college. But they have the same last name, and just their body language. Finn was married.

I nearly jump out of my skin when the door opens. I drop my phone in my lap as I look up.

"I didn't mean to startle you, *cailín*."

"It's all right." I scoot over, but Finn doesn't get in. He bends over.

"Joey's going to take you home. Something came up with an overseas shipping company that lost some cargo last week. I need to deal with this. I'm sorry to cut our date short. I know we were going to..." He waggles his eyebrows.

"Were you married?" Where the fuck did those three words come from?

Finn stares at me, clearly as shocked as I am by what I blurted.

"No."

"Who's Colleen?"

A flash of soul-deep sadness crosses his face before he masks it.

"No. Don't do that, Finn. Don't hide from me. You told me you'll lie to me. You probably just did. Don't shut me out when you don't have to."

"How do you know about Colleen? Did you google me?"

"Yes."

He stares at me for a moment, and he's obviously debating something. He glances back at the restaurant before getting into the car and shutting the door.

"Colleen was my cousin. Dillan's little sister. She was the ringleader of everything. But she was also the kindest soul you'll ever meet. She was a veterinarian."

The fundraiser. *Was?*

"She was murdered nearly four years ago. Dillan was there when it happened."

I feel like the worst sort of bitch. This wasn't something he wanted to talk about. I just picked at a scab. It's clear the wound hasn't healed. His grief is practically palpable. His hands are just resting in his lap, so I cover them with mine. He's not looking at me. He's looking at his lap.

"Finn, I saw a photo of the two you at a wedding reception. You looked so happy and loving with her. She had the same last name. I made an assumption and made an ass of myself because I was jealous. I'm so sorry."

"We're all O'Rourkes. Three sisters married three brothers. Our two sides of the family haven't been closely related in at least ten generations, but there have been enough sons to carry on the name. My mom and aunts didn't have to change theirs when they got married. Joey's an O'Rourke on my dad's side. If you've been investigating, you probably found Liam, Donovan, and Declan. They were O'Rourkes on my mom's side."

I didn't read anything about a Donovan.

"I'm sorry."

"For what, little one? For getting bored because I abandoned you for half an hour during our date? For wanting to know about the guy you're dating? A guy who's a mother-fecking mobster." He spits out the last word.

He appears so dejected along with grief-filled. I tilt my head as I study him. He's sad about more than just talking about Colleen. I let go of his hands, and he makes to grab them as I pull them back, but he stops himself. I push his hands apart and move to sit on his lap. He instantly relaxes. Ah.

"Daddy, I'm not going anywhere. It's scary to hear what happened to Colleen, and I feel awful bringing it up. My heart breaks to hear what you lost. I read the article about the veterinary gala. It makes sense now. The past half hour has given me a look at what my life *will*— not could —not might —*will* be. You have work to do, and Cormac's waiting right now. I'll be waiting until you're free to see me again."

He cups my nape, and his thumb sweeps over my cheekbone as he stares into my eyes. He nods, then we're kissing. My toes curl in my shoes. This one isn't a heart pounding, passion-filled one. It's a heart-stopping, tender kiss. When we pull apart, we rest our foreheads together.

"*Cailín*, there's a good chance you won't hear from me for a couple days. I'll be out of cell phone service."

Where the hell is he going?

"You'll be traveling."

He's back to debating what to say.

"No. There is somewhere here in New York that's a controlled location when we have things to do. I will never tell you where, never take you there. You must not try to find it, Thea. You'll endanger everyone. When I'm there, my cell phone is off. If there's an emergency, call one of the guys. Let me program their numbers into your phone. They'll get in touch with me."

Things to do. Torture. My mind skips back to the article about Liam. Is Finn a sociopath or a psychopath? Neither is a desirable mental condition to have in a partner.

"Little one, I don't enjoy what I do. I can still tell right from wrong and wish things were different. But in this life, right and wrong have vastly different meanings and standards than in the one where you live."

"You read my mind."

"I know what I would think if I were you. It's easy to guess."

"You said it's controlled. That means you're untouchable, right?"

"Yes. Our phones are never on, so we can't be tracked. We have protocols." He hesitates. "Sometimes things aren't under our control. If you're at my place, and I call you to tell you to wait in the guest bedroom, I need you to do that. Don't greet me at the door. Don't offer to help. I'll need space to calm down and clean up. It means I don't want you to see me like that. Not how I'll look and not how I'll act. I'll come and get you as fast as I can, but it might take me a while. I'm sorry."

Biowaste disposal. That would be a more technical name for cleaning off blood and guts. Decompressing is semantics for turning off the psychopathic part of him. No. Yes. I don't know. I think he has remorse in the grand scheme of things— a sociopath. But I doubt he holds any remorse when he's pushed far enough to do what he does —a psychopath.

No. I refuse to see him that way. This isn't how his brain is naturally wired. Conditioned, maybe. Survivalist is more like it.

"Daddy, you can always tell me what you need. Even if it's just space after a crappy day, I will give it to you. I don't have to be up your ass 24/7."

He pinches my ass. "I wouldn't mind being up yours tonight."

"*Daddeee!*" I hiss the word. But my grin is irrepressible. "As soon as you get back."

"I have to go, *cailín*. Joey wound up having his brother take care of your window. He works for Shane's construction company and had a tall enough ladder on his truck. He got what he needed and headed over. I won't press you to tell me what's happening, but if something else does, go to my family. If I come home, and I find out there was another threat, and you didn't go to them, it'll be more than just my hand. Your safety is the one thing you will never get me to budge on. Never."

I'm halfway in love with this guy.

"I understand."

And I'm pretty positive I'm going to disobey.

Chapter Thirteen

Finn

Well, we figured out what the fuck happened to our shipment. The Boston Irish made a move that is going to cost them monumentally. The mob once ran a major part of that city. People up there think they're more Irish than a lass born and bred in County Cork. We usually get along. By that, I mean, we stay the fuck out of each other's way. They keep New England, and we keep everywhere else east of the Mississippi. The exception is Chicago. They have their own ruling family. Their reach is nothing.

"What does Rowan O'Malley think he's doing?" I look at Shane as we stand in my bedroom while I pack.

"Flexing. He's only been in the position as long as Dillan. But he has a massive chip on his shoulder. He has since we were kids. His mommy didn't love him enough." My brother is silently seething.

The lost goods are costing a few million. In the grand scheme of things, that's a lot, but it's not much more than a pinch. It's them worming their way into a place they don't belong. They have their own deals with foreign markets. They don't need to steal from us. It's not revenge because we usually leave each other the fuck alone. They're trying to prove something. Prove they can embarrass us. Prove they can conduct business with impunity. Prove we're their bitches. Oh, how wrong they are.

"Is the jet ready?"

"Yeah. We can go, Finn. I know you have stuff going on here."

"She's not stuff. And I'm not shirking my duties. If Thea and I have a future, then we need to see if we can get through these things. If we can't..." I shrug. The guys might let me off this time, but I can't quit my obligations forever.

I'd rather be with Thea than taking a late-night flight to Bean Town. Being away from her is another thing I'll punish Rowan for. My goal is for this to take only three days. Tomorrow is getting the lay of the land. I need to scout things and meet with my informants. The next day is action. We'll decimate them. Anything less means they'll have resources to attack again. The third day is clean up and my flight home. I pray it's truly that simple.

"I'm headed to the airfield, then. The sooner I get there, the sooner I can finish. I need you guys to keep an eye on Thea. I already spoke to Joey. He and his brothers have a few days off this week. They volunteered to keep an eye on her place. I didn't ask. They volunteered. But that's not enough. I need her to have a shadow."

"Why?" Shane's brow furrows. "Don't you trust her?"

"I do. But someone put a brick through her window tonight. She claimed it was a bird. I pressed, and all she would commit to is it's a family matter. I won't strong-arm her into telling me the full truth, but no one puts a brick through your window without following up. I don't want this mystery fecker to have the chance. If there's more than one, the leader goes to the station. Shoot to kill the rest of them on sight."

The station. It's an abandoned rail station in the Bronx that's been out of service for more than a decade. It has a subterranean level that we've made virtually impossible to access. Only the people who know can find it. We did some renovating and retrofitting. We have a kitchen, showers, and a bunkroom. Sometimes we're there for days at a time. It's our controlled location. We have another place, a house, on Staten Island where we can hold people until we're ready for them at the station. It's not ideal having to transport people more than once, but sometimes it's a necessity. Once a person goes to the station, they aren't walking out on their own. Ash or sludge. That's how they leave.

The other families think their places are secret. The Italians have a garage in Queens, and the Russians have a warehouse there too. The Colombians have a vacant bodega in the same borough. We stay the fuck out of Queens. We all grew up there. It's too fucking obvious. Their places were simple to find.

Everyone shuts off their phones miles away from their place. We track them, so we know everyone usually turns off their phones five miles out. You mark the circumference from that radius and work your way in. Whatever's large, usually close to a river, appears abandoned, and will mask sounds— screams —is the place. The other families think we have a storage facility. We do, but that's not our place. They think we used to use a fake storefront. We never did.

I say goodbye to Shane and head to the town car. Joey's still at Thea's, so I have a different driver. In the privacy of the backseat, it tempts me to text or call Thea. But we said our goodbyes. It's better to leave without prolonging the agony. When Cormac and I spoke, I thought I'd stay in NYC. But that's not an option now. I made it sound like I was staying here. If I call or text her, I'm going to feel guilty not telling her I'm headed to Boston.

I don't want to tell her more lies, and I don't want to cause myself a fresh wave of longing and missing her already.

Ridiculous.

We've gone on two dates. But a day is a decade in this world. A decade is a lifetime. Knowing I could die at any time, day or night means hyper vigilance. It means we must decide in the space of a couple seconds. Anything more gives your attacker the upper hand. That's death.

I've thought about Thea practically every free moment I've had. I think about how much I like her. I think about the danger I'm bringing her into. I think about the things I can share, and the things I'll always keep hidden. I think about whether or not that makes me too emotionally closed off. I think about what a future would look like coming home to her every night. I weigh all the options over and over.

I think about worst- and best-case scenarios with every permutation I can come up with. It always leads to the same place: I won't walk away unless she tells me to. And it's not confirmation bias. It's not me wanting that so much, it's the only conclusion I can come to. I have a shite ton of doubts about this. I have a nearly suffocating fear I'm making the wrong decision. But I can't imagine not being with her now that I know her.

I'm thinking about this as the plane takes off. When we get to our cruising altitude, I force myself to get my laptop out. It's barely more than an hour flight, but I pull up the program I created to track cell phones with a remotely downloaded feature in their operating system. We all have it. We wear trackers built into our watches, but it's a secondary tool if something happens to one of us, and our trackers don't ping. If the phone is on, I can locate it without using any government or law enforcement connected satellites.

It'll be two a.m. when we land, so Rowan is enjoying his last night of sweet dreams. I'll check into a hotel because they will discover I'm here. It's not where I'm staying. We have a house in south Boston. It's a shithole like the rest of the place. But it's also where the Irish dominate. Embarrassing that they've been relegated to the shittiest part of the city. I don't care that my accommodations won't be luxurious like they'd be at the hotel. I often sleep beneath a rail station for fuck's sake. It'll make it faster when I strike. Rowan holds court at a bar near Dorchester.

I get to the house, and my guys— five of them came with me —rack out. We're all exhausted. We had cars waiting for us at the airfield, so we didn't have to wait around, and no one saw us. As far as the FAA is concerned, we never landed there. We have a false registration for that jet. They know the plane is there, but they don't know it's our plane. I'm asleep as soon as my head hits the pillow.

"What the feck is he doing?" I mutter to myself.

Rowan is standing on the sidewalk talking to some motorcycle club leader. The guy is huge, but you can see his arrogance from a mile away. That's his weakness. At least, it's the most obvious right now. Size won't protect him from the stupid decisions arrogance causes.

Rowan and this guy swap envelopes with no discretion. He wants any and everyone to see them doing business. What's he got this guy doing for him? I pull my phone out and focus my camera from the car we're sitting in half a block down. The windows are tinted, but not so much they draw attention.

I like nice things, but I don't have the highest end of most stuff. My cars aren't flashy, but they're fucking expensive even before all the aftermarket parts. My cars' lights and horn do nothing when I lock or unlock them. The dome lights don't come on if there's a bomb. The frames are reinforced, and the windows are bulletproof. I have a few occupational hazards.

My watch isn't flashy since I don't need some fuck nut thinking I'm a good target to mug. It's also where my tracker is hidden. However, my phone is. I have shite programmed in no one will find, but it also has the best camera on the market. I got it for days like this. No one's carrying some hefty Nikon for the world to spot. I snap some pics and enlarge them. They're high resolution, but we're just far enough away that the photos don't show as much detail as I want.

I recognize the biker when he turns toward me. "Tom, hand me the binoculars, please."

I'm in the front passenger seat. I lean forward and focus them. It's just who I thought. Corey Byrne. Fucking sack of shite. He drives around on a piece of crap bike. He thinks the noise intimidates people. He needs to compensate for a micro penis. He rides down to NYC periodically, but he knows to stay the fuck out of our neighborhoods. He knows if we catch him, we'll— at the very least —beat the shite out of him. If he thinks of doing any business in our neighborhoods, we'll kill him. Utterly worthless.

Corey strides over to his bike and lugs his fat arse onto the seat. He uses his size to terrify people, but he hasn't been in a fight in like twenty years. His goons do the manual labor. He has five of them today. He acts like they're his enforcers. They're his bodyguards because there are a few hundred people who would off him if they had the chance. He revs his bike and takes off.

Rowan checks the contents of the envelope he received. He

appears satisfied with whatever's in it. After a quick glance in Corey's direction, he heads to his car. When he pulls out of his driveway, we follow. We make sure we stay three cars back. We only got a few hours of sleep because I wanted to be here before sunrise. Peter, my senior-most guy on this mission, slipped a tracker onto Rowan's car. If we wind up losing him because we need the three-car buffer, we still know where he's going. I have my laptop open on my lap, and his car's signal flashes a dot as it turns right at an intersection. We see the car in time to follow without needing the tracker, but he's merging into morning traffic.

It takes no time to realize he's headed to warehouses they have in Lynn, which is four miles north of Boston. Lynn, Lynn, city of sin. You never come out the way you came in. Jaunty little ditty. We're almost to an industrial park when we pull off. We can watch the parking lot from here. Once he's inside, we'll creep closer. Fucking move your arse. He's standing outside on the phone.

"Are we close enough to get a heat signature?"

"I think so." Nate hands me the heat seeking binoculars. There're at least a dozen people in the building. I can't tell how many might be out back at the loading dock. We'll check before we pull into the parking lot. My informant said they're moving the cargo today. It'll sit here until Rowan finds a buyer. The rugs are nice and all, but I want our motherfucking nanochips back.

It takes another fifteen minutes for Chatty Cathy to finally head inside the building. We wait five more minutes before we head out and make our way closer. We're not dressed in our full fatigues like we are for some missions. We're dressed in casual street clothes, but each of us has at least one gun holstered to our back and knives in our pockets and our boots. You can never be too prepared. We split off into two trios. Three guys head around back to look at the loading dock to see what's going on there. My other two men and I creep closer to the front door.

I wish I still had the heat-seeking binoculars with me. But those are impractical if I have to run or fight. We'll have to make do without. You'd think they would have tinted the front wall of glass, so you can't see inside. Since it's not, it's much easier to get a glimpse of what's happening than I expected. More fool are they as we get closer.

The reflection off of the glass makes it harder to peek inside than I want to admit now that I've assumed it would be so easy. There's a lobby area, but nobody's there. It's obviously a fake front for whatever they have going on in the back. There's some type of pass code door I see when I put my hands to the glass and peer inside. We've already looked to see if there were any surveillance cameras in the area attached to trees, posts, or the building. There're none. Now that actually is foolish of them. My two guys and I turn around and head to the back of the building and meet up with my men who're waiting there.

"What's going on?" I whisper as I join the others at the building's corner. I peer around the side but duck back quickly.

"Something to do with weapons they're selling across the border. They have buyers in Mexico City." Peter fills me in as I risk another glance at the loading docks.

"There aren't any cameras back here either." Tom nudges his chin toward the roof as he speaks.

"They're the only property owners in the area. Half these places are vacant, and the other half are businesses they own."

I checked out all the deeds when I woke up this morning. It wasn't hard to hack into the city clerk's system. I only got three hours of sleep since I wanted that done before we headed out at dawn.

"Get this. We heard them talking about a bunch of iguanas

they have waiting for them at some rich fecker's house in Brookline." Tom smirks and rolls his eyes as if to say stupid, rich people.

Brookline is one of the most expensive communities in Boston. The average home costs one-point-two-mill. Not surprising there's an exotic animal trade running out of there. I'm not into lizards, but they are easier to transport than most animals. We'll snag those and take them to the MSPCA. They'll know what to do with them. That's a nice little afterthought to add to my retribution list.

"What do you want to do, boss?" Nate glances over his shoulder at me.

He and I are the same age. We *hated* each other growing up. We were super competitive, but I always had an edge on him with anything academic or athletic. It used to piss him off like nothing else. It wasn't until our sophomore year of high school, and we got in a fight with Pablo and Juan Diaz that we decided we had to put aside the hate, or we'd both end up dead. Thanks to him, I cracked Pablo's collar bone. He crushed Juan's hand and broke three ribs. We made peace after that.

"I want two of you inside. We need to know what else they have here. I noticed the fire escape on the far side of the building and a roof hatch. Luke and John, you head up there. Text me once you're in. If you can, call me on video."

You couldn't find two brothers who look more different. Luke has almost black hair with blue eyes, and John's hair is nearly bleach-blond. He has dark brown eyes instead. Luke's almost six-and-a-half feet tall while John barely makes it to six feet on his best day. But their mannerisms are so damn similar, you can't doubt they're siblings. I watch them head back the way I came.

It surprises me that no one's noticed us yet. They would if

they had security cameras. The guys in the loading bay haven't glanced in our direction. Makes life easier for us.

JOHN

We're in

It's a few more minutes before my phone vibrates again, and it's a video call from Luke. I answer, but no one makes a peep. He has the camera facing forward as they inch their way down a hallway with closed doors. With their guns drawn, they test each one. They're all unlocked, but there's nothing there. Once they clear all of them, they continue forward. The hallway had carpet, but it turns into a metal walkway over the main warehouse floor.

Both lie on their bellies as they inch toward the end of the carpet. Luke tilts his phone down, so I can see through the slats. There's a shite ton of stuff stashed here. I spot crates marked with a caduceus— the international symbol for medicine. My guess is surgical supplies and prosthetic devices. It's shite that should go overseas as humanitarian relief. I recognize a logo on a crate.

Luke pans his phone around the warehouse, so we can see more crates. I also notice burlap sacks. Grain, rice, and seeds. Those're legit imports from Asia, so that's what I want to get first. I prioritize taking their legal shite over everything else. Once we clear out what we want tomorrow, I'll tip off the feds. What we don't take, law enforcement will confiscate. I want them left with nothing, so the legal goods have to come with us.

The camera angle shifts, and I can tell Luke is commando crawling with one elbow. He's silent as his head and shoulders move over the grated walkway. He's opened his chest to be a target. He rolls to his side, and I can see the other half of the warehouse. Motherfucker.

There're a dozen animal carriers lined up against a wall,

and they each have a spider monkey in it. Iguanas and monkeys. What other exotic animals are they dealing? Is Luke going to turn around and find tigers waving?

He zooms in. Riley O'Malley, Rowan's younger brother, appears on camera. He must have come from an office underneath the carpeted hallway. Since Luke and John are probably holding their breath, waiting to get shot, it's easy to hear Riley when he speaks.

"The buyer's in Florida. We need to get these guys to the airfield tomorrow night. Rowan's going to meet us there with the lizards and birds."

Birds? They have a fucking menagerie going on. It could be Miami, but my guess is Tampa. That's the largest port in the state, and with undomesticated rare animals, people are far less likely to suspect Tampa than Miami.

We haven't seen Rowan since he went inside. Did he slip out the front? No. We would have heard the car, and he definitely would have spotted us. Summoned like the devil, Rowan walks over from I don't know where. The brothers move to a spot where Luke can film them, but he doesn't have to lie on the walkway. He inches back into the darkened and carpeted hallway's protection.

"Finn's in town."

I grin. Didn't take him long to hear. My informant's doing her job. Heidi was a regular fuck buddy, but we weren't even exclusive about that. I've been with Rowan and Riley's sister, Cady, every time I've come up here. The thought that I could fuck her while I'm here didn't come to mind when I sent her a text, telling her to call her brother in a panic. I'm going to have to explain to her there'll be no more sneaking off for a quickie any chance we have. There will be no chances. It won't go over as well as it did with Heidi. She's always believed I'm way more into her than she is me. She thinks that gives her power over me. I haven't corrected her because I haven't cared.

"What? How?" Riley fists his hands as though he would punch anything in reach. He puts them on his hips as Rowan explains, repeating what Cady told him, which is verbatim what I told her to tell her brother. Supposedly, I stopped in town to see her on my way up to Montreal.

The sex was good, but never good enough to schedule a layover. Cady didn't point that out, so she believes we'll hook up before I continue my trip north. She doesn't need to know I'm here for a sole purpose: ruin her motherfucking family.

"So, what're we supposed to do? Just ignore an O'Rourke rolled into town to feck our sister?" Riley's full of questions.

He's known about Cady and me since the first time we hooked up. Rowan didn't find out for like four months. He tried to have the shite beaten out of me for it. He wound up two men short after that.

"Yes, but it means we have to get those rugs out of town tonight. We can't keep them here."

"And where do you suggest we put them? The ship doesn't sail into port until tomorrow morning. Keeping them here with extra security is our best bet."

"We take them to Corey."

That surprises me.

Apparently, it surprises Riley too because he's shaking his head hard enough for his hair to move. "Feck no. I don't trust him, Rowan. He's nothing but trouble."

"He owes me."

"That info about Gallagher isn't worth shite."

Riley jerks his head back as his brow furrows, and he frowns. It's a completely derisive and dismissive expression. He thinks his brother is fucking nuts. Rowan tries to rationalize his stupidity.

"It is to him. He despises his nephew. Corey'll put the screws to the guy and force him to accept help. We'll get a cut of the hush money and another way to fuck with Finn."

No. It better fucking not be...

"You really going after the guy's daughter?" Fear laces Riley's question. He's smarter than Rowan.

"I'm not. That's all Corey. From what I've heard about Finn's lovesick arse, there's nothing he won't do to save her. If he wants to make the threat go away, he cooperates with us."

Not a fucking chance.

"When's Corey headed back down there?"

Back? Did that fucker put the brick through Thea's window?

Rowan shrugs. "Day after tomorrow, probably. Soon enough to get down there before Finn finishes his shite in Montreal."

"How long's he here for?"

"Just tonight. He'll feck Cady a few times, then be on his merry way."

"But he's with Corey's grandniece now."

"From what I hear, it's only been two dates. It's nothing serious."

"Bullshit, Rowan. The O'Rourkes don't just date. They fall hard and fast. If he's gone on two dates, then we should consider them engaged. Look at Dillan. Hell, look at the Mancinellis. They weren't any different from the Kutsenkos. Those New Yorkers are all in or nothing at all. This shite's going to blow the fuck up in our faces."

"Stop pissing vinegar. He won't know shite until after it happens. Corey knows what he's doing. He'll use her to get to her parents. She'll do anything to protect them, and they'll do the same for her."

"I'm telling you, this is the worst idea Corey has ever had. Does he know she's dating Finn?"

"I don't know."

"You don't know?" Riley throws his hands up in the air as he explodes. "You better motherfucking know soon. He knows Corey. He knows the piece of shite is connected to us. They're already pissed about the rugs." He gestures toward the crates.

"Calm down."

Riley steps in front of Rowan. "And I'll be telling you to give a shite at your wake on Sunday. We need to get all of this shite out of here. We need to clear out and not come back. We haven't brought him here, but Dillan knows about this place. He'll tell Finn, who'll stop here on the way home from Montreal and blow everything up."

"No, he won't. He'll rush home to Althea."

"Althea? What? Are we in 1950?"

I want to punch Riley in his junk. I never think of her full name, so it's jarring to hear. I especially don't enjoy hearing it from either of them. So much for today just being about scouting. I pull up John's contact.

ME

Fall back. We need to go.

Chapter Fourteen

Thea

I know I've had a shadow since yesterday morning. I'm positive it's Finn's men since I'm pretty certain I saw Joey as I walked into the hospital yesterday. But I had to make an emergency shift change to come out to my parents'.

"Papa?"

"In the living room."

I don't like how reedy his voice sounds. I dump my stuff on the entryway table and rush toward him.

"Papa! Oh my God!" I'm too stunned to move for a moment, then I'm kneeling beside the sofa as my eyes roam over him, taking in his injuries.

My mom called this morning to say he'd had a cycling accident yesterday afternoon. She'd taken him to the Emergency Room, but she downplayed it. It was a friend who was on rotation last night who called right after I hung up with my mom to ask how he was doing since he knew his patient was my dad. I could only stand there and listen as he said my dad's injuries were serious enough to keep him overnight. They got home a couple hours ago. I was about to leave for work, but I called around to find someone to swap. It wasn't easy, but there wasn't a snowball's chance in hell I was going to work today.

"I'll survive, squirt."

"I can tell, but this is serious." I pick up the prescription bottle on the table. "If Dr. Harding prescribed these, you must be in intense pain or will be."

These are about as powerful as you can get outside an IV drip in a hospital. I put the pills down and scan my gaze over him from head to toe and back up again. He's pale as fuck, and I can tell his skin is clammy.

"The doctor said as long as I take these on time, I shouldn't have any problems managing my pain."

If only it were that simple. His pain is only a fraction of what I'm worried about. My parents gave me access to their health portals years ago, so I could read test results and appointment notes. I saw it all before I left my place. He has a concussion, a sprained right wrist, and road rash on his face, side, and leg. He has bruising from shoulder to ankle on his right side. They suspected two broken ribs and a dislocated shoulder, but it was the massive bruising that caused their suspicion. He got lucky. The CT scan didn't reveal any trauma to his organs, but the notes recommend he follow up with an orthopedist for his wrist and a neurosurgeon for a possible herniated disc in his neck. Thank God he always wears his helmet.

"What happened?" My mom was evasive.

"I swerved to miss someone, and my front tire rolled over something that punctured it. I went flying over the handlebars."

"Do you remember any of it? Did someone call an ambulance?"

"I don't remember much until Mom arrived at the ER. I

don't know who called 911, but people stayed with me until the paramedics arrived."

"Did the person you almost hit at least stay?"

He hesitates a moment too long. "Yeah, he stuck around."

"Papa, was this one of Uncle Corey's men? Tell me the truth."

"Maybe. I don't know. I didn't get a good look before the accident, and I'm not sure if my memory is real or something my imagination made up."

"Did he threaten you before this happened? He obviously knows you lost your job because he came to my place, then went looking for Jamie. You know he won't stop until you're paying him weekly."

I want to call Finn. I want to tell him everything that's going on. I want to lean on him. I want him to fix this— and by fix, I mean make sure Uncle Corey is dead. I may have sworn to do no harm, but that doesn't mean I can't wish it on deserving people. Finn sure as hell didn't make that pledge.

"I'm not giving him a penny."

"Papa—"

"No. This isn't the worst that's happened to me because of him. Granted, I was thirty years younger, so I bounced back a lot easier. He knows he can try to bend me, but I won't snap."

"He knows he's going to have to keep trying until he succeeds."

"Not happening."

I just nod. What else am I supposed to do? "Papa, did you just take a dose? You look like you're getting sleepy."

Did our argument— brief as it was —exhaust him?

"Yeah. About ten minutes ago."

"Can I get you anything? I'll watch TV in the other room. Sleep as long as you can. The body heals while it sleeps."

"I'm good, squirt. Go find that housewives show you like so much."

I like certain reality TV way more than I'll admit. But that's not what I'm doing as I leave the living room. I check over my shoulder to make sure he hasn't moved before walking down the hallway to the front door. I ease it open and shut it quietly once I'm on the stoop. I look around until I spot the car I'm searching for. I make a beeline to it. I'm about to tap on the glass when a man in a charcoal suit winds down the front passenger window.

"I need to speak to Finn."

"Dr. Galla—"

"Someone hurt my dad."

I lean forward and see a guy in the driver's seat who looks just like Joey. The man right in front of me looks a lot like Finn's driver, too. The men glance at each other as they reach for the door handles.

"He's okay for now. He had an accident yesterday, and I'm certain I know who caused it. This is— this is —" I puff an exhale. "—shit Finn knows how to handle. I don't."

I give them a pointed look, and the driver nods. "Give me a moment. I can't call him, but I can text him. Do you have your phone? I'll tell him to call you. It might not be immediately, but he will call when he gets my message."

"Thank you."

"Should we pull into the driveway? Do you want whoever this is to know you have a security detail?" The guy near me isn't looking at me, but at his side-view mirror.

"My mom isn't home yet. She needs to pull in, and I don't want her asking why there're men sitting in our driveway. But there's a spot a little closer. Could you park there, please?"

The driver starts the car as he speaks. "I'm Simon, and this is my brother, Fallon. We're Joey's big brothers. I'm going to call him to come over. He'll bring our cousin Ted. I'd feel better if we have another car at the other end of the street facing this way. Are you spending the night?"

"I don't know. Maybe. Someone's covering my shift today, but I don't know if I can get someone to do it tomorrow."

"Fallon and I will follow you home. Two other guys will relieve us at six regardless of where we are. Joey and Ted will stay here until midnight. They'll have two guys relieve them. I'm certain Joey will insist upon being your guard tomorrow. Unless Finn tells us otherwise, Joey's going wherever you go. No waiting in a car. If your parents go anywhere, we'll have people follow them. Do you have brothers or sisters?"

"Two brothers, and they both have kids." This conversation is reassuring part of my mind, but it's clearly not easing all my fear because my heart is racing.

"We'll call Dillan and arrange all of this. Let Fallon program all our numbers in your phone."

I hand it to him and step back from the car. Simon reverses, then pulls out of the spot. I walk alongside them but on the sidewalk. He pulls into the new spot and parks. Fallon hands the phone back to me just as it rings. Oh, merciful saints.

"Finn." I flash a smile at the guys and hurry back to the house.

"*Cailín*, what happened? Are you safe?"

I know no one can hear me. "Yes, Daddy. But my dad's uncle tried to kill him."

I don't believe for a second that I'm exaggerating. Not with my dad that banged up.

"Corey attacked your dad?"

That grinds me to a halt. It's not Finn's deceptively calm voice. It's his question.

"How do you know about him?"

"I've known Corey for years. I put two-and-two together about an hour ago. Whoever attacked your dad wasn't Corey because I saw him this morning. It was one of his thugs. He's headed back to the city in a couple days. I want you to stay with my parents. If it's really dire, then your parents, brothers, and their families go there too."

"Your parents can't accommodate that many strangers. They don't run a hotel."

"Little one, my family is large and rich. My parents have an eight-bedroom home plus a three-bedroom pool house. You'll all fit."

I stop with my hand on the door handle. That's a fucking mansion, not a house. I can't imagine that. There are only three brothers and their parents. Four bedrooms for them and a guest room. That would be enough.

"Thea, they bought the house after my brothers were born. By then, there were seven cousins. We each have a room, plus my parents. Colleen's bedroom is a guest room now. When my aunts and uncles stay over, they either stay in the pool house, or two of us give up our rooms, and we stay out there. No one in our family uses Colleen's room. Since none of us live at home, there are plenty of places for your family to stay."

"Thank you, Daddy. I pray it doesn't come to that, but I'm relieved to know we have that option. Simon and Fallon are arranging for my parents and me to have guards tomorrow. He said Dillan would take care of my brothers and their families. Finn, Corey won't show up alone. He goes nowhere without at least five guys with him. I don't want to insult your men, but two of them won't even be a speed bump."

"*Cailín*, I need you to have faith that my guys can handle this. Joey and his brothers volunteered to watch out for you while I'm gone. If I had to choose men for the job, they're the first ones I'd go to. They're the ones who guard my mom and aunts. Fallon is usually with Mair these days."

"Hold on a second." I slip back into the house and down the hallway. I put my phone next to my thigh as I check on my dad. He's passed out and snoring lightly. I spin around and head to the stairs. "I'm almost to my room."

When I get there, I shut the door and sit on the bed I've slept in since I was five. I kick off my shoes and lie down.

"My dad's knocked out with the pain meds. He's sleeping on the sofa downstairs. There's no way he's making it up the stairs to my parents' bedroom."

"How serious are his injuries?"

"Bruises and road rash all over his face and body, sprained wrist, and a concussion. They suspected broken ribs and a dislocated shoulder, but that was from the bruising. That's with a helmet on. He probably would've died without it. At the very least, he'd have a serious TBI."

"Thea, I can't leave until at least tomorrow. I'm sorry."

"No. I didn't ask Simon to have you call me, so I could ask you to come home. I—I—Finn, you know the man Corey is. I don't want him to come near my family ever again. I can't make that happen, and neither can my dad." *But you can.*

Those three words are silently dangling in the air. I pretty much just asked him to put a hit on a family member. But Corey's never felt like an uncle, and he sure as fuck isn't family if he could do this. I'm certain he was behind this, even if he wasn't there when it happened.

"*Leanbh,* I'll make sure you and your family are safe."

"What does that mean?"

"Baby."

I close my eyes and breathe easier. I'm certain Finn needs

to go. He's not wherever he is for shits and giggles. But hearing his voice is calming me down.

"Thank you, Daddy. I'll see you when you're done."

There's a moment of silence, then his voice is practically a whisper. But it's not quiet enough for me not to hear the hurt.

"That's it?"

"Finn, you're not on vacation. I know you have stuff to do."

My mind flashes to the place he told me about. My head tilts to look at my bedroom door. Finn told me his phone will be off whenever he's there. Simon said he would text him. He said Finn might not get it right away, but he called me a few minutes later. He's not at that place.

"Thea, there will be times when I might have to go more than a few days without talking to you. I'm thankful that it hasn't even been a full day. Do you have to go? If not, I'd like to hear your voice a little longer."

"You say the sweetest things. I'd like to hear yours too."

"Did you take today off? I know you're supposed to be at the hospital right now."

"I got someone to swap with me, but I'm not sure I'll be so lucky tomorrow. I'll call around in a little while. If I get someone to cover me, then I'll probably spend the night here. If I can't, then I need to go back to my place because my shift'll start at six. I have scrubs and my clogs in the car just in case."

"Thinking about you in scrubs with your white coat and stethoscope around your neck is hot. Do you wear one of those things on your head? Like a bonnet?"

I chuckle. "Yes, a bonnet. I just rolled right out of *Little House on the Prairie* and into labor and delivery. It's called a surgical cap."

"Does yours have like Snoopy and Charlie Brown, or whatever kids like these days?"

"Finn, my patients can't even distinguish my face. They

truly can't see more than a foot in front of them. They don't notice if I have cartoon characters. I have one with all different dogs, one with smiling suns, and one with flamingos. I like having something cheery on when I see parents."

"I admire you so much."

That sends a rush of warmth through me that makes my toes curl. "Thanks."

"What color are your scrubs?"

"I brought lavender ones. I usually wear pastels for the same reason as the fun surgical caps."

"Which cap will you wear?"

"The dog one. Why?"

"And your lab coat says Dr A. Gallagher, Neonatologist?"

"Neonatology."

"What color are your clogs?"

"Black. Are you picturing me in my scrubs? I thought you'd picture me naked." I'm almost offended that he prefers to think of me all covered up.

"I think about you naked all the time. Picturing you in your scrubs is fecking hot as all get out. You're brilliant, and kind, and dedicated, and you use all of that as a doctor. Knowing you spend all day helping sick babies in those scrubs— it's a turn on."

"Daddy." I sigh the word.

"Yes, *leanbh*."

"You're wonderful."

"I want to be for you." There's a wistfulness to that.

"Are you in one of your right off the Milan runway suits or your version of casual?"

"My version of casual? What does that mean?"

"Even in jeans and a sweater, you look like you're ready to make the panties drop off every woman who sees you."

"The only woman whose panties matter to me knows she better not be wearing any."

"I know. I'm not."

I'm wearing yoga pants, so I'm quick to open my camera and pull the waistband out enough for him to see my pussy. I snap the pic and text it to him. A groan is my reward.

"Thea, I'm already hard just talking to you. I can practically feel being inside your pussy. I'm going to enjoy every part of you. I'm going to lock us away for three days when I get back."

I can practically hear his teeth clack together when he realizes what he just said. Get back. He already told me he saw Uncle Corey this morning, but the piece of ass is heading *back* to the city in a couple days. Finn's not here in NYC. It's a gut punch. He left without telling me.

You can't feel sorry for yourself. You knew this could and would happen. You knew he would lie to you about where he is.

"Thea, I had to go out of town. For this trip, I can't tell you more than that. But Corey came up, and I figured out you're related."

Boston.

Uncle Corey might have influence in NYC and Boston, but I can't imagine he matters anywhere else. He let it slip that he left the city, but he just reminded me my great-uncle came up in conversation.

"Are you angry I didn't tell you about Uncle Corey when you saw my window?"

"I'm not thrilled, but you didn't know half of what you know now, and that's not even a thimbleful of what you will learn. I don't blame you for being hesitant to tell me something like that. But I'm glad you called me. I will take care of it. Corey will understand you and your family are off limits."

I fucking hope so. There's more I should tell him, and I

never planned to hide it. But it's not something I want to discuss over the phone. It's too complicated for that, and I couldn't have imagined he'd know Corey or be anywhere near him right now. Just knowing I'm related to the piece of shit is bad enough. I don't know what Finn'll do when he finds out the woman I used to be.

Chapter Fifteen

Finn

We were back at the house when Simon's text came in.

> SIMON
>
> Call Dr G urgent father hurt

What the fuck was I supposed to make of that, that wouldn't send me into a panic? I barely got the words out to tell my guys not to disturb me as I ran to the bedroom I used. I tried to sound calm, and I think I pulled it off. But I was seething the entire time until we changed the subject. I didn't mean to let it slip I'm not in NYC. I never make mistakes like that. Ever. But it shows just how much I let my guard down around Thea. I don't regret it, but I must be more careful going forward.

I'll deal with Corey, but we have to deal with Rowan and the warehouse right now. We're back outside the building this morning. We know the rugs are ready to ship from the warehouse because we followed the truck from their parking lot half an hour ago. We weren't convinced Rowan could arrange for

Corey to hold onto to them last night, so Nick kept watch overnight at the lot where they keep their fleet of trucks and vans. He called when he heard the driver tell another guy where he was headed in an hour. It gave us time to get in place.

The port's not even open yet, but the O'Malleys run the docks in Boston just like we do in NYC. They plan to get the rugs and whatever medical supplies they had stashed at their warehouse into the ship's hold before any customs agents can inspect the crates.

The heat signature shows four people inside. We need those four guys to help load the truck. I have no clue who they are, but we'll know in a flash whether they recognize me. I don't know if they'll know me as Finn or just an O'Rourke thanks to my hair.

I speak into my earpiece. "Peter, go."

He's driving a box truck that he'll pull around to the loading bay. The rest of us jog forward, our rifles at the ready. It's three in the morning, so it's dark with shite lighting around the building. In our black fatigues, we're practically unnoticeable. By the time we're there, one of the O'Malley men is gesturing at Peter to get out of the truck. He's yelling at him, but Peter won't move until I signal him. The fuck nut is making so much noise that I sneak up behind him and put the barrel to his head.

"Shut up." I pull his gun from his hip holster and thrust it behind me, so one of my guys grabs it.

I push a little against his head and nudge him forward, walking behind him to the building. I nod, and the rest of my men jump onto the loading dock while Peter gets out of the truck. He goes around the back of the vehicle and opens the door. It's only a moment later that I hear a single gunshot.

"We're good." I hear Nate in my earpiece.

I keep nudging the idiot in front of me until we get to the

steps. Just as we get to the top, the warehouse bay door opens. The three men who were still inside now stand in the same position as the guy in front of me.

"Move your arses. Load it."

As I issue the command, I can see their empty shoulder, hip, and back holsters. A different one for each guard. They're in shape, but they're no match for the physical strength my men possess. O'Rourke men learn to be light on their feet, considering how heavy most of them are. And it's definitely not chub. They're lean muscle that's as intimidating as it is functional. I pull my rifle away from my captive and put it between his shoulder blades before giving him a hard shove.

I sure as shite don't trust any of them to operate a forklift, so Tom climbs on and gets it running. Geniuses left the keys in the damn thing. It takes an hour, with my guys rotating who's working and who's making sure the O'Malley men don't sprout a backbone, but we get everything in the warehouse loaded. We manhandle the men into the back since we'll need them to help unload the shite, too. We make sure they'll have their wrists and ankles zip-tied every time we load them in. I debate whether to shut the bay door, so it surprises Rowan and Riley when they get here later. I decide to leave it open. It'll be a surprise either way, but I want them to see they've been fucked the moment they arrive.

Since there's no security in the entire place— Nate confirmed that while we worked —we're not in the rush we normally would be. There are three offices downstairs we couldn't see while John and Luke investigated. We do a controlled burn. We light them on fire and watch as the shite burns. We stand out of the fallout range when the windows explode, but before the flames can leap and spread, we put them out. Luke's an ace at cracking safes, so we ransacked theirs before the office turned into smokey rubble. It tempts me to leaving a calling card, but they'll either guess immediately—they should —or they'll chase their tails trying to figure it out.

Peter and Nate ride together in the truck while Tom, Luke, John, and I head back to our SUV. It's always a debate whether I should follow my men or lead them when there's only one escort vehicle. Do I protect them from the front or the back? This truck's large enough to be a battering ram or survive being rear-ended by pretty much anything but a semi. We're sticking to surface streets, so I'm not worried about a semi. The SUV leads.

We head to Brookline and find the house with the animals. We disable the outside motion detectors and doorbell camera. Tom, Nate, and Luke head inside with Luke making a beeline to cut off the alarm system. His day job is to work for a security company. He's in product development, so he has plenty of knowledge. Our men have a variety of day jobs. Not all of them are bodyguards, enforcers, or street hustlers. Actually, most appear like completely average men with average jobs.

Luke comes through my earpiece. "Yes." *You can enter now.*

We keep our talking to a minimum. These guys aren't fluent Gaelic speakers like my brothers, cousins, and I, but they can get by with enough that we only use it if we absolutely have no choice but to speak.

We know there are six people in the house, and the goal is not to disturb a single one. We want to be in and out before anyone's the wiser. The heat seeking binoculars are a godsend. Not only could we tell where everyone is, we also figured out where the animals are. They're cold-blooded, so it was their heat lamps we detected.

Fuck.

There are at least fifty of them down here. Some have more than one in a terrarium, so they're definitely two man carries.

Good thing we have the extra help. We didn't injure any of the O'Malleys. They weren't shot. They were shot at. Very convincing when the bullet enters the wall behind you at ear level. We're in and out in thirty minutes— twenty-five minutes later than I wanted to be.

When we got back to the safe house before raiding the warehouse, I hacked Rowan's email again and discovered the birds are in the same neighborhood. This place has a security gate, but that's simple for us to open. That's one of the earliest skills you learn before your first mission. The security system is off again, and we're in.

Fecking hell. It smells worse than the Queens Zoo aviary. There're birds of paradise, and what I think are cockatoos and toucans— definitely not as fun as the freaking cereal mascot. I don't think Toucan Sam smells like shite. I can't say I feel sorry for Rowan's men who will be stuck with the stench in the truck.

With spider monkeys, lizards, and birds, the back of the truck is noisy. We shut the door fast and head out. Since Colleen was a veterinarian and specialized in working with rescued animals, we have a connection with animal protection up here. Without special permits and licenses, it's illegal to own, propagate, or cultivate exotic animals in Massachusetts. It's already close to seven-thirty, so our connection should be at work by now. I shoot off a quick text and get an immediate response.

Our license plates don't match the vehicles, and we all have ski masks to shield us from the security cameras. I don't give a shite about O'Malley's men since they won't live long enough for anyone to find them. The woman who meets us nearly has a heart attack when she sees how many animals we have. There's barely enough room for all of them. We give her the information about the two homes we took them from. She knows

Rowan and Riley are involved, so there's no need to give her their information.

Our next stop is practically in the heart of the city, just around the corner from the famous Boston Common. We own a boutique near Beacon Hill, the most expensive area of the city. Houses here go for three-point-two mill. This is the perfect place for us to conduct business since no one expects us to be here. The boutique is a legit business that Lisa, my second cousin twice removed, runs. The O'Malleys don't have her on their radar, so they have no idea she's related to us.

When we need to stash shite, we come there. She has plenty of space in the back of her store. Everything goes in, and it'll be safe there until more O'Rourke men can come up from New York tonight and load it up. They'll bring everything back to us. It's risky to have these goods change hands so many times, but it makes it harder to track.

Our last stop for this wave of my plan is a meat grinding factory near Lowell. Morning traffic turns what should be a forty-five-minute drive into just over an hour, but it's fine. Let those men shite themselves, wondering what's going to happen to them now that the box truck is empty, but they're still locked inside. Tom and Peter stay there with the O'Malleys to oversee their disposal while the rest of us look for our friend, Corey.

His security detail is lazy as fuck. They don't notice as I saunter up the path from the sidewalk. They're snoring too loudly to hear me. Silencers on my guns take care of them. Corey's ex-wife left his arse twenty years ago. He can't find anyone to fuck him despite how much he tries to pay women. His sons have their own places above bars they own. I know they're not home. I contemplate kicking his door open to make a statement that nothing's keeping me out. But I opt for a more subtle entrance.

With my lock picking set, I let myself in while my men

spread out to guard the perimeter. I tip toe up the stairs to the second floor. I ease the bedroom door open. How polite of him to sleep on his back with this mouth hanging open. I put my pistol's barrel in his mouth.

"Wake the fuck up." I slam my fist into his sternum.

He jerks awake, his teeth smashing the gun as he tries to snap his jaw closed. His eyes widen as he takes in who's leaning over him. His eyes dart around the room, and I let him look. There's not a damn person here to help him.

"Corey, we're going to have a little chat. If I don't like your answers, I'll blow your brains out. Understood?"

He makes some garbled sound then nods his head.

"Did you throw a brick through my girlfriend's window?"

His brow furrows.

"Oh, so you just assumed you could intimidate Althea with no repercussions?"

His eyes open even wider. I didn't think it was possible. I'll take that as a yes.

"Did you cause her dad's accident?"

He nods.

"Why?" I pull the gun out of his mouth, pointing it between his eyes instead. Terror pulsates off him, and he appears to struggle to put a thought together. He's certain he won't survive this chat. Who knew the harbinger of death was a ginger?

"Because he believes he's too good for his past. So does his slut daughter."

I slam my fist into his sternum again. "I already told you she's my girlfriend."

"Exactly."

Getting ballsy for someone who's about to get his junk blown off. I swing my arm to point my pistol at his crotch.

"Did Althea's father run with your club back in the day?"

The background check my brother Sean ran already told me Thea grew up in Boston but moved down to NYC after med school. Once her younger brother went to college, her parents moved closer to Thea's mom's family. It was the slight New England accent I heard when I met Thea. I know Brandon— her dad —had a few arrests for petty shite, but they were before Thea was born. His rap sheet listed no accomplices. Her dad's background check showed no known associates that concerned us.

We learned our lesson with Mair. Not only do we do more extensive checks on all employees, but we extend it to their family. Sean insisted on that for Thea. I haven't told her yet, but I will. I don't want to freak her out, but I'm going to have to admit I know some shite about her family. I just didn't know this. It makes me wonder if her connection to Corey is what Dillan wanted to tell me, but I said I wanted Thea to tell me on her own.

Her parents' childhood addresses along with where they lived when Thea was a kid weren't in neighborhoods commonly associated with motorcycle clubs. Brandon grew up here in Boston, and Thea's mom— Sandra —grew up in north Jersey. I know Thea's family struggled when she and her brothers were really young, but her dad made good money after he started at the company he works for now. He got a transfer to a site in Jersey, right outside the city. Her mom stayed home with her kids before they went to school, but she went back to work full time once Thea's younger brother was in kindergarten. They were comfortable after that.

Corey's glare is wasted as he answers me. "Yeah."

"But he got out. Why?"

"Because he thought he was too good for us once he became a welder. Doesn't matter that he married a Black woman. He thinks he can pass himself off as something he isn't just cause he doesn't look like her or us. He didn't want to ride with our crew once his mom's side of the family got to him. They thought they were too good for us too, but not for the same reason."

I haven't seen any photos of Thea's parents, but I get what he's saying. Thea's mom is Black, and her dad is mixed. Knowing Corey, Brandon's dad was black, and his mom was white. He's insinuating Brandon's mom didn't want her son running with criminals. Apparently, Corey believes Brandon's reason was easier to see. Whether it was Brandon's job or half his family, Corey is obviously bitter that he couldn't control Brandon.

"Why're you targeting them now?"

"Because I can." He tries to smirk, but I lean a couple inches closer and put the barrel to his skin.

"No, you can't. Give me the real reason."

"I told him Althea's time was up, and her ass needed to get back up here. She has responsibilities and commitments to keep."

What the fuck?

"And?"

"And he refused to deliver the message or make sure she did what I expect."

"So?" I'm getting tired of him not just spitting out the complete story. This is the last prompt I'm giving him before I really hurt him.

"So, I made sure he got fired. He needs his job back, or they'll lose everything. That is, unless they accept my help."

Extortion. Loan sharking. That's his kind of help. He continues without me having to say a word.

"He knows this could all end if he accepts my help or makes Althea come back to where she belongs."

I don't want to give away that I don't know what the fuck

he's talking about. And whatever's in Thea's past, I want her to tell me herself. Not to test her, but because I want her to trust me. That she can tell me anything— good, bad, or ugly. Fuck knows, there's next to nothing she can tell me that's worse than my past and my future. But I need to know what's going on. I don't think I have the luxury of waiting.

"What makes you think he'd sacrifice his daughter?"

"He won't. I can still make her come up here, but I'll force him to use my money before that."

"You think you're going to force my girlfriend to do anything? You woke up to my gun in your mouth. I have it between your eyes now. And you tempted me earlier to blow your dick off."

"Killing me won't stop what's already in motion."

That's true. That's why he's still alive. I'll let him think he's going to die any minute for a little longer. Then I'm leaving. He'll still be breathing, though barely.

"But it sure as fuck would be satisfactory. Call your henchmen off Althea. She has nothing to do with this."

He snorts in disgust. "She hasn't told you about her past, has she?"

I keep my expression impassive as though I already know, so I don't care whether or not he tells me. I want to know right the fuck now.

He laughs at me. "She's a Sweet Butt."

Chapter Sixteen

Thea

It's been a day, and I haven't heard from Finn. I don't know if he dealt with Corey, or if he's still working on the shit that forced him up there. Joey's been at my side since I left my parents' place last night. His cousin drove my car back to my apartment, and Joey drove me in a town car. I didn't put up a fight. If it got back to Finn that I declined the protection, it would not only piss him off, but also hurt him. I don't want him to think I'm rejecting his concern, and frankly, I feel a fuck ton better with Joey so nearby.

I'm in the doctor's on call room and about to heat up a can of soup. I have three hours to catch some sleep. Between what's going on with my family and four extremely challenging deliveries, I'm wiped. I want nothing more than to curl up in my bed. This sofa will do, but it's hardly as nice as my mattress. But I've crashed here plenty of times. I even keep a pillow and blanket in my locker.

When the microwave dings, I bring my soup over to the

sofa and kick off my clogs. My surgical cap is on the table in front of me. It's the flamingos today with pastel pink scrubs. I wiggle my toes in my boring white ankle socks. By the time I'm done eating, I'm practically nodding off. It feels like only a minute after I fall asleep that I'm lifted into the air. My eyes snap open, and I'm staring into Finn's emerald orbs.

"Daddy."

If I'm dreaming, then this is perfect. I try to curl in a ball, but I can't. I open my eyes again because he's definitely holding me right now.

"*Cailín.*"

I sit up and gaze into his eyes before we can't keep our hands off each other and our lips apart. His hand cups the top of my neck just below my braids. His fingers rub at the knots, and the pain is soothing. The tension's easing. His other hand continues to roam over my ass and tits. When he tries to pull back, I fist his hair and press his head forward. He relents and devours me. I tried to take control, and now he's reminding me who really has it. I love it.

When we absolutely have to come up for air, we pant, looking at each other. He presses gentle kisses to my forehead, the tip of my nose, and my cheek. I sigh with happiness. I'm so damn content that I never want to get up. I glance toward the door, knowing someone could walk in at any time.

"How'd you get in here?"

"I know my way around this hospital, and I'm patient. I follow people through the security doors."

"How?"

"I look like I'm on my phone, then like I'm rushing to slip through the doors since they're already open. A grin makes people think I belong."

He cups my jaw and kisses me again. This one is so damn tender. I'm so into him. I don't want to let go. I don't want to get up. I wish we could stay like this. The only thing better would be feeling him inside me.

"I missed you, little one. Any free moment I had, I thought about you."

"Same. I'm so glad you're back. What I told you didn't make you leave early did it?"

"No. I finished what I went up there to do. I couldn't resist coming to see you, but how much longer is your shift?

I glance at my watch. "Forty-four hours."

He groans, and I'm echoing him in my head. I want to strip and ride his cock. I want to make him come. I want to feel his hands on my bare skin and his tongue against my nipple. I really want to feel his cock. It'll be another two days before I can do that. There is no real privacy in here, and I would never fuck at work. It's not worth the risk.

"How long do you have right now?"

"Two-and-a-half-hours."

"I know you were sleeping, and I hate waking you. But I need to talk to you, and it can't wait."

Trepidation fills me. "Should we go for a walk, so no one can interrupt this? You shouldn't be in here, anyway."

"Yeah."

I get up, slipping into my shoes before I put my lab coat and surgical cap back on. When we get to the door, I open it and peer down the hallway in both directions. We slip out and make our way to the elevator. There's an enormous courtyard in the center of the hospital complex. There's plenty of room for people to talk without being overheard.

"Are you okay to be out here?"

"I have my pager." I pull it out of my lab coat pocket and clip it back on to my scrubs' waistband.

Finn slides his hand into mine as we walk to a secluded area. He waits for me to sit on the bench before he takes a seat,

waiting for me in the lounge just outside the unit's security doors. Fallon was here yesterday.

"Dr. Gallagher, am I taking you home?"

"You can call me Althea or Ally."

The look he shoots me tells me that's never happening. Is it protocol for all women, or is it Finn would kill him for being too familiar? I don't know. I'm too tired to think straight.

"She's coming home with me. Take the night off, Ted. Thanks for protecting Thea."

I spin around when I hear the first word. Finn's waiting by the elevators. Even though Ted's right there, I sag into Finn's embrace the moment the doors shut. I close my eyes and let him hold me up. Between the emergencies and my fear about this inevitable conversation, I could fall asleep on my feet.

There's a town car waiting in the basement parking garage. I don't know the guy who gets out and opens the door for me. Finn slides next to me. The moment the door shuts, I'm pushing my pants down, and he's pulling them off my legs. Then he's fumbling to get his trousers unfastened. I'm taking his cock into me the moment he frees it from his boxer briefs.

"Daddy." It comes out choked as I struggle not to cry.

"Nothing you tell me is going to push me away."

"Yes, it will."

His tone changes, and it sends a shiver through me. "I have my cock inside your cunt. I'm going to fill it with my cum. I'm going to carry you inside my building and into my bedroom, so not a bit drips out of you. I'm going to lay you on the bed and fuck you hard enough that you'll probably safe word. You are mine. Unless you tell me this is over, you remain mine."

I kiss along his neck. "But are you going to stay mine?"

I can't stop the tears that fall. I don't want to cry. I shouldn't be. But the whirlwind that's torn through me since Finn woke me has my emotions flying all over the place. His fingers bite into my hips. He yanks me closer.

"Take that fecking shirt off and get your bra off before I burn it. Now, Thea."

To anyone else, he'd sound like a controlling asshole. To me, I want to come just listening to him. I whip the shirt over my head but struggle with my bra clasp. I'm all fingers and thumbs. But I get it off. He pinches my nipples so hard I shriek. He latches onto my right one and bites. Not enough to break the skin or anything, but enough to shoot pain through my chest. His hand rains down a hard spank on my ass, jerking me forward on his dick. My clit rubs against his pubic bone, and I don't stifle my moan.

"That's right, *cailín*. I know what you like and what you need. You like the pain because it matches your mood without you thinking about what terrifies you. It reminds you I'm in control."

He presses me to lean against him, and my head goes to his shoulder as he massages my sore nipple and breast. He's flexing his hip to press his cock deeper into me while I roll my hips.

"Sleep, *leanbh*. Traffic's going to make it at least half an hour before we're home."

We're home. Not my place or my condo or even the condo. He makes it sound as though we both live there. Like it's completely natural to think of it as ours.

He strokes my back, and I'm asleep before I know it. When I wake, I immediately register the feeling that he's inside me. He's still hard. His thrusts are a little harder than before, and I'm moving my hips more. But it doesn't feel like we're fucking. He's just making sure he can stay inside me.

"Thea, we'll be home in ten minutes. It's time for me to fill you with my cum."

It's like he's saying it's time to grab my stuff before we get to his place. Like it's time to put away small hand-held devices, stow trays, and return my chair to the upright position. I nearly laugh. Then he turns us, so my back is on the seat. He thrusts deep, and I'm moaning, not laughing. We move together, and I can't get enough. Warming his cock was comforting. This is life giving.

"Daddy, I need to come. Please."

"You don't have to ask. Come as many times as you can. I want to see you. I want to get off from getting you off."

My fingers dig into his back as I feel my first orgasm. I've come more than once with other men, but never like with Finn. The second is usually not as strong. Every orgasm with Finn feels like an out of body experience. He doesn't let up until I've come three times. Then he surges into me one more time before holding himself in me. I watch his abs ripple as he comes.

"Thea, you know it's more than just getting off."

"I do."

"Then I need you to believe I won't turn against you. I don't want more secrets or lies than there have to be. I don't tell you things for your safety, not because I don't trust you. I need you to trust me, too."

"I do, Finn. I'll tell you everything I know."

He helps me get my clothes back on, and he's true to his word. He carries me into his place, but we stop in the living room. His couch looks like the most comfortable one I've ever seen. He has a *massive* TV mounted on the wall.

"We like rugby."

He reads my mind as I look up there. I assumed it was something like football. I bet you'd think you were on the field watching any sport on it. I notice the library he has. It's an eclectic assortment of books, from academic and professional to travel to classics. His kitchen could rival Martha Stewart's.

"I'm the best cook."

He sits down with me in his lap. I really wish I could nap more. Maybe later. He's quiet, letting me collect my thoughts. This is probably going to be a long ass story, but I start at the very beginning.

"I remember Uncle Corey coming around sometimes when I was really little. I remember the sound of his motorcycle more than I do him. My dad would leave with him, and it used to upset me because he wouldn't be home in time to tuck me in. He did that every night. As I got older, that happened more infrequently, but when it did, my mom would never tell any of us where Papa went or when he would come back. Now that I know you, maybe my mom didn't know. When I was twelve, my parents felt I was old enough to ride on the back of my dad's bike. Neither of my brothers were allowed on it before they were twelve. Mom and Papa believed we understood the danger and took holding onto our dad's waist seriously. I loved it when he'd take me out. We'd ride near the Charles and over the bridges. We'd do a loop around Boston Common, and I'd see all the houses in Beacon Hill. I used to imagine I'd become some world-renowned surgeon at Mass General and have a home there."

I smile and shake my head as I picture those rides with my dad.

"By the time I got to med school, I knew I didn't want to be a surgeon. I also knew I would never live in Boston again. When I was thirteen, I developed a crush on this boy. I was in seventh grade, and he was in high school. I knew him through Uncle Corey. He'd started coming around again, but he never came inside the house. I remember Papa wouldn't allow it. I was walking home from school, and this boy was there. I thought he was so cute. I thought he enjoyed talking to me. He was distracting me, so I wouldn't interrupt Papa and Uncle Corey. We talked for like an hour, and I was in love. Puppy love. When I glanced over at the house a few times, I thought Papa was talking to his uncle and two of his men. I didn't realize until much later they were keeping my dad from getting to me. That Uncle Corey had a gun pointed at my dad's heart and would have gladly shot him if he'd called out to me. I didn't know there was a man behind me with his gun pointing at me and would have killed me right before Uncle Corey shot Papa."

I close my eyes, a vivid picture of that day replacing the happy ones of riding on my dad's bike with him.

"The high school let out thirty minutes before the middle school, so Chris would walk me home. I thought I was the shit because girls who barely noticed me started asking about him. But Jamie found out and lost his ever-loving mind. He's three years older than me and knew the guy from school. He told me the guy not only drank and smoked, but he also tagged people's houses and businesses. He said he got into fights and used a knife to win them. I didn't want to believe him, but the more Jamie told me, the more I realized it was all plausible. I tried to be polite when I told Chris I didn't want him to walk me home anymore. He didn't take it well. He started yelling at me outside a convenience store that had six bikes parked out front."

Another memory I wish I didn't have.

"The two men who were with Uncle Corey the day I met Chris came out when they heard him screaming at me. Rather than stop Chris, they laughed at me. They called me a cock tease and a slut. I was thirteen. I barely knew what those meant. I was so ashamed. The only person I told was Jamie. My brother was three inches taller than Chris and at least twenty pounds heavier. They had gym the same period. I don't know what my brother said, but I know he got in Chris's face and made sure he understood he better stay away from me. Chris's younger brother was in my grade. A couple months after Chris left me alone, Jared started following me around. His friends never sat at the same lunch table as my friends and me, but he kept coming over. He'd just stare at me. He and his friends would hang out near my locker when I got to school, and they'd follow me out of school. I told Jamie, and he started walking me home. After that, no one paid attention to me for like a year-and-a-half."

Then I sprouted tits and an ass.

"When I started my freshman year, I'd developed a lot over the previous summer. A few guys asked me out, but my parents didn't allow me to date until I was sixteen. After six months, no one asked anymore. I figured I'd said no enough times no one wanted to bother. I still think that's a lot of the reason why I dated so little in high school. I got a reputation for being a prude even though I always explained my parents wouldn't let me. That was the same time Uncle Corey came around the house again. He and Papa had some horrible arguments. Papa even pushed him out the front door the one time Papa allowed him in. I don't know what they argued about, but Papa said something one night because when Uncle Corey walked past the living room— they'd been in the basement —he looked terrified. Papa looked furious. The next morning, Chris and Jared were at my locker. They told me they'd beat the shit out of my younger brother, Rod, if I didn't hang out with them that afternoon. Jamie was home sick, so I couldn't go to him. Rod was still in middle school. I believed Chris and Jared, so I agreed to meet them at the park across the street from school. I figured it was close enough that I could scream and run to safety."

I swallow and curl into a ball. Finn holds me tighter, kissing my forehead. His hand runs over the outside of my arm and up and down my back, soothing me.

"They led me to the far side of the park. Way farther away from the school than I wanted to be. I tried to turn back, but they each grabbed my arm and pretty much dragged me. There were a dozen bikes parked on the street, and I recognized several of Corey's men. This guy, Mark, came over and scared the shit out of me with the way his eyes ran all over me. He kept looking at my chest, trying to make me uncomfortable. I refused to show how terrified I was. I looked down my nose at him, which made the other men laugh at him. He reached out to slap me, but this senior I recognized caught his arm in time. He pushed Mark out of the way and told Chris and Jared to fuck off. I didn't trust him, but I was relieved. I'd thought Chris was cute, but Elijah was Shemar Moore level hot. He offered to give me a ride home, but I refused. Not a fucking chance in hell, even if he was fine."

When I said Elijah wanted me on his bike, I felt Finn tense. I stroke his chest, and he relaxes.

"I still don't know how the rumor spread so fast, but Chris and Jared told people I slept with them at the park. They said the men watched us. I'd gotten a new watch for my birthday a few days earlier, and they claimed I got it as payment for fucking them. I told my parents. I explained everything that had happened and that I'd been too ashamed to say anything to anyone but Jamie. They understood that, but they were pissed. My dad left the house that night and didn't come back for two days. When he did, his knuckles were raw. The rest of him was fine, but his fists showed he'd been in a fight. He was gone on a Wednesday and Thursday. That Friday, Elijah told me what happened with my dad."

And this is when shit got complicated.

"Elijah said Papa showed up at the clubhouse— some dive bar in south Boston —and threw a chair at Chris and Jared's dad. It smashed into the guy's head. Before anyone could stop him, my dad had the splintered leg and whaled on this man to within an inch of his life. People tried to pull Papa off, but he swung the chair leg like a club. He broke one guy's nose and shattered another guy's cheekbone. Elijah said Uncle Corey pulled a gun on Papa, so Papa threw the chair leg at his uncle. Apparently, it hit him square in the forehead and knocked him out. My dad spotted Elijah and insisted he tell all the members how Elijah and his cousins, along with Chris and Jared, targeted me— a fifteen-year-old girl who still had braces. Papa accused Chris of grooming me. He called me jail-bait. I guess Elijah's dad was there too, and he used to be super close to my dad when they were growing up. Elijah's dad lost his shit because Papa accused Elijah and the others of planning to assault me. Elijah's the one who calmed his dad down, but not until after Papa broke two of his ribs with another chair leg."

I recall how sick I felt while Elijah recounted this story to me. How I wanted to run straight home and hide. I was certain all of it was my fault. I knew something was off all along, but I still left school with Chris and Jared. I could have called my mom to pick me up or asked one of my friends' parents to give me a ride. But I didn't.

"Elijah appointed himself my bodyguard. He knew I wouldn't get on his bike, and my parents would never allow it, so he'd give me a ride home every afternoon in his car. I played volleyball, and Jamie had a job, so we didn't leave school at the same time most days. There were a few times Elijah said he had to run an errand on the way to my house. He wouldn't let me stay outside in the car, so I went into the stores with him. I didn't know until way later that he was collecting Uncle Corey's protection money. Uncle Corey and Elijah's dad were training him to be an enforcer. I was upfront with my parents about getting rides from Elijah. At first, they weren't pleased. But no one came near me again. Summer came, and I figured I wouldn't see Elijah again because he graduated. I was a summer camp counselor at another school. It wasn't walking distance, so he started giving me rides in the morning and the afternoon."

I sit up, so I can twist and see Finn better. I suspect he has some idea of where this story is going since it's so cliché.

"Elijah was my first kiss. I was still fifteen, but he was nineteen. I thought I was so cool to have an older boy interested in me. I knew it probably toed the line of statutory, but I never planned to go all the way with him, and I didn't. It was at a party Jamie let me go to with him. Elijah was with friends I didn't know. Jamie knew them, so it seemed fine. I didn't drink, but I didn't care that everyone else around me was. I had fun, anyway. Elijah had his arm around me nearly the entire time, and I felt so special. He kissed me off to the side of the house before Jamie took me home. There was so much I didn't understand."

I shake my head and look down at my lap where my hands now rest. I'm a lot older and lot wiser now. If only my fifteen-year-old self knew what my thirty-three-year-old self does now.

"The first couple of weeks after that party, Elijah would sneak a kiss when he picked me up and when he dropped me off. My parents knew he was still giving me rides. When Elijah asked me out on an actual date, I didn't tell my parents. I knew they would never go for that. I lied and said I was going out with a friend. I considered him a friend, so I justified it wasn't a lie. I saw it as a selective truth. He took me to the movies, and we sat in the far back. We made out the whole time. It was all over the clothes, but I thought it was amazing. When we pulled up to the clubhouse— which was more like a roadhouse bar — after the movie, and I figured out where we were, I refused to go in. He guilted me into it."

One of so many things he guilted me into. I feel the old anger bubbling within. I don't think of my teen years often, but when I do, I'm usually able to do it without the rage I once felt.

I might not make it through this story without wanting to throw something.

"I recognized the guys from the party who I didn't think were affiliated. I found out later Jamie had no idea either. They offered me drinks, but I refused. Elijah tried to guilt me into that. When he insisted, I got up and walked toward the door. I could hear the men taunting Elijah about getting his Ol' Lady in line. He flicked them off over his shoulder and wheedled his way into getting me back to the table. But I felt like an idiot with the men taunting me. The next morning, when Elijah came to pick me up, I thought I dumped him. It pissed him off, so he tried to yank the screen door open. I'd made sure I locked it before he arrived. I wouldn't go outside with him. Jamie took me to and from work for the next week. Elijah would call when he knew I was home, but my parents weren't. I could see it was him on the caller ID. I'd pick up the phone, then hang up. He followed a group of my friends to the movies. He sat next to me. I was still angry, but I missed him. When he slid his hand up my leg, I moved my popcorn to keep the other girls from seeing him cup my pussy."

Finn's stayed quiet through all of this. His arms are wrapped around me, and he's nodding his head from time to time. I can't tell what he's thinking, but apparently he knows exactly what I'm thinking.

"Thea, tell me the rest or stop now. Whatever you want. Either way, let me hold you. I may not always show my emotions, but it doesn't mean I don't feel them. I want to know the rest, but I won't push you. But either way, I'm not okay with this. Holding you is the only thing that's keeping me from losing my shite."

That makes me seriously consider not saying another word. But if I don't get the rest out, he'll wonder what I didn't say.

And as shitty as all of this is, telling Finn is cathartic. I take yet another deep breath.

"I asked my parents if I could go out with Elijah, and it was an immediate and emphatic no. They said they trusted him to give me a ride, but nothing more. I found out later, the only reason they agreed to it was because Elijah saw what happened to his dad when he spoke badly about me. Elijah didn't take it well, but I wouldn't defy my parents again. No matter how he tried to guilt me about that, I wouldn't go on another date with him. I wanted to. I really did, but I feared the consequences too much. Once I turned sixteen, I didn't need any more rides. Jamie was off at college, so I got his car. Two weeks after my birthday, Uncle Corey sent men to talk to Papa."

I cock an eyebrow. He knows Corey didn't want his enforcers to chat.

"They followed my dad from work to a gas station. Security cameras captured the entire thing. They jumped my dad, and he beat their asses then called the cops. That didn't go over well with Uncle Corey. Go figure. Elijah showed up and said he would smooth everything over if my parents agreed to him dating me. My dad laughed and shut the door in his face. The house got egged that night, and a brick went through my bedroom window."

Sounds familiar.

"I was so naïve back then. After a few weeks, it seemed like everything died down. I started going out with this guy, Tyler, who was in my grade. He was so sweet and so much fun. I really liked him. We'd been dating about three months when someone slashed my tires in the school parking lot. A month later, someone broke into his car and slashed his seats. My parents wound up paying for the repairs to keep his parents from filing a police report that would inevitably name me as a witness. Needless to say, he and I were through. Something similar happened with every guy I dated between sophomore and junior year. I rarely went on dates because I was afraid. I'd try it when I thought long enough went by that they'd lost interest. They hadn't. It was the perfect shitstorm. Uncle Corey couldn't strong-arm Papa into riding with him like he did when my dad was in his twenties. Elijah couldn't control me and make me defy my parents. And Papa humiliated one biker after another when they came for him. My senior year, one of my friends heard about a cool place to party. The moment we pulled up, I told the girls we had to turn around. I told them this was the worst place we could be. I recognized it immediately and had no interest in going inside the clubhouse. I warned my friends, but they got out anyway. I couldn't just let them go. In the two minutes head start, I walked in to find them surrounded by guys in their forties and fifties. They all knew who I was when I walked in. The mood shifted in a second. They converged on me."

That rage that's been building is crawling up my throat like bile, burning me from the inside out. I don't know how I didn't piss my pants or shit myself that night. I believed they would rape and kill me.

"I spotted Elijah against the back wall, just watching what was happening to my friends and me. I fumbled around in my purse, and when three men stepped forward, I pepper sprayed them. I'd never used it, so the can was full. I shook it and sprayed it toward anyone who came near me. I'd nearly backed out of the bar, and I knew my friends were already outside when I ran into someone. My fucking luck. Uncle Corey blocked the only door. Maybe it was some miniscule sense of family duty or morals, but he didn't let any of his men touch me. But I had to stay until my dad got there. He came in calmly, but the men started lobbing insults about me, my mom, and my dad. They all had to do with our skin color— that my dad and I thought we were too good for the club because we aren't as dark as my mom. He and I ignored them, but a guy grabbed my arm and tried to pull me away from my dad. It was like he went from Bruce Banner to the Hulk in a blink. He broke the guy's nose. When he bent over in pain, my dad plowed a right hook into his temple. It knocked him backwards, and his head hit the corner of the bar. I knew he was dead. My guess is my dad's punch severed an artery in his brain, but the biker's head was also bleeding profusely. Alcohol consumption makes it harder to clot. Anyway, men tried to mob him while I kept pepper spraying anyone who got close. Through it all, Elijah didn't do a fucking thing but watch. My dad grabbed a bottle from the bar that was near us. He shattered it against a man's head, then jabbed him in the throat with the jagged edges. Where he struck was no accident. He got the guy's jugular. He pulled me behind him and withdrew a gun. I knew they banned anything inside but a knife because people lost their tempers too fast for club members to be in an enclosed space with a weapon like that. After that night, no one came near me. I watched my father kill two men to protect me. My friends assumed my father and I would get out alive and took off without me. I couldn't even be mad because it meant they witnessed nothing they could tell the cops about later. Obviously, the bikers wouldn't say shit to the cops."

"When I saw Corey the second time, he said you have duties and responsibilities that you needed to go back to."

Wonderful.

"Uncle Corey came by the house the next day. He came alone, which he'd never done before. He walked up to the stoop but didn't try to come inside. He said that after the previous night and whatever my dad did in the past to protect us— I got a feeling it was a shit ton more than what Elijah told me —they would leave us alone. But only until I was eighteen. Then I was fair game. If I wanted to protect my parents, I would ride with them. That I would be a Sweet Butt with whoever wanted me. My dad shot Uncle Corey in the kneecap. That's why he limps now."

"I thought he was just fat." Finn grins at me, and it lightens things for a moment.

"I graduated early to get away from Boston before I turned eighteen. My mom's family is from Jersey, so they would come down here to see me. I'd stay with my grandmother during school breaks. I went straight from college to med school to residency. My parents moved down here the week after Rod graduated high school. I've been back once, and that was to watch Rod's graduation. I think part of the reason my brothers and I moved to New York was to get lost in the crowd. Until now, Uncle Corey rarely came near Papa. But he collects monthly to let my parents keep it that way. This is his way of getting back at my dad and me. I don't know how he found out Papa lost his job."

"Thea, he got your father fired."

Chapter Seventeen

Finn

I listened to Thea's entire story without interrupting. That was a Herculean feat, considering how much I wanted to demand each man's name. I want to find them and beat them all to death. I've killed far too many times, but it's never been because I desired their death on an emotional level. I wanted men dead because they fucked us over or tried to fuck us over. I wanted them dead because they were an inconvenience. I wanted them dead because they posed a threat to my family, our people, or our businesses. But it was always with cold-hearted detachment. This is different.

"What do you mean he got my father fired?" Thea's staring at me, and I hate being the bearer of this bad news.

"Corey wants you to go back to Boston, and he wants your dad indebted to him. He believes he can get both of you to do what he wants to save each other."

Her gaze remains steady, but I can't tell what she's thinking. I wait, not wanting to rush her as she works things out in her head.

"Finn, I will do anything to protect my family. But I'll kill my uncle before I go back to Boston, so those pervs can pass me around. I'm nobody's bitch— not a biker's or some piece of shit with a Napoleon complex. My dad's already proven what he'll do to protect me, but that was fifteen years ago. His arthritis means he's not as strong as he used to be, and he's in bad shape right now. He's not in a position to fight anyone off."

"I know, little one. I arranged for men to stay close to their house around the clock, and everyone in your family has a bodyguard assigned to them. They won't know unless you want to tell them. But they're there. Your nieces and nephew are at the same school. There are four guards, one on each street surrounding the building. There are two guards outside Jamie and Asher's house while the nanny is there with Skyler. You are not going anywhere without a man in my family with you. I love Joey, and he's my closest friend who isn't a near match to my DNA. But my brothers and cousins know what it means for me to ask them to protect you."

"What does that mean? Don't they have jobs besides—" She gestures in the air not wanting to vocalize our crimes.

"They do. If it's not straight to and from work, Mair goes nowhere without one of us. Dillan would lose his shite if she did. Work is predictable, so we have precautions and protocols put in place. If she deviates from the routine, then at least one of us is with her if Dillan can't be. It'll be the same if I can't be with you."

"But Mair's married to Dillan."

My fingers grip her hips as I lift her and turn her, so she straddles my lap. I slide my hands down the back of her pants and cup her bare arse.

"You've just told me something I doubt you've told anyone

outside your family. You admitted your dad killed at least two people and shot another. You know more about my family than anyone who isn't part of the organization. Would we have confessed those things to each other if we didn't plan for this to be permanent?"

"I..." She doesn't know what to say.

"Thea, I'm not saying we run off to Atlantic City tonight and get married. I don't know what the future holds in store for us, but I think we both know neither of us wants something casual. Everything about this world you're entering is on speed. Hell, some days it feels like this world is on meth. We are not morally devoid like civilized people believe." My tone is mocking. "We have a strong code of right and wrong and swift justice. Corey knows that. He's been skirting the edges since he was a teenager. He wants to play with the big boys while getting a pass for being an outsider. It doesn't work that way. He knows we're together."

I watch her stomach cave at that last bit.

"Did he know when he threw the brick through my window?"

"I don't think so since we'd only been out once. I told him when I saw him in Boston."

There's no point in pretending that's not where I went. I knew she figured it out while we were on the phone. It's obvious since I saw the piece of shite.

"Are you ready to meet my parents, Finn?"

"Yes. The sooner the better. I know you won't like this, but I need to speak to your dad alone."

She doesn't like it, but she nods.

"*Cailín*, what you don't know you can't testify about. Please believe me about this. You're placing all your trust in me, and I'm asking for more. I know that's not fair, but I'm doing it to protect you and the people you love."

"I know, but the unknown is scary."

"How far out are your shifts scheduled? Do you have vacation days?"

"I do, but I'm scheduled for the next month. I have two days off in a week."

I don't like that, but I'll have to accept it. "If this isn't resolved by the time the following schedule is about to be posted, I want you to request vacation days."

"I can't wait that long. If I want a vacation in a month, I should have asked four months ago. I can try, but I can't guarantee it."

I don't want to get too far ahead of ourselves. Part of me wants to say, "you can quit your job because my men can keep you plenty busy stitching them up." But she's not a surgeon, and we already have a doctor on call. Her work is too important to her and the families who depend on her, even if they don't know it yet. I never want her to give that up.

"Would you stay here with me?" *Would you move in with me?*

That's definitely getting too far ahead of ourselves. At least, it would be for her. I hated the few nights I had away from her. I kept dreaming about her sleeping next to me. I'd wake up alone, and it blew big chunks. I want her in my arms when I fall asleep, and I want her still there when I wake. I want to know she's safe, and I want the calm she brings me. Contrary to what it seems, I'm pissed as shite right now, but I'm calm because I'm holding her. It's not that I'm forcing myself not to rage in front of her. It's that I don't feel the need to rage while I'm holding her.

"I'd like that, Daddy."

I cup her jaw, and our kiss is unlike any I've had with anyone but Thea. I stand, and she wraps her legs around me. I walk to my— our —bedroom and into the bathroom. With one arm around her, I push down the plug and turn on the bath. I don't have bubble bath, so I squirt a few pumps of body wash under the faucet.

"We can soak for a while, then eat. I saw the empty bowl on the table in your breakroom. It looked like soup." I put her down, so we can strip.

"Shit! I forgot to wash and put that away after our talk and the patient. Fuck. I hate it when other people do that. Someone had to clean up after me."

"You'll make it up to whoever ended up doing that. Do you want me to cook for you, or do you want to order something?"

"Honestly, I don't mind what we eat. I just want to be close to you."

I test the water before looping my arms around her waist and drawing her against me. "I want you close to me, too. I'm sorry I had to be away from you when you found out about your dad."

"Thanks, but it worked out that you saw Uncle Corey."

"I suppose. I still think it would have been better for me to be here for you."

"You were. You got the message that I needed you, so you called as soon as you could. I got to talk to you, and I felt better for it. The problem isn't solved yet, but I felt more equipped to deal with it after talking to you. Work kept me plenty occupied, but knowing I can depend on you let me stay focused. My patients deserve my full attention, and not being terrified that something else is going to happen to my family let me do that. Thank you, Daddy."

I tip her chin up. "Always, little one."

Something passes between us. A silent understanding that we could date for months— a year— whatever —then commit to a future together. Or we can just admit we've found our soul-mate and start life together. I've already fallen hard for her. I know I'm more than halfway to falling in love. I believe our lives are entwined for good, so I know I'll love her. I don't know if she feels the same way, but I think she does.

We step into the tub once I turn off the water. She leans back against my chest, my legs bracketing her hips. We sigh at the same time, then laugh. Her hands rest on my upper shins, and my arms are around her ribs. I close my eyes, and I can't remember the last time I've been this content.

Then my phone rings. I haven't debriefed Dillan yet. I can't ignore it. I stretch to grab my pants and pull it out. It's Sean. I'm tempted to ignore it, but a wave of doom washes over me.

"Hey."

"Welcome home. Everything with Marco went to shite."

I glance down at Thea, unsure if she heard what my brother said. "Can I call you back in ten minutes?"

"What? No. Finn, we have a shitstorm right now. Steven Russo stole a shite ton of money from us. The FBI-ATF bust went to shite, and Elizabeth got caught up in it. And someone just took out Lorcan Cullen in his office. A fecking sniper. A kill shot better than anyone short of Robert Simms. Oh, and there's another problem. He's dead. We—"

"Thanks for letting me know. I'll call you back in a bit."

"Finn, what the— are you not alone? Is Ally with you?"

"Yes. I'll talk to you later."

Fuck, fuck, fuckity fuck! Holy fuck.

That's a lot to take in. I turned down the volume while Sean spoke, so I know Thea couldn't hear anything else. She sits forward and reaches for the body wash. She doesn't turn toward me as she lathers her arms.

"You need to go, don't you?"

"Yeah, probably. I'll call Sean back when we're done."

"I don't want to keep you from talking to your brother."

"Little one, he didn't tell me the sky is falling." Though it probably is. "We can't stay in here like I hoped, but we can shower, then head to Dillan's."

"We? Your brothers don't want me there."

"How do you know? I'm not leaving you alone here. Not because I'm scared you aren't safe. I'm not leaving you here because I've been away from you for three days, and I want to at least be in the same building as you. And once I find out what's going on, I have to tell the others the gist of what you told me. I won't reveal anything you don't want me to. But everything involving Corey is all knotted together. That means your family's threats and our business problems intersect. If the guys have questions, I'd rather you answer for yourself, but only if you're comfortable. I won't push you, but I don't want to speak for you and get it wrong."

I release the plug, and we stand. She turns on the shower before we switch places, then faces me. Her arms go around my neck, and I want nothing more than to pick her up again now that there're no clothes in the way. I've been fucking hard since I spotted her napping on the couch in the hospital. Sex in the car on the way here was only a temporary fix. As though she reads my mind, she wraps a hand around my cock and strokes. I groan, and she tightens her grip. Fucking hell.

I lift her, and she clings to me. My cock finds her cunt with no problem. I thrust into her, and she squeezes my waist. I support her as she rides me. I kiss her neck and nip at her earlobe. I kiss along her jaw until our mouths meet. Then it's a race to see who can devour the other. When she sucks on my tongue, I nearly explode.

"Feck, Thea. I won't last if you do that."

"I don't want you to. This is a quickie not a longie." She grins at me before kissing me and tugging my bottom lip.

I spank her, pushing her up then letting her drop down on my cock. She rocks her hips, and I can tell she enjoys this. I keep spanking her until she screams my name. I want to make her come at least once more, but I can't stop. I feel my jizz squirting into her. My cock pulses each time. Our kisses are calmer, but they don't last.

I watch her checking out the shampoo on my shelf. "Order whatever you want. Toiletries, food, drinks. Whatever. I know we don't have any of your clothes here. We can grab whatever you need in the morning."

"Finn, I have to be back to work in four hours. I have some clothes in my bag. I always have an extra set of scrubs and some jeans and a shirt. I was on an eight-hour break between shifts. I planned to go home, shower, eat, and sleep for a few hours, then head back. I can go to Dillan's with you, but I have to go back to the hospital."

It's going to take some getting used to this schedule. I thought mine had me coming and going at all hours of the day and night.

"You can stay here and sleep. I'll post two guys outside the door. I know you're exhausted." I feel guilty now. I pretty much barreled over her and decided for her.

She puts her hands on my chest. "I'll go with you. I can nap in the car each way. I want to help if I can. If I can't, I'd still feel better being in the same house as you."

"Dillan and Mair just bought a home in Queens. They haven't finished furnishing everywhere downstairs, but they set up all the bedrooms for us. I have a room you can sleep in."

"That's rude."

"Not at all. They'll understand."

"But—"

"Little one, everyone will understand why I don't want you here alone. And everyone will understand why a doctor needs to sleep." I turn off the water and hand her a towel.

Once we're dressed, we head down to the underground

parking lot. I'll drive since it's faster than waiting for a car to get here. I open the door for her before getting into the driver's seat of my Jag. Traffic is on our side, so it doesn't take us too long to get from SoHo to Queens. When we pull up, I sense Thea's nerves getting the better of her. We're in a gated community and drove into a driveway behind a gate. She sees the armed security guards before she looks up at the house. In all fairness, it's a mansion.

Ironically, all the syndicate couples from each family live near here. The only people who don't are Enrique— the Cartel *jefe* —and his brother and his family. They live in north Jersey in affluent communities. It's like our childhood when we all played peewee sports together. Everyone lives a few blocks from one another. Most of the single syndicate men have lived in Manhattan, but I'm the only one in my family who does. The other guys live in Brooklyn, Harlem, and Queens.

"Now I understand how each of you has a room here." Thea glances at me before reaching for the door handle, but I lean across her and catch her wrist.

"Never get out on your own. If we pull into a house's garage, you wait until the door shuts all the way. You don't turn off the engine until the door is only an inch or two off the ground. When you have a driver, they open the door for you. When you're in a driveway at one of our homes, a guard or a family member opens it. When we're at the condo, I'll walk around and open it, or your driver does."

She stares at me before twisting to look out the windows at the men in black clothes with rifles slung across their chests and various weapons clipped to their belts. Then she turns her luminescent eyes on me. I still find their color transfixing.

"Am I really going to be in that much danger, too?"

"You may rarely be in any danger, but that's because we have safety protocols in place. I'm not a pessimist, Thea. I'm a realist. That means I'll do whatever I think is necessary to protect you and my family. The car doors are one of those things. It's the rule for everyone, especially the women. I'm certain some of the other syndicate wives carry guns, or at least knives, but even if you did, I would still insist that an ounce of prevention is worth more than a pound of cure."

She sighs but nods. Then she thinks better of it and cups my jaw. She kisses me, but it's over way too soon.

"Thank you for taking care of me, Daddy. I have to get used to this, but you could merely insist I obey. You're explaining everything and being patient while I learn. I appreciate it."

"You're going to sacrifice a lot, Thea. More than I wish and probably more than I can predict. I will always give you what you need, and I'll try my hardest to give you what you want."

"All I need right now is you."

And now she has my entire heart in her palm. I kiss her again before turning off the car. She waits for me to come around to her side before getting out. We hold hands as we walk to the door. I punch in the code and go in. If I didn't know we're all meeting— Sean sent me a flurry of texts after we hung up —I wouldn't walk into Dillan's house unannounced. He's a newlywed. Hell, even when they've been married forty years, I won't walk in unannounced. They'll still be all over each other, and that's not something I need to see. And Dillan would gouge my eyes out before letting anyone see Mair uncovered.

She wore a slinky bikini during their honeymoon. They came into the house from the beach not realizing the rest of us — yes; we went on their honeymoon, but as their security detail —were in the dining room. My brothers, cousins, and I have never moved so fast in our lives. Cormac even knocked over the dining room chair as he pushed it back.

I understood then, but I *get it* now. It wouldn't thrill me to have any man see Thea naked, especially if I'm making love to her. Now that's a phrase I've never used before. I've said fuck and any number of euphemisms, but I have never considered what I've done with other women making love. I'm certain I've done it more than once with Thea.

"Finn?"

"Yeah, Shay. I'm coming." Seamus and his brother, Cormac, are built like ox who move on silent feet, but the man forgets what an inside voice is.

I sense Thea's getting more nervous with each step. I lean over to whisper in her ear as I give her hand a squeeze.

"They don't bite, though I might. You're delicious. I know they're a lot, but they know how important you are to me. They're happy for us."

"They won't be once they know my past."

I slide my arm around her waist and pull her against me as I stop. "No one will blame you for your family. We have no leg to stand on. I wouldn't let you meet them if I thought they'd be unkind."

I give her a peck before we walk into the family room. Feck, there are a lot of us. Dillan and Mair are sharing Dillan's favorite armchair. Sean and Shane are on a love seat while Cormac and Seamus have the sofa. I shoot my brothers a look, and they get up. I grin. Still got it.

"Thea, you've met everyone but Dillan."

She walks over as Mair and Dillan stand and shakes his hand. Mair hesitates for a moment, then goes for it. Her hug sets Thea at ease. I don't know that anyone else notices it. Maybe Mair feels it. But Thea shoots me a smile as she steps back.

"I know what you called me about, but Thea has to be back at the hospital in a few hours. She's also exhausted. We need to talk to you. After that, Mair, could she use my room?"

"Of course." Mair turns to Thea. "Would you like anything to eat or drink?"

"I'm all right. Thank you, though."

I won't press the issue, but I'm certain Thea must be hungry by now. She told me while we got dressed that she originally planned to go home, eat, sleep, and shower. She's only done one of those.

"You know I'll be hungry later." I offer Mair a lopsided grin.

"Yes. All of you have hollow legs as Granny would say." She rolls her eyes, then shoots Thea a conspiratorial wink. "You know where everything is. I'll be in my office."

With a kiss on the cheek for Dillan and a beleaguered sigh for the rest of us, she slips out. Normally, we'd meet in Dillan's office. But the family room is more spacious. Having all of us in a smaller space is intimidating. Fortunately, our dads aren't here. Add the three of them to the six of us, and it's terrifying—and loud. She and I sit on the loveseat. I wrap my arm around her shoulders, but she doesn't lean into me. Her hand rests lightly on my thigh, and I think she's trying to appear confident and independent. It's unnecessary, but I can appreciate the need.

The guys look at me, thankfully. I don't want them all staring at Thea at once. I don't want her to feel like I've put her on the spot by bringing her here. The best thing is for me to start.

"I saw Corey while I was up there. We had a chat." Thea stiffens. "I found out Corey threw a brick through Thea's window. Or— it's more likely —he had someone throw it for him. Corey is Thea's great-uncle through her dad's side."

Six sets of eyes dart to Thea before turning back to me.

"He's causing problems for her family. He got her dad fired to extort him. He's threatened Thea to force her dad's hand." I still haven't told her about the background check and what the others already know about her family.

"He wants your parents to pay him to get your dad's job back?" Cormac leans forward, resting his elbows on his knees.

"He wants my parents to take a loan from him. He knows the only reason to take a loan is because you don't have the money you need. If you had the money, you wouldn't go to someone like him. Despite being family, he'll make the repayment terms impossible. My mom and dad know that, so they have no intention of taking a penny from him. My dad'll find a new job if he has to way before taking Uncle Corey's— help."

She says the last word with such disgust.

"Corey wants to terrify you into convincing your parents to accept his offer."

Sean is the quietest of us and the slowest to anger. But when he gets pissed, the universe knows his temper matches his red hair.

"They've said they'll dip into their savings until my dad finds something else. I haven't pressed the issue, but I'll give them the money before they take funds from what needs to support them for probably twenty years after they retire. I'm single and only have rent and my student loans as my financial commitments. I can afford to pause my retirement savings to help them. I will *not* let them take a penny from Uncle Corey and suffer for it. My great-uncle is well connected with several unions, including the one my dad belongs to as a welder. He'll make it exceptionally hard for my dad to find a new job, but Papa's good at what he does. It isn't impossible."

I'm not offering to help yet because I don't want to insult her parents since they don't even know me. I don't know if they know of me. I don't want to make Thea feel uncomfortable by me swooping in with my fat bank account. But helping her parents helps Thea, and there's no limit to what I'll do for her. My expression reassures my family that I'm on top of it.

Dillan asks the question neither Thea nor I are eager to answer. "Why's he coming after your dad now?"

Thea looks up at me, and I see her nerves threaten to overcome her, so I answer. "Thea grew up with Corey popping in and out of her life. Her dad stopped running with Corey and his gang before Thea was born. But he could never sever his ties entirely. When Thea was a teenager, men in the biker club started paying too much attention. She didn't date any of them because her parents wouldn't allow it. Once she understood who they were, she didn't want to."

Thea dives in. I wasn't sure how much more I should say, but at the same time, I hate she's the one telling them something so painful.

"My parents were okay with one guy giving me a ride to and from school until I got my license. He'd protected me when two guys closer to my age tried to hand me off to a group of men. When Elijah wanted more, I said no. When I said no, he got pissed. I wound up at their clubhouse because some friends of mine heard there was a cool place to party. Thinking back on it while I told Finn earlier, it wouldn't surprise me if a member's son didn't plant the idea in one of my friends' ears. It was horrible. I had pepper spray, and I used it. Uncle Corey showed up— likely planned —and made the men stay away. He let me call my dad, who came to get me. A couple guys tried to separate us and attack him. He killed both of them. My dad and I got out of there, and Uncle Corey mostly stayed away. But he issued an edict that once I was eighteen, I was the motorcycle club's. Neither my parents nor I were going to let them turn me into a Sweet Butt, and I had no interest in becoming a citizen wife to any of them."

"What's that?" Shane speaks up, but I don't think any of us know what it means.

"Sometimes a biker will legally marry a woman. They have a normal life away from the club. Kids and everything. She has nothing to do with it and stays out of the way. The biker might have an Ol' Lady side piece. I think Uncle Corey assumed that's what my mom would be. There isn't a chance on God's green earth my father would ever cheat on my mom. My dad was jumped out to avoid any of this. A lot of good it did him."

Gang members are jumped in— often have the shite beaten out of them as an initiation —and *if* they're allowed to leave, they often get jumped out— the shite beaten out of them again.

"Uncle Corey probably figured I'd breed the next generation of bikers. Who knows? He's certifiable."

I don't disagree.

"He thought you'd get married at eighteen?" Dillan's brow furrows. It's not that he doesn't believe Thea, it's just hard to fathom. But Thea thinks he's questioning her.

"I'd rather have been a House Mouse. I guess being family paid off."

"I'm sorry. I believe you. I just can't believe even Corey would force a child bride." Dillan realized his delivery was off for someone who doesn't know him.

It's my turn not to understand. "A House Mouse?"

"Yeah. Sometimes a club will take in a runaway girl. If she can get along with a man's side piece, then he'll give the girl to her, basically. The House Mouse doesn't get involved with most club things, but an Ol' Lady might turn her into a maid and babysitter for a safe place to live and protection. Usually, they don't expect a House Mouse to put out. I'd rather be a maid than forced during a marriage to a man who'd insist he has a right to make me sleep with him. Granted, if she's biddable and trainable, she might become a guy's Mama or Ol' Lady."

"Did you know all of this back then?" Seamus asks what I should have back at our place. Yes, *our*— mine and Thea's.

"No. I didn't understand most of what was going on around me back then. The internet explained it, but I wound up asking my mom because half of it confused me. Uncle Corey likes to claim I was a Sweet Butt or Mama, but I never was. No one passed me around. I wasn't anyone's maid. I didn't hang out at the clubhouse. None of that. He does it to degrade me and intimidate me. I've been back to Boston once since I graduated high school and that was to see my younger brother graduate. I'm not scared to go back, but why would I tempt fate?"

It's a reasonable question. The answer goes without saying. We've gotten to where I don't think there's much to be gained by Thea telling the others everything she told me. But we can't talk about anything else in front of her. I think she senses that.

"I have time for an hour nap. Which room is yours?"

"Top of the stairs to the right, third door down. I'll make sure you're awake in plenty of time."

"Thanks."

I watch her walk out of the family room and to the stairs. None of us say anything until we're certain she can't hear. Even then, we keep our voices low. Mair's office is at one end of the house, and Dillan's is at the other. This family room is in the middle. We don't want Mair to hear anything either.

"I let him live because I think he's still useful. We've fucked Rowan and Riley over, but it wasn't enough. Corey doesn't know it, but he's about to fuck those brothers over. When they come for him, they'll all wind up dead. I want them looking at each other when it happens."

I want a lot more than that, but that goes without saying. Dillan nods, then it's Shane's turn to speak up.

"You know I called Steve Russo to warn him to keep his sister away from Marco. Short of telling him everything, I made it clear things were already in motion that neither he nor *Tres J's* were going to feck up."

Tres J's— Joaquin, Jorge, and Javier — are Enrique's nephews. They're fucking batshit crazy from growing up in Bogota. They moved to America when we were all teenagers. They'd seen some shite way too young. They wanted to fuck Marco over at the same time as us. It was a coincidence, but our plan was in the works way before theirs. Theirs came from Marco fucking over Enrique. Ours came from needing the feds off our backs. We put way too much work into setting up Lorenzo, then Marco. We weren't going to let it go to shite. But it did anyway.

"You said Lorcan's dead." I look at my brothers.

"And we're all better for it. Shite bird." We all share Shane's disgust.

Lorcan Cullen was our godfather. My parents definitely didn't choose him. Our grandfather did. They were friends even though Lorcan was younger than him. Granddad thought Lorcan would be an excellent influence over us. Piece of shite drank too much and spent most of his time finding young gold diggers to suck him off.

"Who did it?" I look at Dillan, then the others.

"We're not sure, but it was marksmanship like only Robert Simms could do." Dillan hated working with Simms, but the man was a necessary evil.

Simms was a mercenary and a fucking great one. He was a ghost. You could only contact him through a burner phone you had to hope he would answer. All payments were in cash— mostly. I dug up some shite on him and his connections to the old bratva *pakhan*. The psychopath before Maks Kutsenko took over. I used that to leverage him into some jobs for us. Then I used Carmine and Gabriele as my dupes. While Salvatore banished them to some shithole vineyard in Sicily for being *idioti*, I routed payments through Gabriele's bank accounts. It was going great until Sumiko Kutsenko— Pasha's wife —figured it out. She's a forensic accountant, just like Pasha and me. There went that plan.

"Sean, didn't you say Simms was dead, too? How the feck did that happen?"

"Elizabeth Russo soon-to-be Mancinelli." Dillan's jaw clenches.

"What?" How did I miss so much in the space of three days away?

"Simms went rogue, even more pissed at her about money than he ever was with us. He got to her while she and her brother were having lunch with Marco and Carmine. Shane, here, didn't mention she's a fecking expert marksman and shoots clay and skeet and whatever other shooting sport there is."

"Don't piss in my direction. I haven't spoken to her in years. Finn's the one Donovan and Declan tasked with following her."

"You make it sound like they tasked me to stalk her." I look over my shoulder toward the stairs before glaring at my brother. "I was there to protect her."

"You never mentioned her competitive shooting."

"How was I supposed to know she'd use it against a mercenary? You're the one who dated her."

"In high school." Shane's about to lose his shite, but so am I.

"I already had Lorenzo break my nose because he thought I was into his wife before they even got married. Marco's with her sister now. Their mother made it very clear about our duty being discharged when Michelle married Lorenzo. So, if anyone shouldn't be pissing in someone's direction, it should be you leaving me the feck alone."

We can argue all day and all night, but our parents would skelp our arses if they heard us swear at each other.

Lorenzo broke my nose a week and a half before I met Thea. My nose wasn't even completely healed when I did. I still had some lingering bruises from our rounds in the boxing ring. My cabinet full of arnica got rid of the bruises on my face. Since there was shite happening that I'd never reveal to Lorenzo, I let him get his punches in. If I'd really defended myself, we'd probably both be dead.

"Can you two stop?" Sean's glaring at us both. We never make him choose sides, but he doesn't like being caught in the middle, which inevitably happens to whichever brother isn't in the argument.

"Fine. In the three days I was away, Elizabeth Russo killed Robert Simms, a man no one's even injured in, like, forty years. Lorcan is dead, and from the sounds of it, probably shot by Elizabeth. And Marco's still free. Marvelous."

Cormac frowns before he speaks. "I don't think Elizabeth shot Lorcan. From what I heard, it was self-defense for Elizabeth. It was a hit on Lorcan. There's no way Marco would have taken her to do a job like that. The shooter took him out from the building next to the bar. It had to be from the fire escape. He would never agree to that risk. My money is on Steven. It was a high-power rifle round. Any of the Mancinellis could have fired it, but only Maria and Nicoletta have that kind of aim. They're no more likely to be there than Elizabeth."

Nicoletta is Luca, Marco, Lorenzo, and Maria's mother. She and her daughter are the best shots I know of besides Laura Kutsenko. It's not surprising they're all women. They say women are far better shots than men because they have patience men don't. Those three— apparently along with Elizabeth now —are proof of that.

"And the money Steven stole? I haven't checked the accounts yet." I'm certain I'll be pissed when I do.

"All the money we let him invest. The Mancinellis have a few million more than they did yesterday." Dillan's mind is going in at least four different directions right now, coming up with some permutation or another to get revenge for their revenge.

"He only had the money I wanted him to see. He thought he had a far larger share of our portfolio than he did. You know I control three-quarters of it and do the trading myself. I tested him, and he failed." I shrug.

If he went after our money and Lorcan to defend his sister, then I can't blame him. But that doesn't mean I won't destroy his career. I'll make sure he loses his license and his job. Shite, if his two sisters weren't Mancinellis now— it's obvious Elizabeth and Marco are like two seconds away from walking down the aisle just like it's a foregone conclusion to me that Thea and I have a future together —I'd tell Dillan to hire Steven as our hitman. We already know he's done some jobs for the bratva. Internal work mostly. I should have known right away now that I think about it.

"That's not all. Finn, they hit McGinty's. The girls got out safe, but no one else did. They already sent their cleaners in, but we know it was them." Sean grimaces, not wanting to be the bearer of bad news. Our Nana started that bar. It's my favorite of all the ones I own.

"How bad is it?"

"They didn't trash it. They went for the men more than damage. But there's still shite to fix."

Fucking hell. I nod because there's nothing else I can do right now.

"Dillan, what do you want to do? Let things go with Marco

or keep pushing?" Seamus has plans for tonight, so I can tell he wants this shite wrapped up.

I glance at my watch. I can let Thea sleep for another forty minutes, then we have to go. I'd like to finish this conversation before that.

"No. That ship's sailed and sunk. *Tres J's* wants to go after him. Let's feed them enough shite to make them step it up. They can do our dirty work for us. We never meant for Elizabeth to get caught in the crosshairs with the FBI and ATF. Is Marco going to deal with them?"

Sean shakes his head. "I don't think so. I think he plans to do what we did. Make them his bitches and get them to do what he wants to come after us."

"Then we need to make sure they're useless. Leak their affair."

Dillan couldn't give any more shites about who someone fucks— gay, straight, everything in between, and all around —than any of us. The scandal is Spiegel's married to Holland's sister. Hollands is the Director of the FBI, and his sister is the Deputy Director of National Intelligence. Rather suss that a lowly ATF agent suddenly got put in charge of busting an organized crime family that's controlled a huge chunk of New York for four generations. Not to mention he's working alongside his lover. It was fine while they were convenient for us. Now they're not.

Shane cracks his knuckles— drives our mom nuts —as he speaks. "That'll only keep Marco distracted for a few minutes. He and his family are going to strike back. What are we willing to lose? We can let that dangle in front of them."

I think about what we have coming and going. I picture our shipments and investments. I consider properties we own. The bratva already went after what we'd thought of as our ancestral home. It's where our mom's family lived when they first immigrated to the U.S. What else do our rivals think we value as much as that? That's what they'll go for.

"I'm not thrilled to say it after going all the way to Boston to retrieve the shite, but the rugs. Let them think they stole them from us. They can have the nanochips. We don't need them that much. Seamus, put the word out to their informants. We can watch them scurry back to Luca and Carmine. The whole shipment is worth one-point-seven. I don't like losing that much, but it's a small price to pay to get them off our backs. We point them in the Cartel's direction too."

The blessing in disguise of chasing those damn rugs was finding out what's going on with Thea's family. Knowing it's Corey means I can protect her better. Thinking about Boston leaves a lingering question for me.

"Why did Rowan think he could come for us? I left him alive for this week. I want him stewing over how we're going to strike next. Joey and his brothers will go up and finish it for us."

That means I need to think about who else to assign to Thea's detail. Part of why Joey's my first choice to guard Thea is because he's so good at what he does. He's not noticeable, but he notices everything. He blends in wherever he goes, so people don't know he's about to strike until they're a breath away from dying. His brothers and cousin are the same way. Their dads trained alongside my dad and uncles. They all worked for Granddad at the same time, and their dads taught them just like my dad and uncles taught us. There aren't too many men outside my immediate family who I trust as much as Joey, Simon, Fallon, and Ted.

Dillan leans away with his elbow on the arm of his chair as he looks over at me. "We still don't know the answer to why Rowan got delusions of grandeur. Someone put Rowan up to it."

"I figured as much, but there was no sign of who. I hacked

his emails before I went to Boston and while I was there. I already dug around their finances. It makes sense why they'd want a high profit item like that tech shipment. But nothing makes sense about why they thought they could target us. Why not another Boston family? Why not a rival down here, rather than an ally? Rowan's arrogant and stupid, but he has enough common sense not to target us unless he believes he has a sure-fire plan. He didn't, but what made him think he did? Or better yet, *who* made him think he did?"

"Finn?" Thea calls out to me, but she must still be upstairs.

"Yeah."

"Can I come down? I need to head back to work."

I stand and walk to the family room's open archway. "Yes. I'll take you."

She hurries down the stairs wearing a fresh pair of scrubs. Mint green. They make her eyes glow. God, she's beautiful. All of her. Inside and out. Fuck. How'd I get so damn lucky?

She takes my offered hand and looks around me to the other guys. She shoots them a smile and gives a quick wave. I hold the door open for her, and before I step out, I look back at the others.

"I'll be back after I drop Thea off."

Chapter Eighteen

Thea

It's been the strangest twelve hours I've possibly ever had. It doesn't even have anything to do with patients. I've gotten three pages to units I have nothing to do with. When I get there, no one knows who sent the alerts. As though that wasn't weird enough, the first was to the ER just as a gunshot wound was being transferred to surgery. The second was to intensive care as a patient crashed. And the third was to surgical recovery where a patient was hemorrhaging and eventually died. It's no coincidence that death was the common denominator. I get that. The strange part is why me? Why today? And who?

"Ted, can you meet me on the first floor? I just got paged to the morgue. Something's going on, and I'm not comfortable going down there alone."

"Are you safe right now, Dr. Gallagher?"

I'm on the phone with my bodyguard for today. Joey and his brothers aren't available, but I like Ted. I think Joey, Simon, and Fallon are doing something else rather than having the days off.

"I believe so. I'm about to get on the elevator. I'll meet you downstairs near the gift shop."

"Okay."

I push the button and wait for it to arrive. I'm on the NICU floor and have five to go down before I can find Ted. A sudden wave of trepidation slams into me as I step onto the elevator. What if someone corners me in here? I can't control who gets on. I keep my phone out and Ted's contact on my screen. One press will call him. My toes are tapping inside my clogs.

Fuck.

"Morning."

"Morning." I don't know who this person is.

Definitely a visitor since no hospital ID. He pushes the close door button, but nothing else. Lovely. He got on at the fourth floor and is riding down with me to the first. I make sure I'm in the corner. But the doors open on the third floor, and two more men get on. Don't any women work here too?

Blessedly, we don't stop on the second floor. I'm in the corner, so the other two people have to step off first. I reach for the door open button as an excuse to get the original man off the elevator before me. The hairs on the back of my neck are standing up, and I don't want him behind me. I'm being paranoid, but I'm a single woman living and working in New York. Situational paranoia is a survival instinct.

I spot Ted, but the first man is standing right outside the elevator, looking around as though he's lost. This part of the first floor is pretty straightforward. Visitors desk, the gift shop, elevators, and snack cart. There's one door outside. When Ted steps forward, the guy pretends not to watch where he's going and shoulder checks Ted. I watch to see if they pass each other something.

I glance down at my phone as Ted steps on. I pull up Finn's contact. I didn't like how that man got physical with my guard. It makes me even more apprehensive. I'm certain that was no accident.

"Are you all right, Dr. Gallagher?" Ted's checking his suit coat pocket, then his pants pocket. He pulls nothing out, but it reassures me he's checking. He must have thought it was odd, too.

"Yeah. That man was weird. He didn't have a hospital ID, and I didn't see a visitor sticker either. He got on at the fourth floor. The other two men were doctors, but I don't know them. They got on at the third floor."

"Yeah. I saw the elevator numbers pause at each stop."

I've already pressed the basement button. I rarely have to come down to the morgue. I can't remember the last time I did. The only dead bodies I've spent much time with are the cadavers in med school. The babies we lose sometimes are still babies to me.

I scan my badge to open the massive security doors. Ted holds it open for me as I step forward. I know he has two guns holstered under his arms because I saw them this morning when he checked in with me. Finn explained on the way here from Dillan's house that they have connections at the hospital that let them bypass regular security and bring their weapons inside.

I look around, but I see no one. This isn't exactly the busiest place in the hospital. And that's just as well. I push through another set of doors that aren't secured. I still see no one.

"Dr. Wazir?"

I call out to the pathologist I know works down here a lot. She's more likely to page me than the medical examiner. Maybe not.

"Dr. Moffet?"

The ME doesn't respond either. No one just wanders around down here, so why doesn't someone respond? I head to the room where I know they take neonates— newborns —and the stillborn. I hate coming down here. Like with the fiery passion of a thousand suns when I think about that. I cried after every visit down here during my first year of residency.

"Ted, I don't know who paged me or why." I look up at my guard, who's scanning the area, doing a three-sixty.

"Should we leave, Dr. Gallagher?"

"Let's check two other places. This is bizarre." It's graduated from strange.

I check the doctors' office and the autopsy room. No one. We head back to the elevator, and it dings before Ted or I can press the button.

"Dr. Gallagher, what are you doing down here?" At least Dr. Wazir greets me with a smile. I see she ran to get lunch.

"I got a page to come down here, but I don't know why."

"I didn't page you, and Dr. Moffet isn't in today."

The hairs on the back of my neck go up again. I pull my pager from my scrub pants' waistband and show it to my colleague. Sure enough. The message is to come down here. I didn't misread or imagine it.

"I don't know who sent that, but I didn't need you or any of the neonatologists. So that wasn't meant for someone else either."

What more can I do than nod? "Thanks, Khadija."

"No problem. Have a good day."

"You, too." What the fuck is going on?

Ted and I ride up to my floor together, and he asks me two more times if I'm all right. I'm not, but I smile anyway. I head into an unoccupied postpartum patient room rather than straight into the NICU and close the door behind me. I unlock my phone and tap on the screen.

"*Cailín*, how are you?"

"Finn, I'm a little freaked out."

"What happened? Where are you?"

Well, that wasn't the smartest way to start a conversation with a man like Finn. I'm certain I just heard chair legs scraping a floor.

"I'm all right, Daddy."

I pray I'm not on speakerphone, and I look over my shoulder in case the door magically opened.

"Then what do you mean you're freaked out?"

"I've gotten four pages today that have sent me on a wild goose chase. They're all to places with someone dying or already dead. But no one at any of the units or the morgue paged me. I don't know who is."

"The morgue?"

"Yeah. The first three pages were to patients in distress or had just died. The one to the morgue is obvious. Ted went to the basement with me. But I met him on the first floor. A guy got on the elevator a floor below me with no hospital badge or visitor sticker. He bumped into Ted as Ted headed toward me. I watched. They didn't exchange anything, and Ted checked his coat and pants pockets. Nothing."

"How did you and Ted wind up on separate floors?"

"I didn't plan to leave the NICU, so he'd just gone down to grab lunch from the food cart. He didn't even get a chance to pick something."

"I'm sending Sean." Something muffles the phone. "Sean!"

"You don't have to send anyone else. Ted is fine. I'm certain—"

"Do not finish that sentence, *cailín*. I'm sending my brother because this shite is fecked-up. And I trust Ted, but only for now. I always trust my brother. I can't come because I'm in the middle of something, but Sean can. I want Sean on the same floor as you until Cormac or Seamus can relieve him tonight."

"They're going to be super bored."

"I don't give a flying feck. This is not normal, Thea. Accept my brother and cousin or call out sick for the rest of your shift. You are not staying there without a family member guarding you."

"Ted is your family."

"You know what I mean. Please, trust me about this."

I sigh. "I do. I'd feel way better if your brothers or cousins were here. But I feel guilty making them babysit me when they'll just sit around for hours in an uncomfortable waiting room."

"They are not babysitting you. They don't see it that way. I don't see it that way. You shouldn't see it that way. Little one, I take this as a threat to you. Maybe it's nothing, and I'm being unreasonable and completely overreacting. But I won't chance it. You mean too much to me to ever ignore something or someone who could harm you."

"Thank you, Daddy. I appreciate it."

"Always, *cailín*. Hang on for a sec."

I hear more muffled voices, so I assume he's speaking to Sean. He uncovers the phone, but not before I hear a language I don't understand.

"You still there, little one?"

"Yeah. What were you just speaking?"

"Irish Gaelic. We're all fluent."

I didn't expect that. But it doesn't take a genius to figure out why they'd speak a foreign language, and especially one that's sorta obscure. How many people in America speak Irish?

"Useful. Please tell Sean I should be on the fifth floor when he gets here. Have him call or text if he has any problems getting in."

"I will. I'll make sure he lets you know when he gets there."

"Thanks. And I'm sorry I started the conversation the way I did. I didn't mean to upset you."

"I know you didn't. I'll try not to stop you going places or doing things you want. I never want you to feel suffocated or controlled outside of sex, but there might be times when my protectiveness is over the top. Just know it's because I have a good reason."

"I know. I'm still new to this, so I'll follow your lead. It's why I called you."

"I'm glad you did. Call me back if you need anything else."

"Okay. I'll talk to you later."

"Bye."

"Bye." I feel better.

Or rather, I'm minimally uneasy now that I've spoken to Finn. I still feel badly that Sean's going to be bored out of his gourd. But I know he's been a bodyguard for the other women in the family. He's probably used to it.

"Medical Alert, Code Pink, fifth floor, postpartum, bed six."

What the fuck?! That's my patient.

I yank open the door and look around. The sirens and lights are flashing, and hospital armed security burst through the door. Code Pink is newborn abduction. The babies are basically Lowjacked. They have a bracelet around their ankles with a sensor that alerts the charge desk if a baby passes through a unit doorway. You can't just take a baby anywhere. The nursery is only for special cases short of going to the NICU, which is down the hall from where I am now. Babies room in with their mothers. There's no reason for an infant to leave this unit unless they are going for a special procedure or going home. Their alerts don't go off for that.

"Suze, what happened?" I yell over the sirens when I spot the charge nurse.

"The mother wheeled the basinet into the bathroom when she showered. She stepped out, and the basinet was gone."

"The bracelet?"

"On the floor."

I look back toward the doors. Family members are sticking their heads out of rooms and milling around the hallway. Babies are wailing from the noise, and I'm certain parents are terrified. It's organized chaos as the safety protocols are put in place for the entire hospital. This could be a non-custodial parent abduction, a premeditated abduction, or— I don't even know —crime of passion abduction?

I take two steps toward the patient room since that baby was under my care at birth. Everything checked out, so I'm no longer her doctor. I still consider her a patient.

"Dr. Gallagher?"

I turn toward a woman holding her baby, jiggling it as she calls for me. The baby isn't moving. Not flailing. Not crying. Not twisting their head.

"Suze, with me!" I practically have to scream as I run below a speaker.

I lift the newborn from his mother's arms and take him to the basinet. The infant is turning blue. I pull my stethoscope from around my neck as I run my gaze over the baby. The heartbeat is irregular, and the breathing shallow. The nurse comes in with a cart that includes oxygen. I get the mask fitted around the tiny head. I keep listening to the heart as I run my hands over the fragile arms and legs. I press with two fingers on the abdomen.

The heartbeat grows steadier and stronger. The breathing remains labored with nostrils flaring with each inhale and quiet grunts, but a healthy color is coming back to his blue-tinged face, arms, and legs. I hear the parents asking what's happening, but I don't stop to answer them. Something made this baby nearly stop breathing. I can feel the muscles pulling in around the ribs with each breath, which concerns me. This little one isn't fully out of distress yet.

Suze and I keep working for another five minutes until I'm more confident the infant is stable, but I explain to the parents that their baby needs to go to the NICU for more observations than we can provide in their hospital room. I hate giving that piece of news. I know they feel like their world is crumbling because the unknown is unquantifiably terrifying right now.

I hurry to catch up with Suze and the baby. Examining and running tests on the little boy consumes the next two hours. I'm finally satisfied that he's stable and recovered from a BRUE— brief resolved unexpected event. I have no idea what happened with the abduction. I barely looked down when Sean called. I pulled out my phone long enough to send a thumbs up text back to him. He must hear what's going on inside, so he knows I'm not ignoring him or being flippant.

I head back to the charge desk with my surgical cap in my hand as I blow out a long breath. I look around, and you'd never know there was a crisis earlier. It's like everything is back to normal. That wouldn't be the case if the abduction was unresolved.

"Terence, what happened?" I stop at the desk and ask a nurse.

"It was a false alarm."

"How? I heard the monitoring bracelet was on the floor."

"It was. Apparently, it was too loose and slipped off."

Bullshit.

"Where was the baby?"

"In a crib in the nursery."

"What? How?"

Occupied basinets have stats on a whiteboard at the foot of them. That would mean there was one too many babies in there if a basinet with no information had a patient.

"The baby who belonged in the basinet— a little boy —was under the bili lights. The baby in the basinet was a girl. She had a birthmark one nurse recognized and knew who she was."

Bilirubin lights— phototherapy for jaundiced babies. That makes sense about an unoccupied bed, but that is— I don't even know. We have one of the best birthing centers and postpartum care units in the state. These types of accidents don't just happen.

I thank him and head to the doors that lead to the lounge outside the unit. I spot Sean immediately. Red hair helps. His back is also like twice as broad as the chair. He has his laptop and looks up when the doors open. He stands as I walk over.

"What happened?" He keeps his voice low since we aren't alone.

"An abduction, or rather a misplacement. A baby went missing from her basinet while the mother was taking a shower with the basinet in the bathroom. Apparently— and I don't believe this for a second —the monitoring bracelet slipped off. The baby wound up in the wrong basinet in the nursery. I just found this out because I had my own patient in distress for the past two hours."

"Are they both okay?"

"My patient is stable and awaiting test results. As far as I know, the— misplaced— that sounds as horrible as it is — baby is back with her parents. I have ten minutes before I start rounds. I'm going to grab a Coke Zero and a candy bar. Would you like anything?"

"Where do you have to go for that?"

"Down the hall to the next unit. Just before you get to it, there are three vending machines."

Sean looks in the direction I point. You can't see the machines from here. He's holding his computer, so he grabs the bag.

"It's just down the hall, Sean."

His look tells me not to even bother.

"Thank you for coming. I didn't handle things well when I called Finn. I should have tempered my wording a bit."

"No. You did the right thing. It would have worried him more if those four pages didn't upset you. He knows you're taking your protection seriously, which means one less thing to worry about for him while he sorts out who threatened you."

"Did he tell you I didn't want to bother you with coming here to sit around and do nothing?"

"I wasn't doing nothing. I was working. I had stuff to do on my computer, and I was guarding you. Ally, we used to call Finn 'Doubting Thomas' when we were kids. He believed nothing without proof. It makes him a stellar mathematician. He excels at investing and playing the Stock Market, and he can root out any accounting discrepancy dating back to the Renaissance. He trusts very few people to begin with. There are eight men he trusts your safety to with no reservation. Shane, me, Cormac, Seamus, Dillan, our dad, and our two uncles. Dillan feels the same way about Mair. My dad and uncles feel the same way about my mom and aunts. We may allow other men to guard you when we're certain the situation is under our control. The moment it's not, the family circles the wagons. You're protected now just the same as my mom, aunts, and Mair. Nobody considers guarding the women who mean the most to our family as doing nothing."

We stop in front of the vending machines, and Sean pulls coins and a couple dollar bills from his pocket. I do the same, and he shoots me the same look as earlier.

"What would you like besides the Coke Zero?"

"A Twix, please."

"That's it? I'm having a Twix, a Snickers, and Reese's Peanut Butter Cups." He grins unrepentantly.

"And you work out twice a day."

"I think you earned at least two treats today." He hands me the Twix and waits. His grin is contagious.

"The pretzel M&Ms, please."

He gets his own snacks after handing the candy and soda to me. We walk to the lounge in silence as we eat. Chocolate really is the soul's best medicine. That and cheese.

I finish my snack and head back into the NICU at the opposite end of the hall from the vending machines. Things are quiet for the rest of the day and the next. I still can't shake the dread over the four pages, and the pessimist in me wonders if the Code Pink was a way to get at me. My respiratory distress patient has a potential nerve disorder, but we need more tests to diagnose that definitively. I'm dead on my feet when I head into the break room for a nap. It feels like a million years ago—not two days ago —that I was soaking in the tub with Finn.

I still can't shake the one question that's been plaguing me. What the fuck is going on?

Chapter Nineteen

Finn

Is someone trying to get to me through Thea? Does Corey's reach extend as far as the hospital?

The hospital still uses an encrypted paging service that doesn't run on Wi-Fi or cellular networks. That doesn't mean it isn't hackable. Sean said nothing to Thea while he was waiting for her, but he was already working on tracing the incoming pages. His own encrypted program allowed him to infiltrate the system and discover Thea's beeper log.

Someone accessed the hospital's system remotely. That's not how it's supposed to work. A doctor can receive messages when they aren't at the hospital, but they shouldn't receive pages sent away from the medical facility. There are a handful of people I know who have the skill to hack into a system and do that. The first who comes to mind is Lorenzo. Considering we've been trying to fuck him over lately, he's at the top of my list.

The next are Anton Kutsenko and Sergei Andreyev— the bratva. They have their Ivy League educations and believe that makes them both superior to all the other families' computer experts. Bully for them they went to UPENN where Sergei got into hacking. My baby brother went to Cornell, which has the highest ranked Computer Science program of all the Ivies right now. He's just not a showoff. Plus, he has that degree in national security and all.

And finally, at the bottom of the barrel is Joaquin. He's by no means an idiot or uneducated. He went to MIT, so he has the training to create the programs his family needs to fly under the radar for everything. He has plenty of experience hacking, too. His shortcoming is his impatience. He doesn't always dig far enough, and he can be sloppy. He's a D's get degrees kinda guy. We know he was at the top of his class, but he's a minimalist when it comes to effort. He sailed through his classes because he's naturally that smart. But when something calls for hard work, he bails or does a half ass job. I'm not convinced he'd attempt to disguise the call routing as much as what Sean explained to me. But I won't discount him by any stretch. The least likely answer is often the right one.

Even if we figure out the who, that doesn't explain the why. Why use Thea to get to me besides knowing it'll piss me off more than anything else? Is that the sole reason? What does scaring her or pissing me off gain them? Do they think I'll be rash and lash out without aforethought?

The questions are on a loop in my mind as I run payroll for all our businesses. If other people didn't depend upon me to get paid accurately and on time, I would have ditched this in a heartbeat and gone to the hospital. I would have been Thea's guard. But I don't have the luxury of being irresponsible like that. Not like *Tres J's* or Carmine— that shitbag. He might appear like he's repentant and matured, but he's still a big bag of arse. Spoiled and petulant since we were all kids. He may have gone to Stanford, but he graduated from USC— University of the Spoiled Child. He's an only, and his parents think the sun shines out of his arse.

How he convinced his wife to marry him is beyond me. He humiliated her at Salvatore's wedding reception about fourteen years ago. He fucked Maria's best friend in the restroom right before his uncle announced his betrothal to Serafina. He was straightening his tie and smoothing back his hair when he walked in. The girl's dress was barely back in place. Carmine and Serafina actually love each other, so it wasn't an arranged marriage after all. Fuck if I know what she sees in him.

Get your mind back on what matters.

Thea.

I have a list of suspects, but no evidence. Sean's still working on it and will keep going until he cracks it. He's the quietest of us, the slowest to anger, and the most patient. It means he's a fucking dog with a bone when he commits to something. Speak of the devil.

I turn from the entrance to my kitchen when I hear someone unlock my door. It's biometric, so not just anyone can come in.

"Hey. Cormac's at the hospital and in place. I don't know how Ally does it. From the moment I got there until the moment I left, she had maybe an hour off cumulatively. I'd be running on fumes."

"I knew she was amazing the moment I saw her. Did you find anything?"

"They originated from a burner in Trenton." What Sean says surprises me.

That's two hours south of Manhattan in New Jersey. "Do we know anyone down there other than the O'Briens?"

If we were a medieval feudal system, they would be our

vassals. They run Trenton because we allow it. We can't be all the places all the time, so we have lesser mob families oversee certain cities. Trenton is one of them. We had some trouble with them a few months ago. Besides fucking the Mancinellis over, we wanted the ATF and FBI off our case after the head of the O'Brien family disappeared. By that, I mean we held him hostage at our place in Staten Island, in the dark with the very least amount of food and water to sustain him, until we took him to the station in the Bronx two weeks later. He's sediment in the Long Island Sound.

People still make jokes about cement shoes and swimming with the fishes in the Hudson or the East River. We know the bratva uses the Flushing River. We prefer the Sound since it's wider and goes out to the ocean. Bodies might decompose faster in freshwater than saltwater, but they never go into the Sound as anything but ash or acid disintegrated sludge.

Sean shakes his head. "The O'Briens are the only ones who've mattered. But it's possible someone's getting froggy and thinks they can make a move on us. Maybe make us think it's the O'Briens."

"How connected are they to Boston?"

"We're all Irish. What do you think?"

Boston's like Mecca for Irish Americans. The O'Briens arrived in Boston around the same time as the O'Rourkes arrived in New York. They stretched themselves too thin when they tried to seize control from us here. They wound up with the O'Malleys taking Boston from them, and us kicking them all the way down to Trenton. They were lucky to survive because the O'Malleys weren't going to let them.

"Yeah, but they're watered down Irish. Their idea of showing Irish pride is ordering Irish car bombs for everyone on Paddy's Day."

St. Patty's to most Americans or even St. Paddy's to a few. Many Irish stick with just Paddy's Day. It's what we grew up saying. And as for Irish car bombs— yes, please remind all of us of the Troubles. Some fucker gave Mair a hard time at McGinty's one night after she'd had a few to drink, and her accent came out. The douche kept offering to buy her car bombs, not knowing she's married to Dillan. She lost a family member in an IRA bombing.

She finally lost her shite when he tried to touch her arse and called her a bitch for not taking the drink. She kneed him and was ready to break a bottle across his face if Shane hadn't intervened. Dillan heard the ruckus in the back, came out to see what was happening, and went completely ballistic. He grabbed the guy by the front of his shirt and practically lifted him off his feet while he shook him. The guy was still holding his crotch from Mair kneeing him. Dillan made him apologize to Mair, who laughed in his face and dumped the car bomb over his head.

He's banned from everywhere a syndicate family owns. We hate each other, and we've done some fucked-up shite to the women in one another's families at this point— even the saintly Kutsenkos. But an outsider comes near our women? We make sure everyone knows, and they get banned from bars, restaurants, and most jobs. That's how far our reach is.

Sean snorts at my last comment. "Watered down they may be, they still like to claim they're more Irish than the rest of us. Having a common last name doesn't make them more Irish. It makes them a dime a dozen."

"Find out what Gareth is up to now that his dad's dead." Gareth is a fucking Welsh name.

"And if it isn't him?" I knew he'd say that.

"It most likely isn't, but he could do with a healthy scare to keep him in his place. Are you still hacking the others?" The others— the other three families.

"Yeah. Still nothing coming from their usual channels. I'm certain they still don't know I found them. Not even Sergei and Anton." He rolls his eyes.

If Sean weren't basically a spook for his mob family, the CIA and NSA would beg him to spy for them.

"I need to deal with Corey. Rowan and Riley aren't an issue anymore now that Joey and his brothers are back. I want to fuck with Corey a bit and make him think I'll get him more pull with Ewan now that he's taken over from Rowan. Let's see how far the apple rolled from that tree. I'll make Corey think it's the price I'm willing to pay to get him to leave Thea alone."

"He has no idea he's about to die, and his club is ours, does he?"

"Nope."

Here in NYC, there's the Iron Order Motorcycle Club. Clean and dirty cops belong to it. Well, if they belong to it, they're not so clean. Tarnished and dirty cops belong, and they love a good rivalry. They'd eat this shite up about a gang from Boston being down here. All I would have to do is wind them up and let them go. That'd take care of the men who rode down with Corey.

I'd cause a fucking riot. I lost my shite over what Tony said about Thea. I'm not going down that road with a bunch of NYC cops going after club members from up north. That's not what this is about. This is about Corey going after Thea. I'll make sure he lives long enough for him to remain useful until I terminate our arrangement.

"You're sure Dillan's going to be cool with all of this?"

It's a reasonable question. Usually everything goes to hell in a handbasket when any of us get a bug up our arse and strike out on their own.

"Dillan's already given me the go ahead to do what I feel is necessary to protect Thea. He knows I'd stop if he ordered me to, but he knows better than to give that order."

"She is your woman, after all." Sean grins at me.

"I dare you to say that in front of Thea or Mair."

He pretends to shiver. "I'll pass. Where are you going to be if I find something new?"

"Corey is gauche as fuck. He got a hotel room at the Waldorf. I'm certain he'll have company, but I'll make sure the hookers are gone before he and I chat. By the end, I'll have him thinking Ewan's a chump he can walk all over. The kid's got brass balls, so that won't play out well for Corey's members still up in Boston. In the meantime, get Seamus over to Rosedale."

I own a bar out there called Connacht. It's named for one of the ancient kingdoms and one of the four provinces of Ireland. It's where our family hales from. Where the O'Rourkes once dominated. I can almost guarantee Corey's men will go to Queens to drink there since it's no secret it's mine. McGinty's is too popular for them to pull off anything. Rosedale is an affluent area where they'll stick out like a sore thumb if they go in their jeans and leather vests.

They'll do that on purpose because they can afford the overpriced drinks and would blend in if not for their clothes, tats, manners, and attitude. But it'll make them easier for Seamus and our guys to spot. As the owner's cousin, it'll make sense for him to be there since his red hair, freckles, and green eyes will make him stand out just as much as the bikers, but for a different reason.

"Anything you want Shane to do? Cormac's at the hospital for the night, right?"

"Yeah. See if Shane can relieve Cormac in the morning if I can't go. I'll call Dillan on the way to the Waldorf and see if he wants to deal with Gareth and the O'Briens."

"Sounds good. Be careful. Corey is fucking batshit crazy if he went after Ally when he knows you're together. That makes him unpredictable."

"I know." We turn toward the door. "Actually, can you have Shane look into Ted? Thea said some guy shoulder checked him at the hospital today. She didn't see them pass anything to each other, and she said Ted checked his pockets. Short of someone else I trust checking them, I won't believe they're empty."

"Sure thing, Doubting Thomas."

My little brother goads me, but he won't disagree. I know he wants nothing to happen to Thea, so he's not being flippant about her safety. He's just doing what little brothers do: being annoying.

We have people working all over the city for us. That includes the highest end restaurants, bars, night clubs, and strip clubs— many owned by our rivals —along with hotels, sports clubs, coffee shops, and cigar and vape shops. Anywhere people with money go to spend it.

It makes it easy for us to get access to places we shouldn't like a hotel's reservation software. It only takes a name for the woman at the front desk to give me a key card to Corey's room. I knock on the door and wait. I hear giggles. Gross. I knock again. Still nothing. Good. He's unlikely to be in a position— literally —to fight back. I let myself in and want to gag. The stench of sex fills the air. It's never pleasant when it's someone else's.

"Corey, we need to talk."

One of three women spins around and recognizes me. She works at one of our casinos. Hmmm. I didn't know she was moonlighting. Her eyes nearly pop out of her head. She runs to grab her clothes.

"We need to go. Now." She's whispering to the other women, but it comes out as a hiss.

"Let's chat on Monday, Stephanie."

She looks like she might be sick. I haven't taken my eyes off Corey since I recognized Stephanie, and she recognized me. I lean against the wall with my arms crossed, and my right ankle crossed over my left shin. I look smug and bored. I can tell because there's a mirror straight across from me. The women are still pulling on their clothes as they run from the room. The moment the door closes, and I see we're alone, I pull a gun from my shoulder holster. I make sure Corey can see I have the other one. I lift a robe off an armchair with my pistol and fling it at him.

"Cover your wee willy before I laugh and can't stop."

"What do you want, Finn? I helped your guys take care of Rowan and Riley."

"Yes. That was restitution for what you've already done to Thea. We still need to talk about staying away from her family and her. We didn't get to that last time. You were a little too distraught."

After I saw Corey at his home, I made another house call on the way to the airfield to make sure he understood I wasn't giving him a suggestion, but a command. He was practically shiting himself when I burst into his clubhouse and started shooting at shite on the walls and behind the bar. Then I started shooting at people until he ran out of the office. I turned my gun on him while my guys blocked him from leaving. I thought he was going to have a stroke from the way the vein in his neck stood out. That was before I discovered what happened to Thea at that place.

"You'd like to live. That means you must continue to be

useful to me. If you're not, then there's no reason for you to breathe. You sure as shite don't matter in Boston now that Rowan and Riley are dead. Ewan couldn't care less about you. If you want to remain relevant, I'd do as I say if I were you. Irrelevant shite gets forgotten when it's gone."

"Ewan knows the deal still stands even if his dad is dead."

"Have you met Ewan? No, it doesn't. He wouldn't give two fucks what his dad or his granddad did before him. He thinks he's going to breathe new air into his family. He thinks he's going to modernize them. And do you know who he's going to emulate? My family."

Rowan got some girl knocked up at sixteen, so his son is already twenty-seven, even though Rowan was only a decade or so older than me. We're all closer in age to Ewan than Rowan, but we can all remember Rowan as a whiny arse little bitch teenager.

I keep my gun pointed at Corey as I walk to the chair across from him. Blessedly, he has the robe on. I look relaxed and comfortable, but he knows better than to believe I am.

"Here's how it's going to go, Corey. You're going to ride your arse back up to Boston. You're going to see Ewan and tell him you heard we have another shipment coming through Belize with more kilos than the last one we sent through Boston. You're going to tell him you can get him an in with the Cardinals and the Dawgs since your members are so similar. You're going to tell him you're the only one who can make that connection. You're going to tell him it was the Viscusos who took out his dad because Rowan wasn't paying attention to anything but revenge for me taking back what was mine."

Ewan won't believe a damn word of this and will know Corey is lying. It's not that Corey is a shite liar. He's actually pathologically good. Ewan's an old soul. He's way smarter—

therefore, potentially a greater threat —than his dad and uncle combined. He and I are cordial, and he'll realize I did him a favor by bumping off his dad. He's been considering patricide for years. I took care of it for him.

After I let Corey set himself up, I'll confirm Ewan's suspicions that Corey is full of shite and that I'm the one who took care of Rowan. That's two favors he owes me for the drugs and diming out Corey. I'll make it a hat trick by letting Ewan fool his men into thinking he was the one who got that shipment off us. He needs something big like that early on to establish he's the new alpha.

"I'll do that for a price, Finn. Get Althea's father to accept my help."

I grin. "You are stupid, but you aren't that stupid. You went after my girlfriend. The only reason you're alive is because you're useful. But you are out of your mind if you think I'm letting you strong-arm Althea's family. You're lucky I didn't put a bullet through your empty head just for saying her name. The only price being paid is the one I'm collecting. Your life is worth what I told you to do. If you don't, then it's worthless."

It's been worthless since the moment he got Thea involved in his club bullshit. He just didn't know it back then.

"You're getting on your bike tomorrow, and you're going home."

I feel my phone vibrate. I dig into my pants pocket and pull it out. A quick glance tells me what I suspected. I tap on a photo and turn it toward him.

"*Alone.*"

I tack that on once I know he's registered the image. Seamus and our guys took care of Corey's posse. It means he'll be rolling back into Bean Town without an entourage. I'm risking him not making it home if the right people see he's unprotected. But I really couldn't care less one way or another. We'll find another way to make Ewan our bitch as payback for his father trying to fuck us over.

I shake the phone before thrusting it in his face.

"Breathe in the Gallaghers' direction, and you'll wind up just like them."

Chapter Twenty

Thea

I talked to Finn half an hour ago, and I feel a lot better. He wouldn't give me any specifics— of course —but he alluded to him reminding Corey my family and I are untouchable. He said Corey was already on his bike and headed back to Boston. I don't think I've ever had such a deep sigh of relief. I'm not convinced things are over with Corey, but at least he isn't in the same area code as us anymore.

Sean and Cormac are really sweet. They both got me food when their shifts ended. Shane's the one in the waiting area now. I wouldn't have eaten much more than the candy bars Sean got me if they hadn't. It's a full moon, and L&D has been crazy. Was it a full moon forty weeks ago? It's been a while since Labor and Delivery has had almost all their rooms occupied. Fortunately, I was only called in twice. The other neonatologist was called in once. That's what I call a good shift. Every once in a while, I go an entire twelve hours without a single call. I count those as miracles. They are few and far between.

I'm reminded every day of what a blessing it is to have a healthy baby when there is so much that can go wrong. It honestly is the miracle of life. I've never been opposed to having my own family, but this job certainly gives pause to that idea. I like the thought of having a family with Finn one day. I haven't met another man I seriously entertained that idea with.

However, the moment I contemplate it, I remember I wouldn't just get Finn. I'd get the mob too. The O'Rourkes would be wonderful in-laws, from what I can tell. But I don't want to imagine raising children in that world, knowing any sons would follow in Finn's footsteps. It's a bucket of ice over my head when I remember that. I want Finn the man, not Finn the mobster as the father of my children. That begs the question: will I sacrifice having kids to have a life with Finn? Right now, the answer is yes. Will it be the same in six months or a year? I don't know.

I know I'm getting way too far ahead of myself, but I have time to let my mind wander. I'm in the doctors' on call room and scrolling social media mindlessly. There are two other doctors asleep in here, so I'm remaining quiet. I needed a change of scenery from the L&D unit and the postpartum one. Just a few minutes to breathe. I haven't received any more inexplicable texts, and I'm grateful for that. It was freaking me out more than I wanted to admit.

When I spoke to Finn a little while ago, I admitted that. I know it bothered him that I'm still scared, but I felt better telling him. Not because I want him to worry more. Just the opposite. I don't want him to think I'm naïve and believe this isn't a big deal. I want him to know I trust him to take care of me and keep me safe. He also understands I need to relinquish that worry to him, so I can focus on work. I can't control what's happening, but he can.

I hit accept when I see an incoming call pop up. It's a colleague who's off today. He left a few hours ago. He was the other neonatologist who only had one baby to attend. I step into the hallway to keep from disturbing the two sleeping doctors.

"Hi, Drew."

"Hey, Ally. I was wondering if you could do me a favor."

"I'll try. What's up?"

"My in-laws just surprised us with a trip to Pittsburgh." Oh, I hear the excitement.

"Sounds—"

"Miserable. I like my mother- and father-in-law. It's the rest of the family that drives me batshit. But we're supposed to leave in two weeks for six days. I know you're on right now. I was wondering if you'd swap your shifts until I leave. I'll cover everything you have now, and you'd cover the days I was supposed to be on while I'm gone."

"Sure."

That's a no brainer. Finn wanted me to take time off right now, and frankly, hiding out at home sounds perfect. A bubble without the outside world would be terrific. I know I'm not entirely untouchable since someone put a brick through my window and fucked with me yesterday. But the brick happened before Finn gave me a security detail. And I had guards yesterday.

"Great. I can be in, in an hour. Does that work?"

"Do you want to sleep before you come back?"

He hesitates. "Yeah. But only two. The more hours I can cover for you now, the less I have to hear from Deena's family about me rushing back to work. They think big money for a doctor. They don't think patients who need their doctor."

"Sounds familiar. I get it." Sounds like Corey.

"Great. You're a lifesaver."

I chuckle. "No problem. It's actually great timing."

"Oh? Is everything okay with Skyler?"

The only time I've really taken off for more than a day or two is when Skyler's had procedures.

"He's doing really well right now. I'd like to spend the time with my boyfriend."

"Tony?" I hear his disdain.

"No. He and I broke up a while ago. That was a mistake. I'm dating someone else now."

"Cool. Well, I'll see in a couple hours."

"Great. See ya."

"Bye."

ME

> A doc just asked me to switch shifts with him for a few days. He has to see family in two weeks. He wants to cover for me now so I'll cover for him then. He'll be here in two hours.

Finn's the first person I think of. I'm excited to tell him. Not for any other reason than I hope we can spend more than a couple hours together at a time. When I think about it that way, I've barely spent much time with him. But when I have, it's always intense. He's intense. It always feels like longer, yet never long enough.

FINN

> That's great. I'll pick you up. Come out when you're ready. I'll switch with Shane.

ME

> I don't want to make you miss work

FINN

You're not

He sends me the kissy emoji. I send him the hearts for eyes one.

ME

Do you have a driver today?

FINN

Yes I plan to say hi to my cailín properly.

ME

I like that Daddy

My pager buzzes. I check it and know I have to go.

ME

Duty calls see you soon

FINN

I'll be picturing you in your scrubs and white coat SO HOT

Silly man. But it makes me feel great that he values what I do. That part of his attraction is that I take care of other people. Take care of babies. He values my intelligence and character as much as he does my personality and body. No other man has made me feel that wholly appreciated. I never felt like I was missing anything. But now that I have it, I want to cherish it.

The next two hours go by as I do my rounds, checking on the newborn they paged me about first. I signed off on releasing three babies today. It's been a one-eighty from yesterday. Things are looking up. When Drew arrives, we do the hand off. I hurry to change, then I push open the doors to leave the unit. Finn is on his feet immediately. Then I'm in his arms.

He gives me a soft but quick kiss. I'm still at work. He takes my bag and wraps his arm around my waist. I'm not shocked when I feel his gun as I encircle his. I rest my head against his shoulder while we walk to the elevator. I want another hug when we step on. I want to burrow against him. But again, I'm still at work. I have my badge on, and there's always the chance of running into people I know.

All bets are off once we're in the car. The ride from the hospital to SoHo isn't that long. But it's long enough. Our pants are around our ankles before Joey has the car in drive. When Finn moves to run his fingers along my pussy, I grab his wrist.

"I don't need that. I'm ready."

He guides me onto his cock, and we both sigh. I've always enjoyed the feeling of a dick entering me. But with Finn, it's like a spiritual experience. It's divine.

"I think you've missed me as much as I've missed you, little one."

"So much, Daddy."

Our kisses are sloppy as I ride him. It only takes a couple minutes for me to come. I can't get enough as he continues to bounce me on his cock, alternating it with the rocking I love. I want to make him come just like he did me. I want to know I do that for him.

"Fuck, Thea. I can't last."

He presses me down, pinning my pelvis to his. I know he's filling me with his cum. He's mine because only I get this. I'm his because only he gets this. Our kiss is slower, less frantic now. His hands roam over me. The back of my thighs, my ass, my back, around to my tits. All of me.

"Thea, I want to spend the next sixty years doing that."

I gaze at him, and he's not saying that figuratively or in the throes of passion. He means it.

"I want that too, Finn. If we're really going to think about doing that, we need to talk more about what our future would look like."

"You work with infants all day every day. You're worried about what will happen to our kids." *Will* not *would*.

"Yes. Mind reader."

"No. It's just what I've thought about ever since I met you. Daughters would only know it as something their father does. They would never be in the middle of the things I know you've guessed. I can't be sure about sons. It's not as simple. None of us wants to pass this life on to yet another generation. But to walk away means to turn power over to rivals we've dominated for generations. It would be a death sentence for all of us. There's nowhere in the world we could go that's untouchable. Especially not with the red hair. A fecking curse."

"A curse that makes you fucking hot as fuck. But yeah, I get it."

"I'm scared to bring kids into this world."

"Scared enough that you don't want kids?"

"I don't know. You?" I appreciate his honesty and can relate to his uncertainty.

"I don't know either."

"Maybe we never do, but could you picture the possibility that we would?"

I pause to consider that. I've been thinking about this, but now that he's posed the question, I don't have an immediate response.

"I can picture the possibility. I want a future with you, Finn. I want all the things that can go along with that. Kids are a maybe, but I'm nearly in my mid-thirties. It's something I only have a few more years to safely consider."

"At least we're equally unsure together."

I press another kiss to his lips before kissing his cheek. "We are."

"Do you have stuff you need to get done while you're off? Stuff you want to do?"

"Besides you? No."

He tickles me, and I can't help but giggle. I feel so light-hearted now that I'm with him. When he smiles, tiny lines form around his mouth. They're invisible when he's not, but they're slow to fade. I like it. He appears youthful because they aren't wrinkles, but it shows he smiles a lot. If he can find things to laugh and kid about despite what he does, then I'm relieved. I'm glad his mob life isn't so oppressive that he finds no joy in life. I worried about that when I first realized who he is.

We arrange our clothes as Joey pulls into the underground garage. Shit. I don't have any clothes besides two dirty sets of scrubs and what I'm wearing right now. I didn't think about going home first. I didn't even think about my place as where I want to spend time with Finn. A while ago, I wanted to curl into a ball and use my home as my protective bubble. Now I want to be wherever Finn is. Not just so I feel untouchable. I feel the weight of the world— life, work, family —lifted from me. He's my bubble.

"Little one, we never grabbed any of your stuff from your place. We can head over there."

"Mind reader. I just realized that, too."

"What do you want to do? We can go there. We can order what you want, and I can have it here in an hour."

Apparently, he's not shopping Amazon Prime if he can get one hour delivery rather than one day shipping.

"We can also walk around the boutiques near here. There are plenty."

Plenty is an understatement. SoHo has some of the best shopping in NYC since it's a commercial neighborhood. But I'm not a boutique shopper. I'm more order online or go to a department store. I can't rationalize boutique prices.

"Next day shipping will work. I'm certain I can find something online."

He nods and doesn't press me. Joey opens my door, and I slide out as Finn gets out on his side. I smile at Joey because I missed him while he was gone. I've gotten used to him as my shadow. I like his brothers and Ted, but Joey's kinda goofy. I know he's there to protect me, and I feel almost as safe with him as I do Finn. But he makes it feel like I'm walking with a friend rather than a detail. Ted, Simon, and Fallon come across as bodyguards. It makes me feel a bit self-conscious. I don't get the sense I stand out when Joey is with me. When the elevator doors close, Finn pulls me against him. As soon as we move, he presses the stop button.

He presses me against the wall as his hand slides under my shirt. He finds my nipple and pinches as he kisses me. When I try to touch him, he snags my wrist with his free hand. He moves it behind my back and keeps it there. I slide my other between my back and the wall. He lets go of my wrist, so his fingers can travel up my ribs, squeeze my breast almost mercilessly, then wrap around my throat. He doesn't squeeze. It just rests heavy.

"If I were a jealous man, I might wonder if you like Joey more than me. But I know my cum is in your pussy right now. I know there's going to be a lot more there and in your arse."

I know he's not serious. We're slipping into a dynamic I crave. I love that he's an alpha. He's not my Dom, and I'm not his sub. But I enjoy being sexually submissive in moments like this. I'm curious what he'll do next. What pleasure or pain he'll offer. What ecstasy or denial he'll give me.

"Daddy, are there cameras in here?"

"No."

"Are other people waiting for it?"

"Don't care."

"I want to suck you off right now. Right here."

His hand tightens around my throat, and he presses me against the wall to where I can't move. I feel how hard he is, so I dare to slip my left hand from behind my back— difficult to do with my weight trapping it. I cup his cock and run my hand down it until I feel his balls. I squeeze ever so slightly, and his hips thrust forward. He nips at my lower lip, tugging with his teeth. I stroke his cock through his trousers. He steps back, and I drop to my knees. I waste no time getting his cock out.

I lick the length of him until he's wet before I flick the underside of the head. Then I slide my mouth down it. I close my eyes, breathe through my nose, and tell myself to let my throat relax. I gag, and he pulls back. My hands fly to his ass and press him until I'm practically swallowing him. I glance up and see he's leaning against his forearms as he watches me.

"Fuck, Thea." I barely hear him as I continue to bob my head.

But it's not enough. Yes, this is a submissive act because I'm on my knees. But I'm the one who has him so hard that he's going to come soon. I could stop and leave him with a hard on and no relief but his own hand. I usually like knowing I still have that control when I'm giving blowjobs. But that isn't what I want tonight.

"Daddy, fuck my throat. Fuck it like a porn."

He groans as his hand comes to the back of my head. He doesn't press hard, letting me go at my pace as I slide my lips down his cock again. Then he holds me there. I remind myself not to panic, not to gag. He pulls back, then thrusts. He does it over and over, sometimes holding my head pressed to his pelvis in between. But he's not rough. He's not using me like he doesn't care about anything but getting off. He's enjoying it. There's no doubt about it. But he's not taking advantage of what I've offered.

"Thea, unbutton your shirt. Hurry."

I fumble but do as he says. I've barely got it open when he pulls out and fists himself. We watch as he sprays my tits. In a porn, the guy would have put it all over my tits and face. I even have my mouth open, but he doesn't aim for that.

He's panting when he finishes. He's staring at my chest, and I'm not sure what he's thinking. I slide my index finger through his cum and lick, then suck. He seems to only half notice that. He helps me to my feet. Then his kiss is almost too much. I was unprepared, so I didn't inhale. I'm pressed back against the wall like before. I don't know where this aggressiveness came from, but I love it because I know he's not doing it to hurt me. It's almost desperation— like he wants more of me or from me, but there is nothing more to give or take.

"When we get inside, I want you in our room, naked. Immediately, *cailín*. If you take too long, I will rip your clothes off you and leave them in shreds. Then I will have you naked for as long as I want. Do you understand?"

"Yes, Daddy."

He presses the start button, and the elevator lurches back into motion. His hug doesn't match the command he issued a moment ago. He's loving and gentle now. He kisses my temple before tucking himself back into his pants and making himself presentable. Though, I don't know why since his place is the only one on the floor, and he has biometrics to get into it. The elevator pings, and the doors slide open. Once we're in the condo, I kick off my shoes by the door and make a beeline for the bedroom. He called it our room, didn't he? I didn't catch that at first.

I'm pulling off clothes as I go. My shirt and bra get wadded under my arm as I unfasten my pants. I'm kicking them off as I walk into the room. An arm snakes around my waist and yanks me back. His hand squeezes my ass hard enough for me to go onto my toes.

"Such a good girl to not have any panties on."

"You told me not to wear them anymore."

"You didn't plan on seeing me today. You might have worn them, thinking I wouldn't know. You could have disobeyed me."

"I could, but I don't want to."

He lets go of me, but when I step away, his hand lands across my ass. Hard. I glance over my shoulder. Surprised and unsure what to do next. I turn to face him, then he prowls forward, backing me into the footboard.

"My cum dripped down your tits and dried on them. I could have come down your throat, made you swallow. I could have forced myself to slow down and wait until we got in here, and I could fuck your cunt or your arse. But I didn't."

"Why not?"

"I wasn't sure until after I'd done it."

"Why weren't you?"

"Because I had to see it to understand some primitive desire. You were being so perfectly submissive. Not because I told you to be. Not because that's how you are in everything. You did it to fulfill something you wanted or needed, but you did it for me, too. You wanted me to take control. Do whatever I wanted because I could. It doesn't take a psychologist to know I marked you as mine. But it was more than that. Seeing my cum on you did more than just confirm you're mine to protect and to pleasure. You were wearing the very essence of what makes me a man. You have all of me. You have me in a way no one else and nothing else can. I want you to have that. Recognizing how deeply I want that was heady— exciting —arousing. I don't remember the last time— if ever —I've wanted something so much."

That's a lot to take in. It shifts something in me. Something primal, too. Our relationship isn't solely about sex. But sex is our love language. It's how we've communicated things too deep to say since the very beginning.

"I have the next six days off. I have nowhere else I have to be, and nothing I have to do. Daddy, you have free use."

Chapter Twenty-One

Finn

Free use truly means just that. She would be sexually available to me for anything I want, any time I want. She couldn't decline. Even when I've done scenes or when I used to be with Heidi, it was implicit some things were off limits. There were things I discussed with my partners that were off limits. If she really means free use, there would be no limits. She'd have a safe word I would respect just like during a scene or any kinky sex we would have. But there'd be a lot more she'd have to accept that she might not normally.

"Thea, you don't have to do that because of what I said."

"I know I don't have to. That's why I want to. Finn, I know you will always give me a choice about everything. Even to an extent about my safety protocols. I know if I change my mind, you'll respect that. I know you'd never ask for something like this. I want to explore more of what we can do together. I'll confess that it's not entirely altruistic. It excites me to feel that desired. That you want me so much that you'll take me whenever the mood strikes."

"The mood always strikes." It's true.

"Can we start right now?"

I'm slow to nod because I still have reservations about this. I don't want to take advantage of what she's offering. And I don't want her to wind up feeling like a sex slave or sex doll I use like an inanimate object I play with until I'm done. But the idea intrigues me, and it sure as fuck is getting me hard again the longer I think about it. My dick might truly explode.

"I haven't been near you nearly as much as I've wanted the last couple of weeks, but I've thought about you nonstop. I've pictured us together nonstop. Not just having sex. I've pictured us falling asleep together and waking up together. I've pictured us on vacation together. I've pictured us at the grocery store together. I've pictured the exciting and the mundane. Sometimes when I picture us having sex, it's vanilla. It's slow and tender. It's more than lust. It's always been more than lust. But there are times when I picture us doing scenes together."

"At your club?"

"At a club. Not one I've gone to in the past. I don't want to see women from my past, and I don't want you forced into a position where you're reminded of it. You are my now and my future. The past taught me what I know, and now that's only for you."

"Do you know you say some of the most romantic things I've ever heard?"

"I say what I feel."

"I know. That's why I— want to be with you so much." What was she going to say when she paused?

"I've done some shopping, *cailín*. Some online and some in stores."

"I'm curious."

I step away and walk to my closet. I consolidated a lot into a couple bags and a box. I didn't want to freak her out if she saw what everything originally came in. I carry it all to the bed.

"I don't expect you to accept everything because I bought it. If there's anything that's unappealing, I put it away, and we don't think about it again unless you bring it up. I will do things to you in a physical sense, but I want this— the intimacy —to be done *with* you not done *to* you."

"I get the difference, and that's what I want too."

From the box, I pull out handcuffs and padded cuffs, a collar, a leather cat o' nine tails with smooth lashes and one with leather barbs on the lashes, a paddle with holes and one without, a flogger, shibari rope, nipple clamps with and without a clit clamp, a Wartenberg wheel, a box with an assortment of butt plugs, a vaginal plug, a vaginal spreader, a vibrator, a vibrating dildo, a vibrating egg, various gags, two spreader bars, and Ben Wa balls.

I watch Thea as I pull each item out and lay them on the bed. I see interest in all of them, but I fear I've bought far, far too much. She must sense my nervousness because she puts her hand on my forearm.

"How fast can we try everything?"

"There's nothing here that's off-putting or you fear trying?"

"Nope. I want it all."

I pick up the collar. "I will never make you crawl or follow me with this. I will use the leash to move your head, but that's it."

"And if I want you to use it as a leash? I'm offering you free use because I want you to have complete control. I want you to stop me from what I'm doing to do what you want. Go where you want."

"You know my desire is for you, not a desire to control you, right?"

"I do. That's the only way I would offer this or agree to it. You want *me*. You could do this at a club with someone else or have a sub if it was just about control over someone. I don't think I'm generally insecure. I think I've grown past most of it. But I think it's human nature to want to feel desired by your partner. I admit— my pride— ego —whatever —wants you to desire me over everything or anything else right now. That this only ends if you're called away."

"Don't tempt fate." I'm quick with that response.

I want nothing to tear me away from Thea right now. I never want to be apart from her, but especially not while we're sharing something like this that bonds us more than I've ever had with any woman and differently from how I'm bonded to my family.

"Are you okay with me being that needy, Daddy?"

"You're not being needy in the least. You're telling me as an equal partner what you want and need."

I move to the bag and pull out various pieces of lingerie. I glanced at her bras a few times to see if I could catch the size on them. I did. That's the only way I knew what to get. There are teddies, sheer camisoles, and bustiers. There's one thing there's none of: panties. The teddies have snap crotches.

"No panties, Daddy? Good."

She grins, and I can't help but offering her a ridiculously eager one back. It's fucking Christmas.

"What do you want to try first, little one?"

"You pick."

"I will this time. But if I ask again, it's because the way I want it is the way you say."

"Yes, Daddy."

I survey the collection in front of us. How the fuck do I choose when I've set up a Smorgasbord? I grab the handcuffs, the Ben Wa balls, a medium size butt plug and the bottle of lube I forgot to pull out, and the smooth whip. I snap the collar around her neck and pick up the leash. Leading her is fucking exciting. I feared how it would make her feel if I suggested it, but it's what she wants. I guide her around to the side of the bed.

"Lean forward, hands beneath you. Feet apart, turned in." My hand lands across her arse as she does what I say.

I appreciate the sight in front of me. She's exquisite. A round arse I can't wait to hold onto as I plow her cunt then come in her arse. Long legs likely toned— at least in part —from all the walking she does. A waist that dips in enough to hold her in place more easily. And I know there are tits beneath her I love to play with.

"I'm going to put this plug in. If it's too much once it's in, tell me immediately. You know better than most the risks with anal."

"I promise, Finn. You're trusting me just as much as I'm trusting you. I don't want to lose that. I know you'll feel guilty and refuse to risk harming me if I don't tell you if we reach one of my limits. I won't put you in that position, and I don't want to stop this. I want us to keep sharing more."

I lean over her and kiss between her shoulder blades. I've always been careful with past partners. But the fear that I could harm someone so precious to me is new and overwhelming. However, this is already an important part of our relationship and how we communicate what we haven't said. Feelings far deeper that most people would say couldn't exist between people who haven't spent nearly enough time together. Feelings that most people would say are just infatuation. It's not. I've been infatuated before. This is nothing like that.

I pour lube over the plug and onto her arse as I spread her cheek. I ease the plug into her and twist it three times. She says nothing, but she pushes her arse toward me. I oblige. I slap each cheek before helping her stand. I give her a moment, and she nods. With the leash, I lead her out to the dining room. I have the handcuffs, whip, and Ben Wa balls in the other hand. When we get to the dining room, I pull out a chair. Mine have a full back, but there is a slat at the bottom. I've never done this before because I've never brought a woman back to my place. It's my sanctuary.

"This shouldn't pull your shoulders too much. But if it does—"

"I know, Daddy." She twists and gives me a peck on the lips.

The temptation to hold her in place for a proper kiss is one I give into. I let go of the leash and wrap my hand around her throat above the cuff. I hold her in place as I devour her mouth.

"You are mine to do whatever I want with. I'll take what's mine whenever I want."

"Yes, Daddy." Her response is more like a sigh.

I steer her onto the chair, drawing her arms behind her back. I wasn't sure, but the bar is at just the right height. Her hands slip beneath it, so she won't have them trapped between her and the chair back. I cuff her, then walk around to look at her from the front.

"Spread your legs wide."

I pull her hips forward and tip them, so her cunt is open to me. I take the Ben Wa balls from their case and warm them between my hands. I slide them into her, rolling them and stroking her g spot with my finger. She wants to squirm, but she controls herself. That is until I rub her clit with my thumb. Her head falls back with a moan.

"Daddy."

"Needy little pussy."

I pinch her nipple, then pull my fingers from her cunt. I

pick up the whip I'd laid on the table while I cuffed her. I step to her right, and she turns her head to watch me.

"Eyes straight ahead."

I decide to stand behind her now that she's seen what it looks like when I'm beside her. I bring the lash down over her shoulder to her left breast. That one is more like a swish. The next is a real lash. I alternate sides and force ten times. I trail the whip down her belly to her pussy. I'm not gentle with this one, and she screams. I wait, but she says nothing. I do it again. This time it's a whimper. A third elicits a moan, so do the next seven. I put the whip on the table and walk away. I go to my office and sit at my desk, but I do nothing more. I can't think about anything besides Thea, and I don't want to. I stare at my watch until five minutes have passed.

I go back to the dining room, studying her expression. I watch her gaze dart to me once before looking straight ahead again. With no warning, I slap her right nipple. She jerks, and the skin darkens immediately. I do it twice more before I pinch hard enough for her hips to jerk off the chair. I stop immediately. I walk to the kitchen and fill a water bottle for her.

"Tell me when you need a break." I issue it as a command.

I put the bottle next to her and head to the bedroom. Fuck. I need to come. It tempts me to jerk myself off, but I don't want to do that alone. Thea can't get off, so I'll deny myself an orgasm just like I'm denying her. I could see her pussy dripping.

I'll always sleep closer to the door in any room we share. I will always be the first target, and I'll always be her shield. I pull the bedside table drawer open where I have a gun. There's always the risk someone could find the weapons I have scattered around my place and use them against me. But I know there's far greater risk that I wouldn't get one out of a safe fast enough. I'll have to reevaluate that if we have a family. I put the things not in use away in the drawer. Always in easy reach when we want them.

I snag the bustier before heading back to Thea. My eyes skim over her with more expertise than I will ever admit to her. I look for any signs of strain or unwanted pain. When I've cuffed men at the station, it's always been to exert pain. That's the last thing I want now. Mild discomfort, yes. That reminds her she has no control. But I don't want to harm her.

I use the key and unlock her cuffs long enough for her to stand. I rub her shoulders and run my hands up and down her arms. I offer the water bottle, and she takes a quick drink. Then I cuff just her wrists together. With a light tug on her leash, I bring her closer to the table.

"Lean over the table and bend your arms."

She obeys immediately. I bring the lash down in a figure eight over and over. I don't bother counting this time while I keep it light. I do count when I increase the force. I give her twenty, watching her dance from foot to foot. But she pushes her arse toward me every time I slow. I pause at fifteen, and she shakes her arse. It tempts me to deny her. But I don't want to deny either of us. I was still dressed when we walked over here. I toe off my shoes and drop my pants and boxer briefs. I'm certain I look ridiculous with a suit coat, button down, tie, and black socks on. Good thing no one— including Thea —can see me.

I put the whip back on the table and tap my cock against her arse, alternating hands while I get my jacket, tie, and shirt off. I will *never* wear just socks to fuck her. I tossed my suit coat on the chair where she sat, but I leave everything else where they fell. I help her up and release the cuffs again. I rub her shoulders and arms.

"Move them around." I don't want her getting stiff.

I'm stiff as a fucking plank, but that's entirely different. I cuff her again with her hands in front of her. I nudge her legs apart, knowing it's a challenge to keep the balls inside her while standing. I thrust two, then three fingers into her, stroking her and making the balls move around them. I don't stop her when she brings her hands up to my shoulder to brace herself. When I rub her clit, she rests her forehead on her hands. Her hips sway until I'm certain she's a second away from coming. I pull back, bringing the Ben Wa balls with me.

When I filled her water bottle, I also grabbed a piece of paper towel. I wrap the balls in that and put them on top of the lashes. She's trembling with need as I move around her. I pull her close to me. My hand on her arse, but not squeezing. I keep the pressure light. My kiss is tender. This is to soothe, not to frustrate. She tries to reach for my cock, but I press her hands away as we continue to kiss. Words I want to say but am too chicken shit to say are on the tip of my tongue. I won't back her into the corner and make her feel obligated to say something she doesn't feel. And I sure as fuck don't want to share how I feel and hear nothing in response. Or worse, some platitude.

"Come with me, *cailín*." I lead her to the sofa.

I fasten the lingerie around her ribs and admire the view. It pushes her tits up. Such temptation. I'll titty fuck her in this thing one of these days. I grab the TV and fireplace remotes from the basket they sit in. I turn on the fireplace even though it's late spring. It's cheery. We sit as I turn on the TV. I scroll the guide until I find something I think she'd like. I'm not a fan of crime thrillers since some scenes are a little too close to reality for me. But I remember something she said in passing.

"Have you seen this before?"

"No." She's watching me in confusion.

"Curl up next to me."

She does as I turn the movie on. I guide her mouth to my cock. I sit in a way that allows her head to rest against my abs, so she doesn't have to support the weight on her own. She sucks, but I rest my hand on her throat.

"You're not getting me off. You're warming my cock. Lie here with it in your mouth. Suck only if you feel me getting soft."

Not that I will with it in her warm satiny mouth. I twirl her plug and ease it in and out as the movie starts. I move to stroking her arse.

"Play with yourself. But if you come, I will cuff you to that chair and leave you there for a long, long time, little one. You come only when I give you permission, and I make you come."

She nods as she moves her hands to her cunt. I watch her fingers play with her clit, rubbing and pinching. I look down at her with my cock in her mouth and eyes closed. This is domestic tranquility in a way I never imagined. I keep stroking her arse as she pulls her fingers away and shudders with need. Self-denial is as powerful as me edging her. She goes through the same thing twice more.

"You can stop rubbing your clit." I'm certain she hopes I'll relieve the ache.

My free hand strokes her temple until I feel her body go completely lax. There's a box of tissues on the coffee table in front of me. I pull the plug out and wrap that in the tissues. My cock is still in her mouth. Asleep, she's sucking. I'm going to come if we stay like this. I ease her off, but she doesn't stir. She's exhausted, and I knew she was. From work and then what I just put her through. I couldn't give two shites about the movie. I pull the blanket from the basket beneath the table and shuffle us until I'm lying on my back with Thea draped over me. I cover us, and I'm asleep within minutes.

I'm awake within seconds when she jerks and screams. I reach for the basket that had the blanket, knowing there's a gun inside. I pull my hand back and scowl as Sean and Shane spin on their heels and face the door.

"What the feck are you doing here?"

I help Thea sit up with the blanket around her. I wouldn't care if my brothers saw me naked if I wasn't with my girlfriend. We shower at the station, and it's not like we each have a private bathroom. Once I'm certain Thea's covered, I rush over to grab my boxer briefs and pants.

Shane speaks as I dress. "We swung by to drop those contracts off. We didn't know you were home. We would have knocked if we had."

"We're sorry, Thea." At least she gets an apology.

"Same rules as Dillan." They know from my tone as much as anything else that this is not negotiable.

We've always had an open-door policy at each other's homes. Since none of us bring women home, it's never mattered. But ever since Dillan and Mair got together, we call from the driveway when we arrive at their place. The guys are going to have to call from the lobby.

"Got it." I know they both spoke, but to anyone else, it's one voice.

Thea looks at me over her shoulder. Her eyes are wide. It's not embarrassment. At least, that's not it. There's fear, and I don't like that. I don't think it's fear that my brothers will hurt her. It's fear of what they'll think of her and that they might see her less than half dressed.

"Wait in my office."

It's at the other end of the loft from our bedroom. They head in one direction while I scoop Thea up in my arms. She leans to whisper.

"The plug, balls, and whip. They've probably already seen them."

Ah. Not embarrassment and fear. Utter mortification. I lean for her to grab the tissue wrapped plug with her cuffed hands before I walk to the table. She grabs the balls, their box, and the whip. Fortunately, the handcuff key is in my pants pocket. I hurry to our bedroom and kick the door closed behind me.

"*Leanbh*, I had no idea they would come over. Those contracts arrived a day early. They never would have walked in if they knew you were home, too. I'm so sorry. They understand what I mean about the same as Dillan. No one is allowed to come in until they've called up to be sure we're decent. If they don't reach me, they'll call you."

I put her down on her feet and hurry to unfasten the cuffs. She drops everything she was carrying onto the dresser. My brothers can fucking wait until I'm ready to see them. But I want Thea free of anything that reminds her that my brothers saw her in such a compromised position. From the elbow to my chest that woke me, I know she'd raised her arms above the top of the blanket. That means they saw them.

She cups my cheeks. "I'm home too?"

I didn't realize I said that. She rises onto her toes and gives me one of those kisses that makes me forget the world around us but also convinces me I'd burn it all to the ground for her. I pick her up, this time with her legs around my hips, and walk her to the bed. I lay her down just long enough to get my fucking pants and boxer briefs down. I'm inside her with a single thrust. Then there's no stopping us now. It only takes a few thrusts to get her off, but I keep going. I want to feel her come again before I do.

"Daddy, come."

"After you, little one."

"With me. I'm so close. I—"

She tenses and arches beneath me, her hands squeezing my arse. I can't hold back. I empty myself into her. Then I'm smattering kisses along her jaw and up and down her neck and behind her ear.

"Yes, you're home. I want you to be as comfortable here as you are at your place. I hope one day your place and my place are the same place."

She strokes hair back from my forehead. "I want that too. And soon. Not because I need your protection. I know you'd post guards around my condo to protect me. I don't want to go home to an empty apartment. I want to come home to you. I want to be home when you get there."

"You don't feel rushed?"

She glances toward the door, knowing my brothers are waiting. I still don't care.

"Thea, they're interrupting us, not the other way around. If it were urgent, they would have said so. Do you feel rushed?"

"No. If anything, it's like things are moving too slowly." She hesitates for a moment. "Do you believe in soulmates?"

"Yes. One hundred percent. My parents are proof. So are Dillan's and Cormac and Seamus's. Three sisters married three brothers. It's not like it was a triple wedding. But there's no denying each couple was meant to be together. I see how Dillan and Mair are together. They're like his parents and mine. I've seen eleven other syndicate marriages. Each couple is undoubtably soulmates. You can't enter a world like this as a wife if you don't commit to your partner to your very marrow. A couple can't survive this life if they aren't. It would tear them apart and leave them both in shambles. I wouldn't have brought you within a mile of me if I doubted you're mine."

"I wouldn't have come within a mile if I doubted you're mine, Finn."

301

"We've known each other a while, but we've had little time together if you were to count the hours."

"I don't think time makes two people soulmates. They are or they aren't. It might take time to realize it, or it might take a few minutes. I didn't fall in love the second I saw you. I did fall in lust, but that's not the point. I saw a lot of your character those first two times we were together. I've seen it over and over, and it's always been consistent. You're kind, generous, fierce, protective, dominating not domineering and you make me happy. I don't think it's infatuation because you're hot. I don't think it's infatuation because I want a bad boy, or I'm curious about mob life. You know my past. You know I should have run far, far away. I only want to run to you."

"When you're ready to talk about living together, I want to have that conversation."

"I thought we were having it right now."

She sits up, and I move out of her way. She scoots back on the bed but glances at the door again. I walk over to it and open it a crack.

"Is this going to take long?" I know they can hear me.

"Five minutes." That was Shane.

"Just need your signature." That was Sean.

I turn back to Thea. "Be back as fast as I can."

I want my brothers out of my place, so I can be alone with Thea. We need to finish this conversation, but I don't want either of us distracted by them being here. I grab my pants, shoving my legs into them before hurrying down the hall until I reach my office. Sean speaks up first.

"We are so sorry. We wouldn't have come in— wouldn't have come by —if we knew you were both here."

"Just call from now on. If you don't reach me, call Thea. She's— going to be here a lot."

Shane snorts. "You're moving in together, aren't you?"

"If we can get this shite done, I can find out."

Shane hands me contracts for an acquisition Cormac negotiated with some Japanese developers. No one would guess Cormac is a corporate lawyer, and Seamus is a criminal defense lawyer. It cost a fucking fortune to get them and Dillan admitted to the bar, but all three are freaking legal eagles. Dillan doesn't have time to practice anymore. I know Cormac's gone through this with a fine-tooth comb. If it's gotten to me, it only needs the numbers run. I skim until I get to the parts I need. My brow furrows.

"No. This isn't right. These aren't the terms Cormac and I offered. It looks like they're offering the amount we demanded, but they've insisted on putting it in escrow. There's no reason for that. It's not like we're going bankrupt, and they want to make sure we can afford operating costs. They know we want to turn it into a shell corp for now. I suspect they guessed we'll break it down and sell off shares to devalue it, then buy them all back at an even lower price. When people see the O'Rourkes buying— us, not a shell corp —they'll rush to buy back or buy in. The price'll rise, netting us the real profit. Not the chump change they want in escrow."

I pull my phone out of my pocket and dial Cormac. "Hey. This contract is bullshite. The escrow part isn't acceptable. Tell them they accept the original terms, cash in hand, or we make this a hostile takeover. And when I say hostile, I mean I will eviscerate them. They don't decide the terms. We do. They can take it. There's no leaving it. If they're taking it up the arse, so be it."

"This is why we have money stashed all over the place and are way richer than anyone realizes. I'll pass the message along." Cormac hangs up, and I look at my brothers.

"We'll go." Shane walks toward me with Sean in his wake. It's Sean who stops when he gets to the door.

"Pass our apologies along. We didn't mean to scare her. I called out your name as we came in because we didn't see you at first. As far as we're concerned, we saw nothing."

"So, there's nothing to remember." Shane turned around when Sean and I didn't follow him out of the office.

Always serious— even if they call me Doubting Thomas — Sean claps me on the shoulder and squeezes. "She's good for you. She's your Mair. Don't feck it up. We like her."

"For feck's sake, could you speak any louder? I thought Seamus was the fecking foghorn."

"I want her to know we like her." Sean grins, and I could throat punch him. It's the smug one he'd give me when we were kids, and he and Shane got away with shite I couldn't as the oldest.

"I'm the one who drank the last of your twenty-seven-year-old Redbreast."

"You fecker. You let me think that was Cormac!"

"I know. He was being annoying about something I can't remember. You'd annoyed me about being a tight wad when we were at Bushmills during Dill and Mair's honeymoon. You wouldn't stop giving me shite that I was only willing to pay for the twelve-year-old and not the twenty-one-year-old. I didn't like the older one. It wasn't the money."

All five of us went as security for Dillan and Mair while they were on their honeymoon. We were discreet and tried to always give them space while being close enough to guard Mair. Dillan should be our top priority as our leader, but the women will always come ahead of any man. We're trained, they aren't.

"Sure." Shane tags in.

"Feck off. I have a beautiful woman waiting for me. You have each other. Get out."

I flap my hand in the front door's direction. They give me

that matching shit-eating grin. I have two fists for those two throats. They let themselves out, and I head back to the bedroom. Thea's on her phone when I walk in. I raise my eyebrows with concern.

She smiles and gives me a thumbs up.

"Okay, Mom. I gotta go. Finn's done talking to his brothers."

"Everything okay?"

"Yeah. Skyler had a cardiologist appointment this morning. No news is good news. The doctor said things are the same as last time. For us, that's a plus."

"Do you ever go to the appointments with your brother and his husband?"

"Sometimes. But rarely, since I never want their doctors to think I'm second guessing them. I only go when I know it's going to be terrible news. News I suspected but couldn't confirm. Their doctors are excellent both with treatment and with parents, but it's terrifying. Sometimes it's just nice that they have a sister who's a doctor to interpret or reiterate what their physician says."

I climb onto the bed, then lift her onto my lap. She still calls me Daddy, but I like her on my lap purely for the physical closeness, not because I think either of us feels she's younger than she is.

"One thing I appreciate most about you, Thea, is you understand family comes first. Sometimes that's hard to do, but it's what you value and want. You get why I feel the same."

"I do. And that's a big part of why I fell for you right away."

I run my hand from her collar bone, over her breast, and down her bustier-clad waist to her hip. I sweep along her thigh and back up.

"I want to do that when we're watching TV together. When we're cooking together. When we're falling asleep and waking up. I don't want to catch a few minutes in between shifts because you have to run back to your place to get things. I don't want to miss any of those minutes because you're on Staten Island, and I'm here. I want a home with you. If that means Staten Island, I think I can survive."

She elbows me. "It's not that bad. It gets a bum rap."

I cock an eyebrow.

"Keep that up, and I'll insist we live in Jersey."

"At least there's no possibility I'll turn into a Guido."

She nips at my earlobe and tugs. "I don't know. Maybe I'll make you into Rico Suave."

"Now there's a reference I haven't heard in like twenty years."

She laughs. "I don't know if there's a Russian equivalent."

"If there is, it's not worth knowing about."

Fucking pious, holier than thou bratva. The shite they've done to women might not have risked their lives, but it still fucked them over. They say women and children are off limits. They just mean no one will touch them. It doesn't mean they won't drag women into our business. Sean's digging points in a few directions, and Pasha is one of them.

"Seriously, though. If you want me to move to Staten Island because you like your place, then I will."

"It's a shoebox compared to here."

"And this place is ridiculously large for a bachelor. It's even too big for a couple. I got it because I could. And I am the best cook out of all of us, so the guys would come here. That's why I have the biggest TV."

"I don't want them to stop doing that because of me. That's the last thing I want."

"Thank you. They just won't drop by unannounced to use my TV or raid my fridge for leftovers anymore."

"You work mostly here in Manhattan, right?"

"I work from home most days. I go to our various businesses to run payroll, and I go to our construction sites to ensure the numbers equal the supplies the foremen claim we have and to check the equipment if they say something needs replacing. I'll go to contract negotiations too."

"So Manhattan still makes the most sense."

"Not necessarily. You work in Queens, and I can work anywhere."

"You already have this place."

"You already have your place."

"I rent. I doubt you do."

"No, I don't. But I grew up in Queens. I'm not opposed to moving back."

"That would be super helpful. At least being in the same borough. We don't have to be right next to it."

"There's Dillan and Mair's neighborhood."

Her eyes light up. Sold.

"If you think we'd find something there."

"Thea, I saw the excitement. Don't downplay it. We'll find what's right for us."

"What's your family going to think?"

"They already understand. Yours?"

"I don't know."

I open my mouth, but my phone buzzes. I check it and don't like what I see.

SEAMUS

Corey never left.

Chapter Twenty-Two

Thea

I can't see what Finn's looking at, but whatever it is, he's not pleased. His expression is neutral, but I can tell.

"What went wrong?"

He looks up at me, surprised. "How do you know something went wrong?"

"I can just tell. You don't seem as at ease as you did a minute ago."

"Seamus just messaged me. Corey didn't leave the city."

That's a kick in the gut. He's near my family. I'm not worried about him being near me because of Finn. But my nieces and nephews. That terrifies me.

"Thea, we still have guards for your family. I think your dad suspects something, but no one else seems any the wiser."

"What do you mean my dad suspects something?"

"My guys say he looks around a moment longer than needed when he gets in and out of his car. If he's with your mom, he makes sure she's half a step ahead of him to protect her back."

"He's barely in any shape to go anywhere right now." He should rest as much as he can.

"Before the accident."

"Accident my ass."

"I didn't want to freak you out and call it an attack." He looks contrite for choosing the wrong word.

"Thank you. I appreciate it. It probably would have freaked me out rather than mildly annoyed me. What's going to happen?"

"I don't know for sure, but I think it's time I met your parents. They need to know how you feel about me. Do they know about the brick?"

"No. They know Uncle Corey came by to see me and that he was going to go to Jamie's afterward. My dad would have lost his ever-loving mind if he knew about that."

"We need to tell them everything we can. If your dad rode with a club, he'll recognize who I am without me having to give my name. He'll be able to tell."

"How? You look like a totally normal guy who probably works on Wall Street."

"And that's what I like people to think. But when you know what to look for, we're easy to spot. He's likely well informed about the Boston mob. When he hears my name, it'll confirm any suspicion."

"I truly don't know how he'll react then."

"I'll stay by your side if you want me there. But if you or they tell me to leave, I'll wait in the car. I won't leave your parents' driveway without you."

"We leave together if it comes to that." I'm already feeling defensive on Finn's behalf.

"I don't want that. I don't want to come between you and your parents."

"Daddy, I know. We're planning for the worst, but let's hope for the best. When do you want to see them?"

"Do you want to invite them out to dinner?"

I glance down at my phone. They are probably cooking already, but maybe they'd come.

"I can try."

He kisses my forehead, and I melt against him. I pull up my mom's contact and put it on speaker as it rings.

"Hi, sweet pea."

"Hi, Mom. Is Papa around too?"

"Yes. We're just about to make dinner. What's up?"

"I wanted to invite you to dinner with my boyfriend. I know it's last minute, but we'd really like you to meet each other."

"Boyfriend?" That's my dad.

"Yes."

There's silence, and I don't know what to say. But I have to come up with something.

"Will you come if we meet you near your place?"

"Is something wrong?" That's my mom.

I glance up at Finn, and he nods.

"I know Uncle Corey hasn't left town. Did you?"

"Yes, he did. He told me he had to get back to Boston because something came up."

"He was supposed to, but he didn't."

"How do you know, squirt?"

I look at Finn again. He points to his chest then the phone. I hand it to him.

"Mr. and Mrs. Gallagher, I'm Finn O'Rourke. I'm Ally's boyfriend."

There's dead silence. I guess they both know who the O'Rourkes are. My dad clears his throat before he responds.

"How long have you been together?"

I chime in. "A few weeks."

Fuck that sounds so ridiculously short for the conversation we just had. We cannot tell my parents we're talking about moving in together. Especially not when they find out how much of those few weeks I've been at work. They will shit a brick.

"Mr. O'Rourke, how did you meet our daughter?" My dad's voice could chill an ice cube.

"Please, it's Finn. I come from a large family with a lot of men. It gets confusing. Ally came into my bar with friends a couple times. I approached her the second time."

"Sweet pea, haven't you been working a lot lately?" I know what my mom's hinting at.

"I have, but I see Finn between shifts whenever I can. Mom, that's not why we called. We want you both to meet Finn. From your silence earlier, I guess you recognize Finn's last name. We need to talk about Uncle Corey. I don't want to do that over the phone, and I don't want you to remain strangers with Finn because Uncle Corey has involved Finn's family, too."

"My guess is the involvement isn't new." My dad is pissed.

Finn might not be able to tell, but just like I sensed something bad happened before we called my parents, I know my dad's distinct tones.

"Mr. Gallagher, it isn't. Ally's told me about your family's past with Corey and his club. When he arrived in town, Ally—"

"Hold on. Finn calls me Thea, and I prefer it. It sounds weird to hear him call me Ally. I don't like it."

Finn is shooting me a look, saying this isn't the right time to poke an angry bear. I shrug.

"When he arrived in town, Thea and I had just started dating. Corey didn't know. He does now. He knows I expected him to leave New York and to leave you alone. He knows exactly what he's risking, and he's done it, anyway. Even if he comes nowhere near your family, I perceive his presence in the city as a threat to you. That's not okay with me. Like Thea said, we'd rather have this conversation in person. There's more to discuss, but a phone is not a good choice."

I was thinking I want my parents to see us together and that we're a normal couple. I think Finn means someone might be listening. My eyes widen as I stare at my phone, watching the seconds tick by. He squeezes my hand. When I look up, he shakes his head. He shoots me a reassuring smile. Does that mean no one's tapped my phone? Could it have been?

"I think that's a good idea. But this conversation will be better done in private. You two should come over." My mom's tone is as even as my dad's, but I know it, and I know we're entering a shitstorm.

"Okay. We can be there in forty-five minutes. Love you."

"Love you too." My parents speak at the same time.

When I hit the end call button, I realize I have no clothes here. I just have the jeans and shirt. I look toward Finn's closet, and I can picture the million dollars' worth of suits he must have in there. There's not a chance in hell I can convince him to wear jeans and a T shirt to meet them. I'm going to look so underdressed.

"If you don't want me to wear a suit, I'll just wear trousers and a button down. I'll leave off the tie if you prefer."

"I like the mind-reading right now, but it's disconcerting. I might not like it when we have an argument."

He kisses me, and I turn to straddle him. We're going to be

late. But I slide down his cock, which has been hard since he put me on his lap. We just sit together, connected as one.

"Your thoughts are your own, and I can't guess them all the time. Only when you're probably thinking what I'm thinking, too. I don't want to appear overdressed when you only have casual clothes. It'll look pretentious."

"We could say you came straight from work. You can't wear your gun without a suit coat."

"I wasn't planning on wearing it into your parents' home. I'd have it in the car, but I won't bring a weapon into someone else's home that isn't my family or doesn't pose a threat to you."

"Me? What about a threat to you?"

"Your safety will always be my greatest concern."

"You make it sound like you don't care about your own. I don't like that, Finn. That scares me."

"Shh, cailín. I have too much to live for now that I've met you. I won't be rash or irresponsible. I want to come home to you too much to get myself killed by not taking the necessary precautions. But I'll still prioritize your wellbeing over mine. I do the same for all the people in my family."

I nod. That's only mildly comforting. He pulls me in close to lay my head on his chest. My arms go around his waist, and he hugs me tighter.

"Daddy, I like this."

"I do too. I like how connected we are. There's no way to tell where you begin, and I end."

"We're discussing some tough shit right now. I need this peace I feel when we're like this. I always feel untouchable with you, but this is a whole other level."

"And I always want to keep you sheltered from the darker parts of my life, but being like this makes me realize how committed I am to that."

"Finn, can we try falling asleep like this some time?"

314

"I'd love that. I know we need to go, but we have to sort some things out before we get there. Do you want to do it in the car, or do you need a few minutes like this?"

"Yes." I smile against his shoulder.

"That doesn't answer my question." His chest rumbles as he laughs.

"We can sort things out in the car since it's a forty-five-minute drive. But I need to be like this for a little longer. Even though that conversation went better than I expected when it started, it was still nerve-racking."

He strokes my back, and I sigh. This has been an intense afternoon. I need to figure out another word to describe things with Finn. Intense is getting monotonous. But it was. The BDSM, his brothers, my parents. It's just a lot.

"I was going to drive us, but I'm going to have Joey come over."

"Why?" I sit up.

"Because we need to get going, but I want us to finish our conversation like this. We can't do that if I'm supposed to watch the road."

"I don't know that I'd fit between you and the steering wheel."

He picks up his phone, which he'd put on the bed when I made my call. He shoots off a text, and one comes back nearly immediately.

"He'll be here in ten minutes. You may need to text your parents and tell them it'll be closer to an hour."

"I know. I can do it once we see what traffic's like. I need to take a quick shower. I—"

"Still have my cum in your pussy. I know."

"There's that, but I also just want to freshen up after being at the hospital."

We head into the bathroom, and we force ourselves to have

a quick shower. It's tempting to have another round of sex, especially since Finn's still hard. I offer to suck him off or give him a hand job, but— with an aggrieved groan —he declines. Fucking responsibility.

By the time we're done and dressed, Joey's here. We meet him at the curb, and Finn slides in from the street side. The moment our doors close, he's pulling at my jeans. I'm trying to get his trousers unfastened. We abandon each other's clothes and get our own off. Then I'm back where I belong. His hands on my ass, cupping them as we kiss. This isn't a passionate one. It's one of our sweet ones.

"Do you want to tell your parents about the brick?"

"I have to. They're going to be angry I waited to tell them."

"Do you want to tell them the truth about how little time we've spent together?"

"No. No one else counts the hours they spend with the person they're dating. I don't want to do that with you. That said, maybe we don't tell them we're talking about moving in together."

"That's probably wise. And that doesn't have to happen immediately. If it'll make it better with your family to ease into that, then we will."

"It's not what I want, but that is the better choice. I don't know how your family will react."

"My parents would probably like me to wait to get to know you a little longer, but they already know about you. They know I'm serious about a future with you. I wouldn't be with you if I weren't. But they know this world and understand it. Your family is on the periphery."

"And if they ask you about your family business?"

"Then I'll tell them all about the legal ones and as much as I can about the other stuff."

"And when they ask me alone about the mob?"

"You tell them what you know and tell them you don't know more than that because I don't believe it's safe. Again, your family will understand that better than most."

"True. I know there's stuff my dad doesn't tell my mom for her safety. But I also know there's stuff he tells her he probably shouldn't."

"I think that's true about all couples in this world. I will always try to think before I speak, but I let it slip that I wasn't in New York. I trust your opinion and advice, so there may be things I ask you about. But it'll be nothing that could implicate you. It'll be nothing someone could force you to tell."

"How worried should I be about the cops coming to me?"

"Aware, but not scared. The feds caused some trouble for Mair, but it was always about getting to Dillan. The same happened to a woman involved with a Mafia guy."

"So, another woman in your family?"

"Don't let the Mancinellis hear you calling any other family Mafia. It hurts their feelings. They're quick to remind everyone that they're Mafia with a capital M. That they're the real ones since their family is from Sicily. They love to take a jab at us because we're 'only' the mob." He uses the air quotes and all.

"The rivalry even comes down to what people call you?"

"The Colombians are the Cartel. The Russians are the bratva. Sometimes people call both syndicates the mafia with a lowercase m, but no one in a syndicate does. Some of the lesser organizations call themselves mafia or mob, but that's because they have nothing better to call themselves."

I hear a hint of humor, but I think he's serious about most of that. I guess I can see why the way they identify themselves is important. Their reputation and appearances are important. I guess it's machoism. But I think it's also a sense of family. They identify as a unified group.

"Do I need to fear the other syndicates?" I think that's a valid concern.

"There's some recent history I need to explain to you, but this car ride might not be long enough. It won't paint my family in a good light. The abridged version is Dillan inherited his position from our moms' cousin who seized it after our uncle on our moms' side died. Dillan was out of town. Uncle Donovan was a pretty good leader once he listened to Dillan, who is a strategic genius. But when he ignored Dillan's advice and went after a bratva wife, it put our family on a slippery slope. Declan nearly destroyed us by going after the bratva again, but after a different woman. Shite we couldn't stop when my generation stepped into our full roles was already in play. We will always put *us* ahead of *them*, whoever the *them* might be. We did some unsavory shite because things we inherited were in motion we couldn't stop. At least we couldn't stop them and still come out alive. The Italians made some shitty choices too that endangered bratva women. They nearly got one killed in Greece. The Cartel's hands aren't clean either. They've gotten away with shite neither the bratva nor the *Cosa Nostra* know."

"*Cosa Nostra?*"

"It means 'our thing.' It's specific to Sicily. There are other Mafia factions in other parts of the country. You met Serafina that night we ran into Maria and Matteo. Her dad's side of the family is Venetian Mafia. Her mom's is Sicilian."

Fuck. That's a lot to digest. No wonder she watched me so closely. She's probably spent her entire life assessing whether people are a threat.

"So, the bratva and Cartel don't hurt women?" Double fuck. "That sounded horribly judgmental. I'm sorry."

"It's a fair question. Neither of them have clean hands. The Cartel's done shite that's endangered women, just not to the extent the Mancinellis and mine have. The bratva says they never target women or children, but that only comes to not physically harming them."

That doesn't reassure me in the least. The disdain in Finn's voice makes me wonder what the bratva did. It feels like it must have been recently.

"Are you going to tell my parents about this stuff with your family or the others?"

"I'd rather not, but if it's appropriate or necessary to, then I will. But you know I won't tell them more than I just told you. You'll learn more with time. That's inevitable. But I'd rather you find out in whatever context it comes up rather than me unloading it now."

I nod. I suppose that makes sense. But what if the context sucks?

Finn's hands on my ass have me rocking on his dick, and it's slowly building my need to come. Like having a vibrator on a low setting and just letting it buzz against my clit. It's going to get hard to concentrate soon.

"Do you think another syndicate has something to do with Corey?"

"Yes. I don't know who or how. But I can feel it."

"I think you better draw me a family tree for everyone when we get home."

His smile is pure happiness. He gives me a peck on the lips. I settle against his chest and run my thumb over his stubbled jaw. I'm happy too. In a sea of trouble right now, Finn's my life raft.

"Sounds like a good idea to me, *cailín*."

"Should I meet you parents soon?"

"Yes. I'd like to introduce you, and I know my parents would like to meet you."

If we didn't think we were serious before, it's getting serious now.

"I have the next few days off. If they're free, now would be a good time."

"Let's figure something out in the morning."

I glance out the window and realize we made great time. We won't be more than five minutes late, and my parents know any time given is an estimate when leaving the city.

"We're almost there."

"My *cailín* isn't wearing any panties. Does she want me to meet her parents with her cunt full of my cum? Does she want that secret?"

"She does. She wants Daddy's cum in her pussy and on her thighs."

We move together until I'm clutching his shoulders, my head tipped back. Fucking hell. Orgasms with Finn are unreal. Except feeling his cum on my thighs as we walk into my parents' house is completely real.

"Mom? Papa?"

I can hear them in the kitchen. Finn's standing beside me, so when he spots my father and Papa spots him, I can tell they freeze.

"I know your father, Thea."

Chapter Twenty-Three

Finn

I never guessed the man standing in front of me was Thea's father. I didn't notice any family photos in her living room the one time I went to her place. If there had been, I would have spotted them as I looked around after noticing the broken window.

Now Brandon Gallagher and I are staring at each other. I didn't know this man's name the two times we've met, and I don't believe he knew mine. When Thea's freezing hand slips into mine, and I feel the slight tremble, I pull my head out of my arse. I walk forward and offer to shake her mother's hand. Sandra isn't unwelcoming, but she looks less than thrilled to meet me.

When Brandon and I shake, there's definitely male posturing as we squeeze each other's hands far tighter than necessary. When Thea shifts restlessly next to me, I know she can tell what's going on. I release her father's hand immediately, and he lets go too.

I don't think she realizes what she's doing when her arm goes around my waist, and she turns in toward me. I think she's monumentally uncomfortable— more likely terrified —and needs comfort. I wrap my arm around her back and hold her against me. Her parents watch us like a pair of hawks. With my hand on the outside of her arm, they focus on my thumb that's rubbing her shoulder.

"Papa, how do you know Finn?"

"We met several years ago." He shifts his gaze to me. "You probably weren't more than a teenager either time."

"I was nineteen."

I'm staying tightlipped for now. I don't know what Brandon wants to reveal to his family. As our gazes lock, he understands what I'm doing. I'm not being recalcitrant. I'm letting him steer the conversation.

"It was one of the times Uncle Corey insisted I ride with him. You were already away at college. He was trying to recruit Rod to get to me. Your brother wanted nothing to do with it, so Corey sent some guys round. I got home in time to be the one teaching them a lesson. But the price of peace was being his muscle at a meeting."

He goes quiet, and I sense I'm supposed to share now.

"I was at a meeting with Uncle Donovan and the man who used to lead the mob up in Boston. That man and my uncle were like oil and water. It's why Corey and his guys were there. Uncle Donovan brought his best friend, a guy named Colin. The man was once a golden glove boxer. He went one too many rounds against Maksim Kutsenko, and it ended his time in the ring. But he was still an enforcer. Uncle Donovan also brought Dillan and me as muscle, too. Sean, Shane, Cormac, and Seamus were still too young. Our dads refused to consider it. It caused a heated argument, and it was our moms who made sure their brother understood it was bad enough our parents had to let Dillan and me go. Uncle Donovan loved to say no to any and everyone. But my mom and aunts were the only ones he never refused. It wasn't fraternal love. It was healthy sororal fear. He couldn't stand up to one of them let alone all three together. We get the red hair from them."

I can't help but grin. My mom and aunts are a foot shorter than all the men in our family. But fucking hell if Uncle Donovan didn't want to piss his pants when my mom or aunts stared at him. That was all it took. The few times I saw him try to say no to my mom and aunts, he regretted it. I don't know what they said to him because it was always behind closed doors, but he would come out a changed man.

I'm not supposed to know this, and my parents would flip if they knew all of us do, but my mom put a hit on one of his guys. She made sure the man lived, but not until she made sure Uncle Donovan understood she had the power to do that. The power to make his men obey her. So much for women not getting involved.

It was when Dillan and I were thirteen, and Uncle Donovan wanted us to go on our first mission. Granddad was still alive and leading the family, but Uncle Donovan had a lot of power as second-in-command— the position I hold now —so he thought he could force my parents. My dad and uncles beat the two men who tried to corner us after school to within an inch of their lives. That didn't satisfy my mom. She wanted to make sure her brother understood her son and nephew would join when our parents said we could. Unfortunately, that was only a little more than a year later.

"Did you talk to each other?" Thea pulls me back to the present.

"No. We stood across a room from each other. I remember asking Colin who the big guy was. He didn't say your name, but he told me you were a welder. That your arms are the size they are from smashing skulls on your anvil. If I'd been a kid, I would've believed him."

Even with the obvious injuries, it's easy to see Brandon isn't someone you want to pick a fight with. He's the same size as Seamus and Cormac. You'd never guess he's old enough to be any of our fathers. He looks like he's still in his early forties. As I stare at him, I realize something.

"I should have known Thea was your daughter the moment I met her. She inherited the same birthmark on her right forearm as you. With the slight Boston accent, I should have put two and two together."

"Obviously, I know who the O'Rourkes are, but since no one introduced us those two times, I didn't know then or on the phone tonight which one you were. I recognized you as fast as you recognized me. You don't look the same as you did fifteen years ago, but it's similar enough for me to know we'd met."

"When was the second time you met?" I glance down at Thea as she asks.

"I won't tell you that." I'm fast to answer.

I don't want Brandon to even hint at the situation. We were at a different meeting six months later, and I shot the man standing next to Brandon. But not before Brandon tried to put a bullet in me. I can't blame him, and I hope he doesn't blame me. That meeting went to shite because Uncle Donovan did the exact opposite of what Dillan told him to do.

"Ally, I won't tell you either. I wouldn't even if Finn weren't here, but if he says no, then I'm going to follow his lead."

Thea'd opened her mouth, but Brandon answered before she could make a sound. She looks up at me, and I see a flash of hurt. Then I watch the resolve come into her gaze. She doesn't pull away, but she stands a little straighter. Is she pulling away emotionally?

"If Finn doesn't think it's safe for me to know, then I won't ask. I can live without knowing."

My sweet, strong *cailín*. She wants me to know she won't demand information I can't and won't give. She wants me to know she's brave enough to accept this first challenge and go with the flow.

"Why don't we sit down?" Sandra gestures to the dining room.

The oven timer is buzzing. Thea offers to help her mom as Brandon and I walk into the dining room. He points to a chair, which I stand behind.

"Mr. Gallagher—"

"Brandon. I don't know your dad any better than I know you. But I knew about your family long before we met. I know about your mom and what happened with Randall O'Keefe."

He pauses for a moment, and I nod. Randall O'Keefe was the man my mom put a hit on. It shocks me that he knows about that.

"I also know your parents got engaged within a month of knowing each other, but they had to wait because they were only nineteen. Dillan's parents met first and were high school sweethearts. Your parents met through them, but not until a few years later. Same as your other aunt and uncle. They got engaged at the same time as your parents. If you're dating Ally, then it's because you intend to marry her, isn't it?"

"Yes. I wouldn't bring her near my life if it was just casual. I wouldn't do that to any woman, but Thea's—" I can't stop my smile. "I knew when I met her. She's the only woman I've ever wanted to let into my life. She's the kind of special you only meet once in a lifetime because there can only be one of her."

"Why do you feel that way?"

"She's incredibly intelligent. You can tell by speaking to her, then you find out she's a neonatologist, and that confirms it.

She's kind and self-sacrificing. She's patient and forgiving. I met the guy she was dating before me. She brings me a sense of peace I haven't had since I was a kid and was too young to know what my life would become. I tell her all the time that I will do anything to keep her safe. I will, and you know what that means. But I feel safe with her. I don't feel like I have to be as guarded. I'm not looking for what's going to go wrong at every corner. I can just be Finn, not Finn O'Rourke."

"She's all of those things. You said she told you about our family history."

"I know what Corey expects of her. I know that you're probably thinking she's jumping out of the frying pan and into the fire. That I'm not—"

Brandon holds up his hand as he glances toward the kitchen.

"I'm glad she's with you. Not because I expect you to shelter her from Corey, so I'm willing to look the other way. In the fifteen minutes you've been here, it's obvious you're both in love already. It radiates from you both. I didn't fall in love with Sandra at first sight. It took longer, but I see in you two what I see when I think about my wife. Ally trusts you, and to a man like you, trust is everything. Once it's gone, it rarely comes back. You won't betray her trust because that's not the man you want to be. I know the O'Rourkes more by reputation than anything else. That reputation is rooted in family. Nothing is more important to your family than one another. You wouldn't bring Ally into yours if you didn't feel that way about her and think they would accept her."

"You can tell all that?"

"There are things from my past Sandra will never know. That my children will never know. I'll tell you if I need to. I understand what my daughter is getting into. Motorcycle clubs aren't all criminal. But the one my family runs is. I've known the O'Malleys my entire life. People always assume it must be my mom's side of the family with ties to the Irish mob since she's white. They don't expect it to be my dad's since he was Black. My dad died of pancreatic cancer when I was fifteen. I looked up to my uncle, and grief nearly destroyed my mom. I did what Uncle Corey told me to because I trusted him. When my mom came out of her grief and realized the crimes Uncle Corey was forcing me to commit, she got me away from him. There was still a price— like an annual tax —for that freedom. He's still trying to claim it. To men like Corey, family are people to be manipulated and guilted into submission."

We don't have time to say more because Sandra and Thea walk in with the food. I lift a platter from Sandra's hands, and she offers me a warmer smile than I'd received in the foyer. I pull out Thea's chair, and she sits. But Sandra is still moving things on the table. I don't sit until she does. Thea's parents stare at me.

"My parents are strict."

That gets a smile from Brandon, a nod from Sandra, and confusion from Thea.

"I don't sit until all the women have. I stand when they do. They always get into the car first. And if I take the first piece of anything, it will be my last piece ever. My parents are old-fashioned."

"I think it's chivalry and courteousness."

If we were alone, I'd kiss her and show her just how courteous I can be when considering her needs. Instead, I grin.

The meal progresses, and I have a great time getting to know her parents. I think they've more than accepted me. I think they like me. But the conversation gets hard again when we move into the living room.

"Corey isn't in Boston like he's supposed to be. My cousin texted me this afternoon to tell me. I don't know why he hasn't left when I'm certain I was clear about my expectations. Has he contacted you in the last two days?"

"Yes." Brandon's scowl is so deep the lines might never fade from his forehead.

"What did he demand?" Thea's leaning against me again while we sit on a loveseat, her hand clutching mine and resting on my lap.

"He wants you back in Boston, and he wants me to ride with him. He said he has a deal going on here, and he needs me to protect his back. I guess he doesn't have the men he arrived with."

Brandon stares straight at me, and I stare back. The implication hangs in the air. My silence confirms it, but I will never admit it aloud. Thea and Sandra are watching us. Sandra remains nonplussed by the exchange, but Thea's getting more anxious. Her hand tightens around mine, she's pressing harder into my shoulder, and her thigh keeps tensing against mine. She's getting some large doses of reality today. I think it's good, though. I'd rather she sees how noncommittal I'll be about certain topics before we move in together or get married. She needs to accept this, or there's no future.

"Did he say where you're supposed to go?"

"Brighton Beach."

It's my turn to tense. But I make sure it's the leg that isn't touching Thea's. Rage boils inside me.

"These people know who your uncle is connected to?"

"Yes."

"And they want to do business with him?"

"Apparently. According to Uncle Corey, they want him to be the middleman for some deal in Boston. He's the go between to keep them anonymous. Rowan was stupid enough to fall for that sort of thing. But Ewan isn't. I don't think they know Ewan well enough."

"Who?" Thea shifts her focus from her father to me.

"The bratva."

"The Russians?"

"Yes. If you hear Brighton Beach, nine times out of ten, it's the Russians. The Kutsenkos run the Ivankov branch. Sometimes Brighton Beach means another Eastern European syndicate, but if it does, the Kutsenkos aren't far away. They're either involved, or they know about it."

Brandon shakes his head. "They're Albanian."

It's my turn to shake mine. "Maybe that's who you're meeting, but the Albanians are weak right now. Here and in Boston. The bratva pulls their strings. The Albanians don't breathe without asking the Kutsenkos' permission."

We got sucked into that fucking Albanian shitshow a couple years ago. It was one of the few times my family hasn't wanted to gut our rivals and was willing to help. However, it all blew back on us thanks to fucking Declan. He started the shite but didn't live long enough to see it through. No one else completely believes that part. They blame Dillan.

We lost our family home— the house we considered our ancestral one here in NYC —because Misha Andreyev lost his shite and blamed us. The circumstances of what happened to Misha's sister-in-law and what nearly happened to Maria Mancinelli meant we had no leg to stand on. We had to take it when the bratva struck back. We had trouble with the Albanians again two months ago when Dillan and Mair were only dating.

"When is all of this supposed to happen?" I need to let my family know.

"Next week. Corey said he'd come back down."

"Next week? Papa, he just got you injured, and he wants you healed enough to ride with him? He's even crazier than we thought."

"I'm more bruised than anything else."

Thea scowls, and I can tell she gets that expression from her dad. "I'm not all right with that. Not as your daughter, and not as a doctor."

"That may be, squirt. But they didn't invite me. They told me. It's part of that annual tax."

"He made you lose your job, so he could loan shark you. When you refused his so-called help, he nearly killed you on your bike. And now he wants you to go with him to some meeting that could get you killed."

I let go of her hand, but she clutches mine. I use my free hand to pull hers off and place it on my thigh. I wrap my arm around her and press her against my side. I won't be over the top with my PDA, but I kiss the top of her head while I squeeze her upper arm. She rests her head against my shoulder.

"Papa, you can't do this." Her voice catches.

God, I wish I could pick her up and put her on my lap. I wish I could slip inside her and hold her until she calms. I wish I could blink and make this all better. But I can't do any of those things.

"Thea, Sandra, I need to speak to Brandon alone."

Thea tries to shake her head, but when our gazes meet, tears fill her eyes. She's guessed what's happening, but I won't tell her a thing until Brandon and I speak to my family. I kiss her cheek and whisper to her.

"It'll work out."

"But not for the best." Her voice is equally soft.

I stand when she and her mom do. I risk her parents annoyance when I pull her in for a hug. I kiss her forehead when all I long to do is press my lips to hers.

"Nothing's planned yet. Don't panic until there's a reason to, *cailín*."

She nods, and we let go of each other. She follows Sandra

from the room. I watch as the door shuts. Then I turn to Brandon.

"I know you killed two men to protect Thea. You shot at me once before. Corey is going to die."

"And I'd like to be the one to kill him." Brandon's so deadpan you'd think he just told you about the weather.

"I can't promise that, but I can try to make that happen. We need to speak to Dillan. First, I need the truth. How much of a liability are you if you ride with Corey or come with us?"

"I'm pretty banged up, but I've been worse. My children haven't seen that, and Sandra's only seen it once. It was when she and I were dating. Her reaction was completely justified, but I swore I'd never put her through that again. I've stayed away an extra day or two to heal enough to not frighten her. Ally and her brothers were too young to remember, or they were away at college. There were a lot of years Corey left us alone. He's been pushing harder since Thea turned eighteen."

"I disliked him but didn't give him much thought until meeting Thea. Now his days are over because he wants to pimp her out."

"No one understands that better than me." Brandon's gaze bores into me.

"And that's why I'll do my best to let you have the kill shot. You don't need to ask to come along. We both know you are. We need to talk to Dillan about logistics, not permission. I will have to explain things to him, but he'll get it."

I pull my phone out and open a group text.

ME

Answer when I call.

They'll know that means it's a six-way call.
I dial Dillan first.
"Hey."

"Hey. Hold on while I get the others."

I tap Cormac's contact, and it doesn't even ring.

"I'm with Shane."

"Ok. Let me get Seamus and Sean."

I get them on the line before I say anything important.

"I'm at Thea's parents' house. I didn't know this until we arrived, but Dillan, you and I met Thea's dad in Boston when we were nineteen. Brandon's on the call with us. We're in the living room."

I'm grateful this is an older home and not open concept.

Dillan responds first. "You have a birthmark on your arm, don't you? I saw it on Ally's arm a few days ago. I remember you now."

"I do."

"How do you know each other?" Seamus already isn't thrilled about this conversation.

"When Dillan and I were nineteen, do you remember Uncle Donovan made us go to Boston with him? Corey and his guys were there when Uncle Donovan was negotiating with Rowan's dad. Remember the firefight six months later? Remember how I almost got shot after killing one of Corey's men? Brandon was there."

I won't confess Brandon was the one who nearly killed me.

"Your future father-in-law nearly killed you." I guess Shane's going to put that out there.

"And I'm eternally grateful I didn't. Finn makes my daughter happy."

There's silence for a moment, then Dillan speaks. I'm confident he'll go along with what I want, but I can't be certain until we hear what he has to say.

"If Finn's calling all of us with you, then you know something we need to. What happened?"

I nod to Brandon, encouraging him to tell Dillan. I don't want to get the details wrong since I can only assume a lot.

"Uncle Corey cost me my job to force me to accept his financial help. I refused to do that, so he's pushing for Ally to go back to Boston. He knows she'll consider it to help me. Neither she nor her mother and I want her anywhere near Boston. If Ally weren't with Finn, I'm certain Uncle Corey would target her and press harder. He caused my bicycle accident as a reminder that he believes he still owns me. He hasn't since I was a kid. Now he wants me to ride with him to some deal in Brighton Beach that's supposed to happen with the Albanians. Finn says it's likely really the Russians."

When Brandon says nothing more, I continue with my hypothesis. I'm not fully convinced and won't be until we're there. But this is what I'm guessing based upon what Brandon shared before this call.

"I think Maks wants us there. Thea had some odd pages the other day. Death was the common denominator. It was a warning. I suspect Sergei or Anton hacked the hospital's paging network or had someone do it for them. They want me pissed off at Corey and going after him to prevent this deal with the Albanians. It's a bit of a stretch, but a logical one. Maks knows Corey would order Brandon to go with him since we took out Corey's men. Maks knows that if Brandon goes, so will I. If I go, we all go."

"How do they know any of this to put it together?" Brandon's question is reasonable, and I don't love the answer I have to give to my girlfriend's father.

"We follow each other, and all of us have informants."

He doesn't look surprised. He nods. But it doesn't take him verbalizing his frustration to know he feels it. It hardly thrills him to know people will follow his daughter. At least when she's with me. Shane shifts the focus when he speaks.

"Do you want to keep Maks from getting further involved? You can let the meeting happen with the Albanians. It can be mutually beneficial for you, Mr. Gallagher, and us."

"It's Brandon. I suspect we will be in-laws in a couple months."

I fucking hate my fair skin. I tan, which is great. But when I blush, I'm fire engine red. He already said Thea and I are meant to be, but that's not the same as knowing we'll live together and all that goes along with that. That's why we were going to wait to tell her parents and mine that we want to move in together.

"As long as Corey is no longer a threat to my family, your family can do whatever you want to the others."

Shane plows on. "Then we need to know when and where. We need to know what the bratva plans to gain. Right now, the bratva and *Cosa Nostra* have put the most pressure on the Albanians. Maybe we should let them know we feel left out."

Seamus probably has his phone out and is already tapping out a text as he adds his thoughts. "I'll speak to Bujar and see what he knows. I don't know if he'll know how the bratva's involved, but he can tell us about the Albanians. He should tell us the where and when. We can confirm that against what Corey tells you, Brandon. He should tell us what goods will exchange hands."

"Victor didn't tell me anything about the bratva getting more involved with the Albanians when he checked in yesterday. I might need to remind him that a selective memory isn't good enough." Cormac's great at refreshing people's memory.

Seamus oversees a lot of our informants since he's also our criminal defense attorney. It pays for him to know his clients. If he's too busy, then Cormac steps in. Bujar has a healthy fear of Cormac after watching my cousin crush his brother's skull with his fist.

I need to know a few things since I'm certain Dillan will let me lead because it involves my girlfriend and her family. I'd beat my chest and roar *my woman* if it weren't such an inappropriate time. But that's how I feel.

"Do you want us to take what we find?" It's Dillan's decision, so everyone knows who I direct that question to.

"Bujar needs to tell us what it is. It might not be worth it."

"I think I know." Brandon's not hesitant to chime in, but he's not boasting either.

He looks at me, and I nod. He can either volunteer it or wait for one of us to ask. The former would be better since the others don't know him, and I'm just getting to know him. It's not a good idea to make any of us beg for information.

"The Albanians want the O'Malleys to launder money for them through their construction companies. In exchange, the O'Malleys sell more product to them. They then pass that product along to the bratva, who sell it at a ridiculously high price in Europe. I don't know if Rowan knew the Russians were pulling the Albanians' strings, and he wanted the deal to mess with you. Or he truly was that ignorant, not caring what happened to the coke once he got paid. My guess is the Boston Irish are skimming at least twenty-five percent off whatever the Albanians want laundered, and they're saving that to make another move on you."

I laugh. "Ewan will take at least thirty percent if not more. He has titanium balls. He's not scared of the Albanians like he should be since he just took the reins. They're bloodthirsty. Plenty of people won't go near them because they're so damn insular and secretive. The best anyone can hope for is a blood feud starts among their families, and another syndicate can capitalize on it."

Sean's been quiet so far, but I know he has plenty of thoughts on anything related to the bratva. "That's what the

Kutsenkos are betting on. With three leaders in as many years, and none of them particularly strong. The bratva's hoping with the Kurti family wrestling power away from the Hoxhas and them supporting the Kurtis, it'll start a blood feud between the two Albanian clans. The bratva will put enough oil on the fire for the Kurtis and Hoxhas to destroy each other, leaving the bratva with even more power."

"Complicated." Brandon mutters the word, but we all hear it. I don't blame him. Maybe I can sorta explain it.

"If you think of the various international regions as wheels, the Four Families are the hubs. All the lesser syndicates are spokes. Now, imagine the four wheels are all racing downhill, bumping into each other and crashing. The goal is always to send your wheel on the straightest, fastest path without falling over. But while you're in this race, the finish line keeps moving, so the four wheels take turns being in the lead."

Brandon nods his head, so I guess that means my analogy made at least a little sense.

"Cormac, Seamus, how long will it take to get that information from your CIs?"

Dillan's probably thought of four plans while he's been quiet. That means he's also thought of their permutations for how things could go wrong with each one and the needed solutions.

"Give us a day. Right, Shay?"

"Yeah. I already sent a text to Bujar, saying we need to meet."

"Brandon, when is all of this supposed to happen?" Sean's probably already hacking Sergei's and Anton's computers. I'm a strong hacker, but it's mostly in the financial realm. Once we fully decide what to do, I'll be the one who makes the money disappear.

"In five days. Finn said Corey is still in the city. He told me he was headed back to Boston until this rendezvous. My guess is he thinks I'll let my guard down, and he'll be here and ready to spring the trap."

That's my guess too. We finish the conversation with a couple more logistical concerns, but we have everything in place for now. We end the call, and I'm left staring at Brandon.

"You might get the kill shot, Bandon. But I deal with Corey first. If you can't handle seeing the worst things you can imagine one person doing to another, you won't be the one to kill him."

Chapter Twenty-Four

Thea

It's been a subdued three days compared to how things have been. They've been what normal couples would consider the usual. For us, it's been bliss. Nothing's happened, so Finn and I are inseparable. It's a fairytale come true. He's charming without trying, and he's incredibly considerate. I don't think it's to woo me. I think that's just who he is. We've cooked together, cleaned together— apparently, none of the guys have maids because their mothers guilt them out of it —and fall asleep in each other's arms. We've taken more naps than either of us has since we were toddlers. And sex. Lots and lots and lots and lots of sex. And then some more.

The one downer was a call from Maria Mancinelli. She warned me about some imaging results Jamie and Asher were going to get. She couldn't be specific because of HIPPA, even if no one in my family nor I would ever report it. At the end of the call, she brought up Finn. She didn't explicitly warn me away, but the meaning was clear. I was as polite as I could be when I told her to mind her own fucking business. She's a friend, and she was looking out for me. I can appreciate it, but part of me wondered if the men in her family put her up to it just to spite Finn.

I reminded myself that Maria is not someone anyone can force. She won't do what she won't do, especially if she thinks it'll hurt someone else. Now I might know that she's a Mafia daughter— Finn said no woman in any of the syndicates wants to be called a princess —and married to a mafioso, but she's still one of the very most kindest people in the world. Like as kind as anyone could be.

Besides that, and the looming issue with Uncle Corey, it's been wonderful. I don't think it's because Finn and I have been on our best behavior to impress each other. I think we just live well together. We like the same things, and we often think of the same things. The mind reading is uncanny. Sometimes I can't find even a smidge of a hint to what he's feeling. I know not to push that. He's had a few calls that made him reserved when he came out of his office. He said he hadn't a clue what the conversation was about that I had with Maria because I was just as reserved. Finn said he likes not knowing what I'm thinking because if he can't guess, then no one can. It'll come in handy.

I'm meeting his parents tonight, and I'm only mildly petrified. His father is a mobster, and his mother is married to one and raised three. What if I completely underwhelm them? We're back at his place right now after spending last night at my apartment, and I'm staring at the closet with the clothes I brought over yesterday. As though meeting his parents isn't enough, it's Sunday dinner. That means *all* of them will be there. Finn's brothers and cousins plus Mair and Finn's parents. But that's not all. Oh no, let's toss in his two uncles and two aunts.

"Little one, you could go in a paper bag, and they'll still love you."

Finn wraps his arms around my waist and holds me against him. He kisses my shoulder before pulling my towel off me. I reach for a shirt, but he turns me away. Without a word, he guides me to the bed and sits. He opens his legs and points to the floor. I drop to my knees and open my mouth. He presses my head forward as he guides his cock to my mouth.

"Warm it. *Cailín*, they will adore you for you. You're everything any parent could hope for their child's partner. You're genuine, and they will know that the second they meet you. You don't need to put on a show to impress anyone. Just be you. They know how important you are to me. They know our future is together. They'll be happy for us. I know you're nervous. I was practically queasy meeting your parents, but it will go well. I promise. Suck."

We've kept going with the free use, and it's been wonderful for both of us. I've never felt more desired and needed in my life. Finn enjoys letting me know how much I mean to him. Anyone looking in from the outside would argue it's pure lust. But it doesn't feel like that. Yes, sometimes we just want to bang. But even when we're into bondage or impact play or whatever else, the emotions run deep.

He pulls away and helps me to my feet before guiding me to lie with my chest and stomach on the mattress. He spanks me. Hard. Like enough to push me forward on the mattress. He does it four more times until I'm dancing from one foot to another. He squeezes my left ass cheek until I whimper. He doesn't let go, and I don't want him to. He hovers over me.

"Who's in control?"

"You, Daddy."

"Does that mean I'm going to take care of you, *cailín*?"

"Always, Daddy."

"Who gets all my cum in her cunt?"

"I do, Daddy."

"Why?"

"Because you care about me."

"It's more than that. Why?"

"Because you like me."

"More than that. Why?"

What more is there to say short of saying he loves me?

"Why, Thea? Answer me." He spanks me again.

"I don't know, Daddy."

He gets me back on my feet before lifting me to wrap my arms and legs around him.

"*Daddy.*" It's a hissing whisper as he slides into me.

"I know, *mo ghrá.*"

"What does that mean?"

"My love."

I stare at him for a moment before I tighten my whole body around him. Is he saying...?

"Thea, I love you. I will always take care of you the best I can. I will always do everything in my power to give you what you need. Tonight, you need the reassurance everything will be okay. That you can trust me to only take you somewhere I control who's around you. That you will only be around people who'll accept that your family connections are older than you are. You're letting me control how we make love because you trust that I'll know what you want and give it to you. I'll always do that. Until my last breath."

"I love you, Finn. You understand me in a way no one else does. You get what I need and want without me saying a word. You're hilarious, but you're also silent strength when I need it. My feelings for you are so vastly different from any I've had before. I've been infatuated, and you know I loved my college boyfriend and the one in med school. This doesn't feel like any of that, so I can only attribute it to a deep and lasting love. I want you to know I will give you everything you need and do my damnedest to give you what you want."

"You already do. You are my refuge. You're who I turn to now. Even when I can't tell you things, you're still who I turn to. You're who I want to be with when things are great, and when things are shitty. I haven't told you about other stuff going on separate from your uncle. I can't, and I won't. But you have helped me immeasurably just knowing I'm coming home to you, or I'm walking out of my office to you. There are two absolute certainties in my life. I can never change being a mobster, and I will never change loving you."

"There's a third one. Family. We are each other's, but now we both have twice the family we did before we met."

He carries me to the bedside table as though I weigh nothing. That is not the case. I've been called thick more than once in my life. But he told me about carrying Cormac up the stairs when his cousin had a concussion a few months ago. He couldn't let Cormac's head bounce around like it would if Finn had fireman carried him. Nope. He said he carried his heavy-arse— his words, not mine —cousin across the threshold like a bride.

He grabs the smooth paddle and walks to where he can see us in the mirror. I can't. I see the wall behind our bed. He's gotten me used to calling everything in the condo ours. He's even gotten me used to calling all the cars ours. And yes, all. He has four. He has a Wrangler he takes off roading like a little toy Tonka. He has a pickup truck from when he was just out of college and worked construction for Donovan while going to grad school at night. He has a Jaguar convertible. And he has an electric car that I've never heard of. It looks like a prototype that only he has because he's richer than the Vatican.

I drive a Beamer, so it's not some old clunker. But it hardly lives up to his cars. He says I'm wiser than him since— except for the electric car —I picked a far more practical car that's the most fuel efficient of ours.

I'm unprepared for the paddle to land against my ass. I jerk up as my thighs squeeze his ribs. With the arm wrapped around me, he presses me back down his dick. I don't stifle my moan. I knew the spank was coming, I just didn't know it was coming right that moment. None of the spanks are punishment. They're purely for pleasure.

"Count them and say thank you."

"One. Thank you, Daddy."

Smack.

"Two. Thank you, Daddy."

Smack... Smack...Smack...

I count and thank him each time until we get to ten. I'm ready to crawl out of my skin, needing to come. He turns back to the bed and tosses the paddle aside. He pulls my arms from his neck as he lays me down. My back barely touches the mattress before he's pounding his cock into me.

"Harder."

"I will hurt you."

"Harder, Finn." He always holds back a little, and that's the only thing that's frustrated me since we met.

"If I harm you, I will—"

"Fucking hell, Finn. I'm fucking thirty-three years old. If I want you to fuck my brains out, then I know what I want. You will never totally lose control. Even if you think you have, your subconscious will always keep you from harming me. Now, please, Daddy, fuck me harder."

He growls. He wraps his hand around my throat and squeezes. He increases the pressure incrementally, knowing I'm still not used to breath play. But I like it. He grinds his pubic bone against my clit. My nails graze his biceps as I try to

There was no way any of their children wouldn't be born with red hair. The older men's blue eyes are as brilliant as their wives' green ones. Since Finn and all the other guys have exactly the same shade of emerald-hued eyes, they clearly came from their moms.

The couple near the fireplace walks over to us while everyone else watches. I feel the spotlight on me. The woman kisses Finn's cheek, then the man hugs him. They turn expectant faces to me.

"Mom, Da, this is Althea. Ally for short."

"Except he calls her Thea. No one else gets to."

I look around Finn's mom to where Sean smirks. I glance at Finn, and I'm absolutely positive he'd give his brother an obscene hand gesture if his parents, aunts, and uncles weren't in the room.

"Thea, these are my parents. Breda and Ronan."

"Hello. Thank you for having me for dinner."

Wonderful.

That sounds like they're about to skewer me and serve me on a platter. That's about how I feel.

"We're so happy to have you. I can tell already. You and Mair are such an improvement on these heathens."

Breda offers me her hand, and I shake it. Her smile makes her eyes crinkle where lines weren't a moment ago. She's beautiful, but her smile makes her radiate something more than skin deep. She reminds me of my mom.

"Ignore Frick over there. Frick and Frack are just jealous their older brother still beats them at everything." Ronan grins, and I'm seeing an older version of Finn who could be his brother not his father.

"I never said I wanted a girlfriend."

I'm pretty sure that was Shane muttering. I'm positive when Cormac pushes his shoulder and laughs. He gets a jab in.

"Don't pout. Nana used to say you'll trip over that lip."

I suck my lips in and try not to laugh, but Breda whispers to me, and I fail.

"Go ahead and laugh. You'll pop if you don't."

It comes out somewhere between choking and snorting. I want to sink into the ground.

"You feel better now, don't you?" Ronan waggles his eyebrows.

What have I walked into? I ask myself that a second time. My family jokes around, but nothing like what I've seen in the five minutes I've been here. Finn was right. They accepted me when they heard about me. Putting a face to the name was just a technicality. I feel part of the family already. Finn guides me to one of the three sofas in the sprawling— what else do you call a space this large —family room. Before we sit, the other two couples join us. The women kiss Finn's cheek, while the men hug him. All four offer me kind smiles that match Ronan and Breda's.

"Thea, this is Auntie Siobhan and Uncle Tate. They got stuck with Dillan. And this is Auntie Saoirse and Uncle Kieran. They claim their sons are the nice ones. Seamus and Cormac just never got caught."

"So, they're the smart ones." The comment pops out of my mouth before I know what I'm saying.

Cormac and Seamus walk over. Seamus snags my hand and gives it a little tug, so I step away from Finn, but I'm still holding his hand. They give me a kiss on each cheek, then smirk at Finn. Cormac has all the jokes tonight.

"I think we made Finn cry."

"You must have been the ones who stole everyone else's toys." I test the waters with that one.

"They did." Dillan chimes in before his wife playfully

covers his mouth with her hand, leaving only a garbled sound coming from him.

"See why we like her as much as Mair." Sean's the picture of an angel, which clearly fools no one since his parents don't even look in his direction. Breda speaks to me instead.

"I'll say the same thing to you as I did Mair the night she met all of us. They weren't raised in a barn. They just spent all their time there. Ignore their nonsense. Come and have a seat. Dinner's almost ready."

Finn and I sit on the empty loveseat, and there's a lull for a moment. Blessedly, Mair comes to the rescue.

"Are you busy at work?"

"No more than usual. We've had a few particularly challenging cases, but we've also sent several babies home in the last two weeks. That makes up for the long days."

"You're a pediatrician?" Saoirse sounds genuinely interested.

"A neonatologist. I specialize in babies born with complications."

Saoirse's expression turns sad for a moment before she glances at Seamus. "Shay was nine weeks early. He spent a month in the NICU. We had a fantastic neonatologist who explained everything at least three times for our sleep deprived—and my hormonal —brains to understand. Thank God for the nurses who would play with Cormac while we were with Seamus. Cor was just over seven months old. Irish twins, I know. You'd never guess Shay was a preemie then or now. He weighed four pounds six ounces."

My gaze jumps to Seamus. You'd never believe the man who looks like he eats bodybuilders for breakfast was considered very preterm. Babies born at thirty-two weeks, the cusp of very and moderately preterm, are usually just shy of four pounds. At thirty-one weeks, he probably looked gigantic in the incubator. He catches me looking at him and flexes his pecs like Terry Cruz.

"Showoff." Saoirse sounds playfully exasperated with her son.

I hear a timer go off in the kitchen. Ronan, Tate, and Kieran rise and head into the kitchen. I shouldn't find that surprising, but I do.

"Kieran's the best baker in the family." Saoirse is about to say more when Seamus cuts in.

"Because Cormac's such a whiner." The younger brother looks like he'd stick his tongue out at the older brother is they were five.

"My body is a temple."

Dillan snorts. "You were praying to the porcelain god last Halloween. I'm damn positive that whiskey wasn't vegan."

"Before my son ever so rudely interrupted his elder—" Saoirse cocks an eyebrow at Seamus "—Kieran enjoys it, and he's been making the boys' birthday cakes since they were little. Cormac is the cleanest eater of all of them. He avoids the processed foods that are clogging the other boys' arteries."

I look at all the men in the room. None— not a single one from either generation —looks like anything but the picture of good health. Ronan pokes his head back in to say everything's ready. It's a lively meal, and I feel like I've been part of the family for decades not a couple hours.

When we finish, the younger men gather everything and head into the kitchen. Mair leans back in her chair, raises her wine glass to me, winks, and takes a sip. I hear them moving around, loading the dishwasher, washing things in the sink, and wiping down all the surfaces. Now I get what Finn meant when he said their moms guilted them into not having maids. They can do it all, and I'm certain the kitchen's spotless now.

Another hour passes in the family room before everyone

says their goodbyes and heads out. I sit curled on Finn's lap in the car. My eyes are drooping shut.

"That went well, *mo ghrá*."

I love hearing the Irish term of affection. I curl my toes in my shoes and burrow closer.

"I thought so too. Everyone is so nice."

"And normal."

"Yes. I wasn't sure I should say that. But they are. Is it to balance everything else?"

"Our parents decided when each couple married, the mob ended at their front door. No one can change who and what we are. But our homes are for family and friends. We're close knit by choice as much as by necessity. The six of us guys grew up more like brothers than cousins. When Colleen died, and Dillan became an only child, he and I gravitated toward each other even more. Cormac and Seamus have each other, and Shane and Sean showed up as a package deal."

"What about before Colleen died? Were you the odd one out?"

"I suppose I could have been, but Colleen always made sure I wasn't. She was our leader even though Dillan and I were older. She got us out of as much trouble as she got us into. Seamus and Cormac always came out looking squeaky clean when the seven of us lined up in front of what always felt like the firing squad. No one ever narced on the others. Not even when we were really little and didn't yet understand that family comes first. We were born and bred loyal. But Cor and Shay still got away with everything. Colleen doled out her own brand of justice once our parents were gone. She was having none of our cousins' innocent act when she knew they were in the thick of it with the rest of us."

There's a tinge of sadness in Finn's voice as he reminisces. It makes me feel shitty all over again like when I demanded to know if he was married. That car ride seems like a million years ago.

"You would have liked her, little one. You remind me a lot of her. You both committed to a life of service."

I press his cheek to turn him, so I can kiss his lips. "I won't ask to learn Gaelic because I'm certain your family is fluent for a reason other than tradition. But what can I call you?"

"I appreciate your thoughtfulness, but Mair speaks fluent Gaelic as do the moms. We're always conscious of who's around us. Is there an English word or phrase you want the equivalent of?"

I think about the term he used and practice it in my head before I say it aloud. *Moh graw.*

"You said my love is *mo ghrá*. What about sweetheart?"

"*Mo chroí* is my heart."

I repeat that one in my head too. *Moh kree.*

"*Mo anam cara* is my soulmate."

I try repeating it. "*Moh anum cair-ah.*"

"Excellent."

"That might take some practice."

"Good thing you have a lifetime. *Mo stór* is my treasure."

Moh store. Simple.

"What about something like my darling?"

He chuckles as he pulls out his phone. He unlocks it and pulls up the notes app and types as he speaks.

"That's the least phonetic of any of them. *Mo mhuirnín.*"

"Say that again. There are too many letters."

He chuckles again and says it slowly for me. "*Moh wur-neen.*"

I can say it, but it's butchered. "It's going to take me a while to get the accent right."

"I think it's cute how you say them. And I appreciate you wanting to learn."

"I want you to know your feelings are never one-sided, *mo stór.*"

"Very good."

He puts his index finger beneath my chin and lifts it. His kiss leaves me all gooey inside. It's interrupted by a phone call. I didn't see who it was, and I can't hear anything. Finn's watching me until he hangs up.

"I have to go out tonight."

Chapter Twenty-Five

Finn

That was Brandon. Corey and the Albanians moved up their meeting. It's happening tonight. When Thea and I get back to the condo, I'm rattling off instructions as I get dressed in all black. I have on cargo pants, a black turtleneck, and black boots. She's listening and nodding, but I'm not convinced she'll remember it all. I pray she never needs to remember it all.

"Give me your hand. Do you feel that ridge? Press it."

I slid all my suits aside, so I could run her hand over the back wall of the closet. She finds the little latch and presses it. We hear a soft click before I push the door with my hand over hers. I reach inside and down, grabbing the flashlight. I hand it to her. She looks over her shoulder at me then flicks on the light.

"If anyone ever breaks in, or our guards tell you someone's on their way, you come straight here. Go inside."

She steps forward, and I follow her. This isn't some magic *The Lion, The Witch, and The Wardrobe* shite. This is a fully stocked panic room. I watch her as her gaze sweeps the small enclosure. It's big enough for about four people— normal size people, not the men in my family sized people.

"There are nonperishable foods over here. There's a case of water I switch out once a year. Have you shot a gun before?"

She shakes her head. That's something we're unfortunately going to remedy. She may need to carry one sometimes.

"This is a gun safe even though it doesn't look like one. It's biometric just like our front door. There's not much that can get through our door, but it's not completely impenetrable. Don't worry about what's in here. If anyone in my family is with you, they know how to get into it, and they know how to use what you'll find."

"Like your mom and Mair?"

"Yes. Mair isn't that experienced yet, but Dillan's taught her enough that she can protect herself and others. She's still learning."

"Will I to have to learn?"

"At least the basics. Thea, I know this might be contrary to what you believe as a doctor, but I won't bend on you at least knowing how to use them. You don't have to become an expert marksman. I just need you to stay alive until I can get to you."

"I understand, Daddy."

She's scared, and I don't blame her. Scared, tired, or playful are what she's feeling when she calls me that. Otherwise, it's Finn and hopefully now some Gaelic terms of endearment.

"If you come in here, make sure you push the door all the way closed and hit this button. Do you see how it snaps these reinforcements around the door? They only unlatch from in here. Never open this for anyone who isn't in our immediate family. Not even Joey. Not even his brothers or Ted. No one, Thea. If they don't share my DNA or gave me DNA, you do not *ever* open this door unless they give you our code word. We need to come up with something I can tell the others to use if they ever need you to come out of hiding. If they don't use the code word, you remain silent and hidden. It means it's either not safe because they aren't alone or because it's someone pretending."

"What's the code word?"

"We need to come up with that. It has to be something easy enough to remember under stress, but not obvious."

"Gavage. It's a medical term for feeding with a tube that passes through the mouth to the stomach. It's easy to say, but who would use it except a doctor or nurse? Even then, it's not common in most specialties."

"All right. I'll tell the others."

I lead her out of the panic room and into the living room. I grab my go bag out of the hall closet and put it by the door. She stands quietly and watches. I open my arms, and she falls into them.

"I don't know how long I'm going to be gone. If it's more than two days, my dad or uncles will come and get you. I want you to stay with my parents. If all goes to plan, this won't take long. If I call you on the way home or from the lobby and tell you to go to the guest bedroom, I need you to do that without question. I need you to stay there until I come to you. Don't offer to help me. Please."

I remember to tack that last word on there. I lean back enough to see her face before I continue.

"Most things are under our control, but not always. If I call you and tell you to give me space, it's not because I don't want to see you. I'll always want to come home and go straight into your arms. It means something went wrong. I need to get cleaned up or calm down. Sometimes both. I promise as soon as I'm ready, I will come to you. I swear."

"I believe you. I'll remember all of this. I promise. I know you'll be careful, so it should go without saying. But I can't help it. Please be careful. I love you."

"I will, and I love you too. I'm coming home to you, Thea. Always."

I shouldn't say that. I shouldn't make that kind of promise because I can't guarantee tomorrow, let alone always. But it's what I want. Our kiss is over far too soon, but I have to go. We exchange another I love you, then I'm gone.

That motherfucker.

"Who is that?"

I swung by and picked up Brandon on the way to Dillan's. It came as a surprise to everyone that things got moved up by several days and is no longer happening in Brighton Beach, but I believed Brandon when he called me. I wanted to tell Thea her dad would be with us, and I'd watch out for him. But I can't promise anyone coming home alive any better than I can promise I am. I didn't want her to panic, either. I remember when I was really young— like four and my brothers were still toddlers —how my mom would try to entertain us when my dad went out at night. I didn't understand why my mom would look at the door and windows so often until I was much older. Those nights are some of my earliest memories. My mom was waiting for my dad to get home. She was checking the windows to make sure no one who wasn't a guard was near her children. I don't want that fear for Thea.

"That's Gareth O'Brien. He's the new leader down in Trenton." I point to a guy to the far right. I don't see any of his men around.

No mob boss likes the official term skipper. I don't know who thought nautical terms would be impressive titles for various members of the mob. And the fact that we don't have the same hierarchy as the Mafia or the bratva leaves us as the butt of plenty of jokes. The cartels aren't as rigidly structured as the Mafia or bratva, but they have more than we do. Hence the name mob.

"Did you expect him to be here?"

"No. Not at all. This isn't the bratva or the *Cosa Nostra*."

So that leaves one more motherfucking option. Fucking *caremonda*. Face of a penis. *Fucking carechimba*. Face of a vagina— cunt. That one fits.

"Is that Pablo?" Sean wants to know as he comes to lie on his stomach next to me.

Brandon's on the ground, too. He made it down without a single groan or gasp considering his bruises. It's a testimony to his past and running with a gang. He's more like us than I guessed.

"Yeah. What the hell is he doing here? How is he involved?"

I'm thinking out loud as all seven of us— my family plus Brandon —lie on the ground facing a warehouse. None of us has an answer to that since no one expected him to be involved. Pablo Diaz is equivalent to me, Luca in the *Cosa Nostra*, and Aleksei in the bratva. Second-in-command. He's Enrique's heir. The next in line to be *jefe* of the Colombian Cartel. He's been a motherfucking pain in my goddamn arse since we were kids. Whiny little bitch. He wouldn't shut up about his loose tooth when we were seven, so I knocked it out for him.

We have dark camo paint on our faces and ears with black beanies on our heads. Our green eyes are recognizable enough. We don't need our shock of red hair giving us all away. The camo paint makes our eyes stand out more, but from a distance, people often can't make out the difference between our eye color and the ice-blue the Kutsenkos and their Andreyev cousins have. They just see sets of two glowing, floating circles coming toward them. With camo paint on, the darker eyes the other two Kutsenko cousins have, along with most of the Mancinellis and Diazes, appear like soulless empty pockets. Fitting. Empty eyes, empty heads.

Unless we're not wearing our NVGs when we move in, Corey will know our green eyes in an instant, which means I have to be doubly sure my future father-in-law stays behind me.

Dillan's on the other side of Sean, but we all have ears like dogs, so I hear him when he whispers to me. "I thought you believed Joaquin wouldn't be interested enough to hack anything."

I look at my cousin. "I still don't think he is. I think this was Alejandro and one of his minions."

I glance at Brandon because I'm certain he's confused as fuck by all the names. I would be because there isn't a small family among us. Three of the Four Families are Roman Catholic, and the other is Eastern Orthodox. We joke that's why our families are so big. No one wants to admit the truth: three of the families knew they would need more soldiers.

"Alejandro and Pablo are cousins. Their uncle, Enrique, is their *jefe*. Enrique has a younger brother who's Pablo's dad. Enrique also has two younger sisters. One spawned Alejandro, and the other spawned Javier, Jorge, and Joaquin."

I won't get into how Pablo had a younger brother, Juan, who fucked up so badly the Kutsenkos made sure he could never go near Maks's wife again. That's an entire story of its own.

Brandon's still confused, and I don't blame him. I'm going to have to share a little more of the Diazes' inner workings. Motherfuckers.

"Pablo's Enrique's heir, same as I am Dillan's for now. He's a jack of all trades, master of none. Alejandro heads their security. He's the top enforcer and plans a lot of their missions. This is a business transaction, so not his usual role. Joaquin is a hacker, so he's their intel gatherer. Jorge is a CPA like me. He does the active accounting and investments, but he's also a forensic accountant like me. Javier is an attorney like Enrique."

I can tell Brandon wants to know what roles we each have as he looks around. He's going to be my father-in-law, which is all the more reason I want to tell him as little as I can about our family jobs. Less he can testify about if the feds pressure him and less he'll confess if any syndicate captures him.

"I'll give you a copy of the family trees I'm going to make for Thea. I knew something was in the works when Thea got those pages at work. Someone was trying to scare her away from me. I wondered if Joaquin was the one responsible for hacking the hospital system and heading whatever operation they were sucking Thea into. I still don't think he did it. He's too lazy for that when I know he has other stuff already keeping him busy."

"Then who did?"

I told Brandon about the pages Thea got and the brick through her window when Corey first arrived. It didn't thrill him to find out about either. Before I can answer, my phone buzzes in my back pocket. I turned it on dark mode and dimmed it all the way while we were getting ready. We all do it.

It's a web search results alert. This explains so damn much. The more I've thought about the hospital messaging system, the more I became convinced it was an inside job. It's also why I didn't think Joaquin did it. But someone did, and it wasn't for their own shits and giggles. So, I did a little digging into the background of the fuck nut she was dating when I met her at McGinty's.

Tony isn't short for Anthony. It's short for Antonio. I said nothing to anyone when I met Thea because Tony disappeared from her life. But I wanted to keep an eye on him just in case. I found out his last name and did a background check on him. That's usually Sean's job, but any of us can do it. Some drunken disorderly showed up, which came as no surprise. But nothing more significant triggered the DOJ or FBI.

"It was the nurse Thea dated. Tony De Luca. His family were Maldanodos."

That draws everyone's attention. Brandon's super pissed.

"She was friends with him for a long time before they dated. She hung out with him outside of work, and I met him at a baseball game. Bastard."

After the fucked-up messages came to Thea's beeper, I dug some more. Thank you Church of Jesus Christ of Latter-day Saints and their meticulous ancestry records. Still less noticeable to hack their system than the commercial ancestry databases. Tony De Luca— forgive me for not guessing that a douchebag with the most Guido sounding name might not be mostly Italian American.

Oh, no. He's only like a third Italian. He's a jumble of other shite, too, but out of that jumble one part of his ancestry stands out. His mother's grandfather was a Maldonado. Sounds Italian to some, but it's a Spanish last name. Not just Spanish, but fucking Colombian in his case.

I catch myself before I run my hand over my face in frustration. I didn't dig deep enough. I let my immediate fear for Thea's safety distract me from finding the fuller explanation. I'm slipping up, and it's going to cost us if I don't get my shite together. Thea's not the distraction. It's not knowing what to do with all these feelings that are new to me. It's too much time thinking about the future and not enough time paying attention to the present.

This is my fucking fault. Or at least part of it.

Brandon leans close enough, so only I hear him. "This is

not your fault. It's that fucker's. I know what you're thinking because I'm thinking it about myself, too. But we didn't do this. He did."

I nod, but I don't feel any better even if he is right.

I scroll the full results to make sure I miss nothing. I have time because Pablo's here with his henchmen, but Corey hasn't shown up, and neither have the Albanians. Fucking way past fashionably late. But the Albanians want the Colombians to wait for them, thinking it makes their balls bigger than they are. Corey probably doesn't want to step foot here since I'm certain he went for Brandon and couldn't find him. But he'll show. He just doesn't want to be alone with the Trenton mob, the Cartel, or the Albanian syndicates. The moment he isn't useful, they'll kill him. The goal is to get Corey away from either side while we run the bust, so we can deal with him.

I lean forward on my elbows to see Dillan. "His family's been around since the Cabreras."

Looks like the Maldonados married into the Cabrera family. Enrique's father, Josue, was still in Colombia back then. He killed the Cabrera *jefe* and took control. From the dates, Enrique was still super young. Like preschool young. It was Enrique's uncle who moved to the U.S. and took out the Cabreras up here to become the New York *jefe*. Enrique arrived in America to attend boarding school when he was twelve.

From this point, I know the story clearly. His uncle went down for racketeering in the U.S. He had a shite ton of crimes in Colombia, so the U.S. government let Colombia extradite him because they wanted him out of America. The feds figured the Colombians would kill him faster than they could. He lived and is the *jefe* down there because rivals murdered Enrique's father twenty-five years ago. It's questionable as fuck whether it was fratricide. In the meantime, Enrique stepped into his position as the NYC *jefe* when they dumped his uncle's arse back in the Amazon.

Shane keeps his head down, but I hear him on the other side of Brandon. "How?"

"Tony's Maldonado family bent the knee and kissed the ring when Enrique's uncle assassinated the Cabrera *jefe*. By then, they were lesser Cabreras. It's Tony's maternal side that wound him up as a De Luca and growing up in Trenton. She never married his father, so he got her last name. From what I can tell, both sides of Tony's family have been out of organized crime for two generations. That begs the question, how the fuck did he wind up working for Pablo?"

It does explain why he knew the families when I named them at McGinty's before I called Enrique, Salvatore, and Maks.

One thing I looked at along with his DOJ and FBI records was his bank account. Nothing raised an alarm. I could account for where all his money went. He wasn't a cash guy, so the records show where he blew his paychecks, and it was all on entertainment. None of the places belong to the Diazes. Most were ours until I banned him. A few were bratva owned. After I called the other families, there were no transactions at any establishment the Four Families own. Just chain restaurants or liquor stores.

Fucking-a.

"It was when Margherita was in the hospital. Tony's an oncology nurse. He must have met Pablo when his mom nearly died. She got out of the hospital a few days before those pages came in. She's still recovering at home. Our moms just sent a ton of meals over there like three days ago."

That takes some huevos. Pablo accepts food for his barely alive mother from my mother while using my girlfriend to fuck us over. I can't fucking kill him, but I can make him wish he was dead.

Sean elbows me and jerks his chin in Brandon and Shane's direction. I watch Gareth jump from the loading dock and run to his car. Its engine has been running the entire time. He's driving away the moment his door closes.

Cars flick off their headlights about a hundred yards away and roll into the loading docks with rifle muzzles sticking out windows. Then there's Corey. His fucking bike is a goddamn homing beacon. I see Pablo step forward and say something to Corey right before the bike goes silent. We keep watching in silence as Pablo talks to Corey and the Albanians' newest leader. We aren't moving in yet because we're waiting for a few more people to show up to the party.

It's another five minutes, but Ewan O'Malley joins what should have been a tête-à-tête between Ewan and the head of the Albanians, their *kyre*. Instead, Corey looks like a fucking Ping-Pong ball between Pablo and the Albanians. Ewan's ignoring Corey entirely. That means they already consider Corey disposable. Fuck. One of them's going to kill Corey before Brandon or I get to.

If I were five, I'd stomp my foot and hold my breath because it's fucking unfair. But I'm not. I signal all of us to move forward. My family and Brandon lead the way with thirty of our men coming out of the trees surrounding the warehouse in north Jersey. They call it the Garden State for a reason. Perfect hiding places. Everyone has their NVGs on since we're in the pitch black to make our arrival more of a surprise.

I'm not interested in anyone but Pablo, Ewan, and Corey. Even the Kurti fucker can die for all I care. Our men know to leave Ewan and Corey alive, and it goes without saying they can't kill Pablo.

On my signal, still in the darkness cast from the trees, my men do their job. One Colombian, Albanian, and Boston Irish drop after another. Faster than any of them can return fire. Our men know how to line themselves up with their targets to make sure they waste no bullets, and no one's left standing.

Once friendly fire won't hit us, Dillan and I step forward. I have my rifle raised and my goggles still down. So does Dillan. Pablo knows one of us is Dillan, but he can't be sure who I am. Ewan takes a step to the left, and I shoot between his feet.

"I didn't miss, *buachaill leanbh.*" Baby boy.

Ewan doesn't speak fluent Gaelic, but I'm certain he knows that phrase. Dillan and I keep creeping forward, not taking for granted the possible arrival of more men from any of the three syndicates. When we're as close as I want to get for now, I stop. I flip up my goggles.

"What the feck, Pablo?"

He laughs. I didn't expect much more from him. We use feck around the other syndicates on purpose. Let them think we're a bunch of twats clinging to the motherland. We prefer to be underestimated.

I twist to my right and put a line of bullets from the front fender to bumper of his Maybach. The top end of Mercedes luxury cars. I know the rounds didn't pierce the metal since it's reinforced like all our cars, but it'll be a bitch to fix.

"You didn't answer my question. I'll ask it only one more time. What the feck, Pablo?"

He crosses his arms and stares. I shoot off his driver's side-view mirror and make a perfect circle around the hub caps on each tire I can see.

"I know you're pissed now that I've fecked around with your favorite toy. That's just payback for you breaking my fecking remote-control car when we were nine, you stupid feck. Do you really want me to keep going?"

I aim for him now. He knows I won't kill him, but I will fecking shoot him. I've done it before.

"What do you want, Finn?"

"Well, Santa, I've been on the nice list this year. I want Corey. My future father-in-law gets to kill him. I want Cormac and Seamus to beat the shite out of Ewan. My brothers can have your Albanian playdate. You and I are going to talk about you being such a little bitch that you used my fiancée to get to us."

I haven't proposed yet, but she will be.

"You're not engaged yet."

"How would you know? I flushed the last bug you tried to put outside my door. I know you've gone nowhere near my place since you killed the last guy working security at my building. I've watched all the footage. Since Thea's always with me at my place, you didn't get shite from hers. I'm certain you weren't in bed with us because I've never been good at sharing with you. You and I are gonna chat."

I signal my brothers and cousins to move forward. The rest of our guys fan out to guard the perimeter. I hear Dillan whisper into his earpiece. As he and I inch forward and the others pass us to get to Ewan, Corey, and the Albanian *kyre*, three truck engines roar to life. By the time my family's dragging the three men back toward the unlit area, the three trucks are pulling up. More of our men pour out and load the full contents of the warehouse. It's an Albanian one, so it's not that big. But there's plenty for us to take. Yup, the hosts of the party were fashionably late. Did them no good.

Dillan and I go up opposite sets of steps to get onto the loading dock. Our rifles still point at Pablo. I come around in front of him and put the barrel to his forehead while Dillan strips him of all his weapons. We know where to look. When Dillan's tossed everything far enough away that Pablo has no chance to get them, I shove the barrel forward, pushing Pablo back three steps. I swing it around and ram the butt into his chest. He stumbles back, but Dillan pushes him forward.

"Why, Pablo? We cut you some fecking slack because of your mother. You use her being in the hospital to go after a woman. Does your *mamasita* know how big a shitbag she raised?"

"Don't talk about my mother, *hijueputa*."

"Considering you have a gun at your chest and one at your back, I wouldn't call me a son of a bitch. I think I'm in a better position to talk about your mother than you are mine. Why Althea?"

"Since you're sniffing after her like you're the dog in heat, I decided you could chase your own tail."

I pull my knife from my pocket and flick it open. I hold it up for Pablo to see. It's the same one that gave him a scar from his right collar bone to his sternum. Dillan sees me lower my gun, so he grabs Pablo's arms and pulls them behind Pablo's back. He wraps his right calf around Pablo's legs and pushes him to the ground. He gets zips ties around Pablo's wrists faster than a cowboy can lasso a bronco. I grab Pablo's shoulder and pull him back while Dillan moves to Pablo's legs. He puts his boot on Pablo's kneecaps and starts increasing the weight. Before Pablo can try to wrestle away from us, I rip his shirt open and slice from his left collar bone to his sternum.

"Stay away from my woman. Maybe your dad shouldn't have taken so many field trips to Colombian jails. Maybe he wouldn't have raised two *pedazos de mierda malparido*." Despicable pieces of shite.

Malparido means badly born, but it translates to despicable. It's more insulting in Spanish than it sounds when I use it in that context. I put my blade to his cheek and nick the skin.

"Do you want a scar to match Luca's?"

Luca has one that runs from his cheekbone to below the collar of his shirt courtesy of his former best friend.

"If you won't give me an answer to why you targeted Thea, then tell us what you hoped to gain by getting involved in this shitshow between the Albanians and the Boston Irish. How'd you get the feckers from Jersey involved? You know we're going to crow like fecking roosters to Maks about this."

"He already knows."

That gives me pause. I glance in the direction where my brothers dragged the *kyre*. "He can't kill him, so he's letting you. What're you getting out of that deal? The chance to feck us over? Sounds like Maks is getting twice the deal you are since you have no product left. We'll make sure the Kurti family knows their leader died doing a deal with you. They'll go after you, which does the bratva and us a favor. All the while, you're still everyone's little bitch."

I slam my fist into his nose, barely jerking back in time to avoid the blood splatter. I kick him in the ribs as Dillan transfers more of his weight to Pablo's kneecaps.

"This all ends with just this if you tell me why you went after Althea instead of just me or any man in my family?"

"I told you. You're sniffing after her like you're the one with a cunt. She was easy bait."

I jerk my head, and Dillan removes his foot. I nudge Pablo's legs apart until my right foot is between them.

"You're an heir, so you're expected to have an heir. Hard to do when I smash your balls." I draw back my foot.

"Fuck you."

"No, thanks. I don't think you'll get it up."

I drive my foot into his junk. But it's nowhere near as hard as I could. He tries to curl into a protective ball, which is the usual reaction to getting hit in the nuts. But I'm still standing in the way. Dillan kicks his injured shoulder to get him flat on his back again.

I speak into my earpiece. "Brandon, finish Corey. I'm having too much fun with Pablo. We're gonna be here awhile."

I prepare to kick him again, and I will make him puke this time. He knows it too.

"I'm sorry."

"I accept. But that's not enough. You are going to make a motherfucking goodwill tour. You are going to apologize to Althea. You are going to apologize to Laura because she's going to lose her ever-loving shite when she finds out you went after a woman. And you are going to apologize to your mother for taking advantage of her near-death in the hospital to use one of her nurses to target a syndicate woman. I am going to be there for each and every one of them."

I slam my boot into his balls hard enough that he curls over again and gags. I put my boot on them and push. He pukes. I step away from him. I didn't make him a eunuch, but he's going to be in pain for days. I grin when I think about him trying to piss.

"Meet me at Maks and Laura's tomorrow morning at seven. Their twins will have them up. I'll make sure Maks doesn't shoot either of us before we get on the property. You will apologize to Althea in front of Laura. Then you will apologize to Laura. Once she's done with you, we'll visit your *mami* and *papi*. Don't worry. I'll make sure Enrique knows why you're late for work."

I dig his cell phone out of his pocket and take it to the far end of the warehouse. I come back and zip tie his ankles. He can call for help if he makes it to his phone.

"Don't forget. Seven a.m. If you're late, I will tell Laura everything you've done rather than sticking with you tried to scare my fiancée."

I kick him in the gut for good measure. Then Dillan and I jump down from the loading dock. Two trucks are gone with the dead bodies to deal with. Ewan is wishing he was dead by now. The third truck has the cleaners in it. They're our men who will make sure there isn't a single trace of a crime scene. They'll drop the Cartel bodies off at a Mancinelli construction site and call the police with an anonymous tip. The Albanians will wind up as ash in the Sound. Ewan's men will get dumped at one of the O'Briens' sites down in Trenton with a call to the cops. That'll remind both of them who their feudal lord is. They'll know it's us, and there isn't shite they can do. I have plans for Corey.

"Brandon?"

"Over here."

Corey is alive, but just barely. He's got three gunshot wounds and at least two knife wounds. I crouch over him, tempted to spit in his face.

"I gave you a chance to survive. I told you to leave Ally alone and to go home. When we say family first, it means you protect them above all else. You don't make them your targets before anyone else. The Gallaghers are my family. You should have gotten the hint. Now you die."

I move out of the way as Brandon puts the barrel of a shotgun in Corey's mouth. I know a taxidermist who asks no questions. He'll take care of Corey's body since that's all that's left now. Once it's stuffed and preserved, I'll have it delivered to Corey's motorcycle club and have it mounted over the bar. It'll remind his men to stay in Boston where they belong.

I step away from the others and pull out my phone. There's only one call I need to make. I don't hear it ring.

"*Cailín*, it's over. I'll be home soon."

"Daddy! Thank God, Finn. Do you need space when you get here?"

"I need you naked and in our room. You don't go back to work for another three days. We still have a lot we haven't played with yet. Be sure to grab a water bottle on the way. You're going to need to hydrate."

"So do you. I plan to suck you dry."

"Do you really want me hard in front of your dad?"

"Ew. No."

"Then don't say things that make me want to do dirty, dirty things."

"Hurry up, Daddy. I'm already naked."

Epilogue

Thea

I ease the preemie back into her incubator and smile. This little one is going to be all right. She had a rough entry into the world, but she's already proven she's stubborn. I leave the NICU and wave to Seamus, who's my guard today. I still wouldn't have guessed he was once the same size as the baby I held a few minutes ago. And from his size and his brother's, you'd never guess Seamus and Cormac are the politest and shyest of the men in the O'Rourke family. But they are.

"You ready to go?"

"So ready. Let me grab my stuff."

"Does Finn have any idea what you're planning?"

I stop dead. "He better not."

He throws his hands up in the air. "I didn't say anything."

We keep walking until we get to the doctors on call room. I slip inside and grab my bag. I fold my lab coat and push that in along with my stethoscope and pager. I don't know what Finn did to Tony, but it's been three months, and he hasn't been back to work. I asked around. He's on medical leave. Finn came home in the middle of the night after he dealt with Pablo and Corey. Those are the only two I know about. We caught a couple hours of sleep, then we headed to Maks and Laura's house.

I thought I was going to be Finn's human shield when Maks came out to see him. I'm pretty sure he had plenty more to say, but he bit his tongue when he saw me in the car, too. I wish I could be Laura's new best friend. She reminds me of Mair. It's a shame they can't be friends either, since their husbands run their syndicates. What keeps them apart is what makes me wish they could be. They're in the same position and must have the same fears and duties.

Laura took one look at Pablo, who showed up with his uncle and went back in the house. She got a butter knife and came back outside. They didn't invite us past the driveway. I didn't understand the full reference when she waved the knife in Enrique's direction and told him to roll up his sleeve. Something about her initial and her sister's on a cross with Pablo's initial that's on Enrique's forearm. She warned him about something, and that if any women were involved, she'd dig her and her sister's initial out of his flesh. Nothing about her anger made me think she was kidding. It made me wonder if she really runs the bratva, and Maks is there for intimidation.

It was the opposite when we got to Pablo's parents' house. His mom is still super frail, and Pablo looked like shite as he explained as much as he could in front of women. I stepped in at one point and made Pablo stop. Margherita looked like she was having chest pains. I checked her out, made her put her oxygen mask on, and told Pablo he had three more sentences before I stopped him for good.

I join Seamus in the hallway, and we head to the SUV waiting for us. It's not long until we get to the house Finn and I just bought in Queens. It's not as big as his parents', but it's big enough to have plenty of house guests. I love it. We knew the moment we pulled up. We barely made it through the tour before Finn made a cash offer. We signed the paperwork two hours later.

I run up to our bedroom and take the fastest shower I probably ever have. I put on my makeup and hurry to my closet. I've just slipped on my heels when I hear Finn come in from the garage.

"Thea?"

"Upstairs. Hang on. I'll come down to you."

He's waiting for me at the bottom of the stairs. His smile could light up Long Island. He offers me his hand as I take the last step. I'm wearing the dress I had on at our wedding rehearsal a month ago. I didn't expect all Four Families— apparently, that's what they go by these days. One of the Mancinelli wives coined it— to be there. At least, they were only at the reception. It was the most perfect day thanks to Finn, even if the reception was more about showing off than us. I didn't care because Finn warned me.

But I only had the next two days off. I had to cover for two doctors who both had deaths in their families. We found out the day before the rehearsal, so that was a bummer. Finn still made everything perfect. I can't believe he's real sometimes. Our wedding night was— holy fuck-a-moly. Every fantasy we've talked about, we enacted as best we could in the hotel suite. We slept in, which neither of us does. Then we spent the two days at the beach in the Hamptons. Shane has a mansion out there. Not exactly the bachelor pad you'd expect.

"You look gorgeous, *cailín*."

"Thank you, Daddy. I have plans for you."

"For me?"

"Mmhmm. Come on."

I lead him to the French doors leading to the backyard. It's dusk, and the sunset is beautiful.

"What's all this?"

"The beginning of our honeymoon. I have the next eight weeks off, Finn. I cashed in every day off I have. Stop staring at me. We'll be late for our dinner reservation."

I tug his hand as I lead us to the bottom of our garden where the helicopter waits. That took some serious negotiating to convince Cormac there was enough clearance for him to land and takeoff. I swear he came out here with a tape measure. It came out in conversation one day that he and Shane are both pilots. He flies helicopters, and Shane flies small planes. I stored that nugget away, and now it's come in handy.

"Reservation?"

"Yes. And you need to put that fine arse in gear, so we aren't late."

I lean back and spank it. Full granite back there. He pinches me in return.

"Cheeky, little one."

"You can see my cheeks later. Come on."

I playfully tug him as we walk along the path with pavers. He helps me in, and Cormac hands me headphones. We're off the ground a moment later, and the view is breathtaking. Cormac takes us for a scenic tour over the city, which is wonderful but confusing for Finn. Perfect. It's dark— unfortunately —as we fly over DC and when we land in Northern Virginia. There's a car waiting for us with two SUVs, one in front and one behind.

"Thea?"

"Hmm?"

"What're you up to?"

"You'll see."

"Are those my brothers and cousins?"

"Yes. I knew you'd flip if we went anywhere without a security detail, and I knew you'd have a coronary once you find out my plans if that detail wasn't your family."

We arrive at an estate that's nestled away where you wouldn't expect to find a restaurant with three Michelin Stars. The inside of the inn— a completely understated name for what's like a castle —is luxury to the hilt.

"Welcome Mr. and Mrs. O'Rourke. It's a pleasure to have you stay with us tonight. Your suite is ready as is your chef's table."

A young man leads us to the restaurant where people must wonder if we're foreign diplomats or celebrities as Shane, Sean, Seamus, Cormac, and Dillan spread out. Not exactly unobtrusive, despite how I know they try.

When our wine arrives, I hold up my glass.

"Finn, I love you."

"I love you, too, Thea."

"The best decision I ever made was one I feared I'd regret. I went back to McGinty's a second time. Thank you for the life we're building together. I never imagined I could feel so complete, but it's like the missing piece I didn't know wasn't there is now in place. As happy as being with you makes me, I'm happier that you can just be Finn with me and not Finn O'Rourke. I get the man at the end of the day, not the family accountant."

I can't say mobster in public. He knows what I mean.

"Thea, I couldn't stop looking at you the first time I met you. Not just because you're the most beautiful woman I've ever seen. I knew you were so much more. I never imagined anyone could be as special as you. You are my safe harbor wherever we go."

Our glasses clink before we take a sip.

"Speaking of places to go. You know that island off Bimini that you were talking about?"

"Yes."

"We're headed there for two weeks."

I pause when I see Finn's expression. It isn't surprise. It's fucking straight up a shit-eating grin.

"We can read each other's minds even when we're not in the same room. Thea, I bought the island three days ago. I planned to whisk you away this weekend."

We laugh and clink our glasses again.

"I hope you can read my mind all night, Daddy. I've been thinking a lot."

Don't miss Sean's story when the ruthless mobster falls for the enemy's daughter.

Preorder your copy of *Mob Princess* and have it waiting for you on release day.

Would you like an extra sex scene with Finn and Thea? Would it surprise you that they don't even make it to the wedding reception without keeping their hands off each other?

Subscribe and get your free download here.

Get A Bonus Epilogue

Enjoy this free bonus epilogue with a scene from *Mob Star*.

Check out this extra sexy scene with Finn and Thea when you subscribe to my newsletter. Get your copy now.

Don't miss the next installment
Preorder so you don't forget!

I might be the quiet one in the family.

I might be the patient one in the family.

Push me too far, and you'll find out.

She fell into my life.

But I'm the one to catch her.

Now I won't let go.

Try to make me. I dare you.

I'll push her to her limits with more pleasure than she can
dream of.

Then I'll hold her when we're done.

I won't let anything get in the way.

Preorder now.

Thank you for reading Mob Star

Sabine Barclay, a nom de plume also writing Historical Romance as Celeste Barclay, lives near the Southern California coast with her husband and sons. She loves her days at the beach soaking up way too much sun, a good Netflix binge, and a strong hot chai. Her heroines are independent women who can defend themselves but love their Alpha heroes who want nothing more than to protect their soulmates in her Mafia Romances. She's Gen Y/Oregon Trail and loves creating engrossing contemporary romances that will make your toes curl and your granny blush.

Subscribe to Sabine's bimonthly newsletter to receive exclusive insider perks.

www.sabinebarclay.com

Join the fun and get exclusive insider giveaways, sneak peeks,
and new release announcements in
<u>Sabine Barclay's Facebook Dubious Dames Group</u>

Do you also enjoy steamy Historical Romance? Discover
Sabine's books written as Celeste Barclay.

The O'Rourke Brotherhood

Mob Boss
BOOK ONE SNEAK PEEK

Dillan

I hate meetings like this. I don't need to wear pants from some shitty off-the-rack suit that are too tight to *try* to make my dick look bigger. I'm secure in my cock size, and I don't need to show how big my balls are for people to know I run this part of the city. I loathe strip clubs too. I'm past the point where naked women make my jimmy do jumping jacks. I can appreciate a hot bod and gymnast level strength, but it does nothing for me. These douchebags? They're practically ready to come in those cheap arse pants. Why am I here? I keep asking myself that. Seamus and Shane are doing just fine with these negotiations. I'm just here to look good. I'm the muscle today. Or rather my name and my position. Who the fuck thought— way, way back in the day —that giving the mob hierarchy nautical names was a good idea? Fucking Skipper. This isn't motherfucking Gilligan's Island. None of these numb nuts are the Professor, even if they think they're fucking Mr. Howell.

But who is that? If this is *Gilligan's Island*, then she's Mary Ann.

I glance at Seamus, but he's focused on the Albanian he's trying not to lose his shite at. Shane smirks at me when I dart my gaze to him. I cock an eyebrow as the waitress walks over. She's definitely not a dancer. She has too many clothes on. But you can barely call the pieces of thread she's wearing clothes. She's got on a bikini top that's barely more than pasties, and the skirt she's wearing would make my Catholic grandmother do somersaults in her grave.

It's the standard uniform for this place, but somehow it doesn't look right on her. Not because she doesn't have a banging body because she does. Not because she's a butter face— but-her-face —as in great bod, not so great face. She's beautiful in a super understated way. That's part of what makes her look out of place. She has next to no makeup on. I think those are even her real eyelashes. The natural beauty is drawing way too much attention.

"'Scuse me."

She tries to step around Zef Hoxha, the *kyre* of the Albanian mafia here in New York. When he reaches out to grab her wrist, I'm out of my seat with my hand around his. He never gets a chance to touch her because my hold is so tight he can't bend his fingers. I keep squeezing until it must feel like I'll snap the bones.

"No touching."

Zef drops his arm as much as my hold allows. I let go and stare at him before I tilt my head toward the waitress. I narrow my eyes, and he knows what I expect.

"I apologize, miss."

"That's all right, sir. Here's your drink."

She's polite as she hands him his glass. Unfortunately, to put down the rest, she has to bend forward, giving everyone a view of her glorious cleavage. Tits and arse are what sell here, and she has them in spades. I'm certain it's why my cousin hired her. If I sit down, everyone will know I'm just as guilty as these fuck nuts because she's made my dick do something that hasn't happened in a strip club since I was like twenty-three. I'm now thirty-three.

Mob Boss
Mob Star
Mob Princess
Mob Saint
Mob Bride
Mob Knight

Do you also enjoy steamy Historical Romance? Discover Sabine's books written as Celeste Barclay.

The Ivankov Brotherhood

Bratva Darling
BOOK ONE SNEAK PEEK

Laura
As I sit across from the four Kutsenko brothers, I press my lips together to keep from drooling. No four men should be so strikingly handsome. Not all from the same family, anyway. I fight a valiant battle against letting my gaze drift toward the eldest, Maksim, whose ice-blue eyes bore into me. After years of negotiating billion-dollar investment contracts while facing countless ruthless businessmen, I've learned to keep my expression studiously blank. But it's a true struggle today. Instead, I focus my attention on the squirrelly lawyer sitting across the conference table. While he's disingenuous with each comment, he's a good negotiator. But I'm better. How cliché am I?

While I feel Maksim watching me, I focus on Dmitry Yakovitch as he continues to argue the merits of the venture capitalist company I represent, RK Capital Group, merging with Kutsenko Partners. What he means is the merits of Kutsenko

Partners acquiring RK Capital Group, then stripping it and making it another money-laundering shell corporation. While most people in New York have little awareness of the Russian mafia, I do. The Kutsenko brothers' names appear on no titles or deeds anywhere in New York City, but it wasn't difficult to determine which shell companies likely belong to them. Their assumption that I'm unfamiliar with them is proving beneficial to me as they continue to whisper amongst themselves in Russian. I think they may even believe they're convincing me that they don't speak much English.

The senior partners of RK Capital Group know who I'm negotiating with, though they may not know I'm aware of these Russians' more nefarious operations. They've given me the go-ahead to agree to a merger with an eventual acquisition, but only for the right price. A price to the tune of twenty billion dollars. Considering an investment firm like Goldman Sachs is worth nearly one-hundred-and-twenty billion dollars, my clients' asking price appears reasonable.

"Mr. Yakovitch, I shall stop you now." I raise my left hand, pen caught between my index and middle fingers. When I have his attention, I lean back in my chair and casually twirl the pen over my index finger and thumb. "Fifty billion is my clients' asking price. You know that. Your clients know that. RK doesn't oppose the merger. What they oppose is the insulting offer you've made. It's nearly noon, and I'm hungry, Mr. Yakovitch. I have a delicious ham sandwich waiting for me. I even have three chocolate chip cookies waiting for me. If we aren't going to make any progress, I shall let you go, so I can move onto my eagerly anticipated lunch."

I cant my head just enough for me to appear as though my gaze rests solely on the opposing attorney's face, but I can see each Kutsenko brothers' reaction. My face battles yet again against showing my emotions as I fight not to smirk. Their muted but surprised expressions confirm what I already know.

"Please tell your clients to make a reasonable counteroffer, or I will conclude this meeting and enjoy my ham sandwich and cookies."

Dmitry glares at me before turning to Maksim and his three brothers. In rapid Russian, he doesn't interpret my suggestion. Oh no. There's no need for that. I can't catch every word because his voice is too low. But I catch something along the lines of "The bitch refuses to budge. What now? A fucking ham sandwich. More like a stick up her ass."

Maksim swivels his chair to look at his brothers. In Russian, he says, "Fifty billion is ridiculous. She's not so stupid or naïve not to know that. My guess is they'll settle for twenty billion. We offer fifteen."

"That's barely better than what we already offered," Aleksei, the second-oldest brother, argues. "She'll be eating the fucking sandwich and dipping her cookies in milk before we walk out the door. We need the buildings."

"We offer twenty, Maks," Bogdan, the youngest, insists.

As I watch the brothers discuss, their voices barely lowered, I pull my lunch sack from the black leather satchel by my feet and set it beside my laptop. It's a ridiculously pink floral bag with an embroidered monogram, the L and D overlapping. It's an empty prop, but they don't know that. I watch as five sets of eyes narrow. I offer a smile that would appear innocent in any setting other than this meeting. It's patronizing, and I know it.

Bratva Sweetheart
Bratva Treasure
Bratva Beauty
Bratva Angel
Bratva Jewel

The Mancinelli Brotherhood

Mafia Heir **BOOK ONE SNEAK PEEK**

Luca

This asshole is pissing me off. We've been going around in circles for five minutes, and the longer we stand out here, the greater the likelihood someone will spot us. I have a sixth sense about these things. It's why I'm still alive at the ripe old age of thirty-one.

"Espinoza, enough already. Either sell to us or don't, but we set the price. Your tequila is good, but it isn't nectar from the gods." I'm watching Carlos Espinoza, some lackey for the Mexican Culiacán Cartel, try to maneuver me into paying more than the agreed upon price. I know it's so he can skim off the top.

"It's as close as you're going to get. You've upped the order, so the price per case goes up."

My uncle, Salvatore Mancinelli, is the New York don. He negotiated this deal, and I warned him it was a bad idea. But what do I know as his underboss and heir? I'm not backing down.

"Haven't you ever heard of a bulk discount? The more I order the better the price should be. No one else around here is buying from you. You know we're your only choice in three out of five boroughs. You aren't going to the Bronx because you won't get more than pennies there. You aren't going to Queens because you don't want to run into the Colombians. You aren't going to Manhattan because then you face the bratva along with us. And what are you going to do in Staten Island? Sell to us anyway? We control Staten Island and Brooklyn when it comes to liquor stores, so take the money and go."

"Luca, there are plenty of liquor stores in Brooklyn that aren't owned by Italians. I'll go there."

We aren't friends. He's patronizing me by using my first name. Fuck him and the horse he rode in on. I have other solutions for this shit.

"And I'll just take what I want from them for free. That's not a half bad idea. The deal's over. Take your shit with the worm in it and go."

"Motherfucking racist. Not all tequila has a worm in it."

"You're selling Mezcal. It's known for the fucking worm. I wouldn't start calling me names, you *penche hijo de puta*."

Fucking son of a bitch.

He has twenty-five crates of stolen tequila that he's trying to offload because he knows he can't sell it at his own liquor store.

"What did you call me?"

Carlos takes what he thinks is a menacing step forward, and his two bodyguards do the same. Not smart. Neither of my two bodyguards nor I react, but the three men in each of my cars open their doors. They won't do more than that. It's just a reminder that the Culiacán can try, but the *Cosa Nostra* still run New York City.

"This is the third and final time I say this. Sell or leave."
Every head turns toward the liquor store's back door as it opens.
A gorgeous blonde steps out, and I wish I had the time to
appreciate her beauty, but she's about to die. Carlos and his
men draw their guns and pivot toward her. My men pull their
weapons too, but we keep them pointed at the Mexicans. The
woman stands like a deer in the headlights for a second before
ducking behind the industrial garbage dumpster like a frightened rabbit. Three shots hit the metal almost at the same
moment. That's all it takes for my men and me. The two bodyguards standing with me aim for a guard each, and I set my
sights on Carlos. We squeeze our triggers, and the men fall.
Screeching tires tell me Carlos's driver takes off. I hear more
gunshots as at least one soldier in my cars tries to shoot the
escaping vehicle. Glass shatters, but the sedan keeps going. I
hear more tires squeal as one of my SUVs takes off and chases
the guy. I holster my gun and wave my men to do the same.
I inch forward toward the trash can, but I see the shadow shift.
The woman bolts from the other side. She's still the frightened
rabbit, but I'm the fox pursuing her. She's fast, I'll give her that.
But she has to be at least a foot shorter than me. My legs are a
lot longer and cover a lot more ground with each stride.
She weaves among the cars, most likely believing it's harder to
hit a moving object. She isn't wrong, but I have no intention of
shooting her. I push myself harder and pounce as she darts out
and tries to cross the last stretch of parking lot to reach a better
lit area near a bus stop. I lunge.
"Stop running, *piccolina*. I won't hurt you."
I wrap my arms around her and pull her back against my chest,
but I'm quick to spin her around and put space between us as I
grasp her arms. Of course, she fights me.
"If I wanted you dead, I would have shot at you, too."
"It doesn't mean you won't kill me after."

She's breathless as she continues to struggle. I almost let go to take a step back, insulted at what she implied. But I can't blame her. If I were a woman, I'd be terrified of the same thing.

"I'm not going to rape you. I'm going to talk to you."

"Talk? You are not a man who talks if you just killed a guy."

"To keep him and his men from killing you. I told you, if I wanted you dead, I would have shot at you too. And I wouldn't have missed."

She stops struggling against me, but her eyes continue to dart from one place to another, trying to find somewhere to flee. I know I can keep her in place with only one hand, so I release her left arm. I still have a firm hold on her right one, but I haven't held it nearly as tightly as I could.

"I'm Luca. I know you figured out you interrupted something you shouldn't have. Did that man know who you are?"

"Yes."

"What about his driver? Would he know you?"

"Yes."

"Do you have a name?"

"Yes."

"*Piccolina*, we won't get very far if yes is all you can say. Are you willing to answer me with more than one word?"

"No."

I knew that was coming, and I grin. I can't help it. I wasn't wrong about her being gorgeous, but I doubt she wants to know that's what I think. At least, not if I want her to know I won't assault her.

"Fine. I have more than twenty questions I can ask that you can answer with one word. Do you work at the store?"

"Sometimes."

Ah, an improvement.

"Did Carlos know you were still working?"

"No."

"Do you have a car, or do you take the subway or bus?"
She raises her chin and remains silent. Smart but counterproductive.
"The subway or the bus will get you killed. You're too easy to find and follow. Do you have a car?"
"Yes."
"Can you stay with someone instead of going home?"
She refuses to answer.
"If that man knew you and you sometimes work in the store, then he knew where you live. If he found that out, so will someone in his cartel."
"I know. Let me go. The longer I stand here, the more likely someone is to come back for me."
"No one will touch you while I'm here."
"Arrogant. If he shot at me, he would have shot at you."
"And he would have died, anyway. What's your name?"
"Jane."
"Look, I know you won't get in one of my cars and let me drive you somewhere. In most cases, I would say that's a smart move. But you did nothing wrong tonight except for leave work at the wrong time. I know that, and you know that. But the Culiacán won't see it that way, *piccolina*."
She freezes for no more than five seconds before she trembles so much that I can see it. I don't know what drives me next, but it's the same instinct that's made me call her little girl three times. I pull her to my chest and tuck her head against it. I stroke her hair down to her shoulders, rubbing my hand up and down her back. This is the most inopportune moment to notice she isn't wearing a bra. I will my body not to react.
"What does that mean?"
Her voice is barely more than a whisper, but I know what she's asking.
"It means little girl."

"I should be insulted, but the way you say it…"

"It has nothing to do with your height. I know you're not a child."

God, do I know she's not. She feels amazing. Her tits are soft as they press against me, and I can see she has the most delectable ass. I'd love nothing more than to cup it and squeeze until she goes up on her toes and begs for me to wrap her legs around my waist and fuck her. For fuck's sake. Stop, you disgusting asshole. That is not what you need to be thinking about.

"Why didn't you shoot me? Whatever you were talking about, if it was with a Cartel member, then it wasn't completely legal. Carlos didn't want me alive to talk about seeing you together. Why are you letting me live?"

"I told you. You did nothing wrong but try to leave work. He should have checked the building before starting the meeting. That was on him. The only thing I take issue with is you leaving by yourself and walking into a dimly lit parking lot. I suspect you do that often, and that's too dangerous. Jane Doe, I don't hurt women."

Mafia Sinner
Mafia Beauty
Mafia Angel
Mafia Redeemer
Mafia Star